Praise for *WHATEVER LIFE THRO[WS AT YOU]*

"Loved this book! Great characters, grea[t]
—Cindi Madsen, *USA Tod[ay]*

"[A]llows readers an all-access pass into
and their families.

"An addicting and gritty story about family, friendships, falling in love, and choosing to follow your own path. *Whatever Life Throws At You* is a story that combined my love of sports and YA romance in a way only one other YA author, Katie McGarry, has done." —*Mundie Moms*

"Julie Cross once again delivers with this swoon-worthy, laugh-out-loud romance between a sexy rookie baseball player and the new coach's daughter." —Yara Santos, *Once Upon a Twilight*

"An irresistible story about family, first love, and following your heart."
—Jen, Jenuine Cupcakes

Praise for *CHASING TRUTH* by Julie Cross

"An enjoyably twisty, romantic, and thoughtful prep-school mystery."
—*Kirkus Reviews*

"A fun whodunit for teens. It has more depth than most teen mysteries and could be recommended easily to fans of Harlan Coben, Ally Carter, and Jennifer Lynn Barnes." —Charla Hollingsworth, HNGC Library

"Fans of *Veronica Mars* are going to love this!"
—Jaime Arkin, *Fiction Fare*

"A whodunit-style read that had me clicking the pages all through the night." —Erica Chilson, *Wicked Reads*

"I love the witty banter Julie always incorporates in her novels, and the swoon-worthy chemistry that always occurs between the two main characters has her books making my favorites list again and again."
—Kirby Boehm, *The Preppy Book Princess*

OFF THE ICE

a Juniper Falls novel

JULIE CROSS

Also by Julie Cross

WHATEVER LIFE THROWS AT YOU
CHASING TRUTH

JULIE CROSS

OFF THE ICE

Entangled Publishing, LLC
2614 South Timberline Road
Suite 109
Fort Collins, CO 80525

Entangled Teen is an imprint of Entangled Publishing, LLC.

Visit our website at www.entangledpublishing.com.

Edited by Liz Pelletier
Cover design by Clarissa Yeo
Interior design by Toni Kerr

ISBN: 978-1-63375-655-7
Ebook ISBN: 978-1-63375-656-4

Manufactured in the United States of America

First Edition February 2017

10 9 8 7 6 5 4 3 2 1

To Nicole for following this book on its long and seemingly endless journey.

Prologue

-TATE-

Something cold and wet hits the side of my face. My braces clank against Haley's, and we both jump apart. I hear giggling coming from several feet away. When I turn my head, my sister, Jody, is sitting on a log, a clear plastic cup of ice in her hand. Her friend Claire O'Connor smacks her on the arm. "You are so mean."

"He's my little brother. I'm supposed to torture him."

"Sorry," I mumble to Haley.

The bonfire in front of Juniper Falls Pond is bright enough that even in the dark, the color in Haley's cheeks is clearly visible.

"I think it's adorable. Little Tate is all grown up," Claire says.

"You act like you're ten years older than me instead of one year," I tell Claire. She does nothing but lift an eyebrow. A challenge, I think. "Oh, I get it. It's a college thing, right? Your high school friends are all little kids now?"

Claire's leaving Juniper Falls to do some fancy dual-credit, early-graduation program at Northwestern University, specially designed for talented people like her—the singing, theatrical type, probably ones who live in tiny towns where hockey is all anyone talks about and musical theater is a foreign language.

"I still remember Tate racing you in your mom's red high heels," Claire says to Jody, and they both start laughing.

My face falls into my hands and I groan. Haley stifles a laugh, and I shoot her a look. "I was nine."

She smiles at me and pushes herself up to her feet. "The cupcake supply is getting low. I'd better replenish it."

"Little Man Tate," a familiar voice says from behind me. "Did I just see you making out with this beautiful girl?"

My jaw tenses. Fucking Luke Pratt.

He grins at Haley. "Hope he's being decent to you. If not, you let me know, and I'll remind him how we treat our girls around here."

Yeah, no thanks, I'll pass on getting advice from a guy who can't go a week without cheating on his girlfriend. Ex-girlfriend now, so I heard.

He plops down beside me, and I force a grin. "So…when do you start practicing?" I ask.

Luke graduated last spring. He's got a spot playing on a junior hockey team somewhere down south. He takes a long drink from a flask. "I leave next week."

Across the fire, Claire flips her long red hair over one shoulder, her face lighting up at the sight of Luke. I roll my eyes and catch Jody doing the same. Luke notices her watching and grins.

"All this for you, O'Connor?" He waves a hand, gesturing at the fire, music, the table of cupcakes Haley made with musical notes and those theater masks on them.

Claire shrugs. "Everyone's excited to get rid of me."

Aside from Haley, my sister, and me, I'm not sure people are here to celebrate Claire's achievements so much as they're here to celebrate, as in hang out and get drunk. Most people in Juniper Falls know Claire best for being Davin O'Connor's daughter—the guy with the coolest hockey bar in the state of Minnesota, famous for the walleye horseshoe.

"Is that right?" Pratt says. And then he looks at her in a way that… Well, I doubt he's really seen her before, but he sure as hell is now.

My stomach turns. I can't take any more of this. I get up and look around for Haley. Seconds later, Jody is at my side, walking with me.

"I hate that guy," I whisper.

"Me, too." Jody shrugs, like this isn't a big deal. She looks at me and says, "What? She's into him. He's finally noticing her, and she deserves that. I voiced my opinion. Can't do anything else."

He's finally noticing her? I hate him even more now.

I move behind Haley, catch her around the waist, and squeeze her against me. It's chilly out tonight, and she's not wearing a jacket. "Cold?"

"I'm fine," she says, before her teeth start chattering.

I pull off my hoodie and put it around her. I'm about to ask her to go for a walk with me so we can make out without ice being involved—I get enough ice at hockey practice—but Jody interrupts me.

She's reading a text on her phone. "Dad wants you back at O'Connor's."

I rest my forehead on Haley's shoulder. "Do I have to?"

Haley reaches up and pats my cheek. "It's cute that you watch football with your dad."

"Cute" isn't how I would describe it.

"Plus…" Haley adds. "Don't you have to hang out with him?"

It's so obvious that Haley lives in a two-parent home it almost makes me smile. She doesn't get the divorce stuff. Any of it. "Jody and I haven't had to do weekends at Dad's for years. Not with his living several hours away during the hockey season."

She turns me to face the bar across the street. "Go. He came all the way from Michigan to watch football with you."

Right. His visits have nothing to do with his royalty among the alumni in town or wanting to get drunk and play King of the World or relive the state championships of '94. People around here worship my dad. Still.

I glance over in Claire's direction. Luke has moved to sit beside her. "Should I even bother saying good-bye?"

Jody shakes her head. "She's busy living out her fifteen-year-old self's fantasy."

Yeah. TMI. I give Haley a quick kiss and leave her with my jacket and my sister. Despite Haley's arguments in favor of quality Dad time, I take the long way over to O'Connor's and run into Mike Steller, our varsity goalie, and his girlfriend, Jessie.

"Saw you at practice the other day, T-Man," he says. "Your glove is getting pretty quick."

"Thanks." I keep my eyes on my shoes, trying to hide the excitement. Right now, Mike Steller is *the* goalie to recruit. And he's only a junior. I'll be a senior before I take his place. Which is good because I'm nowhere near ready yet.

When I finally open the door to the bar across the street from Juniper Falls Pond, a cheer erupts. The Vikings just scored a touchdown. A table of out-of-towners follows the cheering with a few boos and "Fuck the Vikings." From behind the bar, Davin O'Connor, Claire's dad, flexes his muscles and flashes his tattooed arms at the idiot guys cheering on the Bears. That's all it takes to cut them off.

My dad walks to the bar and orders another beer. I glance at the TV—it's only the second quarter.

"Tate," Dad says. "Glad you're here. Larry and I..." He points a finger at Larry Jones, another big hockey legend in town. "We were just goin' on about your teammates, Jamie and Leo. Are they talking to any coaches yet?"

"I don't know." I shake my head. "We have different practices. Plus, it's not like you can sign them—"

"Hey, Tate," Davin calls. "Got something to show you!"

Relieved to have an excuse to leave before I become a coconspirator in NCAA violations, I turn quickly and head back to the bar. Davin is crouched down, messing with the beer taps. "You gotta see how I rerigged these. It's twice as fast and half the cleaning."

I walk around behind the bar counter and check out the redesign. Football isn't exactly my thing, and Sunday night games can last hours. Over the years, I've learned all kinds of things about soda fountains, beer taps, commercial ovens, bar sinks.

"Probably a good idea if you stick around," Davin says, keeping his voice low. He slides a set of keys across the bar to me.

My face heats up. I stuff the keys into my pocket and keep my gaze focused on the hoses running beneath the bar.

"You have your license, right?"

I shrug. "A few more days."

Davin waves a hand. "Close enough."

Yep. Not that it's stopped me from driving before.

After I help with the beer taps, Davin sends me outside to toss some stuff in the Dumpster. That's when I see her. Claire.

She's tugging Luke Pratt toward the outside staircase

that leads to an unfinished apartment above the bar. I hide myself halfway behind a Dumpster and watch them reach the top landing. My stomach ties in knots. I don't like this. Not Claire. Not with Luke.

I mean, it's not like Claire is… I shake my head. Haley is my girlfriend, and she's great. But Claire is Claire. She's something *other*. Other in that way where a girl is completely unattainable because she's seen you racing around in your mom's red heels. But that means I've seen her, too. Claire in the backyard chasing a firework. Claire belting out a solo from *Les Mis* during the middle school talent show. Claire making up hip-hop dances in my living room with Jody— wearing only a sports bra. I know I don't have any right to these feelings, but it's like she's given me a piece of herself.

I should stop this. If Davin knew…

Go back inside, Tate. Forget about it.

I guess maybe it's good that she's leaving Juniper Falls tomorrow.

−CLAIRE−

It takes only seconds after we close the door for Luke to kiss me. I've imagined this moment for years, but in my head, it went slower, it built and built to something…something more.

I wanted it to be everything.

Thirty seconds later, my shirt ends up on the floor. I try with everything in me to get lost in this. He and his girlfriend are finally over. I've wished for years for them to break up— in the kindest way possible, of course. And it's my last night at home. Last night to have the kind of experience girls are supposed to have in high school. Last night to leap or…not.

But now I don't want to be alone up here with him, with a queen-size bed only a few feet away. And I definitely don't want to end up on that bed. "Hey…" I push lightly against his chest. "Slow down."

He pulls back and looks me over, forehead wrinkled. "Slow down? I thought you wanted…"

My face heats up. I shake my head. "Not here. Not like this."

I don't know what I want anymore. His touch, his scent, the feel of his lips—none of it is anything like I imagined or anything like I saw with him and Kara.

"Relax." The beautiful grin returns, and he's found a wall to push me up against and skin on my neck to kiss. "Close your eyes. Then the room doesn't matter."

"Wait… Just—" My heart pumps loudly in my ears. I shove him harder and duck under his arm to escape. This quick move seems to put Luke off balance.

He stumbles back into a coatrack and bangs his head. "Jesus! What the fuck?"

This is all going so wrong. "Sorry—"

"You drag me away for this? I left a bunch of girls back at the party." He works at straightening his shirt, now tangled in the coatrack. "What is wrong with you, O'Connor?"

"You left a bunch of girls?" I repeat. "I thought you and Kara just broke up…"

I thought you were heartbroken and needed comforting. Or finally free to notice someone who's spent way too much time noticing you.

Those words stay locked in my head because in this moment, I know they aren't true. This Luke Pratt I've created is just an illusion. He's not real. How many times had Jody told me just that and I hadn't believed her, hadn't let myself?

"I'm just here because someone said you were into me," he replies. "And you're kinda hot—weird but hot. And I thought…" He rubs his head where he banged it and seems to get pissed off all over again.

I squeeze my eyes shut, hoping to lessen the impact of his words. But they still hit like a slap across my face. *Weird.* I'm the weird girl to him. I snatch my shirt from the floor, holding it in front of me, covering my chest. I march over to the door, throwing it open, and allow the cool night air to hit my heated face. "Go ahead, then. Find those other girls. Have fun with that."

He shakes his head, looking me over like I'm insane. I feel insane. "Singing school? Who the hell goes to school to sing? I bet my lucky hockey puck you end up down the street at El Margarita singing 'Happy Birthday' with a fucking sombrero on your head!"

"Just get out," I whisper. I can't speak any louder or I'll start crying, and I'm not gonna cry in front of him.

Finally, after tossing me one last disgusted look, he storms out. I slam the door and lock it behind him. The second I hear his feet land on the ground below the staircase, I slide down the wall and let myself cry. What the hell did I just do? God, I'm an idiot.

This is what happens when you spend more time with someone inside your head than in real life.

The Luke Pratt in my fantasies would have stuck around, talked to me. Tears stream down my face. I wipe my nose on my sleeve and try to pull myself together. I can't go back to the party like this. I can't go anywhere like this.

Except college. I have to go tomorrow.

What if he's right? Will I end up at a Mexican joint singing "*Feliz Cumpleaños*"? What the hell is so great about me that will get me out of this town when so many other people fail to? What if the "singing school" fantasies inside my head are just like the Luke Pratt fantasies, and it ends up being awful?

I give myself a minute to climb down from this emotional mountain and reach far in the distance for some logical reasoning. This isn't about school. School will be fine. This is about Luke Pratt. Who has turned out to be just another varsity hockey player *player*. I shouldn't even be surprised. But I really had thought he was different—one of the good ones.

Maybe there aren't any good ones.

I spend a little while longer up in the storage/apartment convincing myself to stop crying and then crying all over again. And when I finally lock up, I'm back to being ready to get the hell out of this town.

"Get off me!"

I freeze at the bottom of the outside staircase, recognizing Keith Tanley's voice but not the sharpness it carries. I peer around the corner, spotting a stumbling Keith with scrawny Tate, trying to hold his dad upright.

"Dad…just…can we please—"

Keith spits out a string of swearwords and struggles out of Tate's grasp. Even though they can't see me, my face heats up. I'm embarrassed for Tate. Embarrassed for Jody, despite her absence. Embarrassed for anyone like me who has only seen the completely together, always charming version of Keith Tanley.

I should hide out until they're gone. That would be easier for Tate. Easier for me, too.

But then Keith shoves Tate hard. He falls on his side onto the gravel parking lot. Dust floats around him. Mr. Tanley reaches down, grips Tate's arm, pulling him to his feet. He tugs him along, flings the passenger side door open, and attempts to shove his son in. But Tate holds himself in place. He reaches out and grabs the bed of the truck, his feet skidding in the rocks as his dad pushes him harder.

"Get in the truck!" Mr. Tanley says. "I swear to God, kid, if you ever touch my goddamn keys again..."

My heart pounds, my hands shake, but I have to do something. I walk toward them and shout, "Tate!"

Both of them turn their heads in my direction. Tate's eyes are wide, his mouth falling open. Panic fills his face. He doesn't want me here.

Keith shoves Tate against the truck then releases a frustrated groan. "See what you did? You get in the truck when I tell you!"

A glass beer bottle swings in his hand—how did he leave with that?—and his anger seems to tip over the edge. He gives Tate a hard kick to the stomach, sending him backward. Tate hits the ground hard, reaching out an arm to break his fall. Even in the dark, I see him wince, pain evident on his face. Keith flings the beer bottle at the gravel parking lot. I dive between them, not knowing what else to do. We both manage to dodge the bottle, but Tate is still on the ground, shaken. I reach down for him, tugging on the sleeve of his shirt.

Keith yanks my hand from Tate and suddenly, Tate is on his feet again, staring down his dad—fierce and angry. Looking so much older than he is. Mr. Tanley, for a brief second, has a flash of fear in his eyes. Then he stalks around the truck, gets in, and takes off, leaving Tate and me alone in the parking lot.

Tate rushes over to me. "Claire, I'm sorry. I'm so sorry."

I'm a couple of inches taller than him, but still, I grip his arm for balance and dip my head to look at him. "What was that? Is he always like that?"

Before he can respond, I release a gasp that's close to a

scream. His left sleeve has just slid up, revealing his arm and it's—well, it's not right.

"Oh my God," I say, and he looks at me, alarmed. "Tate, your arm."

−TATE−

It's like Claire flips a switch, turning on the pain in my arm. It throbs instantly, but it's nothing compared to the nausea that sweeps over me when I actually look at it. My entire body turns cold, my teeth suddenly chattering. I hold my arm out in front of me, not sure what else to do.

The color drains from Claire's face, but she gets to her feet. "Your dad…he pushed you and you must have—" She shakes her head, stopping. "You need a hospital. Like, five minutes ago."

"But my mom…" I'm still holding my arm out like it's not part of me anymore. This seems to keep the pain at bay. "She's there."

My mom is an ER nurse in our tiny local hospital. She's working all night tonight.

"Tate," Claire says, resting a hand on my uninjured arm. "You can't fix a broken arm without your mom finding out."

Yeah, that makes sense. Wait…broken?

I look at it again—God, it's messed up. "Okay, you're right—hospital."

Claire nods and then somehow, what feels like seconds later, she's behind the wheel of her mom's car, driving the two miles to Juniper Falls Medical Center. I lean my head against the headrest and put all my effort into breathing normally.

My arm is broken. The same arm that grips my hockey stick.

The darkness fades as we approach the bright lights of the ER entrance. All six parking spots out front are empty. Claire shuts off the engine and looks at me. For a moment, I'm completely free of pain. My mouth falls open but no words form.

Finally Claire says, "It'll be all right."

My stomach twists and turns. I don't know what that means. And I'm too afraid to ask. I swallow back the fear and use my good hand to pull the door handle.

Inside, the ER is dead. So, of course my mom spots me right away. Her eyes widen, gaze bouncing between the blood on Claire's face and the deformed arm I'm holding carefully against my chest.

My mom is still for a long second before she rushes over. "What happened?"

Claire gives me that look again—the one she wore moments ago in the car—and now I know what she was trying to say. We're going to lie. Both of us. Together.

I just don't know why she's doing this. For me. Because I'm too afraid to tell the truth? That my dad did all of this?

"I tripped on the wooden stairs at the bar," Claire spits out. "And then Tate—"

"Tried to catch her," I add. "But obviously that didn't work out."

My mom gets a good view of my arm and, despite her medical training, she goes pale like Claire did. "Oh God, Tate."

There's sympathy in her eyes. The kind that tells me I'm not playing hockey for a while. The nausea returns, and I glance around for a place to sit down.

But then Claire slips her hand in mine, and I'm okay again. For now.

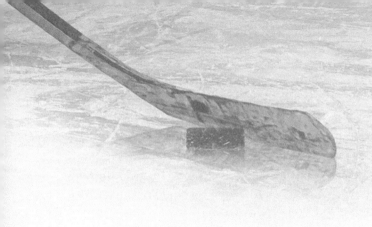

Chapter 1

−TATE−

ONE YEAR LATER

keep trying to sit down, but every time Northfield takes a shot, I'm up, twisting myself into position like I can actually stop a puck from here. It's impossible to watch a game from the bench where my glove and stick are completely useless. Especially after Mike Steller, our starting goalie, just let the Northfield Badgers score their second goal. In our first home game of the season.

Practically the entire town is packed into the arena right now. And after losing game one last week, the boosters and alumni have gone from smiling ass-kissers to using the stiff *we'll give you one loss but that's it* look. The place is so tense it's like the walls are closing in on us with every minute the opposition dominates.

The buzzer goes off, signaling the end of the second period. With a score of 2–0. Them.

I hold my breath and wait for Coach Bakowski's reaction. He flings his clipboard down the bench, and several of the guys on the team jump back.

"Goddammit, Steller!" Bakowski shouts. "What the hell is wrong with you?"

Mike's skating up to the bench, his helmet tucked under his arm. If it were me, my gaze would be glued to the ice. But Steller's staring right back at Coach.

A silent argument seems to flow between them, and then Coach turns to the rest of us. "Get in the locker room, boys. Now!"

I stand up, start to follow my teammate Red, but catch Bakowski say to Mike, "You either get your head in this game or get out of my rink. I'm done with you and all your personal bullshit."

Red catches me eavesdropping and grabs the front of my jersey, pulling me away. We file into the locker room and, given the heavy silence, I can tell I'm not the only one who heard Bakowski's ultimatum.

Mike Steller's spot on the bench in front of his locker stays empty. I sit there rotating the stick in my hand, testing out my left arm—a habit more than a necessity; the bone is fully healed and has been since about a month into last season. But I have to keep myself busy, waiting for the door to swing open.

"This is bad," Jake Hammond, a junior, too, mumbles beside me.

Our senior captain, Leo, speaks up. "Steller may have let a couple of goals slip by, but that doesn't mean we can't score some of our own. Offense wins the game, right?"

Right. And the goalie loses the game.

Some grunts of encouragement follow Leo's pep talk, but they're cut off when the locker room door swings open. Coach

Bakowski and his shiny black dress shoes, but no Mike Steller.

I glance beside me at Red.

Coach stops in the center of the locker room, folds his arms across his chest, and turns slowly in a circle. The dude is freakin' intimidating.

"You listen up, boys," he says. "We have one period left to play, and I swear to God if any of you even so much as thinks the name Mike Steller when our asses are on the line like this, don't even bother showing up at practice tomorrow. Got it?"

Wait…if we aren't mentioning Mike, does that mean…?

Red taps his stick against my skate and says, "Dude. You're in."

My heart pounds so loudly I'm sure everyone in the locker room can hear it. This is what I get for wishing earlier that I could play. I mean, I *want* to play, it's just…fucking varsity.

"Tanley!" Coach swivels around quickly, stopping in front of me. "Number ten has a mean backhand, so watch out for that. Twenty-two likes to go high glove side."

Everyone in the arena will flip when they see me in goal instead of Mike. I can't be Mike Steller. Not yet. It isn't my turn.

Except it is.

Breathe, Tate. Just. Fucking. Breathe.

Coach goes over plays, tosses around insults and errors until everyone is wound so tight the guys practically explode off the benches and out of the locker room.

Me, on the other hand, I'm hoping for a minute alone so I can go barf up the thirty-two-ounce Gatorade I downed in the first period. I try to stall, but Coach grabs my helmet from the bench and shoves it into my chest.

"Let's go, Tanley, get warmed up. You ready?"

Fuck no. "Yeah, Coach. I'm ready!"

The whole walk out onto the ice is a blur, with a few moments of sharpened focus breaking through. Like passing by the Otters's Wall of Fame. I've seen these names a thousand times, but tonight they take on new meaning. Those guys walked down this same hall, suited up in JFH green and silver, then went on to play in the NHL, the Olympics, or for top NCAA teams.

My stomach twists into a tighter ball of knots. The cheering of the crowd, the familiar Otter chants, turns my attention far from the wall back to the ice.

I'm not sure I can do this. I mean, I knew I'd play in a varsity game eventually, but Steller's the senior. He's the one with college and NHL scouts watching. He's the one in the spotlight this season. Not me.

I close my eyes and draw in a deep breath. *He'll be back. Mike will be back.*

Except I don't actually know that for sure. He's been missing practices lately, and we lost last week. And there's his girlfriend and their—

Come on, Tate. Focus.

I can't hear the Otters radio broadcast from inside the arena—especially with all the loud chanting—but I hear the announcement inside my head, dictating the play-by-play for the rare few locals not here: *Otters substitution, number forty-two Tate Tanley in for number ten Mike Steller. I'm not sure what Coach Bakowski is thinking bringing in a cold goalie when we're down by two goals. Let's hope he's got some magic planned.*

In warm-ups, Hammond gets three shots past me, and even Red, who plays defense, sinks the puck low on my glove side. I can feel the crowd growing restless.

"Come on, Tanley, move!" Leo says after I miss his shot, too.

Jesus Christ, what the hell is wrong with me?

I stop to adjust my gloves and glance up into the stands—my mom's still in her nurse's scrubs. Roger is beside her with his five-year-old daughter, Olivia, on his lap. Roger, my new stepfather, whose boxed-up possessions are currently scattered all over my house.

And a couple of rows down from Mom and Roger, my ex-girlfriend is all cozy with a sophomore from JV.

I shift my gaze to the section where all the former Otters in town gather. At least my dad didn't show up today. Last week he popped in on our away game, and I had to put up with all the guys on the bench going on and on about how great Keith Tanley is.

Okay, enough looking up in the stands. *Hockey. Ice. Puck. Glove.*

But before I even have a chance to get my head on straight, the ref is blowing the whistle. Leo and Northfield's player face off and then a few passes later, the puck is sailing toward me. I manage to stop it, but my stick gets knocked out of my hand by my own defender and I can't clear the puck out. Luckily, Jake Hammond is ready and sends the puck flying past the blue line.

I let out a sigh of relief and hold my position while the guys make the other goalie work a little. After a killer pass from Hammond, Leo blows the doors off the opposing goalie with a wicked slap shot from the point. And the Juniper Falls Otters are officially on the scoreboard!

Over the next ten minutes, my teammates help me out, clearing the puck when I'm in the wrong place. Even after we've managed to tie up the score, I can't seem to find my rhythm. I'm hesitating too much. I'm not calculating shots like I should be. I'm thinking too hard instead of just *doing*.

With one minute left, Northfield calls a time-out. The

crowd boos in response and then more chants erupt, feet stomping. The ice is practically vibrating. Leo skates right over to me and wraps his finger around the cage of my helmet. "Look at me, Tanley!"

I look him in the eyes, trying to calm my erratic breathing and slow my sprinting heart.

"I'm gonna go down there and score a goal, and you're going to keep that puck out of our net, got it?"

I nod, and Leo gives me a shove and taps my leg pad with his stick. "That's right. You fucking got this. *We* got this."

True to his word, Leo takes twenty seconds to score, and then my heart is sprinting again. Number ten skates toward me, sliding and shifting the puck all the way. I talk myself through his possible shots and then I shut off all the chatter inside my head, my glove raising on its own.

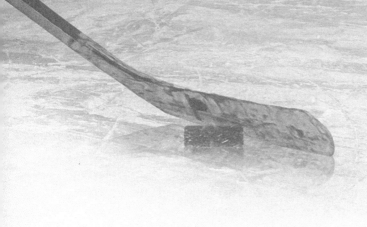

Chapter 2

−CLAIRE−

It's, like, post-Rapture vacant in the bar right now. Which would be awesome if it weren't for the flood of green-and-silver-covered Otters fans on their way over any minute. I wipe down table twelve for a fourth time. Aunt Kay gives me a funny look from her spot behind the bar. I just got back last night. My dad finally got released from the Mayo Clinic in Rochester where I've been camped out all summer and fall. I don't exactly know how to be here. Again. And like this. Working.

My year away at Northwestern University somehow made me forget what the bar is like on game nights. Before the crowds race over here. I'd never been one to watch every single home game, either. I went to enough; I'm not that much of an anti-joiner. Most people assumed if I wasn't at the game, I was here helping my dad, and that was mostly true. He didn't give me much work to do, but we talked a lot. Often about things I wanted to do outside this town. Things that took me far away from here at the most crucial moments.

The game commentary hums across the bar via 107.5: Otters Hockey LiveOnAir playing from the ancient radio behind the bar, but I can't make out specific details, like which period we're in or what the score is. I don't have anyone at the game I can text, either. My desire to get out of town last fall was so strong that I didn't exactly do the best job of staying in touch with anyone.

With a heavy sigh, I toss the overused rag into the bucket of soapy water. Any more table washing and I might break out the choreography and do a rendition of "It's the Hard Knock Life." I grab my coat and put it on over my personalized O'Connor's Tavern apron.

"I'm gonna check on the game," I yell to Kay.

I move briskly through the cold night air, my breath coming out in white puffs, my ugly kitchen-safe shoes pinching my toes as I cross the parking lot that sits between O'Connor's and the ice rink.

The arena is packed—no surprise there. Betty, the old lady who owns the Spark Plug, a coffee shop and bakery down at the end of the block, is leaned against the boards, watching the game.

"Is it me or is this game taking extra long tonight?" I ask.

She shushes me with a raise of her hand and swings her big old-lady purse higher on her shoulder. "Tie game, one minute left…"

One minute left. There's my answer. I'm about to turn around and head back to the bar, but my gaze zooms in on the goalie right in front of me and, more importantly, the name on the back of the jersey: Tanley.

Tate is playing goalie tonight?

"Where's Mike Steller?" I ask Betty.

She shakes her head, her wrinkled face tensing. "I don't

know. Just got here. Someone said he walked out of the building still in full gear—skates and all."

Maybe he's hurt and went to the hospital. But I know Mike Steller, and I don't see him agreeing to a trip to the hospital if he could still walk.

The ref blows the whistle and then proceeds to argue with Northfield's coach over sticking or tripping or something. I turn my attention back to our goalie. Maybe it's all the pads, but I can't see any sign of the lanky, skinny arms he used to have. He looks close to six feet now. A flash of the younger, shorter Tate from last fall hits me.

I told him not to change. He promised me.

"Promise me something, Tate?"

"What?"

"Don't change, okay?"

"Yeah, I know. You wrote that in my yearbook."

"But I mean it now. Promise me you won't become another varsity hockey player."

The crowd erupts in a fit of desperate cheers. They're already panicking at the tie game, and I can feel a rush of nerves.

Leo comes over and gives Tate a loud pep talk, and then the clock starts again. My eyes are glued to the goalie. Tate stays moving and alert while his teammates are at the opposite end of the ice. And then Leo scores a goal. The crowd jumps to their feet and Northfield's five players charge at us. Well, they're charging at Tate, but they look huge and fierce and it feels like they're coming at Betty and me. She reaches over and grasps my hand, her grip tight.

Two of Northfield's players are screening Tate, blocking his view of number nine, who is about to shoot. I suck in a breath and lift my free hand, half covering my face. There's a space near Tate's left skate, but he quickly spreads his legs apart, covering the area, and then his glove rises, meeting the puck right on time.

The buzzer goes off, and the volume from where we're standing magnifies to an almost intolerable level. The Otters pile on top of one another, tossing their sticks onto the ice while the fans in the bleachers cheer and dance to the school's game-winning anthem the pep band is playing.

Betty releases my hand and then pats it once more before turning to face me. "Well, that's a relief. Nothing worse than Saturday morning customers after a loss at home."

I groan. "Nothing worse than *Friday night drunks* after a win at home." It's all coming back to me now. Of course I know that we need the business. The off-season is always hell for my parents' finances, but add a huge stack of medical bills all during the slow summer months, and yeah, things are bad.

"Okay, you got me beat there, dear." Betty smiles, and then it quickly fades. "How's your father doing? Did he get the pastries I sent?"

He got the pastries. Not that he ate them. Or much of anything. When I left the house this morning, the entire island in our kitchen was covered in casseroles, baked goods, and freezer meals. Haley Stevenson, along with her mom, was walking over from their house two doors down, each carrying a large dish. When I get home later, all of it will probably still be there, untouched.

I plaster on my *grateful for life's miracles* face. "He's doing better, and he said thanks for the treats."

While the guys celebrate the victory, I notice Tate still staring at the puck in his glove. Leo and Red skate over to him, ripping off his helmet and attempting to lift him off the ice. He allows his helmet to fall on top of the net but shakes out of their grip. Then he turns around to grab it, and suddenly his gaze meets mine.

I take a couple of steps backward. My heart picks up speed.

That's definitely Tate. But it's not Jody's scrawny little brother with a mouth full of braces. That kid couldn't have stood under these bright arena lights carrying the weight of all six thousand people in town like this new Tate did.

With his eyes on me, his mouth falls open, either in shock or because he's about to say something to me through the Plexiglas wall. But then three of his teammates pounce on him, and before he can even anticipate what's happening, he's on the bottom of an Otters pileup. I guess his arm healed. I wonder if he ever told anyone about—

I shake my head and quickly exit the arena.

My dad is recovering from a supposed-to-be-inoperable brain tumor, enduring radiation and chemotherapy treatments, "just in case they didn't get it all" during the surgery. My school friends are all knee-deep into the fall quarter without me. Northwestern fall musical auditions have come and passed already—no Claire O'Connor on the cast list. The only place I'm singing now is in the shower.

I can't get caught up worrying about Tate Tanley and something that happened a year ago.

Chapter 3

−TATE−

Jamie Isaacs, one of our senior defenders, takes a foot off the frozen pond and steps in my direction. "Tanley, where's the fucking chainsaw?"

I've got my cell in one hand, a can of beer in the other. I glance over my shoulder at Jake's truck and then back at my phone, quickly reading a text from earlier.

HALEY: need to talk about NYE asap! call me back or I'll find u after the game

I stuff the phone in my pocket and head over to the red truck backed up just feet from the edge of Juniper Falls Pond. I'm not responding to Haley. Even though I'm not willing to say it out loud, I'm still too hurt and confused to be around her. She's the one who said two months ago that we needed a break, so why do I need to discuss New Year's Eve with her? This is Haley's thing. She doesn't know when to give in. But tonight, it's not working. I've got a different girl on my mind.

Claire O'Connor.

I'd heard she was coming home, but I haven't seen her since last fall. Since that awkward moment in the car after my broken arm had been straightened out, when she called me cute and innocent and made me promise to stay that way.

"Get the tape measure, too," Leo shouts, his skates slung over his shoulder.

The chainsaw is easy to spot in the bed of Jake's truck, but the tape measure takes longer to find. I toss a rope around my neck, just in case anyone needs rescuing. A lot of beer combined with a possible—but not definitely—frozen pond can equal trouble.

"We had a half inch last week, right?" Jamie asks. "It's gotta be ready."

"Especially considering it's fucking cold out here," Red says while he blows on his hands. He's not wearing a hat or gloves like the rest of us.

"What do you think Steller's doing right now?" Jamie asks, out of the blue. "Think that trailer he's been squatting in is heated?"

All of us stop to look at Jamie. Beside me, Leo tenses. So far Mike Steller has managed to stay out of tonight's conversation. Leo shakes his head. "Doesn't matter. We can't fucking ask him. We can't fucking talk to him. Bakowski would kill us." He looks around at each of us. "You guys got that?"

Another beat of silence hangs over us, and then Jake takes the chainsaw from me and steps a foot onto what appears to be solid ice. "The average temperature has been twenty-two for a week, so that should give us at least another couple of inches of ice."

"Assuming we've had some wind and the snow hasn't slowed things down," I add. We need four inches of solid ice to skate, fish, or play hockey. Five inches and we can drive our snowmobiles on the ice. I've got an old beat-up one that sometimes runs. Jake Hammond's got a brand-new one. I was on it last weekend. Not on the pond, though, since it wasn't ready yet.

I live about three miles from here, on an inlet, so I've got my own ice to skate and fish on, but it's not Juniper Falls Pond.

"I'm waiting for you two to start calculating mathematical formulations," Jamie says, shaking his head at Jake and me. He reaches for another beer, pops open the can, and chugs half of it. "How about I just go out there and jump up and down a few times? If it holds, then it's ready."

"No," Hammond and I both say automatically. Leo reaches out and grabs the back of Jamie's jacket, just in case he's drunker than we thought.

Jake is tipping back the last of his beer, preparing to start up the chainsaw, when we hear a new set of feet crunching through the snow.

"Good evening, boys."

Both Red and I toss our beer cans into a bush a few feet away. Jake dives behind a tree. Leo and Jamie, who are standing a little ways from Hammond's truck, tuck their beer cans behind their backs.

Sheriff Hammond strolls over to us, shining his flashlight in each of our faces. "I'm sure those weren't beer cans I saw you tossing into the bushes, right?"

We all know better than to answer that question.

"And that wouldn't happen to be my nephew cowering behind a tree, would it?" He points the flashlight accusingly in Jake's direction. "I'll tell you what I'm gonna do…"

We all hold our breaths as he spins around to face us again. "Hand over those car keys and walk on home, and we'll keep this between us."

Leo and Jamie also drove here but parked on the street. I rode with Leo. Red came with Hammond. The three guys with keys reluctantly slap them into Sheriff Hammond's palm. He grins at us like this is the most fun he's had all evening. "Go on, boys, get yourselves home and come by the station around noon tomorrow to pick up your keys."

My hands are freezing even with my gloves on, and we haven't even started the three-mile walk home.

We distance ourselves from the sheriff—he's busy returning the chainsaw to Jake's truck. Jake points to the woods. "You guys want to come over?"

From here, assuming you cut through the woods, it's less than a mile to Hammond's place. Beats the three miles to mine. But Leo and Jamie shake their heads and Jamie says, "I'm not fucking walking through the woods at night."

Jake shrugs, and Red turns to follow him. Those two usually stick together.

"See you guys later." Jake gives me a nod. "Great save tonight, Tanley."

I look out at the dark night in front of us and sigh. So much for varsity player perks.

Leo, Jamie, and I head on foot in the opposite direction, out onto James Street.

"You know what?" Jamie says, slurring his words a little. "We need fucking girlfriends." Jamie zips up his letter jacket until it's practically strangling him. "That's where the rest of the guys are…with their girlfriends probably fu—"

"Tanley *had* a girlfriend," Leo says.

Jamie laughs. "Haley fucking Stevenson…how the hell did you screw that one up, Tate?"

I roll my eyes. It's not that simple. Haley didn't really want to break up. But she wants me back on her terms, and I'm not willing to agree to them.

Leo looks at me and laughs. "Fort Knox, huh? The wound still fresh?"

I just shrug. I'm not getting into this tonight.

"No worries, man," Jamie says, which means I must look upset or stressed. "You won the game for us tonight. You're about to have a fucking line of girls who are completely into varsity guys. I bet pretty soon you'll have too many admirers. Maybe you can send a couple of them my way?"

My silence only encourages Jamie to keep going on this topic.

"Let's see...we've got Hammond, who's too picky," Jamie rattles off. "Red's trailer-park ass is from the wrong side of the tracks. Tanley is apparently taking his time choosing a rebound girl." He gives a nod in my direction. "And Leo's a bit...*confused*."

Leo's face darkens, and he shoves Jamie hard, causing him to trip over a stick on the ground. "Dude, what the hell?"

I feel my jaw drop open and then quickly clamp it shut. This is one of those situations where it's probably best if I play dumb or pretend I didn't hear anything.

Luckily, when we walk through the parking lot of O'Connor's, Jamie drops the topic in favor of his stomach.

"I smell fried fish," Jamie adds. "Can we eat?"

I lift my gaze to the brick building and inhale the scent of fried food. Leo does the same and says, "Think they'll let us in now?"

"Probably not," I say. But honestly, I would love to see Claire again. See how she's doing with everything. Or maybe she's not even here. Maybe I imagined her standing there watching me at the end of the game tonight.

Jamie snorts. "Duh. We won tonight. They'll probably serve us drinks, too."

"Only one way to find out." Leo is already heading for the door.

Chapter 4

–TATE–

Claire is leaning against the bar, loading a tray of beer glasses. Her long reddish-brown hair is falling out of its ponytail, and the many orders of cheese fries she probably took tonight have left evidence on the side of her T-shirt and on her black pants and green apron. My gaze follows her swaying hips and tall, slim figure as she walks the drinks out to a table of gritty-looking guys.

One guy whistles when Claire places the beer in front of him, which she completely ignores. Another dude openly stares at her ass.

"Don't tell me that's why you didn't want to come in here?" Jamie says, watching me.

The thing is, part of me did want to see her, make sure she's okay. And the other part of me is still humiliated from the events of last fall. A night I really haven't been able to shake off over the past year.

My neck heats up, and I look away from Claire. "Didn't

know she was working here now."

"Heard she dropped out of school," Jamie says.

Leo shakes his head. "Just a semester off. You know, 'cause of her dad."

"Oh, right." Jamie looks over at Claire and back at me. "Didn't she used to have sleepovers at your house?"

"Yeah. With my sister." I bury my nose in the menu. "Should we get two or three horseshoes?"

Claire's mom makes her way over to us, and we put in our orders right away. I want to ask her about Davin, but it seems too public here. Too intrusive. The second she's gone, Larry Jones and the alumni table spot us. Of course they wave us over. Jamie and Leo jump at the chance to converse about the game.

"Look at the glove hand on that kid," Rusty Lucas, an old teammate of my dad's, says, whistling at me. "Little Tanley saves the game. Can't believe Keith missed it."

I grit my teeth and continue following my teammates across the dining room. Luckily my dad had only made it to a handful of JV games over the last two seasons. I have a feeling, with my playing varsity and his living a little closer now, that's gonna change.

"Bet you're glad to have him closer, though," Larry says.

This statement has been made about a hundred thousand times since last fall. I bet I can guess what comes next. *U Mich is too damn—*

"U Mich is too damn far away," Rusty shouts. "So is Minneapolis, but he was destined to be an SMU Hawk…"

We haven't even reached their table yet and they're already at the part where they go on and on about how unfair it was that my dad got knocked out and permanently injured before he even played one game for SMU, a top NCAA Division I team for hockey, and how no one deserved that scholarship more than Keith Tanley, *blah blah blah*. I'm at the point where I tune it out and remind myself that I want to play and how little that has to do with my dad.

I step toward Claire while she's serving drinks to another table of whistling, ass-gawking dudes. I slow my pace, unable to look away.

"Come on, baby. Bet I'm better than that other pansy," the whistling guy says. He mimes pinching her ass behind her back, then grabs it for real. My blood boils, my fingers tingling.

I'm behind the guy in two long strides, snatching his hand out of the air and twisting his arm behind him. Beneath my fingers, his entire body stiffens. I lean down, getting a whiff of stale beer and dead fish.

"If her daddy were here tonight, he'd do a lot more than break your arm," I say into his ear. He tries to shove me back with his free hand, but I tighten my grip and hold him firmly in place. "Keep your hands to yourself. Got it?"

He glares up at my letter jacket from over his shoulder and attempts to throw a punch that might have hit my nose if I hadn't dodged it. I keep my grip on him tight so he can't even rise from his chair.

"Get off me, kid! You want to take this outside? I'm sure my friends will help me out."

He nods toward the two guys at the table with him. They look way drunker than he is. From the corner of my eye, I see Leo and Jamie standing nearby, arms folded over their chests. The three of us combined aren't exactly lacking brute strength. Not that we have any desire to engage in a bar fight with a bunch of idiot fishermen.

"Let's get out of here," one of the guys says.

"Great idea."

The sound of her voice pushes away the cloud of anger. I glance up and see Claire standing there wide-eyed, her gaze bouncing between the ass-grabber and me. The whole place has gone quiet.

I'm startled when Larry Jones touches my shoulder. "All right, son, let the asshole go before you get yourself in trouble with Coach Bakowski."

It's always about getting in trouble with Coach. Player eligibility first, criminal law second.

I release the guy, shoving him in the process. He nearly falls backward out of his chair. They each toss some bills onto the table and stumble toward the door. It helps that all five alumni guys are glaring at them, along with my teammates and me.

Larry clasps a hand on my shoulder. "Come and sit down with us."

I shake my head, too much adrenaline rushing through my veins to respond. I turn to Claire, whose expression is now a mix of shock and exasperation.

Chapter 5

−CLAIRE−

What the hell just happened?

When did Tate Tanley get such a deep voice?

And when did he start rescuing girls from drunk creepers in bars?

And then there's Larry Jones resting a hand on his shoulder and calling him *son*. Jesus Christ, a lot can happen in a year.

Larry Jones takes Tate by the shoulders, steering him toward their table, and then calls over to Leo and Jamie. "Come join us, boys!" He shoots a glance in my mom's direction. "Anna, bring these gentlemen some food and put it all on my tab, will ya?"

Tate looks like he wants to protest, but it's not easy to tell Larry Jones no. Pretty soon he and the other players, plus the alumni, are all seated at a table. Minutes later, my mom serves them drinks and our famous walleye horseshoes.

We fill up three more tables while I'm trying to eavesdrop

on the hockey conversation, and I get pulled away to serve drinks to a few more fishermen plus a bachelorette party taking up two tables.

A tap on my shoulder sends me spinning around, and suddenly I'm face-to-face with Tate. "So…" he says, leaning an elbow against the bar. "Are you rich and famous yet? Headed for Broadway? I should probably get your autograph now before the paparazzi start chasing you."

I laugh and then give him the full once-over for, like, the hundredth time tonight. This is getting out of hand. Jody would probably freak if she caught me looking at her little brother like this. "When and how did you become…" I wave a hand dramatically in front of him. *"This?"*

"What?" He glances down and tugs on the front of his hunter-green thermal beneath his unzipped jacket. "Someone who wears earth tones?"

"No! Th-that," I sputter, blowing hair off my face, "tall and…not skinny… And the voice…"

His eyebrows shoot up, a grin spreading across his face. "Oh. *That.* My mom calls it puberty, but she's just a nurse. What does she know?"

I relax a little. Something about Tate mentioning his mom is a familiar comfort. "Puberty is when you lose the ability to look a girl in the eyes. And when you discover internet porn. *This* is something entirely different."

Mom bumps her hip into mine. "If you're gonna chitchat, take it back in the kitchen. Tell Manny he can come out here and serve. We'll see if any creeps try to grab his backside."

"Tate, get over here!" Leo says. He's at the alumni table now, along with Jamie. Both look pretty comfortable there. "You're missing the ninety-four-season story."

Ninety-four…? Oh, right. The year Keith Tanley made the game-winning shot at State Finals.

Tate drops his gaze to the floor and swears under his breath. There's tension and darkness in his expression that I don't remember being there the last time I saw him. Clearly he's changed. I glance down at his jeans—they hug him just right. *Clearly.*

He looks in the direction of his friends' table. "I should probably get over there." He turns to head toward their table but stops abruptly after seeing our newest customers walk through the door. Tiny blond Haley Stevenson, still in her JFH cheer uniform, her parents beside her.

I'm about to wave to them and thank them for bringing a casserole we probably won't eat, but Tate is spinning me around. "Actually, let's go have that chat in the kitchen."

With him walking behind me, I'm even more aware of his height and broader build. I'm only a few inches shy of six feet myself, so I notice when guys are taller than me. I also notice when guys are so blatantly avoiding their girlfriends.

In the kitchen, Manny's seventy-year-old body is hunched over the fryer, his hand gripping the basket handle. "Got a hen party for you to serve, Manny."

Manny laughs and, without question, heads out of the kitchen. After he's gone, I assess the orders pinned above my head—two horseshoes and a BLT.

"Careful, that's hot," I warn when Tate leans against the grill. I point to the empty counter on my other side, and he walks around me, brushing his elbow against my rib cage. I shake off the shiver that runs down my spine.

"When did you get back?" Tate asks.

"Last night," I say right away. And then I'm silent for a couple of minutes, too busy tossing bacon onto the grill, while Tate tries to hide the fact that he keeps glancing out into the dining room. Eventually I say, "I saw your mom at the game earlier." His eyebrows lift like he's waiting for me to bring up our little moment of eyeing each other. "She was with…"

"The new husband," he finishes.

I quickly assemble the plates and ring the bell before tossing them up to the counter. I wipe my hands on my apron. "How's that going?"

"What?" he asks. "The stepfamily? Or living with Roger 'The Critter Crusader' Cremwell?"

I laugh. "Yeah. *That*. All of that."

"It's weird, you know? I mean, he's an exterminator. Critter-killing supplies have taken over my garage. And then there's Olivia…she's always either refusing to talk, eat, or sleep, or she's lying on the ground throwing a tantrum. I mean, she's a little kid; I guess that's what they do so whatever. It's just weird. Especially without Jody here to offer her rational solutions."

Jody's away at college now. Just started this fall. I don't even know how she's liking it so far. It's amazing how easy it is to get out of touch with people, even ones you'd like to keep in touch with.

Aunt Kay yells for me to go upstairs and get the giant boxes of toilet paper stored there. I roll my eyes but snatch the keys from the wall anyway.

He looks out into the dining room again and then quickly says, "You want some help?"

"Sure, if you don't mind?" Soon we're both outside by the Dumpsters, heading up the very staircase that supposedly caused Tate's broken arm last year. I grit my teeth, hating Keith Tanley all over again.

When I open the door, revealing the apartment, Tate looks around, amazed. "What happened here?"

"My dad's project last year after I left for school." I head straight for the unfinished storage area and open the door so I can crawl in and get Aunt Kay's toilet paper. "We're trying to rent it out, make a little extra income."

After I toss out two big boxes, I emerge, dusting off my clothes as best I can. "This could be my new life now, refilling toilet paper. Especially if I keep abandoning my tables."

"Sorry, I'm distracting you." Tate picks up one of the boxes. "I just meant to ask you about…"

"What?" I prompt.

"Game night." He smiles. "Next game night. You know the team dinner? Before the game. It's been pizza two weeks in a row, and we're all pretty sick of it, especially before a game. Maybe we can work out something with O'Connor's and…"

The fact that it's obvious he's making this up on the spot is only drawing my attention to the fact that Tate is now a guy flirting with me. A guy who I thought had a loyal girlfriend, but maybe not anymore…?

"Nice playing tonight, by the way." I stand and lift the remaining box. "What happened to Steller?"

He shrugs but says nothing. The dismissal isn't unfamiliar. It's incredible the fortress of secrets these hockey boys keep. *Whatever*. I'll find out elsewhere. Mike and I were friends last year. I can ask him myself.

We're outside again, on the landing. I'm digging for the key when someone whistles from below. Jamie and Leo are outside, probably waiting for Tate. Tate looks over at them and then sets down his box. "Maybe we can talk later…about the team dinner stuff?"

The part of my brain not in shock or still ogling Tate remembers the medical and credit card bills I sifted through this morning. Matching last year's in-season revenue isn't gonna cover those expenses, not even close. "Anything to drum up business during the off-hours is on my to-do list. I can call you if you want?"

He pulls out his phone at the same time that I realize I

don't have his number. With Jody always between us, there was never a need for it.

"Yo, T-Man, let's go!" Jamie shouts up at Tate. "Stevenson's gonna see you."

Okay, so I'm beginning to think he and Haley are no longer an item? I glance down at Jamie and Leo again; they seem to be in a hurry, so I take Tate's phone and quickly punch in my number.

"Thanks, Claire." He gives me that familiar Tate Tanley smile again, but it's so different from a year ago.

Or maybe it's just my reaction that's different.

Chapter 6

-TATE-

I glance back at the bar one last time before walking away. Claire is already inside, greeting the newest customers. When I turn back around, Jamie and Leo are both staring at me.

"What?" I demand.

"Dude, what the hell was that?" Jamie says, sounding both annoyed and fascinated.

"Nothing." I shake my head. "What do you mean?"

"Claire O'Connor," Leo says. "You were putting the moves on her."

"What moves?" I don't have moves.

The wind picks up, and all three of us groan in unison, zipping our jackets.

"You did that leaning-on-the-counter thing. You found an excuse to touch her arm. Twice. And then you got her number," Jamie rattles off like he was keeping a list.

Leo gives me this look that says, *Seriously?* "No offense

or anything, T-Man, but you can't handle that shit right now. We need you at a hundred percent."

"He's right, dude." Jamie kicks a chunk of ice with his toe, sending it out into the road. "Look at how much this Haley stuff is fucking with your head… Plus, are you guys really broken up?"

"If it's not common knowledge," Leo chimes in, "people will talk."

"Okay, I get it," I snap. "It's all about hockey. Thanks, Captain."

"Don't be a smart-ass," Leo says, but he's dropped the authoritative tone. "We're just trying to help."

I ignore Leo and wave at a truck slowing down as they pass us. It's Kyle Stewart, one of our varsity defenders. We're getting a ride.

Stewart rolls down the window and whistles at us. "Look at you boys, hot stuff! Get in the back and let me have my way with you."

None of us hesitates. Once we're in the back, Leo bangs on the window, signaling for Stewart to take off. He's yelling something at us that sounds like, "We're headed to Benny's."

We don't bother trying to tell him that we already ate, because most people are just there to hang out. Plus, knowing Jamie, he's probably twenty minutes from complaining that he's starving. Again.

Sitting in the back of the truck might actually be worse than walking home. My entire body is numb by the time we're tumbling out.

But a little while later, we're thawed and seated in the middle of a crowded table. I must have been silent for too long because eventually Jamie snaps his fingers in front of my face.

"You okay, T-Man?" Jamie asks.

I dunk a fry into ketchup instead of responding to Jamie's question. I think he and Leo got me paranoid. All I can do is replay my entire interaction with Claire tonight and think of a million ways I fucked it up. For one, I didn't even ask her how Davin was doing. All my information on him over the past several months has been hearsay and third-party. Would have been nice to get it right from a reliable source. And *was* I flirting with Claire? Is she gonna label me as just another varsity player *player* guy? I promised her I wouldn't be like that. Last fall, after the emergency room while we sat in the car talking.

"I promise. For you, I won't turn into Pratt."

"Why for me?"

"Because you deserve that."

Stewart plops down at our table with a bag of burgers and fries. Stewart's girlfriend is Haley's best friend, so I'm already braced for Kayla to hop over here and glare at me on behalf of Haley for ignoring the calls and texts earlier.

"Tanley!" a guy from my trig class shouts from across the diner, interrupting my thoughts. "You're the man!"

A few more yells of "Tanley!" echo the first, but before I can react, two girls from the volleyball team slide into the bench seat beside me. Leo nearly topples off on my other side.

"Hey, Tate," both girls say in unison.

"Great game tonight," the taller brunette—Jessica—says.

"It was, wasn't it?" Jamie looks at the girls and then at me, lifting an eyebrow as if to suggest more.

The other girl, Renee, used to play rec hockey with me years ago. Her dad coached us for two seasons. He was pretty cool. Renee turns to me. "My dad would not shut up about your last-second save. He's claiming he taught you how to use your glove."

I laugh. "Um…it's possible, I guess."

I mean, I've had more than a dozen coaches since I started playing in kindergarten. One of them must have taught me how to use my glove.

"So what the hell is up with Mike Steller?" Jessica asks, leaning in like it's a gossip session.

My eyes drop to the fries in front of me, Jamie stuffs a bite of burger into his mouth, and Leo stares out at the wall behind Jamie. Stewart is focused on Jessica's cleavage. I kick him under the table and he jolts to life, lifting his head and searching the restaurant for Kayla.

Renee shakes her head. "Hockey boys and their secrets. Nothing changes around here."

"Except Tate." Jessica reaches out a hand and pets my cheek. "Look, you have facial hair."

I try to lean back, but I'm trapped between two girls and Leo. I move Jessica's hand from my face and look over at Renee. "Is she drunk?"

Renee shrugs. "Probably."

"I'm just trying to figure out why Haley dumped him." Jessica comes at me again, petting my face with both hands this time. "He's so pretty."

Jamie snorts and Leo sprays soda all over Stewart. If these are the "varsity perks" Jamie mentioned earlier, then I might ask for my bench spot back.

It's well after two a.m. when Stewart finally drops me off. I figure Mom and Roger are in bed by now, so I tiptoe in, stepping over boxes in the kitchen.

I walk past Jody's room and stop in the doorway. It's been emptied out, plastic now covers the carpet, and a bucket of pink paint sits on the floor. My stomach turns over, Benny's greasy fries rumbling around in protest. I guess I knew Olivia would need this room and her six-year-old tastes have to be different from my eighteen-year-old sister's, but seeing it empty…it's like it's finally real.

My mom has a new husband, a new stepdaughter. My sister is moved out.

My parents have been divorced for years and all these other changes are happening inside my house and yet, I'm still stuck being "Little Tanley," son of Keith Tanley. All because of a game we both happen to love playing. And our town happens to love watching.

Chapter 7

-TATE-

"I hate Saturday practice," Jamie groans when the three of us come out of the locker room in our gear.

Yeah, Saturday afternoon practice sucks, especially following Friday night games. Especially when we're forced into taking a long walk to retrieve car keys before practice.

Red and Hammond sidle up beside me, and I ask Jake, "You got your truck back?"

"Not without some Uncle Oz blackmail," he says, keeping his voice low. "'The sheriff' can't make me clean out rain gutters in exchange for his silence, but apparently my uncle can."

"Sorry, man. That sucks."

Jake Hammond might have more money than most of us in this town, but his uncle is the sheriff and his dad is a state senator. He's not exactly allowed to get in trouble.

"You ready for this?" Leo asks, tapping a poster hanging on the Otter Wall of Fame.

My dad's face is taking up most of the paper. A microscopic me is way down at the bottom. I suppress a groan. I can't believe it's almost time for the winter clinic already. Last year, Jake and his dad were the "featured pair," but a couple of months ago, my dad and I were asked to be the poster pair this year. Should be a blast.

"Let's go, boys!" Bakowski shouts from center ice. He pulls the whistle to his lips, blowing one short signal to start our sprints even before all twenty of us have made it out onto the ice.

There's an extra layer of tension in the arena today. Bakowski obviously wasn't kidding when he said we weren't even allowed to think Steller's name.

Throughout warm-ups, I keep telling myself to be nothing but focused. The puck. My glove. My stick. That's all there is.

When Coach whistles for us to get into position, there's a definite and dramatic pause while everyone stares at Mike's usual practice goal. It isn't easy for me to take my place at his goal. My stomach knots. Is he gone for good?

Is that what I want?

I don't know. I don't fucking know.

Jamie and Leo are watching me closely, probably anticipating that I'd have this breakdown. And they need me to be on. They've gotten verbal offers for college, but they haven't signed anything. We need to make it to State. That doesn't happen with a shitty goalie. Ever.

Playing in Mike Steller's goal today, instead of at the other end with the second- and third-line guys, I'm up against some shots I've never seen before. Pretty soon, I'm drenched in sweat, my body aching, while I dive for pucks coming at me from every direction.

"Watch the five hole, Tanley!" Coach shouts after Hammond sinks one in the net.

I shove my knees together, causing the next shot to bounce off my leg pads. At the other end of the ice, Ty, the assistant coach, is calmly offering up tips to the JV sophomore who's taken *my* place. I'm not used to Coach Bakowski breathing down my neck for an entire practice. It's enough to jerk me out of my bubble of focus. That and the sight of Claire O'Connor entering through the far door of the rink with an armload of takeout containers.

I follow her with my eyes, and my glove hangs limply at my side while two pucks sail over my shoulder into the goal.

"Dammit, Tanley! Toss that glove in the garbage if you're not gonna use it!" Bakowski's face turns a shade of purple that we all recognize as his tipping point. "All right, that's enough. Get the hell off my ice. All of you. Monday morning. Seven."

Once my helmet is off, my eyes are glued to the ice. I hate being the reason for that pissed-off dismissal. Before I make it to the boards, Coach Ty grabs my sleeve. "It's not you, kid. Relax, okay?"

It's Steller. I get it. Coach is grieving the loss of his star goalie and taking it out on me. The problem with that is, it's screwing with my head, and that's screwing with my game. I mull over the possibility of Steller coming back. I need to find out one way or the other.

When I skate off the ice, Claire's at the rental counter delivering food. Her gaze travels over to the poster on the wall, the one for the winter hockey clinic with the tiny photo of me at the bottom.

"The new poster boy, huh?" she says to me.

"Crazy, right?" I lift a hand to keep her from stepping in my direction. "Trust me, you don't want any of this near you."

Claire laughs but takes my advice and remains a couple of feet away. She checks out the poster again and then turns back to me. "Who's providing lunch at the clinic?"

"Not sure. Last year I think it was Pizza Henry's…" I scratch my head. "Maybe that was two years ago?"

"You think they'd let O'Connor's do it?" Her face lights up in this way that makes me want to give her anything she wants. "That's a Saturday, right? We're always dead on Saturdays until late afternoon, so it would be a perfect time for catering."

I'd suggested something along those lines last night when we exchanged phone numbers. Though I kind of made it up in the moment. Maybe if I can help her with this, last night's idea won't seem so far-fetched.

"Ty's in charge of the clinic. We should ask him." I glance around. He's gathering cones on the ice. I wave him over, and by the time he reaches us, Claire's got a tiny notebook and pen out. "Claire wanted to know about the winter clinic, if you've got food lined up—"

"We can do kid food," Claire says, taking over. "Chicken fingers and fries. Or if you think a healthier option might impress the moms, we can do pasta and veggie trays…"

Ty hesitates before saying, "I did give Gale's Hoagies a maybe, but she doesn't serve at all, just drops stuff off, so if you could—"

"Definitely," Claire says right away. "We'll do everything. Let you focus on the hockey."

They continue to hash out details, Claire scribbling furiously in her notebook. I head for the locker room because I'm in need of a shower, but I catch Claire mouth a *thank-you* to me. I'm smiling down at my skates like an idiot when someone shoves me from behind.

"Nice one, Tanley," Red says, loud enough for Claire to hear. Her eyes widen but she keeps up the conversation with Ty.

"Not a bad pick for a rebound girl," Red says, once we're inside the locker room.

Wait...what?

"Don't know who you're talking about." I peel off my jersey and then get to work on unlacing my skates. My glove hand is cramped and throbbing.

"Really?" Red challenges. "Stewart says he saw you two coming out of that apartment, looking a little flushed..."

My mouth falls open. "What?"

"You saw him last night?" Jamie says to Stewart. "Right before you picked us up? Were you smokin' up in the parking lot again?"

His truck had arrived with suspicious timing.

"Come on," Stewart says to Red, completely ignoring Jamie's accusations. "It couldn't have been what it looked like. A few minutes ago, Tanley missed an easy shot 'cause he was watching Claire walk ten paces fully clothed."

"Claire O'Connor..." Frankie, a senior defender, says. "I always thought she was kinda weird. Or maybe it's just the theater people she hung out with. Those guys are weird as hell."

"She's smart, too," Owen Jensen says. "Freshman year I cheated off her in civics all the time. Best grade I've gotten so far in high school."

"She's only been back for a couple of days," I say, needing to put an end to this conversation. These guys don't have the right to suddenly take notice of Claire when I've seen her, admired her for years. "I went up there to help her carry boxes of toilet paper."

"So you did go up there," Red says at the same time Stewart says, "Is that what they're calling it these days?"

I can feel all eyes on me. I toss a skate into my bag. "It wasn't like that." I look up to make sure they heard me, then stand to my full height, fists clenched at my sides. "I'm serious."

"Sheriff took our keys, then we froze our asses off walking home, so we stopped at O'Connor's for food. Then Tanley, Jamie, and I helped carry boxes down from upstairs before Stewart swung by and picked us up," Leo says. He's looking right at me, shaking his head, doing his responsible captain duties to keep any fighting directed at other players, like from other teams. But I can practically hear his thoughts right now: *I told you, man. This shit's fucking complicated.*

"You guys got a ride?" Red throws his smelly jersey at Leo. "Fuck that! Me and Hammond walked home through the woods. I swear some critter bit me on the ankle."

"A twig." Jake rolls his eyes. "It was a goddamned twig."

Stewart clanks his stick against the locker, drawing attention his way. "Why don't you get Tanley's new daddy to check it out? He's a certified critter-bite professional."

I open my mouth to say something to him, but Leo grabs the back of my undershirt and steers me toward the showers, away from our benches and lockers. "Ignore him."

"They know we didn't... I mean, we really were carrying boxes," I say to Leo when we're in the shower area. "What the hell is the big deal? Jesus."

"It's something different," Leo rationalizes. "Claire's more interesting now. She's, like, an outsider, being away and all."

Claire's always been interesting to me. But I keep that to myself, knowing how Leo feels about the subject.

I change quickly, ahead of Leo, my ride, and then I duck into an alcove on the far side of the rink beneath the bleachers. I pull up Mike's number on my phone, glance around once more, then hit call.

He answers on the first ring.

"Mike, hey..." I exhale. "Are you okay, man?"

The two seconds of silence nearly kill me. "Yeah, T. I'm sorry."

Sorry for leaving or sorry for not coming back?

"Hey, you'll be fine," he adds, giving me my answer. He's not coming back.

I sink down on the ground, leaning my back against the wall. This is it. I could try and persuade him, but what kind of asshole would do that? He's got real shit to deal with and, well...I'm just chicken shit.

"Yeah... No, you're right. It'll be fine," I spit out. "I got this, no problem."

We hang up a minute later and I stay there for a while, staring at my phone, finally letting it sink in.

I'm goalie this season. Me. I'm it. Time to fucking grow into my jersey.

Chapter 8

–TATE–

When I get home from practice, I notice a familiar car in the driveway. A tan Honda Accord. Haley.

I quietly inch my way toward the garage where my snowmobile is waiting. But before I can hop on, Mom pokes her head out the front door and spots me. "Tate, get in here." I glance between her and the garage, debating a rebellious runaway. But Mom narrows her eyes and, with a sigh, I head into the kitchen. It's bad enough that I have to see Haley at school. Why does she have to be at my freaking house on a Saturday?

Haley's standing in my kitchen decked out in a poufy, long white formal dress that looks vaguely familiar.

I glare at Mom. "Thanks for the warning."

My mom rolls her eyes, but there's a hint of guilt on her face. *Good.*

"Are you sure Jody won't mind?" Haley says to my mom.

Okay, so maybe that's why she wanted to talk to me yesterday. She's wearing my sister's dress even though we broke up. Jesus Christ, she made it sound like a matter of national security.

"Of course not, honey. When is she gonna use it again?" my mom says.

This was Jody's dress when she was nominated for Juniper Falls Princess—yes, we have royalty in small-town Minnesota—a town-wide tradition in its hundred and something year. Every November the Juniper Falls Women's League chooses six members of the JFH junior class—four girls, four guys—to be part of the court. The Prince and Princess are announced at the town New Year's Eve ball. Its sounds silly—kind of is to me—but it's a huge deal around here. And it's all Haley has talked about since near the end of sophomore year.

Both Mom and Haley are staring at me like they've been waiting forever for me to come home. Haley and her big brown eyes and blond hair. Haley, who couldn't be with me anymore unless I became "more committed to her goals."

"What?" I snap.

"Keep your voice down," Mom warns me. "Olivia's asleep on the couch."

"We were just…um…discussing what color tie you're going to wear for the ball." Haley lowers her voice and adjusts the top of the strapless dress, forcing me to glance at her boobs. "I'm thinking about pink shoes, you know, 'cause we're supposed to have a splash of matching colors, but only if you're okay with wearing a pink tie."

Wait…what? My brain is moving at high speed, trying to catch up. "Why would my tie need to match your shoes for a dance I'm not even going to?"

I hadn't actually thought about bailing on the ball—I've

gone every year for my entire life — but it sounded like a great way to regain control of this situation. Because clearly people are making plans without asking me.

"You have to go," Mom says. "The hockey team is required to attend."

Damn. She's right. Varsity players have to go. "Well, I'm not required to attend *with* a date."

And Tate Tanley blocks another shot.

Haley looks like someone just slapped her. "But you can't… You have to — "

"Excuse us for a minute," I tell Mom.

Haley stumbles on the hem of Jody's dress when I tug her across the kitchen and into my bedroom, closing the door behind us. "What the hell are you doing?"

She's all wide-eyed and confused. "Your mom offered to loan me this dress a while back, and you know my parents can't afford a new dress for every event."

How are we supposed to have a real breakup when this fucking town is so small we can't get away from each other?

"This" — I gesture a finger between her and me — "is not happening. I'm not gonna show up at some big town event wearing matching colors and smiling like we can actually stand each other."

"I thought we would be over this by now. You know how much I need to win Juniper Princess. I need the scholarship and the letters of recommendation — "

"What's wrong with taking your new boyfriend?" I thought that was what she'd been trying to tell me with all the texting and the "we need to talk about New Year's Eve" messages.

"He's not my boyfriend and he's not a junior. He won't be nominated." She moves closer and rests her hands on my arms. "Besides, you know a varsity hockey player has won Prince for the last fifty-something years."

So she doesn't just want a date for the dance, she wants a court member for a date.

I remove her hands from my arms and step back. "I'm not in the running for Juniper Prince."

Haley rolls her eyes, like I'm a huge idiot. "Your dad is Keith Tanley, both your parents were Prince and Princess together, and you've just taken Mike Steller's spot as goalie. You're a shoo-in."

I look her over carefully—there is no doubt that Haley Stevenson is one of the hottest girls in our school. But all I want right now, all I've wanted for way too many months, is to see that freshman girl I kissed for the first time in the periodical section of the school library during study hall. That girl would have spent New Year's Eve day with me playing pond hockey or *Minecraft*, throwing on any random dress right before the ball. She used to be fun. We used to have fun. I don't really want to go back to us being dorky freshmen with braces, but I can't go forward with this version of Haley, either. I can't talk to her about things that matter. It's just too different now.

"I'm not going with you," I say so firmly she flinches. "Here's what will happen if you don't secure another date: I'll be home faking the flu and forging a doctor's note for Coach Bakowski. Hell, I'll figure out how to give myself the flu for real if I have to."

Her expression turns into a scowl, and her voice rises loud enough that I'm sure the entire house can hear her. "I can't believe I gave you my virginity!"

She flings open the bedroom door, the tears already forming at the corners of her eyes.

"It goes both ways."

"That is so not the same thing!" She's full-out crying now, sniffling and walking toward the kitchen with me trailing behind her. "You know how important Juniper Princess is to me! I never thought you could be so vindictive, Tate."

"Vindictive? *You* dumped *me* and now you're trying to fake date me so you can win a stupid town contest. That's messed up, Haley." I brace myself for the backlash.

Haley's near the kitchen door now, still wearing my sister's dress. She spins around to face me. "You think you're so much better than everyone. You're above all the bullshit. That's just great. You keep it up and we'll see how that works out for you!"

I shake my head in disgust. "Screw you."

"Tate Tanley!" I hear my mom shout from the living room. I probably went about five steps too far just now. But I'm too furious to care. I feel like we both showed our true colors for the first time since breaking up.

I needed that. I needed to be sure. Because underneath the anger I had for her, some part of me still missed her, wanted her back. I almost told her that moments ago. That if we could go back to normal, I'd be with her again.

Not wanting to face my mom's wrath, I head out the door and into the garage. My snowmobile takes a few tries to get started, but soon enough, I'm flying through my backyard and then the neighbors', leaving tracks behind.

My phone vibrates in my pocket, but I ignore it for now. It's probably Mom. I'm sure she's pissed. She likes the idea of Haley and me so much that she's not willing to listen to my side. *Just fix it, Tate. Just make it work. She's such a sweet girl.*

I head straight for the woods once I'm far enough away from my house. My mom would kill me if she knew I was going this fast around all the trees. She'd lecture me about the head injuries she's treated in the ER.

By the time I'm calm enough to think straight and to slow down a little, my hands and face are frozen solid. I emerge from the woods, just a couple tenths of a mile from the main part of town. I hop off the snowmobile and head over to James Street on foot.

A few minutes later, I walk through the door of O'Connor's Tavern and glance around for Claire. It's much quieter than last night but not completely dead. Mrs. O'Connor is behind the bar today. She spots me and grins so widely I have to glance over my shoulder and check to see if there's anyone else.

"She's not here," Mrs. O'Connor says. "I sent her home to play chess with her father."

How does she know I'm looking for Claire? "Um, okay, well, thanks... I'll just, you know, come back later."

I'm already turned around when she calls out, her voice muffled. "Tate?"

"Yeah—I mean, yes?" I spin in place, and Claire's mom is now ducked behind the bar.

"Do you know anything about sink drains?"

"Sink drains," I repeat, glancing at the door again.

A handful of random tools gets dumped onto the bar counter. "It looks like I can just open this pipe thing with a screwdriver and pull out whatever is clogging it..."

"Hold up..." I rush over and walk behind the bar. I pluck the screwdriver from her hand. "Probably better if we don't flood the place."

She rights herself, standing up straight and brushing hair from her face. "I like how you think."

I focus on the sink—or I mean to at least—but then I'm looking at the beer taps and thinking about Davin O'Connor keeping me busy while my dad got drunk and watched the Vikings play.

"I worked on this last year," I mumble after I've successfully opened up the pipe, and Claire's mom raises an eyebrow. "With Davin. The beer taps."

She gives me a long look and nods. "He'll be glad to hear I got an expert to help."

"At least I know where to hide out if the game goes badly next weekend," I say, only half joking.

She laughs. "Always. We don't judge at O'Connor's. Winners and losers welcome," she recites from the sign on the door.

I wonder if Mike would be welcome. I wonder if he can show his face anywhere in town without harassment or the cold shoulder.

As if reading my mind, Claire's mom says, "How are you holding up after last night's game?"

I nod. "Okay. It's a great opportunity. Playing in Mike's spot." God, I sound like a phony.

She gives me a long look, searching like moms do when they already know you've broken something and are waiting for you to turn yourself in. "I heard you helped us book the catering for the hockey clinic next month?"

"That was all Claire's idea. I just pointed a finger at the person in charge." I'm not being humble. It's the truth. I literally pointed a finger at Ty. "But if you're looking for more stuff like that, I can put in a good word if I hear anything." Okay, now I sound desperate. "The cheerleaders plan all our pregame dinners; definitely talk to them because they get pizza literally every other game and the guys are always complaining…"

I stop. I don't want to make the team sound like ungrateful assholes—though some of us are.

Mrs. O'Connor looks surprised by this information. "I will most definitely check with the cheerleaders. Thanks for the tip, Tate. O'Connor's is always dead right before a game anyway."

"That's what Claire said." I return to fixing the sink,

pleased that I could help again.

Right when I'm about to pack up the tools for Claire's mom, we hear a loud thump above our heads. Mrs. O'Connor grins and points a finger at the ceiling. "Looks like someone got bored with chess and went looking for a keyboard buried in the unfinished storage space."

She got all that from a thump in the ceiling?

But I'm not too stupid to miss the hint. I make my excuse to leave, and even though I curse myself for doing it, I check around outside to make sure no one sees me walking up the steps. That was hell in the locker room today. Don't need any more of that shit. I'm about to knock on the door, but the music coming from inside stops me.

Claire. Singing. Playing the keyboard. Loud, perfect, beautiful. And suddenly I'm eleven years old again, standing in my backyard on New Year's Eve listening to Claire belt out a ballad in a way that was both effortless and careless. That year I made a silent wish, one I'd kept secret. I wished for her. Just Claire. All of her. Red hair and pink cheeks and long, thin legs like a graceful spider.

My hand falls to my side. Instead of knocking, I lean my ear against the door, close my eyes, and listen.

Chapter 9

−CLAIRE−

"Claire O'Connor! No way."

I drop a box of cornstarch on my toe, my heart racing.

"Oh, come on, don't look so disgusted. Luke Pratt is hot. I'd do him in a second and let him bring two friends if he wanted."

"God, Pratt is old news. Why is anyone bringing that up again? But do you really think she had an abortion when she got to school? I mean, she'd have to do it there, because someone around here would find out and…"

I did what? And who the hell told these girls that I hooked up with Luke?

"Who knows? Let's just hope she's learned her lesson and uses protection from now on. Like with Tate. Or was it Tate and Jamie? Or Tate and Leo? I can't remember. Could it have been all three? That doesn't seem possible."

"Leo says they were helping carry boxes of toilet paper,

but seriously, they can't come up with a better excuse than that?"

"Because it's probably true."

"What did Haley say when you told her?"

"She said it was bullshit. She would know, so it's probably bullshit."

I press my back against the aisle, my gaze darting side to side. Kayla Donald and Leslie Rhine. Juniors. Friends of Haley Stevenson. Obviously not her most intelligent friends, considering the fact that Maple Tree Market is two blocks from my house and they're not even attempting to whisper.

I scoot down the aisle, testing the distance, seeing if I can get farther away from them.

God, I did not miss small-town life one bit. In a big city, on a big campus, gossip just isn't possible most of the time. But seriously? Who told them about Luke? Besides Jody and Pratt, no one else knew where I took him when we walked away from that party last year.

Except that's not true. That night in the car with Tate, after the ER trip, I didn't want to think about it, but I could tell he knew. He must have seen us heading upstairs from inside the bar.

But why would he tell anyone? Especially knowing the secret I've kept for him. I lied for him. *Against* my better judgment. No way would Tate say anything.

Unless he thought that I wouldn't be back. That it wouldn't matter.

If so, that makes two of us.

After fifteen minutes of skirting Kayla and Leslie, I finally grab my needed items, check out, and head home. My mom has sent me two frantic texts asking me to hurry up. She needs to get to the bar and she needs me to babysit Dad. I don't even get a chance to explain what happened before she's out the door.

This morning, I'm supposed to be doing speech therapy exercises with my dad. I glance over at Dad, now seated at the kitchen table amid way too much neighborly food, and sigh. This is who I need to focus on. Everything else is petty. I grab the materials from the speech therapist and spend the next hour pushing Dad even harder than I had in the last session.

"Try moving your tongue to the roof of your mouth." I lean closer and watch my dad attempt to form the word "stove" for the hundredth time. His tongue drifts to the left instead of up and only a sputter of nonsense sounds emerges.

With his left hand, he scratches furiously at the side of his head where a patch of hair is now growing over the incision. His lips press together, forming "buuuttt…" He squeezes his eyes shut and shakes his head. He picks up the marker beside him and sloppily writes: DONE.

"Come on, Dad. You can do this. *Stove.*"

His left biceps bulges, proving that he hasn't lost all his muscle. He drops his gaze and attempts to trace his right index finger over the Celtic-themed tattoos lining his forearm. The finger swerves and fails to follow the path of the gold and green ink.

Frustrated, he smacks his right hand hard against the table, and I jump.

"Stove," I repeat, not wanting to back down.

The look of anguish taking over his features turns my stomach. He's tired. I'm tired. And we're both failing at this. I wait, holding my breath, as he tries one more time.

"Buuuutt…" Dad's fingers wrap around the coffee mug, and before I can even anticipate his move, the mug is flying from his hand, smashing against the kitchen wall, shattering to pieces.

He pushes away from the table and makes his way out of

the kitchen, his much weaker right side slumped and barely keeping up with the left.

I blow out a breath, close my eyes, and wish for my dad to wake up tomorrow morning and be his confident, capable self again. If anyone could use another medical miracle, it's my family.

God, I'm selfish. I mean, he's alive. I have to remember that.

When I open my eyes again, preparing to clean the broken mug, Haley is walking up my front path, wearing a long skirt and wool tights, probably right from Sunday mass. And she's got another dish of food in her arms. Great. I quickly swipe the loose tears from my face and stand just as she rings the doorbell.

I plaster on a fake smile before flinging open the door. Innocent until proven guilty, right?

"Hey, Haley."

"Hey," she says. "I just talked to your aunt after mass. She said you'd be here watching football with your dad. Did I come at a good time?"

Well, my therapy session with Dad is definitely over. Maybe that constitutes a good time?

"Oh, um, yeah. Totally."

The cold air causes me to shiver, and I open the door wider, inviting Haley into the kitchen. Her gaze drifts in the direction of the broken mug. I shake my head and wave it off. "I totally wiped out walking across the kitchen floor. I was just about to get a broom before you came by…" I hesitate and then add, not wanting to allow her room to ask more questions, "So what's up?"

"Wow." She's fixated on the table and counters now. They're covered with…well, I don't even know what all of it is. "This is out of control, Claire."

My face heats up. "I'm sorry. It's just, we're at the bar all the time, and my dad isn't eating much—"

"Because of the chemo, right?" She clears a space on the counter to set her dish down and then removes her coat, tossing it over a chair. "My grandmother had to have chemo a couple of years ago. She's doing okay now, but during treatments she wasn't eating a thing and couldn't stand the smell of food cooking in the house. That sucks that he had to have chemo even though his tumor was removed."

I let out a breath, relieved to not have to make up more excuses. "Chemo and radiation. Just in case any cancer cells were left. Only a few more weeks to go, thank God."

"Well, he'll be good as new in no time. You'll see." Haley moves around the kitchen, lifting lids, sniffing some of the dishes, sorting things into piles. She reads a note on top of a container of frozen soup and then immediately drops the whole thing into the garbage.

I stand in the kitchen, shifting from one foot to the other, uncomfortable with Haley in my house, seeing the mess everywhere. I know my dad had a nearly inoperable brain tumor and it's a miracle he even survived the surgery, but I still can't help being embarrassed by the lack of order in my life.

"You take care of the broken glass and I'll take inventory." She tugs a notepad and pen out from under a plate of cookies.

"Haley, this is really nice, but—"

She waves a hand to stop me, her head already ducked, making a list. "Don't worry, I'm putting you to work, too. I was hoping you would go over the band auditions and set lists for the ball with me. The Women's League ladies are great and all, but they're…"

"Old?" I supply. Last night, after Tate and his teammates left, Haley asked me to be on the music committee with her for the New Year's Eve ball, promising some advertising for O'Connor's in exchange for my input. I couldn't say no.

"You said it, not me." Haley lifts her head and grins, but the smile fades seconds later. "So glad you're giving me something to do. I had a huge fight with Tate yesterday. He's being so…" She bites down on her lower lip, searching for the right word. "I don't know what. But I think I went about it all wrong. He's not the same guy. Maybe I took that for granted, you know?"

I don't know exactly, but I nod anyway.

Haley continues sniffing dishes and containers while I sweep up broken porcelain. When she's made a list long enough to fill a page, she claps her hands. "Ready to get rid of some of this food?"

"You mean like throw it away? My mom would never get over the guilt." But man, wouldn't that make my life easier. Poof, it's gone. Counter space returned.

"No wasting, I promise." She reaches for an empty cardboard box near the recycle bin. "My grandpa's in a poker tournament over at the senior center; we can start there. They've got a microwave, too. And I bet Mike and Jessie would take some of this off your hands. Pretty sure they've been living on pizza rolls and ramen."

"Mike and Jessie?" I ask, and then realize she's talking about Mike Steller and his girlfriend, Jessie. I don't know her well, but we had gym together one year. She was always nice to me.

"Uh-huh." Haley piles dishes into a box, and I work on another one. By the time we're done, the kitchen table is visible and so are two countertops.

We load the items into Haley's car and then come back for her coat. I look over the almost-clean kitchen, amazed. "Are you available tomorrow?"

She smiles, looking pleased. "Only if you promise to be at the band auditions."

"Yeah, sure, anything."

"I'll need the moral support, since Tate and I are both going to be nominated for Juniper Falls Court tomorrow." She squeezes her eyes shut for a second. "Pretend I didn't say that."

So despite his many efforts to get out of it, Tate is gonna be nominated. Another bit of our conversation in the car last year comes back to me, when Tate and I sat eating greasy burgers from Benny's, his broken arm already splinted.

"Haley's going to freak."

"About your arm? Why?" I unwrap my own burger and examine it. "God, this is so not an O'Connor's burger. How is it they get all the high school crowd?"

"We aren't picky about our grade of beef," Tate says. "And yeah. Haley. Freaking out. She's probably gonna have a panic attack tomorrow." He looks at me and then sighs before explaining. "She's got us on a plan."

I lift an eyebrow. "A plan? Like Paleo? Low carbs?"

"A prince and princess plan." Tate's cheeks flush and he diverts his gaze out the windshield. "For junior year. Photos in town hall and all that. But that plan is contingent on me making varsity next year."

"Is that what you want?" I ask him, careful not to insert my own opinions.

He shrugs. "Steller's a senior next season. If I make varsity, I won't get to play much. Might get rusty or...you know, fat, sitting on the bench."

"Especially if you eat this much Benny's all the time," I joke even though Tate has always been really skinny. "But what about the rest? The photos in town hall and all that?"

"Maybe." He shrugs again. "I don't know."

"So basically you're doing it for Haley," I summarize.

Tate releases a short laugh. "Pretty much."

"You really like her." I take a drink of his soda without even thinking about asking. "That's kinda sweet."

"She's fun, you know? Easy to talk to." He chances a glance at me. "You think it's sweet? I figured you'd be completely against town rituals like that."

"Yeah, I am." I laugh. "And I know you well enough to know you are, too. At least a little. That's why it's sweet. You don't want to do it but you're going to anyway."

Tate turns serious, his gaze now locked on mine. "I don't really know what I want to do. You know?" He shakes his head. "Maybe you don't know. You've always had it figured out."

Tate had been so wrong last year. I haven't always had it figured out. I sure as hell don't have anything figured out right now. But this planning committee Haley's talked me into means more time around Tate. I've definitely figured out that that might mean trouble.

"Last stop." Haley sighs. We've managed to unload food on three different organizations thus far. "I'm so not ready for Monday. Stupid me had to vent about my fight with Tate to Kayla and Leslie. I just really thought he'd be done with this breakup stuff by now. I think Kayla and Leslie are gonna use it against me. In the race."

The Princess race. Sounds like I dodged a bullet not being around for my junior year.

Haley pulls the car up beside a small trailer and reaches in the back for one of the pans. Mike Steller comes bounding out of the trailer, a big grin on his face. "Claire O'Connor!

What the hell are you doing here?"

"Here in town or here at your place?"

"Both. Duh." He's barefoot and not wearing a coat, but still he runs up and lifts me off the ground. I'm straightening myself out again when Jessie peeks outside, not braving bare feet on the cold ground like Mike. Her face is rounder than the last time I saw her, but when Haley and I get to the door with all the food we brought, I can't look at her face anymore. All I can do is stare at her giant stomach.

I glance at Haley. What? No warning?

About two miles from here, Mike Steller's house is probably lit up, three nice cars in the driveway. And yet he's here in some poorly insulated trailer—with his pregnant girlfriend.

I can't help but think our town's obsession with high school hockey is to blame for this somehow.

Later, when we're back in Haley's car and I'm sorta over the *Mike Steller is a father to be* shock, I decide that Haley can probably figure out how the teenage population of Juniper Falls seems to be suddenly interested in a hookup that happened a year ago.

I explain the conversation I overheard in Maple Tree Market. Haley proves herself to be a bad Catholic girl—we have that in common—by stringing together half a dozen swearwords in a very creative combination.

"God, what idiots. And bitches," Haley mutters. Then she looks at me and guilt is all over her face. "I swear on the Bible, Claire, that I only told Leslie with good intentions."

My throat goes dry, my heart picking up speed. This doesn't sound good.

"So last Christmas, Luke came home to visit," Haley continues. "And we were at Stewart's party and Leslie was totally about to hook up with Pratt. So I had to tell her."

"Tell her what exactly?" I say through gritted teeth.

"About you…" She looks at me, and when I don't give any indication that I know what she's talking about, she explains further. "How you and Luke went upstairs and then later he stormed out."

Technically she saw Luke talking to me at the party, but I'm sure she hadn't seen us leave together. I'd been careful. Clearly my subconscious predicted a possible return to this town and prepared well. Now I need to know who screwed things up for me.

"Okay, but where did *you* hear this from?" I press, my patience wearing thin.

She focuses on the road and hesitates before saying, "I can't even remember. I'm sorry…"

It's hard to tell if she's lying. I mean, who would she be protecting? Jody? Tate…? She's pissed at Tate, so why would she protect him?

Haley peels her eyes from the road and looks at me. "Are you okay? I know it sucks to hear those bitches saying your name in the middle of the store." Her face grows weary. "It's possible Luke did some talking. I haven't heard anything, but maybe the guys on the team have…or Kayla told Stewart— they're dating, so yeah…"

"Basically what you're saying is," I conclude, unable to hide the bitterness in my voice, "that most likely everyone in town knows I hooked up with Luke Pratt the night before I left for school."

"I doubt it's really a big deal," she says.

But it's a big deal to me. Maybe it shouldn't be, but it is.

Chapter 10

—TATE—

ME: *Heard O'Connor's is catering the winter clinic. Glad it worked out!*

I hit send just before Mrs. Powel, our very elderly, but also gifted at seeing, English teacher catches me with my phone out. I tuck it under my thigh and pretend to pay attention to her lecture.

The PA system screeches and all of us stop talking, knowing an announcement of some kind is coming. Hopefully it's not another tornado drill. My legs are killing me from practice this morning, and I'm not in the mood to squat in the hallway for twenty minutes.

The principal's voice booms over the speaker in our classroom. "I have the news you've all been waiting for… the nominations for Juniper Prince and Princess."

Good. Maybe when Haley's name is announced, the girl clan will stop feeling sorry for her—and stop glaring at me. She must have cried to all her friends about our fight two days ago. At least a dozen girls have given me the evil eye today. And it's only fourth period.

Three junior girls are named first followed by Haley. And there it is. Her lifelong dream came true. Maybe now she'll stop blaming me for ruining everything.

"And the nominees for Prince," the principal continues, "Kennedy Locust."

"Academic slot filled," Jamie says from the seat in front of me.

Kennedy is number one in our class and also junior class president and pretty much the biggest douche in our entire school.

"Jake Hammond."

More cheers in our classroom. Jake is sitting beside me. He leans back in his chair, giving a half grin—neither arrogant nor surprised. Neither am I. His mom is vice president of the Juniper Falls Women's League and they choose the court every year.

"Paul Redmond."

Red.

Beneath my thigh, my phone vibrates. Claire. It has to be her. I glance at Mrs. Powel and she narrows her eyes, watching me like a hawk.

"And Tate Tanley," the principal says.

Wait...what?

I sit there, numb with shock. Jamie turns around and punches me in the shoulder. "You go, T-Man. I figured they had to get one football player on the list, but look out, three hockey boys in the court. That never fuu—freakin' happens."

Ron, our football team's largest linebacker, is right behind me. Jamie glances his way and retracts his statement. "No offense, dude. I gotta support my teammates, right?"

Lucky for all of us, the bell rings. I'm out of my seat so

fast the girls from the back of the room, approaching me and Jake, don't stand a chance of catching me. But my teammates do. Out in the cramped hallway, I can feel everyone looking my way. Jamie slings an arm around my and Jake's shoulders. "I'm going through the cafeteria line with both of you. A royal court member beside me…I'm bound to get an extra-large scoop of mashed potatoes."

The volume in the cafeteria rises above the noise inside my head. I take one look at the jam-packed room and turn right around.

"Hey," Jamie calls after me. "Where you goin'?"

"Library." I don't look over my shoulder or wait for a response. I need some air. This place is suffocating me.

I glance at my phone while walking and read the text Claire just sent in reply to mine.

CLAIRE: Yep

Huh. I don't know if I'm just paranoid, but something about that reply seems cold and distant. Maybe I should just talk to her in person? What if she took those rumors seriously? Or thinks I spread it around that we hooked up last Friday night? Claire's not an idiot, but still, it's an excuse to talk to her.

I shove Leo's clear directions to stay away from Claire far out of my head, push the doors to the school open, and step outside into the cold midday sun. But when I cross the high school and ice rink parking lot, my plan is quickly squashed.

Claire is leading a guy up the steps to the upstairs apartment. I recognize him from years of high school hockey games, before I played for JFH. He's probably twenty-one or twenty-two.

I stand there for way too long watching Claire smile at the guy with her, rest a hand on the front of his jacket. I don't know what this is, probably just another apartment showing, but regardless, I don't like where my head is going. With Claire, I can kid all I want about the reasons for this impromptu need to see her in the middle of the school day, but it doesn't change the fact that I'm not thinking straight. And this is the worst time possible for me to become a head case. Well, more than I already am, anyway.

And I can't help thinking that when I was eleven, wishing for Claire, she was probably wishing for Luke Pratt.

Chapter 11

–CLAIRE–

The trio of old ladies finally makes their way off the stage and out the back entrance of the great room in town hall. Haley and I simultaneously groan.

"I can't take much more of this," she grumbles while I write a big *no* under The Sparkle Gals's name on the auditions list. "Who's next?"

We've been auditioning bands for three days now. It's getting to both of us. Not all of the groups have been awful, but none are versatile enough to play familiar tunes—from several different decades—for the five hours required of the New Year's Eve ball. I scan the list. "We Love Shawn Mendes."

"What? That's not a band name." Haley leans over to read the name for herself just as the doors nearby are opening again. Four middle-school-age girls stride in, decked out in what is probably the result of a recent trip to Duluth to hit up Justice. Haley sinks back in her chair. "We're doomed. The entire Juniper Falls Women's League is gonna rip up their votes for me, not to mention the letters of recommendation I asked for…"

"You never know; these girls might be good." I watch them lower the mic stands and adjust their hair and tops.

The tallest in the group, a five-foot-nothing blonde with a side ponytail, walks up to our table and hands me an iPhone I stare at it. "Um, what's this for?"

"Just plug it in and hit play." She flashes me a pageant-worthy smile and flips her hair over her shoulder before joining the other three onstage.

I turn to Haley. "Plug it in and hit play?"

"I'm too tired to think about this." She rolls her eyes and then attaches the iPhone to the soundboard.

A teenybopper song blasts through the speakers. The girls attempt to sing along, but they're a bit too focused on the corny hand gestures and swaying in time to the music to think about the singing part. I've heard my fair share of children auditioning—I've been that kid auditioning—I should be more tolerant of this. But it's been a long week.

"Stop them, please," I plead to Haley under my breath.

She maintains a warm smile for the girls but says through her teeth, "Let them finish one song."

I glance over my shoulder, feeling eyes on us. At the very opposite end of the great room, which is pretty far away, an old British lady is giving more etiquette lessons to the members of this year's Juniper Falls Court—including Tate Tanley. Before anyone sees me looking over there, I drop my eyes to the table.

Finally, the song ends and Haley yanks the plug out of the iPhone. She puts on her sympathetic face before addressing the girls. "That was really…"

"Interesting," I supply.

"But for the New Year's Eve ball, it's very important we

have a band."

"We *are* a band," Side Ponytail Girl says.

"A band that plays instruments," I add.

The girls look around the stage, as if just noticing the keyboard and drum set. They all drop their heads and mumble *thank you* before shuffling off the stage.

Haley's pressing her pen harder and harder onto the page of notes, obviously stressed. I drift wistfully into the world she gets to live in right now, where these band auditions and the competition for Juniper Falls Princess are responsible for the majority of her anxiety.

With a sigh, I turn back to the audition list. "Midlife Crisis is up next."

"Well, they should all be over thirteen, right?" Haley says. We only have to wait a couple of minutes to find out, and when Haley sees the band members, her face fills with shock and then she shakes her head over and over. "No! No way!"

Mr. Stevenson, Haley's dad, lifts his hands in surrender. "Roger and Artie needed a percussionist."

"A drummer, Dad!" Haley jumps up and walks toward the stage. "It's called a drummer, not a percussionist. If I wanted to book the marching band, I would have called you."

Roger Cremwell, still wearing a tool belt and a *Critter Crusader* T-shirt, takes his guitar out of its case and blocks Haley from getting to her dad. "He's telling the truth. We all just decided to do this a couple of days ago."

"Sounds promising." Haley folds her arms over her chest and glares at her dad. When no one moves for several seconds, she finally throws her hands up and says, "Fine! Play. Might as well, since you're here and we're already prepared to beat our heads against the table."

Midlife Crisis preps for another minute or two, and when they play the first few bars of their song, I straighten up in my chair, recognizing the tune. Finally, a group that actually picked a song from the Juniper Falls Women's League set list. The music major in me is also quite impressed with their arrangement. They get all the way through the first verse and chorus of "Jesse's Girl" before I tap Haley and say, "Is it me, or are they sort of good?"

"Figures." She pushes to her feet again and waves a hand to stop them.

The guys look startled but cut the music off quickly. Behind us, Leo and Red have appeared.

"Hey," Leo says. "I was enjoying that."

Haley ignores him and walks in front of the stage again. "Okay, so you've got one good song. You're gonna need way more than that."

Roger lifts an eyebrow. "Play something else?"

"Oh! I know!" Kayla has popped up behind us, too, and the others are drifting this way. Looks like etiquette class may have finished. "Vampire Weekend!"

"Remember last year at the ball when we got the mayor singing 'Do you wanna build a snowman'?" Leslie says.

Haley spins around to face us. "None of you are helping."

A hand grips the back of my chair and I'm distracted by the warm fingers and the swinging arm now beside me. My gaze travels up the swinging arm until I'm looking right at Tate.

He releases his hold on my chair and shifts his weight to the other foot. "Sorry. My leg's asleep."

"It's fine." My cheeks heat up, and I quickly turn back to the stage. Roger begins playing an acoustic version of "Just Dance" by Lady Gaga. Already they've achieved the status of most versatile.

I try to sit still and not notice the fingers only an inch from my back, but soon it's all I can think about. I look up at

Tate again, dying to know what he thinks of his new stepdad singing. His face is flushed. Maybe this is embarrassing him?

"Dude, the exterminator can sing," Jake Hammond says.

A lot of eyes turn in Tate's direction, and he quickly drops into Haley's seat, ducking his head. Leo comes up on my other side and squats down. "How's your dad doing?" he says in a low voice.

"Better," I whisper, the answer comes out almost robotic.

I've nearly got my emotions in check when Tate picks up the pencil near my fingers and jots something down on a piece of paper, then folds it half before sliding it over to me. I look around, make sure no one is watching, and then stuff it in my apron—I came here right from working at the bar.

I brave eye contact, and that, along with the proximity of our chairs, sends my stomach flipping around. He's the intense Tate from last fall.

"…you can't cover the set list without a keyboard player," Haley argues with her dad and Roger. "Asking people doesn't count unless they can play and they agree to play at the ball. This isn't some amateur event."

The note in my apron pocket is practically burning a hole, but I ignore it for now. I jump to my feet and stand in front of Haley, giving her a salute. "Keyboard player at your service." If this gets us out of here sooner, I'm willing.

"But…" Haley's mouth falls open in protest, probably because I already have a job on the planning committee. She leans in close to me and whispers, "Are we really going to end up with the high school band director, local hardware store owner, and the town exterminator providing the music for the New Year's Eve ball?"

"If they're the best." I shrug and look the guys over. "Plus, the ball is formal. A tux can really do a lot."

"I guess," Haley concedes.

"That's a great idea!" Mr. Stevenson says, waving a hand between the keyboard and me. "Claire can fill in now until we find someone."

"See?" I grin at Haley and step up on the stage. "I'll fill in, we'll finish the audition, and all the big hockey muscles can pack up the equipment for us and—"

"We'll be done." Haley's face lights up. "God, I wanna be done."

"That makes two of us." I clap my hands. "Name that tune, Haley."

I look out at the table where Tate is still seated. He leans back in his chair and stares at me. My hands freeze over the keyboard. What did he write on that piece of paper? I shake my head and focus on the song Haley's just asked us to play.

A little while later, when the Juniper Falls Court is busy helping pack up the band equipment, I get reminded yet again why ignoring Tate is the best plan.

Haley is whispering to him, her head ducked, her eyes shiny. She wraps a hand around his arm and he immediately jerks out of her grip, and then he's across the room, out the door, carting a mic stand. Haley stares after him, and then Leo comes up beside her, both of them within hearing distance.

"You gotta back off, Stevenson," Leo says. "He's not gonna be your date. Take Hammond. He'll keep it drama free."

Haley drops her face in her hands and groans. "When is he gonna be out of this tortured, brooding phase? I just want things to go back to the way they were."

The way they were? Like at my going-away party?

I sink back in my chair, realizing the truth. Tate does seem different now. Not just the varsity status. He's not the lighthearted, happy kid he was when I used to hang out with Jody at the Tanleys' house. And I can't help wondering if things with his dad have gotten worse than last fall. I shudder at the thought of what that could mean. I had heard that he took a coaching job at SMU. That's a lot closer than Michigan, where he'd been working. Maybe he pops into town more often? And with Jody away at school this year…it can't be easy dealing with Keith's visits. According to the poster at the ice rink, Keith and Tate are running that hockey clinic together, so he'll be in town for that. With Tate nominated for Prince this year…there's a carnival, parade, the shoot-out with alumni—Keith played in that game two years ago.

I squeeze my eyes shut, forcing away all this concern and curiosity. *He's not your problem, Claire. You've got enough of your own problems.*

Later, I pull Tate's note out from beneath the table and read it.

IF you EVER WANT TO TALK ABOUT STUFF…THIS TIME I'll BRING THE MINIVAN, you BRING THE BURGERS.

My insides warm; my vision blurs. I can already see us sitting in Mrs. Tanley-Cremwell's minivan in the middle of the night, with decent burgers this time. Me spilling all my problems, everything I'm now petrified of, and Tate listening in that careful, intense way he did that night last fall.

I look up at him again and wonder, not for the first time, if we're past the point where we could go back to being like we were last year. Maybe I'm past that point. Maybe I want to be alone with him for different reasons now.

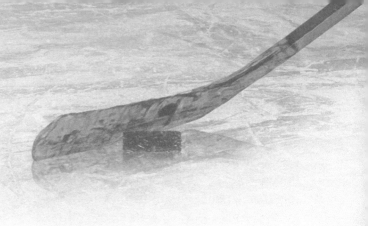

Chapter 12

–TATE–

"What'dya get, T-Man?" Jamie asks me.

I glance inside the top shelf of my locker and pull out the clear container with green and silver ribbon tied around it. I lift it up and spot the slices of yellow. "Pound cake."

Jamie's stuffing cookies in his mouth from a tin his locker buddy left for him. I remove the card from under the ribbon and open it up.

Tate.
Good luck tonight! I'm so proud of you!
Love.
Haley

She also left a thirty-two-ounce bottle of my favorite Gatorade, lime green. Last week there was no cake, just an orange Gatorade—the only other flavor I can't stand—and a note that said:

To: Tate
From: Haley

I flip this week's note over a couple of times, searching for a punch line on the back or another request to be my date for the New Year's Eve ball. Bakowski walks into the locker room from his office, and I quickly stuff the gifts back on the top shelf. Everyone goes silent and turns to face Coach. It's so quiet, I can practically hear my heartbeat. I try to hold my hands still, but the second I stop wringing them, my leg bounces up and down. Beside me, Jake takes his stick and presses it to my skate, stilling the hyperactive leg.

Bakowski paces a straight line down the length of the locker room, pivoting each time he reaches the end. He stops and glances at something near the door, out of my line of sight. "I'm gonna let one of the Otters's most distinguished alumni talk to you about how important it is to get a great start early in the season."

Okay, not something. Someone.

Before he even steps inside the locker room, a cold feeling sweeps over me. Sure enough, my dad strides in, his dress pants, shirt, and tie perfectly pressed for the ceremony later at the winter carnival.

"Keith was the lead scoring forward my last year as assistant coach," Bakowski says. "And he's this year's recipient of the Otter Lifetime Achievement Award for his work as assistant coach for two Division I hockey teams."

I lean forward and make myself busy re-lacing my skates. Even without looking up, I feel the eyes on me. I'm supposed to be excited about this, proud, even, I'm sure. Dad is grinning widely, enjoying the whistling and clapping from all the varsity guys and the "Big Tanley!" shouts.

Dad points a finger at Owen Jensen's mop of hair that

nearly touches his shoulders. "Still haven't located any scissors?"

Everyone cracks up. Owen made it onto the All Hockey Hair Team last year. It's something only the "cool" alums know about. Something we teased Owen about constantly last season.

"I heard a rumor Longmeadow is planning to dunk their heads in bleach," Dad says, earning more laughter. "You boys will need a counterattack."

Coach clears his throat, and all the laughter is cut off immediately. Dad turns in his direction and gives a sheepish grin. "Right. Speech time. I get it."

"Dude, your dad rocks," Red whispers from my right side.

I bite back words of protest and focus on lacing my skates again.

Dad puts on his charming, *I'm important* face. "As many of you already know, I'm assistant coach for the SMU Hawks and before that, I was assistant at U Michigan."

One of many assistants. But whatever. No one seems to ever look up that shit.

"Here's the thing," Dad says. "I don't know where all of you are headed after you're done with this team, but I know from personal experience, you'll never be more appreciated and respected than you are right now, right here, playing this game for this town. Some days, I don't feel like driving two hours just to be here to watch a game or accept an award. But the second I step into this arena, I'm cursing myself for forgetting what it's like to be someone who played for this team."

I look up from my skates and glance around the room. A sick feeling washes over me. I should be eating this up, I should be getting pumped for the game, but I'm too busy faking those things to actually feel them.

"…Every game you play, every time this town gathers to watch you boys, is a memory for someone. Doesn't matter if it's not the playoffs yet; doesn't matter if we aren't ranked yet. All that matters is this game. This could be the best moment of your life, right now."

I rub my sweaty palms on my jersey. I don't want tonight to be the best I'll ever play. No matter how it goes. I want more than playing in this town. Something bigger. Something all my own. Without my dad.

The idea of ambitions beyond high school hockey freaks me out enough to shut those thoughts down. The last thing I need right now is to let my head float away. I've seen it happen enough times. Guys win a few games, get famous in town, and then assume the rest of the world is waiting for them. And then it turns out that they aren't good enough. I'd rather get through tonight's game before I start letting myself dream too big.

All the guys leap to their feet, yelling and cheering. The floor is practically vibrating in the locker room. I grab my stick and helmet and follow behind Hammond and Leo, but Dad catches my jersey before I can escape.

"Listen, Tate," he says, keeping his voice low. "Coach Redeck is pressuring me to recruit. If I can provide him a couple of good players for next season, I might get bumped up a rank. I could really use the promotion."

"Good players?" I keep my eyes trained on the door. "Like who?"

"Leo and Jamie."

My head snaps around to face Dad. "They've already given verbal at St. Cloud and Michigan."

"They've given word," he repeats, an eyebrow lifting like I'm supposed to follow his thought process. "Nobody signed any contracts. Didn't even involve their parents."

That's because Jamie and Leo are the rare players on the team whose parents have little to do with hockey. Lucky them. "They're not just gonna change their plans because you wow them with SMU facts."

"If both of us wow them…" he hints.

"Tanley! Move your ass," Bakowski shouts from the hallway.

I shake my head and back away from Dad. I can't process this right now. "I have a game."

A game that could be the best moment of my life. God, I hope not. And is this what it's gonna be like for me soon? Our town, especially our coach, is known for holding back players from varsity, from the spotlight, for as long as possible to keep all this recruitment stuff from going to our heads. The hunt can be toxic, or so I've heard.

But with Mike Steller out, they're all going to see me now. Now until I graduate.

When I skate out onto the ice for warm-ups, I can't shake the feeling that everyone is watching me, wishing I were someone else, writing me off before the game even starts.

Don't think about it right now. Think about the game. Or something else. Anything.

Claire's long red hair flashes in my head, the look she gave me when I wrote her that note the other night. I'd take five hundred etiquette classes just to be there again, in that moment.

I'm deep in thought when Jake and Leo both take warm-up shots on goal. Two pucks soar through the net before I can react. My heart speeds up, panic rushing through me.

"Goddammit, Tanley!" Bakowski shouts. "Get your head out of your ass!"

Yeah, that's probably good advice.

Chapter 13

−CLAIRE−

"I can't believe Tanley missed that save! He wasn't even looking in the right direction! Bakowski better get these boys straightened up before we end up with a tie on our hands."

Man, these radio broadcasts of the game can be more intense than watching it live. I hold my gloved hands over the portable heater at our booth. Instead of being stuck inside, washing down empty tables tonight, O'Connor's has gone mobile for the winter carnival, which will be a pretty grim event if this game doesn't turn around.

After the game is over, the mayor will introduce this year's Juniper Falls Royal Court, light the bonfire around the statue of James Juniper, then he'll gather all the children around the fire and proceed to tell them the story of how our town was founded.

Behind me, Uncle Ned turns the knob on the radio, raising the volume.

"*And we do not want to give a win to Longmeadow. I'm sure all of you remember the last time that happened…five years ago. And then we ended up losing to them in the first playoff round of the state tourney. We lose tonight and the season is cursed.*"

My phone rings, and when I answer it, Ned turns the radio volume back down. My stomach churns, having seen the hospital business office number before answering. I try not to panic when the woman on the other end spends ninety full seconds listing, without empathy, the various expenses we owe for Dad's treatments.

I walk a short distance from the booth, trying to get away from the noise. She probably thinks I'm out partying while my dad's sick and racking up medical expenses.

"Is there some kind of payment plan you could put us on?" I ask, desperate for good news and smaller numbers on the bills.

"Yes," she says. "We could agree to nine hundred a month for twelve months, but the hospital needs a five-thousand-dollar payment now to keep your account from going to collections. I can extend that deadline a couple of weeks if it helps?"

Jesus Christ. No wonder my mom had stopped opening those bills. This is hopeless. How the hell are we supposed to come up with five thousand dollars in the next two weeks, let alone the "generous" deal of nine hundred a month?

Today, my dad had a major breakdown during physical therapy. I think he'd expected things to return to normal even more than Mom and I had. And when his assessment revealed no improvement on his weaker side…well, let's just say it didn't go over well. I'm still partly stuck in that room at the doctor's office, listening to numbers that brought only bad news. I don't think things could possibly get any worse.

I finally tell the woman we'll take her offer—what else am I supposed to do?

When I return to our booth, Kay and Ned are watching me, waiting for bad news. We're all used to it now. But I shake my head and they have enough sense to go back to yelling about the game.

"They're winning!" Aunt Kay shouts at the radio. "He's acting like it's all over. Idiot."

People around here don't like change. God, I hope they win. Celebration equals more food and drink purchases later into the night.

My phone is now vibrating with a new email and a text—most likely more bad news. I check the email first. It's from the Northwestern bursar's office. I skim over my schedule—classes I'd registered to take this fall, long before my dad got sick—but stop when I reach the bottom:

Total Tuition & Fees for Winter Quarter: $16,208
Amount you are responsible for: $2,652

I used to think I was lucky, being gifted enough scholarship and grant money to cover nearly $14,000 of tuition every quarter. But now, the remaining unpaid balance blinks at me over and over until I have to close the email. My parents will need to take out one of those parent loans to cover things. And probably another loan to cover hiring someone to do the work I'm covering for free at O'Connor's. I move on to the text and quickly realize that today is not a day for good news.

CELLULAR FREE MSG: We've been trying to reach you. Your account is past due. Make payment to avoid service interruption.

Shit. The cell phone bill. It must have slipped through the cracks. And I barely made all the basic payments for November. Oh God, am I about to be one of those "temporarily disconnected" numbers?

I tuck the phone away before Kay or Ned can read the message. I need to do something big to dig us out of this hole.

An idea occurs to me seconds later, as a group of high school kids is walking past our booth toward the rink. "Hey!" I shout.

They stop and look over at me. A few exchange looks.

"You guys should stop by after the carnival." I plaster on a giant *I'm cool* grin. "We're staying open until five on game nights now."

"We are?" Aunt Kay and Ned say at the same time.

I turn and shoot both of them a look to shut up. Benny's stays open twenty-four hours. We can run with them. After the kids have walked away, I turn to Kay and Ned. "I'll stay late. I'll close up."

Kay lifts an eyebrow but doesn't object. "Guess you won't need a bartender if that's your late-night crowd. Or should I say early morning?"

"Do you have any idea what our profit margin is for soda and cheese fries?" I point out.

Kay covers her ears. "I can't do numbers, you know that, Claire! Headache already coming on…"

I'd tried to teach her Excel the other day…big mistake. She kept asking, why were letting these damn sheet spreads add everything up.

I laugh. "I won't bring up the sheet spreads anymore."

Instead, I pull out my phone and send a text to a bunch of high school kids in my contacts, like Haley, Leo, Jamie, and a lot more.

ME: O'Connor's is staying open 'til 5 a.m. tonight/tomr morn just for you guys! The kitchen, too! Come load up on

greasy food after getting loaded :)

The scent of Betty's freshly brewed Spark Plug coffee drifts in my direction from the booth across from ours. I elbow Kay in the side. "Do I have time for coffee?"

She shrugs, and I glance at my cell to check the time. All thoughts of coffee immediately leave my brain when I catch the mayor heading toward the stage with a big sign that has the name KEITH TANLEY printed on it in bold block letters.

My heart jolts. Of course he's here tonight. It's the winter carnival. He's probably part of the ceremony. But God, I haven't seen him since last fall and...*Jesus*, if I feel this way, what's Tate feeling?

And suddenly I have to see him. Playing. I need him to look at me, because I think I'll know exactly what he's feeling. Heat rushes to my face. Feelings, as in about his dad. The game. Not anything else. Definitely not me.

Chapter 14

−TATE−

L eo's playing the game of his life. We were up by five goals, and now Longmeadow is only trailing us by two. So basically, I'm ruining Leo's best game. Among many other things. I'm sure I'll get to have a nice father/son chat about it at the carnival later. Can't wait for that.

"Goddammit, Tanley!" Bakowski's voice booms over all the other sounds inside the Longmeadow arena. "Open your eyes!"

I close my eyes briefly, waiting for the clank of his clipboard hitting the bench. I knew that last guy would shoot high glove side. I watched him warm up. I studied his shots. It wasn't rocket science. And then right as he approached, some buried voice in the back of my head called, *Low glove side, low glove side.* At the last second, I dropped my glove.

And the puck soared over my shoulder into the net.

Leo skates past me and smacks the side of my helmet. "Quit thinking so hard. You got this!"

Yeah. I got this. Obviously.

I don't know what makes me glance into the stands after that screwup; it's the last place I should be looking, considering all the glares probably thrown in my direction, but it's like I can feel her there. Claire. She's standing in the aisle, green apron dangling from under her coat, hands stuffed in her pockets.

Her gaze locks with mine, and I just stay there for several seconds, momentarily free of every burden. I rewind back a year and replay the way she looked at me before I got out of her car, my arm in a splint. It's different now. It's not just me now.

Leo skates up behind me and nudges my shoulder. I tear my gaze from Claire, and all the worry and panic hits me again. Leo gives me this look, like, *See what I mean? Don't go there, dude.*

But what if I already have?

Forty-five minutes after the game, I'm still in the locker room. I mean, we lost. Because of me. So yeah, not in a hurry to get to my own execution. I do the slowest job ever buttoning my green dress shirt before reaching for the silver tie hanging in my locker. The only one left in here is Leo. He's leaning against the wall, his own tie already perfectly in place.

"About to collapse from starvation here," Leo says. "I get why you're stalling and all, but you gotta head out there eventually."

With a sigh, I pull myself together, gather up the dress coat, gloves, and hat my mom forced me to bring, and then head outside with Leo. A large black tent, white lights draped around it, sits at the end of the square on James Street. This is my first winter carnival being allowed inside that heated tent with its tables of delicious homemade food and envious onlookers. If it weren't for my dad's presence, I'd be pretty damn excited. Well, more excited if we'd won.

I stop at the entrance, already hearing Dad's voice, while he has an animated chat with his club of Otters Hall of Famers.

"Dude, I was totally feeling that pregame speech." Leo points in my dad's direction.

"Yeah?" I glance at Leo, hoping to see sarcasm on his face, but he's serious. Of course he's serious. I grab the sleeve of his shirt, holding him back. "So, you're gonna sign that commitment letter soon, right?"

Leo shrugs. "My parents want me to wait until April."

My stomach drops. "Why?"

"Don't look so freaked." He grins and shoves me toward the buffet. "Lots of players wait. It's a thing."

"But if you know you want to play for U Mich, why wait?" From the corner of my eye, I see Dad grab two beers from a cooler and hand them to Jamie's parents. "Or are you considering other teams? Maybe play juniors?"

"My dad made me apply to the dental program he graduated from and..." Leo sighs. "They just want me to have all my responses before I make anything final."

Leo's dad is a dentist in town and his mom is a dental hygienist at his office. They aren't sports enthusiasts and are all about education and job security. And an NCAA commitment letter is a binding contract.

"Between you and me," Leo adds, "I gave my verbal intent to U Mich, and that's where I want to be."

Internally I sigh with relief. I just don't trust my dad and therefore don't want my friends on his team. Hopefully Leo's confidence in his choice will stay this strong. But Jamie…his situation is different. His parents love that he plays hockey, but his dad didn't play; they don't have experience working the system. They also didn't go to college. And Jamie's not exactly the best student—he's barely passing anything—and NCAA teams can only let so much slide. If Dad makes an offer to overlook his academic record more than other schools have…

From across the tent, Haley spots Leo and me. She grabs a sash and the famous antler crown from a table near her and walks toward us.

"Your crown, Mr. Prince." She places the tree antlers on Leo's head despite his protests. He is the current Prince, after all—it's his job. At least until New Year's Eve, when his reign ends and the new guy—hopefully not me—takes over. As a nominee, I get a white satin sash tossed over my head. Better than antlers, I guess. Haley nods in my dad's direction. "Pretty cool, huh? Otter Lifetime Achievement Award…"

"Yep." I stand there looking straight ahead, wishing I could bolt. Maybe go back to the rink and practice. And then I glance at Haley.

It occurs to me now that she has her own version of an Otters jersey that she's growing into. Princess of Juniper Falls. Town socialite. The kind of girl who dreams of going away to college just so she can return back to Juniper Falls, get married, raise her kids here, be a hockey mom or an officer for the Women's League. I'm not sure that plan is for me.

I think all the faking I've had to do with Dad made it impossible to do the same with Haley, going to all those Juniper Women's League events and pretending like I can't wait for my picture to be up in town hall. And her breaking things off with me made me realize that you can love someone and be happier without them. Haley used to be my escape, the fun part of my life, and as soon as that changed, everything changed.

"Tate…" Haley starts, but before I can panic about another discussion (aka, fight) over the ball, Leo grabs Haley and steers her toward Jamie, telling her something about his needing help with his buffet etiquette.

"Good call," I mumble to Leo when he returns, with a nod that's meant to reassure me as well as him.

"I got your back." He hands me a plate and takes one for himself.

By the time my plate is loaded, Dad has spotted me. He yells for me to come over, but I'm rooted to the ground. Leo gives me a nudge in that direction and I have no choice but to go over there. Now I *really* miss playing JV. I loved that world—all game, no drama.

"Tough game tonight, Tate?" Larry Jones says, the positive exuberance from last Friday night vanished from his voice. "I'm sure you remember what happened five years ago…?"

"The last time we tied with Longmeadow," another alum about Larry's age adds. They're all using this careful warning-type tone like this is a lecture on why drugs or cutting class are bad.

"If our defenders worked a little harder, maybe the goalie wouldn't play such an important role," I hear Dad say. He goes for another beer and my jaw tightens. I can't do this. "Tate, what if scouts or recruiters had been here tonight?"

Besides him?

Not too far behind me, my mom is listening to Kyle Stewart's mom go on about Dad's important job. She's nodding and smiling like they're the type of divorcées who remain friends forever. Honestly, I don't know what they are, but I know that Mom has to have seen Dad's ugly side at some point. Did he treat her like he treated me? I've always been too afraid to ask. I'd have to tell her things I've decided never to tell anyone. Jody worships our dad. It's different for her. He's different.

"Excuse us for a minute," Dad says.

At first I'm thrilled that I might be kicked out of the game recap conversation, but then he's steering me away from the other guys to a vacant part of the tent.

"Listen," he whispers. "I need you to plan a little overnight trip to Minneapolis and bring Jake Hammond along. The sooner we get our hooks in, the better our chance of scoring him."

I stare at him, shocked. "Jake's a junior, Dad."

Recruitment trips aren't allowed until the first day of senior year.

"Unofficial visit, that's all." But he glances around as he says this, making sure no one is listening.

"You want a top pick for next year?" I ask. "We've got one right here in this town, completely unsigned, uncommitted anywhere."

Dad's forehead wrinkles. "Who?"

"Steller," I say, keeping my voice low. He's dropped out of school, working three jobs, about to be a father, and is barely staying afloat. Jody was born while my dad was still in college. Maybe Mike doesn't have to give up everything. "He's got more talent than Jamie and Leo combined. Can't you work something out for him? There must be some kind of family housing at SMU—"

"Can't do that," Dad cuts me off. "I'd lose my pull around here. Everyone's pissed at Steller."

"But—" I argue.

He's looking over his shoulder now, making eye contact with another Otter alum. He flashes a grin and then turns back to me. "I'd better go hang out with Jamie's parents some more. They're almost ready to crack."

I can't stay in here and listen to Keith Tanley the Great stories on top of hearing everyone's advice and warnings about next game. I storm out of the tent and stand in front of the bonfire. My phone is blowing up in my pocket. I pull it out and read a group text from Claire about O'Connor's staying open later on game nights. Dozens of responses follow her text. I glance sideways at the O'Connor's booth and then shut off Leo's voice inside my head. My feet move on their own in her direction. This isn't going away anytime soon; might as well stop fighting it.

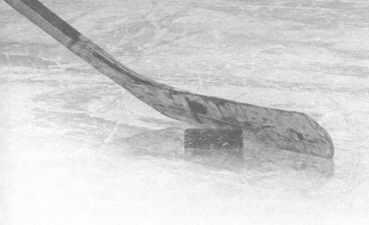

Chapter 15

-CLAIRE-

I hate the way my stomach flutters when Tate approaches the booth. My body is betraying me. The carnival is in full swing now, live music, bonfire, people everywhere.

"Hey," he says, giving me that smile again. The one that's still younger Tate and yet it's morphed into something sexy and dangerous.

I nearly drop the paper plate in my hands but manage to get the walleye horseshoe to the customer. I keep my gaze focused on the cash box while I'm placing seven dollars in it. "Hey…"

"So, I got your text—"

"Right," I say. "I sent that text to everyone."

Why did I have to point that out? Like I'm covering up something.

"I figured." He looks right at me, so direct and purposeful, like when he'd spotted me in the bleachers at the end of the game. Except much closer. "So what's that about?"

I stare at Tate's hands, resting on the counter of our booth. "Uh, yeah, late-night hours. Thought it might be a good thing on"—the catcalling gets louder and I trip over my words— "game days—I mean nights."

Ron, a linebacker for the football team, and Kyle Stewart, one of Tate's teammates, walk closer.

"Nice costume. What time do you hop up onstage and give us a weird little jazz-hand show?" Ron winks, and the grin on his face turns my stomach.

Kyle coughs back a laugh. "I hardly recognize you without your gang of misfits."

"Misfits?" I ask.

He waves a hand toward the choir kids who Mrs. Stevenson is leading in a candlelit version of "O Holy Night." I performed the same song two years ago.

"I hardly recognize her without the back of Pratt's head in her line of sight."

On the counter, Tate's fists are now clenched. Today is a terrible day for these idiots to mess with me. Especially after that therapy session with Dad, the call from the hospital billing office...I need someone to blame for all the bad.

I fold my arms over my chest. "I've learned a lot about brain injuries over the past few months. You know what happens to people who take too many pucks to the head?" Both of them snicker at this, and it only fuels my fire even more. "They end up with permanently flaccid male anatomy. There's a nerve in the brain that connects to the—"

"Claire," Ned says quietly. "Break time?"

The immature asshole hockey/football players act like I've just been called to the principal's office. I toss my apron onto the ground and exit the booth.

I move quickly away from town square, down the block. I reach the movie theater, which only shows hockey films during the season, and push open the door before diving inside. Leonard, who runs the place, is absent from the ticket and snack counter, probably to join the carnival while a movie is playing. God, it felt good to snap at them, but I need to get my head on straight before I go back to the booth. Ned was right. It is break time for me. Unfortunately, the more I lean against the wall, replaying that interaction, the more pissed off I get. Like I need to punch something.

I only get a second to myself before Tate walks in, looking around for me.

"God, I hate this place!" I push off the wall and pace around the theater lobby. Standing still isn't helping. "I hate the stupid ice sculptures, the special varsity hockey tent that's heated. What the hell is up with that?"

Tate approaches me slowly.

I point a finger at the door. "You know what that is out there?"

"A carnival?" he guesses.

"Nothing." I shake my head, still fuming. "It's nothing. And Stewart and Ron? You know what they are?"

Tate nods. "I can think of a few adjectives."

"They're future DUI holders," I snap. "In fifteen years, they'll be living paycheck to paycheck, stumbling out of O'Connor's at closing time after a long night at the alumni table, driving snowmobiles to work because their license got suspended. And then our wonderful town will give them a special award on the stage at the carnival with all the kids looking on, proud and ready to be them in twenty years." I glance at Tate, who opens his mouth to speak, but I cut him off again. "It's so stupid. Caring about this stuff, making it important when people can…they can just—people have bigger things to worry about than a high school hockey game. Some people—" I can't finish. The lump in my throat is too big to speak. I don't want to fall apart. I'd rather be pissed off. I need to be pissed off. We should all be pissed off.

"Hey…" Tate moves closer, like he might touch a hand to my shoulder, but I must have seemed freaked by this because he stops right in front of me. Unlike me, Tate speaks softly, calmly. "You're right. Fuck them. I'm over it, too. Who cares what anyone thinks?"

He looks at me with those big green eyes, his forehead wrinkled. I take a deep breath that seems to pull me closer to Tate; my feet shuffle a few inches in his direction. He lifts a hand and I follow it as he reaches out and rests it on my arm. Just the weight of it heats my skin, even through my jacket and sweater. "I'm sorry I haven't asked if you were okay. I should have asked. Things were so weird between us that all I could think about was—"

I place a hand over his mouth to stop him. He looks so genuine and stressed. I can't listen to more of this guilty speech. I'm full of a million different kinds of guilt from my dad's situation and from what happened with Tate and his dad last fall; watching someone else suffer the same fate is too much. So much for misery loving company. "Consider yourself forgiven."

"Thanks." He exhales, his fingers still wrapped gently around my arm. "Have you seen him tonight? My dad."

My muscles tense at the thought of running into Keith Tanley. "No, I haven't had the pleasure of bumping into him. Not since last fall."

"He won't remember that night," Tate says in a rush. "He never remembers—"

My eyebrows shoot up. "So it *wasn't* just a onetime thing?"

"No," he admits. "But it was really bad that night."

I nod slowly, trying to reassure him, but inside I'm thinking, *God, this is* not *okay*. I look him over and watch his hand drop from my arm. I step closer and slide my fingers along the silver tie around his neck. "You look so grown up."

The seriousness vanishes from his face. His mouth quirks up in that sexy half smile he's recently developed. "Yeah?"

Another step closer. My heart picks up speed. He smells like smoke from the bonfire—one of my favorite scents. "And you're taller than me now."

"I noticed," he says, dropping his voice to almost a whisper. "Claire?"

"Hmm?" My fingers are still gripping his tie.

"Last year…" He takes a breath. "I hated seeing you and Pratt walking off somewhere alone."

His gaze is so intense I'm momentarily speechless, caught up in this haze of Tate and his perfect words. But then… Wait— "You saw us?" I mean, I was pretty sure, but when he looks down at his feet and nods, the idea is cemented. "Did you tell anyone?" He lifts his head, worry all over his face, and I know. God. I suck in a deep, frustrated breath and reword my question. "*Who* did you tell, Tate?"

To his credit, he looks me right in the eyes and says, "Haley."

"Haley," I repeat with a nod. "That's great. Just great. Why the hell would you tell Haley? I know I didn't give specific directions not to tell anyone, but seriously? I can't think of any possible reason for you to tell her."

That smell…the campfire. It's bringing me back. Except things look different now.

"Haley was at my house that night." Tate lifts a hand, rests it on the back of his neck. "Jody called her when she found out about my arm, and she came over. She and Jody waited up for me. When you didn't drop me off right away, I didn't want her to think…"

I blink a few times. "Think what?" I put myself back in

the car that night and try to untangle this mystery.

"Claire," I hear Tate say. He looks all serious again. "Promise me something?"

"What?"

"Promise you won't settle for any guy who doesn't think you're perfect." He drops his gaze to his hands. "Because you are. Perfect."

My eyes widen. I turn to face the windshield, uncomfortable with where this conversation has gone.

"I mean perfect for someone," Tate corrects, clearing his throat. "Sorry. That was weird."

I release a nervous laugh and look over at him. "Probably the pain meds talking."

He scratches his head. "Yeah, probably."

"Nothing. There was nothing for Haley to think." Color creeps up Tate's neck. "You're right. I shouldn't have told her. It was stupid. I'm sorry, Claire."

My heart bangs against my chest. I'm not sure I want the truth. I'd rather blame someone else, but still, I press him further. "I don't get it. You walked into the house at two in the morning with a broken arm, Haley was there waiting, wanting to make sure you were okay, so how did Luke Pratt end up in the conversation?"

His eyes roll upward, toward the ceiling. "I just—I felt guilty, I guess. Maybe over nothing. I mean, I knew she was waiting for me. Jody texted me while we were at the ER. So I told Haley that Luke was an asshole to you and you were upset and needed to talk." He looks at me again, squeezes his eyes shut for a second. "I'm sorry."

I stare over his shoulder, my breaths quick, erratic. Tate told Haley that I needed his help. After I kept all his secrets. And she believed him. If there was ever a reason to knee someone in the balls, it would be this.

"I think…" Tate says, slowly, carefully, "that I wanted to be there with you. In that car. More than I wanted to be with Haley and—" His eyes meet mine. "And that's why I felt guilty. You were leaving, and I needed things to be okay with Haley. I needed her back then. It was confusing, and that's not a good excuse, but—I'm sorry, Claire."

My desire to punch something fizzles out with his confession.

"So you—" I stop and then start again, barely able to hear myself speak over the pounding of my heart. "So back then you…had a crush on me?"

He nods. "Immensely."

My breath catches in my throat, sticking there along with any words I may have thought about uttering.

Tate releases a nervous laugh. "Can't believe I just admitted that."

The banging in my chest grows louder, faster. I lift a hand, resting it in his hair. When our eyes meet again, his face is inches from mine. His gaze drifts to my mouth.

I shift my hand to his cheek, then to his tie, sliding my fingers down it. He really does look so much older, so much like…like someone I could kiss. For real.

But the door to the theater opens and Leo pokes his head in. I drop my hands from Tate's tie and take a giant step backward as the cold air whooshes between us.

"There you are," Leo says, sounding relieved. "Dude, we gotta do the ceremony thing."

Tate peels his eyes from me. "Huh—oh, right. The ceremony."

I bite my lip to keep from laughing. He looks so disoriented.

I'm expecting him to take off, but he angles himself in a way that blocks Leo's view of me. Between us, his fingers brush mine and he leans in to whisper, "You can be mad at me—you probably should be mad. But I really am sorry. If I could do it over…"

I swallow the lump in my throat and then give his fingers a squeeze. Relief fills his face before he turns around to follow Leo back outside.

My body falls back against the wall. I cover my face with my hands and groan as loud as I can. It helps. A little.

On my way back to the booth, I smack right into Haley. My face heats up just seeing her, knowing… Ugh.

"Shoot, sorry, Claire!" She bends over to pick up the event program she dropped on the ground, and when I get a good look at her face, she's all red-eyed, mascara messed up. Her eyes widen, seeing my reaction. She sweeps a thumb underneath her eyes. "I'm a mess, right?"

I grab a paper towel from our booth and wet it with a few drops from my water bottle. Haley holds still while I fix the mascara issue. "Everything okay?" *Did you happen to walk past the movie theater a few minutes ago?*

"Yeah, I guess." She shakes her head. "It's just Tate…and the game… I can't talk to him and I can't stop that *I love him; he needs my help* feeling, either, so basically, I don't know what to do."

She loves him.

My insides twist with guilt. But why? I didn't really do anything wrong. Suddenly it becomes clear why Tate lied to Haley last year. Until now, I hadn't realized how guilty you can feel from…not what actually happened but what didn't happen. Because I wanted it to happen.

Want. Present tense.

Chapter 16

-TATE-

ME: *want to hang out?*

Six hours later and Claire still hasn't replied. If I could take that text back, I would. I thought that's where things were headed after last night. I thought— It doesn't matter. Instead of hanging out with her, I'm staring at my parked snowmobile, trying to figure everything out. The door swings open and my mom appears in the doorway.

"Why aren't you calling your dad back?" she demands. "He said he's been trying all morning."

"Huh." I turn my attention to the tools on the floor in front of me, pretending to search for the perfect one. Behind Mom, Roger is working his way into the garage with two huge raccoon traps.

"I'm not playing middleman between you two," Mom says. "Be a grown-up, Tate, and call him back. He wants you to come for a visit. I think that's nice. He's been there a year and you haven't been down yet. Any college visit is a great opportunity."

I sigh. "I just don't have time, okay?" Then I play to her pushy academic side. "You were right, junior year is hard. And now that I'm taking Steller's place…"

Her shoulders drop an inch, her face relaxing. "But why not communicate this to your father? He works for a college, surely he'll understand."

Yeah, right. "I tried."

"Fine," she concedes. "I'll talk to him. During the holidays you'll visit, got it?"

I shrug, not committing one way or another. This seems to satisfy her. For now at least. She heads back to the house and Roger enters the garage and places the traps in the corner.

He pauses by the door, turning back to me.

"Have you seen Mike Steller recently?" Roger asks. "I ran into him at the Stop and Shop the other day."

Since he walked out of the game, he means to say, I'm sure.

"Uh…" I dip my head to wipe at an imaginary smudge on the side of the snowmobile. "Not exactly."

"Bakowski really did put a ban on seeing Mike," Roger says, not as a question, so I don't respond. Then he adds, "You know, I doubt anyone over at the trailer park pays attention to people coming in and out. I bet Mike worked all night and is probably there now…waking up soon."

It took a while for word to get out about Mike being the father of "that pregnant girl over at the trailer park's" baby, but since his big exit from the game, pretty sure everyone is now in the know. And it's another reason to shun him.

I chance a sideways glance at him. Is he really doing this? Telling me to go see Steller? Is something wrong? All I do is mumble, "Good to know." But later, after Roger's left the garage, I pull out my phone and punch in a text.

ME: want to hang out?

Unlike with Claire, I get a reply within twenty seconds.

MIKE: sure. U got a death wish?

I laugh. Apparently I do.

ME: be there in 20

"Don't move a muscle," Mike directs me. "Listen. Watch."

I'm standing behind a homemade goal the little kids in the trailer park built for the pond close by. The second Mike stepped a skate onto the ice this afternoon, all ten or so of them in their beat-up skates went wide-eyed and cleared out quick. I don't know if they were starstuck over Mike or if it was more out of fear of the new town outcast.

Mike skates toward the goal. His puck-handling is smooth and fluid for someone who's been a goalie for years. "Tell me where my shot is headed."

I lift my glove, bringing it toward my face. I'm feeling vulnerable all of a sudden even though I'm behind the goal, with the net between Mike's shot and me. But I'm not in full gear, only skates, a glove, and a helmet. Mike—who probably hasn't had a ton of recent shooting practice, considering he played goalie—is about to launch the puck somewhere.

"Don't move!" he reminds me.

I drop my glove hand and focus on standing still while Mike maneuvers his way to the goal. I stumble over my words, shouting three different guesses as to where he might aim his shot. My first guess was right. Mike says nothing as he backs up, dragging the puck by his stick, and then he's moving forward again.

"This time," he tells me, "only one guess."

My anxiety levels rise, watching Mike attempt a few different fakes, throwing me off. I do my best to not move and keep my answers to one guess while he attempts another shot on goal, followed by another and another. Finally, when I'm wound so tight I'm actually getting tired from standing still, Mike says, "All right. Now you can move if you want. But no talking. Keep your guessing to yourself."

"Want me to grab the rest of my gear?"

Mike shakes his head. "Nope. Stay behind the goal. You're not gonna touch the puck."

I shake out my stiff limbs and get into position behind the goal. The relief of not having to tell him where I think he'll shoot is instant. He comes at the goal from an angle and pulls off a damn good shot for a goalie. My glove hand rises, lining up perfectly with the pocket of the net the puck sinks into.

Mike nods and grins. "Didn't I tell you your glove was getting fast, man?" he says, reminding me of that night last fall during Claire's going-away party.

We keep this up for another twenty minutes, and instead of feeling drained, I'm energized. Mike stops to take a swig of his water bottle before tossing it to me. "Your head sucks, T-Man. You gotta figure out how to shut that voice down. You know?"

I kick at a divot in the ice and nod. He's right. It's not supposed to be so hard…not for someone like me who's had the training and the practice. I'm wearing myself down thinking too much. "I guess I didn't realize how much I wanted this. To be good. Maybe even great."

Mike takes the water from me again and stares out at the pond. "It's tough admitting that. Then you gotta be compared to everyone else. Even—"

"My dad," I admit.

"Yep. Fucking Dad. The only thing I ever hated about hockey." He nods. "But you know what? Fuck that. Forget him. Forget his jersey on the wall or whatever. You're not him."

I look down at my skates. God, I hope I'm not him. But all that temperamental shit I've been pulling lately...not exactly an apple falling far from the tree. I lift my head and glance out at the trailer park across the road. Less than a year ago, the Stellers hosted a hockey team party and I walked around their huge house, shocked by the size, the view from the private inlet, the wood interior and fancy appliances. "How's it going there? You got heat and all that?"

"In the trailer?" he asks. "The heat sucks. Most of it sucks. But it's ours, and I don't have someone breathing down my neck, telling me I'm a screwup, so that makes this shithole the happiest place on earth, in my opinion."

I'm about to ask him how Jessie's doing, but she appears across the street, a large plastic container in her hands. Mike grins and walks over to meet her, but I can't seem to do anything but stare at her giant stomach. I haven't seen her for a few months so it's like, okay, this is real now.

When Jessie gets close enough, she smacks the side of my head. "It's a fucking baby, not an alien."

I rub my head where she hit me and lift an eyebrow. "You surc it's just one?"

She laughs. "Yeah."

"What are you doing out here? It's freezing." Mike leans against the front of my mom's minivan and pulls Jessie against him.

"The TV went out again." Jessie sighs. "Well, I can hear it, I just can't see a picture. And I think the kids next door figured out our password again because the internet is running super slow."

I look away when Mike slides a hand inside Jessie's coat. "It is an alien in here. There's an elbow poking out. T-Man, you gotta feel this."

My attention snaps back to Mike and Jessie. I lift my hands up in the air and back away. "Dude, I'm not feeling your girlfriend's stomach."

Mike seems to think this over a minute. "Yeah, guess that is kinda messed up."

Jessie rolls her eyes. "Why? Everyone else, stranger or not, loves to touch my belly and tell me how many ways I'm already killing my baby. Did you know if your underwear is too tight—"

"What strangers?" Mike demands. "Who's bothering you?"

She smiles and rests her head against his chest. "All those other guys who might be my baby daddy."

I choke on the drink of Mike's water I just took and spray it everywhere. Jessie seems to think this is hilarious, but Mike looks more haunted by her joke. He glances at me. "My dad. That's what he said when I told him. That it's probably not mine."

Jesus.

I wipe the water from my face and absorb that news. I don't even know what to say. No wonder they couldn't stay with the Stellers.

"You're right. It's cold out here." Jessie pushes up on her toes and kisses Mike. "But I thought you guys might want these."

She hands off the container to Mike, who pops the lid, revealing a couple dozen cookies. "Claire stopped by again?" he asks.

"Claire, these cookies, and three more casseroles." Jessie turns to head back across the road but calls over her shoulder, "See ya, Tate."

"Bye, Jess," I say, but I'm focused on the cookies. "Claire made those for you?"

Mike shakes his head, his mouth full. "She's got food coming out her ears, apparently. People keep bringing stuff and nobody eats it."

The mention of Claire makes my stomach knot with… what, I'm not sure. I wonder when she brought this stuff over? Maybe we almost ran into each other.

Mike is watching me closely. His left brow shoots up. "You still got a thing for O'Connor, huh?"

"What?" I shake my head in protest. "No."

"Come on, I'm not an idiot," Mike says. "I've seen you admiring her, talking…"

"It's not like we ever hung out together on purpose," I argue. "She's my sister's—"

"Friend," he finishes. "Yeah, I know. But Jody's gone and you're here asking about her, so what am I supposed to assume?"

I reach out and grab a cookie. "Want me to look at that TV?"

"I get it." Mike holds his hands up, surrendering. "Can't afford the distraction, right? I'll let it go. For now. You really think you can fix the TV?"

I bend over to unlace my skates. "Maybe."

"Dude." Mike laughs. "You so have a thing for Claire."

"I thought you were letting that go?" My jaw tenses and I yank a skate off, tossing it onto the snowy grass. If I'd known this would turn into more locker room talk, I wouldn't have come over. "We didn't hook up. We didn't do anything."

Mike's forehead wrinkles. "So what if you did? What's wrong with that? Because Claire hooked up with Pratt last year she's suddenly the town vixen? Jesus Christ. Before Jessie, I…" He closes his eyes for a second and exhales. "Let's just say I'm a lot different now. But back then, no one said shit about me. Now they do."

I stuff my foot into a boot and look up at Mike. "I hate that you can't play, but I get it. I'm sorry. About everything."

Sorry that my dad's a selfish asshole and won't do shit for you.

"But you're in now," Mike points out. "Don't think you're fooling me; I know you want it. At least a little bit."

My nonresponse says everything. I do want it. But being in isn't enough. I want to be great. "So...the TV?"

"Right." Mike laughs and we head across the street once my boots are on and Mike's skate guards are in place. "You know..." he says before we reach the trailer. "It might change the tide a bit if people knew that you're into her."

"I never said I was—"

"Save it." He holds up a hand to stop me. "Fooling around is one thing; really liking her is another."

"I think she's going back to school in January." We walk in silence for a minute and then it hits me how weird this conversation has been. "What's with the fatherly advice? Are you reading a parenting book or something?"

Mike bursts out laughing. "Yeah, right. Jessie reads. I pretend to listen to her yap about the reading. To me, it's not that fucking complicated, the whole father thing—don't be an asshole, listen, find your own glory instead of living off your kid's."

"That sounds about right."

Mike looks me over. "Hey, your dad's definitely got the legend thing going on—that's a shitload of pressure for you—but at least he's cool, right?"

"Right." I clamp my jaw shut and nod. "But Claire...she's not—I don't think she's interested."

Except she was. For a moment. But maybe it was a weak moment for her, or maybe she pretended I was someone else. Someone older. Someone else she crushed on for years.

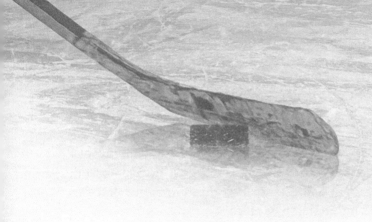

Chapter 17

−CLAIRE−

'm driving back from the cell phone store, after having to coerce the girl behind the counter to turn our phones back on for half the bill, when the pings of forty-eight hours without cell access start coming in. The first one I read is from Tate.

TATE: *Want to hang out?*

Maybe it's fate or maybe it's me finally giving in to whatever this is, but moments later, I pass Benny's. Through the front windows, I can see Tate seated at a table with Leo and Jamie. I don't give myself a second to chicken out. I pull into the parking lot and hop out of the car.

Benny's on a weeknight luckily isn't too bad. The place is only about half filled.

Jamie and Leo both spot me and wave. Tate, on the other hand, slides all the way to the far side of the booth, near the window. He makes eye contact for a second and then looks down at his tray of food. No *hey, Claire* or a wave or anything. I thought he wanted to hang out?

I turn to Leo and Jamie. "What do you guys think about Game Night at O'Connor's? You got my text, right?" With the phone bill issue, I guess I can't be sure it made it through. Late Night at O'Connor's went so well last Friday that I'm working on some more themed nights. Gotta get that five grand to the hospital billing office.

And another two grand to Northwestern, I remind myself, my stomach tumbling at the thought. I've been dismissing that tuition money lately, like it's not a real bill. Like I'm not really going back. But I have to.

"We got your text, but..." Jamie scratches his head. "I don't get it?"

"Game night on game night," I repeat. "With the Otters."

"Like hockey after hockey?" Leo asks. "Probably not a great idea."

I shake my head. "I was thinking more like card games or anything you can play at a table."

Jamie points a finger at me. "Go Fish!"

"Sure...if you want." I give Tate another glance, waiting for him to chime in. The memory of his hand on my arm, my fingers in his hair, two nights ago is still fresh and full of feelings. He continues eating his fries but says nothing. My enthusiasm for this hangout session he requested is quickly dying. "Or even Poker or Blackjack or that board game everyone is crazy about—Ticket to Ride. You know what? Don't worry about that; I'll come up with a plan. Just say you're in? I need maybe five or six of you."

I glance hopefully at Tate but he's still sitting there looking bored.

"What are we getting out of this?" Leo asks.

Jamie nods. "Yeah, what he said."

Uh…good question. "Well…" I stall for a few seconds before coming up with an angle. "You get a few extra hours of being worshipped by a table full of middle school kids and probably freshmen."

Jamie narrows his eyes at me, then a grin spreads across his face. "Dude, I'm so in." He holds his fist out for me to bump.

"Me, too," Leo agrees.

"Think you can get a few more?" I ask, then look at Tate yet again. "Like the new starting goalie, maybe?"

Leo reaches across the table and slugs Tate on the shoulder. "T-Man, you in or not?"

"Um…" Finally he looks at me, and something on his face tells me he's embarrassed or…I don't know.

Leo gives Jamie a look and then both of them jump up from the table, claiming to need milkshakes ASAP. Tate tries to join them, but Leo pushes him back into the booth. They converse silently through a series of warning glances from Leo and exasperated ones from Tate. Finally Leo looks at me. "Chocolate, right, O'Connor?"

"Um, sure."

After they're gone, headed for the counter to order shakes, I give the diner a quick look around and then slide into the booth beside Tate. "You said you wanted to hang out…so here I am."

Tate stares at me. "That was Saturday. It's Monday."

Ah. Makes sense now. And the disconnected phone mishaps just keep on coming. I steal a fry and dip it in ketchup. "Better late than never, right?"

Tension hangs in the air between us while Tate ponders this. Finally, I sigh. "Something happened with my phone. It— Well, it…" My face heats up. Of course. Dammit. "Stopped working. The company stopped it." I wave a hand. "Doesn't matter. I just got your message."

"It's fine," he says, shaking his head. "You don't have to reply. It's no big deal."

My thigh brushes against his, giving me that stomach-fluttering feeling again.

He traces a finger over the long crack in the old plastic table. "I shouldn't have asked. It's weird, right?"

Yeah, but that doesn't mean I don't want to. "So, what's new in the rumor mill?"

He flinches at the mention of rumors but says nothing.

I lift an eyebrow. "Please tell me you haven't gotten in any more fights over any of that stuff?"

He hesitates long enough to get me worried.

"Tate! Seriously?"

I shove his shoulder with one hand, but he catches my fingers in his, stopping me. My breath catches in my throat. Tate, on the other hand, appears completely at ease with his fingers around mine. "No fights. I promise."

"I don't believe you." My fingers are hot where he's touching them. "You hesitated. Clear indication of lying."

"Really?" He walks two fingers from my palm to the inside of my wrist. "Your pulse is awfully fast for an honest person."

My face flushes, and I focus on our linked hands. "It's always like that. All those stage performances, they've put me in a constant state of adrenaline rush." I tug my hand free and look up at him again.

He's wearing the sexy smile from the other night. "So… you and me, hanging out? You don't hate the idea?"

"I'm here, aren't I?" I sit up straighter, my composure regained. "How about hanging out next Friday night, after the game? At O'Connor's."

Tate laughs and then nods. "Yeah, fine, I'll play Go Fish or whatever."

Jamie and Leo return with four shakes, and Tate puts a respectable distance between us. Leo slides a chocolate shake my way.

Headlights shine right into the window beside our booth and Kyle Stewart's truck comes into view. I drop a hand on Tate's knee beneath the table. "No fighting."

His eyes widen, gaze flitting down to his lap and then back to my face. My cheeks flush again, probably enough for Jamie and Leo to notice. I had only meant to hold him in place. I draw my hand back, but Tate catches it again and returns it to his knee. *Jesus.* He is way gutsier than I am.

Just don't check my pulse again.

Chapter 18

-TATE-

She started this. She put her hand on my knee. How am I supposed to think about anything but that right now? I shake my head, attempting to refocus. Kyle Stewart, his girlfriend, Kayla, plus Leslie and Haley walk into Benny's. Haley's stumbling and slurring her words. I can hear her poor attempt at ordering food all the way from our booth. She bends over to rest her head on the counter and Stewart laughs really hard. Then Kayla and Leslie follow.

I swear under my breath and Claire quickly draws her hand back for the second time. Leo eyes me from across the table. "Don't, man. You gotta chill out."

Haley manages to get herself to an empty table. But then more headlights appear outside the window. A group of guys who I know are friends with Luke Pratt walk in next. Beside me, Claire stiffens, watching the guys who just entered. Not for the first time, I want to ask her what happened that night. But Pratt isn't with his friends tonight.

Leo and Jamie wave to the guys but neither moves to talk to them. They head right over to Stewart's table. One of the guys puts a hand on Haley's shoulder. "Stevenson, where's the princess smile tonight?"

The girls crack up and so does Stewart. Haley rests her head against her hand, eyes already fluttering shut. I let out a huge sigh and then look at Claire. "Can you let me out?"

She looks surprised but hops up quickly. I head over to Haley's table, Jamie's and Leo's protests ringing in my ears. I glare at Kayla and Leslie. "You guys are supposed to be her friends."

They both look incredibly guilty but neither one apologizes. As gently as possible, I pull Haley out of her chair and onto her feet. "Come on, let's get out of here."

Her eyes fly all the way open, and she takes me in and then jerks her arm away. "No! I ordered food... I'm staying at Leslie's."

I wrap an arm around her waist and bring her close enough to whisper in her ear. "Kayla and Leslie are two seconds away from posting drunk pictures of you on Instagram."

"They're my friends," she argues, trying to break away. We've got everyone's attention now. "Unlike you. You're not anything anymore."

I should just say, *Okay. Fine.* And leave her. "Your friends who would do anything to beat you for Juniper Princess," I remind her, keeping my voice low enough for only Haley to hear.

Haley's jaw drops open. "Those little—"

"Save it for when you have balance." Luckily she doesn't fight me. I manage to walk her out the door of Benny's.

Claire follows beside us. "Want me to take her back to the apartment above the bar?"

The offering is tempting. Very tempting. But I know how

to sneak Haley in through the basement door at her house. I know her parents are sound asleep because they're teachers and get to school at, like, five in the morning. "Nah. I'll drop her off. It'll be fine."

"You sure?" Claire stops not too far from my mom's minivan and waits for me to answer.

I open the door and shove Haley into the passenger seat. She slumps over, closing her eyes, with her legs still hanging over the edge, preventing me from shutting the car door. I give Claire a nod and she leaves us, walking behind me and heading toward where Leo and Jamie are standing in the parking lot.

Haley swats at my arm when I try and get the seat belt around her. Then she's all wide-eyed and panicked, clutching my arm. "I can't go to sleep. I keep having dreams about the antlers…they're stabbing me."

I tug at the seat belt again. "Come on. Just put your feet in the car."

I've done this with her before, so I know what's coming. Which means I'm not in the least bit shocked when Haley starts sobbing uncontrollably. When she gets like this, sometimes she hyperventilates. She freaked out once while we were studying for a world history test freshman year and I thought she was dying. Luckily my mom was home to teach me the breathing-into-a-paper-bag trick. I don't have a paper bag tonight, so I have no choice but to calm her down.

"Antlers… The crown?" I guess.

Haley nods between sobs. "I'm gonna lose. And everyone will see pictures of me losing. And you're going to win, Tate, and we're not even gonna get married. I'll have to look at your picture in town hall forever and be like, I love him and he hates me."

I rub my temples. Claire was smart to take off.

"Haley, relax or you'll pass out."

She begins listing every test, assignment, cheer practice, and Juniper Princess commitment she has this week, and she's speaking so loudly and in such a rushed voice, I don't even hear Claire drive off.

Finally Haley stops crying for a few seconds, giving me an opportunity to get a word in. "You're gonna make yourself crazy with all this stuff you're doing. Is it worth it?"

She wipes her face with her T-shirt and swallows. "You're really not going to the ball with me, are you?"

I hesitate and then shake my head slowly.

Haley pulls in a shaky breath but nods. "I didn't even want to break up. I thought we were taking a break. What's wrong with me? I mean, you used to love me. I know you did."

For the first time since Haley broke up with me, I feel the ache in my chest I'd expected long ago. Heartbreak, maybe. But more because I can't do it. I can't be this person she thinks I am. And that means we can't have back what we used to be together. "Nothing is wrong with you. You're perfect, I promise. Just not for me."

And even saying that makes me wish it weren't true. But that's the thing. It was always easy with Haley. Until it wasn't. But I don't think it's supposed to be easy. Not real love. Haley would say that we've been through so much together, but really, what would that be? Losing our virginity? Her mom finding out about said virginity? That was a bit rough, but nothing like…

Nothing like standing in that parking lot with Claire, realizing my arm was broken in three places. Again, I'm reminded of the fact that I don't have to pretend with Claire. We may be dancing around something at the moment, but when it comes to real things, important things, she knows me.

With a heavy sigh, I close the car door and then hop in the

driver's side. It takes a while to get Haley inside her house and eventually in her bedroom, which is always a complete disaster, but I manage to navigate strewn items on the floor and make my exit without getting caught.

Later, at home, while I'm struggling to finish my trig homework, I pull out my phone and send Claire a text.

ME: got Haley home. No parentals woken

CLAIRE: good

ME: so...about that hanging out thing. When can we?

CLAIRE: idk. It's late

ME: not now. But sometime

CLAIRE: Maybe it's not such a good idea

My heart picks up, palms sweaty. I almost chicken out and play it cool, but then I remember once again that I don't have to pretend with Claire.

ME: what's wrong?

CLAIRE: nothing. I'm just...I don't know. Need some space

My heart sinks. I stare at her words for way too long and finally type a reply. The only response my pride and self-preservation will allow.

ME: I'm here if u change your mind

An hour passes. I fall asleep with my phone still in my hand. When I wake up to move my books off the bed, I check it again. No response from Claire.

Chapter 19

–CLAIRE–

From the steps leading up to the apartment above the bar, I spot Tate and Jake Hammond flying toward Juniper Falls Pond on snowmobiles. They park near the pond and hop off, Tate with a drill in his hand and Jake with a tape measure. For a moment, Tate looks over this way and I quickly conceal myself, sliding to the far side of the steps. He really does seem like he belongs here, on that pond with whatever varsity hockey players he's hanging out with. But I know that's not completely true. I know Tate shares some of my *I don't belong here* feelings because we talked about it that night in the car, last fall.

My gut twists. I blew him off. I'm sure he's confused as hell, but I'm a disaster. And Haley loves him and he obviously still cares about her if he made the effort to get her home safe a couple of weeks ago. A couple of weeks. Has it really been that long? God, I need to get over this and focus on paying those bills, on getting myself back to school.

"Are these stairs safe?" the middle-aged woman says from behind me. She's finally ended her phone call, after making me stand here in the cold for nearly ten minutes waiting to show her the apartment. "Have you had the fire department inspect them?"

"No."

"No, they're not safe? Or no, you haven't had them inspected?" she demands.

I sigh. I already know how this will end. I turn to face her, plastering on a smile. "How about we check out the actual apartment?"

She exhales, shaking her head. I glance at the time on my phone. I'm supposed to be at Haley's house for band practice in forty-five minutes. I have a feeling that won't be a problem considering this woman is already dissatisfied with the stairs.

When the lady brushes past me, I'm forced to put Tate in my line of sight again. For a second, I let myself imagine us back in that booth at Benny's, my hand on his knee, his fingers brushing my palm gliding over my wrist—

"You're going to unlock the door, I assume?"

"Oh, right. Of course." I peel my gaze from Tate and head up the rest of the steps.

Once we're inside the apartment, she complains about the heat—and yeah, it's not working at 100 percent, can't seem to get the temperature above sixty-two—then she opens the cabinet under the bathroom sink and gasps.

She closes the doors again and rights herself. "I don't do mildew."

With that warning, the woman stomps out of the apartment and clambers down the steps. I stare at the cabinet doors, not really too excited to open them. I debate going across the street to ask Tate to check it out for me but even if we were on friendly terms at the moment, I don't think I could bring myself to engage in such a cliché girlie act. I take a deep breath, squat down in front of the cabinet, and slowly open the doors.

I have to flip on the light and get a closer look to see the problem, but when I do, I can't help groaning. Shit. This is the last thing we need right now. I slam the cabinet doors shut and exit the bathroom and the apartment.

Aunt Kay and Mom are in the bar right now, and I really don't feel like telling them about another failed apartment showing. So instead of going inside to get one of their car keys, I decide the nearly one-mile walk to Haley's is worth not having to face them.

Everyone is already in the garage when I arrive, the band equipment set up. Roger and Artie are in the middle of a debate about guitar strings. I keep glancing their way, waiting for my chance to get Roger alone.

"So…" Haley says to me, and she's got that look like she's about to sign me up for another committee. "We've decided that you need to be the keyboard player. And lead vocals."

"That's what I'm here for." I look over at Roger again and then stand behind the keyboard, powering it up.

"I mean for the ball," Haley says. "I know you've got a lot going on and you're heading back to school in January, but this would be before all that. Plus, Roger's crew says they'll split the two grand with you—"

The music book I've just picked up slips through my fingers. "Two grand? For playing at the ball?"

She nods, a smile on her face. "I really pushed to make the music budget a priority this year. So that's a yes?"

"Uh, yeah. Duh." I mean, how could I say no to that? But wait… "Lead vocals? Roger's got a great voice. I don't think—"

"Shared lead vocals," Haley clarifies. She pats me on the

shoulder. "You'll be great. I'm so excited about this band."

I watch her walk away, grabbing her clipboard to jot down notes. After hearing her a couple of weeks ago, sobbing and listing everything she needed to do, I almost want to ask her how she does it. How does she put on the I've-got-it-all-under-control face for everyone? And I want to ask her if anything happened with her and Tate. She looks happy. Maybe they got back together?

I hate the punch-in-the-gut feeling that follows that thought. I should be glad if that's happened. She loves him.

Haley tells us it's time to get started, so I have to set aside my questions for Roger. She starts off by having each of us suggest a song we could sing well that wasn't on the set list. Roger surprises me by picking "Blurred Lines." I don't even have to think about my choice.

"'Feeling Good,'" I tell her. "By Nina Simone."

It's a song I've loved to sing for as long as I can remember. One Jody and I would belt out in her living room. I have a flash of New Year's Eve six years ago…Tate lighting fireworks, this song playing through a speaker resting on the Tanleys' snow-covered grill.

I have this sudden ache for Tate, to have him around. Which doesn't even make sense. It's not like I've been around him much since I got back home, but something about him… he's my constant.

But when we finally begin rehearsing the song I picked, the one filled with dozens of warm memories, my entire mood shifts.

A hint of that fire, the adrenaline rush I used to get regularly, hits me. Performing, just thinking about being onstage again, the hard work of rehearsals, the hours spent backstage waiting for your turn to practice, the butterflies during auditions—God, I miss this feeling. More guilt punches me, but I shove it aside for now and pour my heart into this song.

When we finish, both Haley's dad and Roger are staring at me like I've grown another head. Artie is the one to speak first. "Your pitch is killer."

Roger shakes his head and proceeds to tune his guitar. "Not killer. Perfect. It's perfect."

My face heats up. "I got a little flat in the second verse." I shuffle sheet music around, not wanting to look at any of them.

Haley's dad clears his throat. "Band director here. Don't insult my professional integrity. Roger's right, it was perfect. A year at Northwestern and you're beyond all of us."

I duck my head. I'm not. Plus, I don't want to think about what that year away cost me. Time with my dad.

Haley seems to sense my shifting emotions because she claps her hands and tells us to move on to the next song.

But now I'm stuck in that place where I can't completely love this because I know what it's taken from me.

Chapter 20

−TATE−

"So, when are you and Claire going to be done with the secret looks and secret everything?" Leo asks.

My body tenses. I really don't want to talk about Claire right now. "She said she needed space." I adjust my helmet and wait for someone to take a shot. We are here to play hockey, right? "That's code for not gonna happen, last I heard."

Jamie scratches his head. "Space?"

So far "space" has translated to *I'm ignoring you but trying not to make it look like I'm ignoring you.*

I glide side to side in front of the goal, trying to smooth out the ice on the pond. Jake moves in a blur in front of me, preparing to shoot. "Come on, Ham, don't hold back. Not here."

Jake spins in one direction, hops over the puck, and then shoots from the side opposite to his normal shot. Leo and Jamie both release a loud cheer. I pull off my helmet and stare at Jake. "What the hell, Hammond?"

"Show me the intergalactic moves," Leo begs. "I need a new trick shot."

It's a testament to Jake's ability that he has no problem teaching his shot to Leo. Probably because he's got a dozen more, and if those don't work, there are a hundred more on standby. Senior year for Jake is gonna be amazing.

We play for a while longer, mostly because I'm pushing them to keep going. Last night's game went okay for me. The cold gets to us after a while and we end up huddled in front of a small space heater Jake brought from home.

Roger's Critter Crusader van pulls up near the pond. He hops out and walks toward us.

"Uh-oh, what'dya do, T-Man?" Jamie says.

"Nothing." Still, I'm tense as Roger approaches us. I've probably done something.

"Need a ride?" he asks.

"Sure," I say, grabbing my stuff.

"Mind swinging by the junkyard on the way home?" Roger says. "Didn't you say you were looking for a carburetor for the snowmobile?"

"Yeah." I'm surprised he remembered that. I mentioned it to my mom this morning. He had just been passing through the kitchen on his way out. I switch my skates for boots and get into the Critter Crusader van with Roger.

"So…" Roger says. "You guys play out at the pond a lot? It's not too cold?"

I shrug. "Sometimes it's too cold. But it's fun. You know, no boards to run into, really different game."

"Huh. I don't know, I've never played much hockey. Or skating."

"Oh, right." I nod like I get it, but I can't imagine growing up around here without playing hockey. I mean, did he always want to be an exterminator? I can't ask that.

"Did you do any other sports?"

Roger's reply is cut short as he slams on the brakes, his eyes huge.

The van comes squealing to an abrupt halt. A man with tattooed arms nearly gets sideswiped by the hood of Roger's van.

My heart jumps up to my throat, and Roger releases a string of swearwords. The man is already taking off, not deterred by his near-death experience. Once I've caught my breath, I give the guy a closer look and realize he's not dressed.

Well, aside from the white boxer briefs covering his ass.

One half of his body appears to be hurrying down the street, while the other side gets dragged behind him.

I sit upright again after having been thrown forward. "Isn't that Mr. O'Connor...?"

Roger pulls the van over to the side of the road and throws it into park. He hops out and I follow quickly behind him.

"What do you think he's doing out here?" I ask. The Davin O'Connor I know doesn't walk around in his underwear in the middle of winter. We're at least a mile from Claire's house.

Roger shakes his head and grabs his phone.

"Mr. O'Connor!" I shout, jogging to catch up. Cars are coming toward him, and he seems oblivious. Maybe he sleepwalks? When I reach him, I touch his arm, and he spins to face me, his expression livid and wide awake. He jerks out of my grip and continues on to wherever he's going.

"Davin," Roger says, cutting him off from the front. "Where are you headed? We'll give you a ride."

His face contorts and he spits out a bunch of sounds that don't make any sense but seem to take a great deal of effort.

Wait…he *can't speak*? Why hadn't Claire ever mentioned this? Or her mom. We talked about Davin while I fixed the sink.

He moves past Roger and is off again. I shift uncomfortably in my spot. This seems like a much-too-personal inside look into Claire's family, and I'm not sure she'd want me around for it. Especially given her *I need space* claim.

Roger goes after him again, but I stay firmly in place watching the two of them.

Sheriff Hammond pulls up beside Roger and rolls down the window. They exchange words, and I finally move in that direction. My hands and face are freezing. I can't imagine how cold Mr. O'Connor must be in just his underwear.

More cars rush past us and then slow to a stop, taking in the situation. Most of them stare and then move on, but a couple of people roll down their windows and ask if we need any help. Meanwhile, Claire's dad seems determined to go somewhere.

By the time Roger and I reach him again, the sheriff has turned around and a gray SUV is barreling toward us, jerking over to the side of the road. Both Claire's mom and her aunt tumble out.

Claire's mom is crying, arguing with Sheriff Hammond, or at least she's emphatically explaining something.

"He gets up and he forgets everything. Thinks he needs to go to work," she says.

Roger finally steers Claire's dad toward the SUV. Instead of wide-eyed and angry, he now looks shrunken and lost. I hang back, putting a few feet between us, not wanting to get in the way.

"You left the damn pain pills out in plain sight," Claire's aunt Kay yells at her sister-in-law. "He probably took too many again. Or he got into the liquor."

"You were supposed to be in the room with him!" Mrs.

O'Connor shouts. She glares at Kay and then lets out a frustrated sigh before pulling a cell phone from her purse. "Claire, honey, he's fine… No, you will not! You know he wouldn't want you to see him like this… He isn't naked…not completely… I don't know if he took too many pills… Yes, I realize I can count them!"

My stomach churns. I don't want to hear any more of this. It's too much. I knew Claire was home because of her dad, I knew he was struggling, but I had no idea how this "medical miracle" was tearing her family apart. She's supposed to be far away having all kinds of big-city adventures.

Since things appear to be sort of under control, Roger walks over to me and suggests we take off. My mind is far away when we climb back into the van and leave the two ladies and the sheriff with the nearly naked Davin O'Connor.

Chapter 21

-TATE-

After that whole debacle and sending Claire three texts and getting no reply, I just need to see if she's okay. I hop on my snowmobile and end up at O'Connor's.

A blond chick is at the hostess stand and Claire isn't anywhere in sight. "Is Claire around?"

The girl looks down at the menus in front of her, shuffling them into a neat stack. "She's not working in the dining room tonight."

"Is she back in the kitchen?"

"Nope." The girl jumps at the chance to seat a family that just entered.

I notice Petey behind the bar. He's always been around for Sunday night football with Dad. "Hey, Petey? Where's Claire?"

"Storeroom, reorganizing," he says after glancing up from the beer glass he'd been filling.

I shrug when the hostess girl glares at Petey. From the corner of my eye, I spot Pratt and some meathead friends of his eating at a table in the back. Maybe that's why Claire is hiding out?

In the kitchen, Manny waves to me and lets me pass through without questions. The cold storeroom is such a contrast to the overheated kitchen that I shiver after walking in. I glance around and Claire's nowhere to be found. I'm about to leave when I hear sniffling coming from the far corner of the room. I walk slowly past shelves of liquor and canned ingredients.

Claire is hiding behind a tall stack of boxes. She's sitting on the floor, knees pulled to her chest, her apron sprawled over her legs. Her eyes are red and her face wet with tears. And she's got a bottle of Jack Daniel's in one hand. With a decent amount of the liquor missing.

"Oh great," Claire says when she sees me. She lifts the apron to her face, attempting to wipe it dry.

I squat down in front of her, assessing how drunk she is. Her speech was pretty clear, but she only said two words. I shiver again. It's like a fridge in here. "It's freezing. Let's get you out of here."

She laughs. "How about we go upstairs? I can give you a private showing. Isn't that what Haley's cheer friends are saying about us?"

I sigh and then slide into the space beside her. Clearly we aren't going upstairs and we aren't going in the dining room. *That* would be a disaster. I touch the bottle in her hands with one finger. "Are you sharing?"

I'm kind of over being the responsible sober one.

She reluctantly hands it over and I take a swig. It's bitter and burns going down. "I think today would be a great day to run away with the circus," she says.

I hand the bottle back and press my shoulder against hers. "I'm in."

She chugs another gulp of whiskey and then puts the cap on. "You want to know something?"

"What?" There's a case of bottled water beside me. I snatch a bottle and pass it to Claire, hoping she'll drink some. She does.

"You know how I'm working at the bar now?" Claire says, and I'm quickly doubting her ability to put one foot in front of the other, but I nod anyway. "Well, I'm doing the bills, too. And I keep paying and paying stuff and it just won't end. My phone is about to get shut off. Again. Oh, the power bill is past due. I have a feeling people want heat and electricity when they go somewhere for food or drinks. And I'm too afraid to remind my parents. I mean, what the hell are they going to do that I haven't thought of?

"And then my dad was running around town naked and I couldn't even go and help him because he can't deal with me dealing with him like that. How is he supposed to deal with the money stuff? I'm so sick of nodding and smiling when people ask me how he is. I'm sick of this lie… He can't fucking talk. He can hardly feed or dress himself."

She's furiously wiping away tears. My stomach is a ball of knots. I pick up the whiskey from the floor where she set it down and take a couple more drinks.

"Claire…" I lean my cheek against the wall, waiting for her to look at me. "I have no idea what to say."

"You don't have to say anything. Why would you? You haven't done anything wrong." She shakes her head. "But me? What am I doing while my dad's trying to figure out how to talk again? I'm living out my pop-star fantasies playing keyboard with the town exterminator's band. What kind of person does that?"

"It's a paid gig, right?" I overheard Roger say to my mom that his band and Claire were splitting the two-thousand-dollar payment. Not exactly chump change.

"But I don't have to enjoy it, you know? What the hell is wrong with me?" she snaps. "And while we're on that topic... you know what I'm sitting here thinking about? Not my dad or the bills, not completely those things, but freakin' Luke Pratt. Why did he have to be right? You know what he told me that night when...well, you know?"

Jesus. We're back to Luke Pratt again. I'm gonna need more alcohol. "What did he say?" I prompt.

"He said I'd end up wearing a sombrero and singing 'Happy Birthday' in Spanish." She lifts her hands. "One look at me tonight and I knew that was what he was thinking. That he was right."

"I saw him out in the dining room. If I wasn't so worried about finding you—"

"No more fighting over me," she groans.

"Yeah. Okay." I pick the skin on my thumbnail. "But he's a prick. Forget about him."

There. That should work. Not.

"I had a crush on him for years," Claire admits, though I already knew this.

I reach for the whiskey again, taking an even bigger drink. "You have terrible taste."

She glares at me and steals the bottle back. "It was the only alcohol my mom hasn't inventoried yet. Underage beggars can't be picky."

"I wasn't talking about the booze."

"Whatever." She rolls her eyes. "Everyone had a crush on him. But you know what I learned about long-term unrequited crushes?"

"What?" I ask, even though I'd love to change the subject. Especially considering what I admitted to her in the movie theater the night of the carnival. "They turn into assholes and then keep showing up for walleye horseshoes?"

"Well, that, too. And that it's so much better in your head, you know? I had this vision of what it would be like to kiss someone after imagining it for so long." She leans her head against the shelf beside her and closes her eyes. "I was such a child. I wanted him to make me feel like the most important person in the world, but it was all so calculated and mechanical."

Her eyes are closed and I can stare as long as I want at her face. And that does things to me. My heart picks up speed. Because I've imagined the same thing with Claire, but there's nothing calculated about it.

"Before my dad…" Her voice breaks, but she swallows back the tears and continues. "Well, before that night with Luke…I didn't really date anyone or hook up much. Everyone around here always seems to fall into this trap and get stuck in some cliché relationship."

"Like cheer captain and varsity hockey player?" I suggest.

She gives me this look like, *Oops, sorry*. "I was talking about other people. And about my expectations. They've always been too high."

"I don't think your expectations are too high." I don't know what exactly she wants or wanted, but regardless, she should have it. And yeah, I'm fucking glad Luke Pratt failed to meet Claire's expectations.

She shakes her head. "Maybe nobody really treats people like they're special. Or they do but only for a little while. That's some idealistic version of love that I ditched last fall. But Haley…"

"Haley?" I ask

"Haley." Claire opens her eyes, looking at me again. "She's not the monster you made her out to be."

"I know that." This is about as fun as talking about Luke

Pratt. "I never said she was a bad person. I just can't deal with her sometimes, and I choose to hide out instead."

"She loves you," Claire says. "I heard her that night at Benny's—"

I sit up straighter. "You were listening? I thought you left."

So Haley was the barrier. The reason Claire "needed space."

I angle my body to face her, but her eyes are closed again. "Claire, look at me." When she does, I take a deep breath. "Haley doesn't— She and I—it's not hard. It's easy and comfortable. We're barely penetrating the surface." I think for a minute, digging for the right words, hopefully avoiding more unnecessary use of the word "penetrate." Claire looks doubtful, and I'm fighting the urge to shake her and make her understand what's trapped inside my head. For the first time since Haley and I broke up, things are making sense. "It's like scooping a jar full of water from the top of Juniper Falls Pond and claiming to know the contents of the entire lake."

Claire groans, like I've clearly said the worst thing possible. "Oh, is this where you justify the need to experiment with lots of girls? You gotta fill a bunch of glasses?"

"No!" I release a frustrated breath. "Why do you keep doing that? Why do you keep assuming I'm like that? You practically predicted it for me a year ago. You've been gone, so what the hell do you know?"

Okay, that came out way harsher than I meant it to. But seriously? What the hell?

Her eyes widen and some fresh tears slip down one cheek, and I feel like an asshole again. "What did you mean, then?"

"Haley and I…we didn't push each other to…to…" I'm still grappling for words. What is this thing that Claire and I are doing? It's painful and messy but also exhilarating, like seeing colors for the first time. "We didn't rip each other open and look inside, you know? We didn't bring all the ugly stuff to the surface."

"Because that's hard," Claire says slowly, trying each word out, picking them apart.

I nod, relieved that she gets it. "Yeah. It's hard."

"But hard is awful," she protests.

"The past several months with Haley," I admit, "I had to pretend more than I didn't. I don't have to do that with you."

"Tate, I'm a sinking ship. I can't do anything without stressing and changing my mind twenty times. Or pissing someone off. Look how much damage carrying a box of toilet paper downstairs for me has done. People expect you to be with Haley; they see you as a regular hockey player guy. I guess I want you to have it easy. Is that so terrible?"

That's why she pushed me away. She wanted to help me. My mind drifts back to Davin O'Connor and how lost he looked standing outside in his underwear practically freezing to death. She's got all this shit to deal with and she wanted to help me.

When Claire sets the whiskey and water bottles down beside her, I find myself scooting closer, then sliding a hand up her arm. She eyes my fingers, watching them slowly make their way higher. "Can I tell you something?"

My fingers reach her neck and then her cheek. I brush my thumb just under her bottom lip. The thud of my heart is blaring inside my ears, but I watch her mouth open slowly and then she whispers, "Yeah...okay."

I trip over my words, too distracted by the feel of her skin beneath my fingertips. How many times have I imagined this? Too many to ever admit. Her unrequited crush theory is completely inaccurate. "I'm... I mean, this is...you and me—I've thought about this. A lot. For a long time."

A question forms in her mouth but I shake my head. I'm

not done. I follow the curve of her jaw until my hand is in her hair. "And the more of you I saw, the more I wanted this. That's how it should be. No one is perfect up close, but it's the only way to know."

I lean in and touch my mouth to her forehead. I slide over and kiss her temple. Her eyes widen and she stutters out a few words. "T-Tate, what are you—?"

"Do you remember when you stayed over with us on New Year's Eve that one time? I think your parents went somewhere…" With my free hand, I search around for Claire's hand near my leg. I lift it, pressing her palm over my heart. "You made Jody and me write down our New Year's wishes, and then we sent them up with fireworks attached to the dolls…"

"Rocket Barbie," Claire whispers, her eyes fluttering shut.

"I watched you writing down your wishes so carefully and then lighting them up. I remember my heart racing, just like this." I press her palm more firmly against my heart. "It scared me. That anyone could pull those feelings out of me. I get it. The Luke thing. But if you had watched him, if you'd seen him for real…"

I pull back enough for our eyes to meet. Claire looks like she's hanging by a thread, no clue what she wants right now. But I'm here, tangled in her life just as much as she's tangled in mine. There is only one way to get out of this seemingly dead end we've hit.

"Remember last fall, in the car after the hospital when I said you were perfect?"

She nods slowly.

"This is what I wanted to do then—what I *should* have done a year ago." I lean in again, her lips barely brushing mine. "This is me being a grown-up."

Chapter 22

−CLAIRE−

'm not only caught off guard by Tate's mouth touching mine, I'm surprised by how warm his lips are. The room is spinning around me, even with my eyes closed. But this, this is frozen. Suspended in midair.

Just the slightest brush of his lips against mine and my insides thaw. I hold perfectly still, releasing a much-too-enthusiastic sigh. "Tate, I don't think…"

But my argument fizzles out when his fingers grip the back of my neck so gently it makes me want to cry. My heart flies, my stomach cartwheels. His mouth moves to my cheek and then my neck.

And then he holds my face in his hands, his lips returning to mine, his tongue teasing my lips until they open. His mouth moves slowly with mine, his fingers wandering aimlessly, touching any skin they can reach. My own hands drift to Tate's back, gliding under his shirt, feeling the shiver that runs down his spine when I touch him.

God, this is so…so…more. It's more. It's everything. It's never going to end. I won't let it.

Slowly, with such ease, he pulls his mouth from mine. One hand drifts from my face to my hair. He touches his forehead to mine, both of us breathing hard.

Something twists inside my chest. My own heart is breaking. No, it's gluing back together. It's doing both. I don't know…

I just know that I got my wish. I got the kiss I've been dreaming about for years.

"Claire?" Tate still has his arms around me. He might be holding me up. I'm not sure. "You're freezing."

I lean in, wanting nothing more than for my lips to touch his again. "No, I'm warm."

He pulls back and looks me over. "Your teeth are chattering."

They are? God, the whiskey must be kicking in.

"Come on, I'll take you home," Tate says, his eyebrows pulling together. "You don't mind snowmobiles, do you?"

"I was planning on crashing upstairs tonight. I open in the morning." I touch my thumb to his forehead and rub the wrinkle that formed between his eyes. "You look so worried, like I'm gonna get hypothermia. It's fifty-five degrees in here. You can't get hypothermia in fifty-five degrees."

"Actually, you can." He tucks the whiskey bottle behind a box and stands up, pulling me to my feet along with him. The room spins, and I reach out for something to hold onto, but after a second, I'm reoriented and balancing on my own. "I'll walk you upstairs, then. I promise I'll leave as soon as you're safely deposited inside, okay?"

"Okay," I say, meeting his green eyes. "But don't leave."

I lean in, wanting—no, needing—to kiss him again. But far in the distance, practically miles away from this cold storeroom, I hear my mother's voice.

"Claire!"

Maybe not miles away. Maybe from inside the kitchen.

Tate jumps, his eyes wide with panic. My heart sprints again for an all-new reason. I don't want my mom finding us back here together.

"What should I do?" he whispers.

I shove him behind the boxes. "Stay here. I'll drag her out the door and then you can sneak out."

I'm about to run for the door, but Tate grabs my hand. "Claire…"

My eyes meet his again and we're both full of hundreds of words, all forming sentences ending with question marks, but there's no time for that. "I'll text you when it's all clear."

He gives me one quick nod, but I can see he's afraid I'll retreat back into that place where I need to push him away to help him. Maybe I will. Probably I will. When the whiskey is out of my bloodstream.

But still…that was the best freakin' kiss ever. Can't deny that.

I hurry into the kitchen, my phone already in my hand ready to text Tate an "all clear" message so he can leave me to replay that kiss alone upstairs.

But the second I step into the kitchen, I get a glimpse of Mom's face and release my phone, letting it fall down deep into the pocket of my apron.

Oh no.

No, no, no…

Chapter 23

−TATE−

I never got an "all clear" text from Claire last night. Eventually, I stacked up boxes near a window, propped it open, and climbed through. I tried to call her a dozen times. It went straight to voicemail.

While lining up for the winter parade at seven o'clock this morning, I'm shifting between pissed off at Claire and hurt, and then I'm calling myself an idiot for kissing her when she'd obviously had a ton of whiskey. It was too much, too soon.

I'm stuck on the drunken-kiss issue when Haley walks toward me, her nose bright red from cold, a giant card and pen in her hands.

"Want to sign the card for Claire O'Connor's family?"

My stomach drops. My heart speeds up. "What happened?"

"Davin O'Connor caught a cold." Kennedy snorts beside me. "That's what happens when you run around naked in thirty degrees."

Haley gives him the death glare of all death glares. "Shut

the hell up, you insensitive prick."

I can't even process this argument because I need to know more. "What happened?"

"Claire's dad is back in the hospital," Haley explains. "He's got some kind of infection. They flew him in a helicopter to the Mayo Clinic last night."

Feeling even more nauseated, I stumble away from my group and the line I'm supposed to be in, ignoring Haley's card. I grasp my phone in one hand, staring at the screen, trying to figure out what to say to Claire.

No wonder her mom was yelling her name like that last night. It had sounded urgent, but I think I'd dismissed that part as my own panic at us getting caught.

No wonder she never texted me last night.

I sigh with relief that Davin's alive. That Haley's card isn't a "sorry for your loss" card.

ME: I just heard. I'm so sorry. Pls tell me if you need anything.

We're stuck standing outside the movie theater for twenty minutes before it's time to start the parade. I'm just about to hop on our giant float covered in JFH green and silver when she replies.

CLAIRE: ok

I try to read something about her state of mind in that two-letter answer but come up empty.

The head of the Women's League walks up to me and my teammates before our float has started moving. "How much time do you boys need to get ready?"

"Ready for what?" I ask at the same time Jake says, "Five minutes, tops."

Haley elbows me in the side and whispers, "The shoot-out, Tate."

The shoot-out? Oh…the Otters Past and Present shoot-out. I didn't even think about it. Of course someone has to be goalie. Jesus, that means—

I lean sideways, looking around. Two floats up from ours is the alumni float, and sure enough, my dad's old letter jacket with the number sixteen on the sleeve is clearly visible.

"He's got gear to put on," Leo answers when I don't speak up. "Probably ten minutes, right, T?"

I nod. "Um, yeah, sure."

"Don't look so excited," Kennedy says from behind me. "Only the entire town will be watching. I'm sure the alumni will go easy on you. Especially considering all the trouble you're having with your hand."

I spin around to face him, my forehead wrinkled. "Nothing is wrong with my hand."

"Oh." He fakes surprise. "I thought that was the reason all the pucks keep sinking into the net above your shoulder. Figured you couldn't lift your glove hand or something. Guess you just suck."

Obviously Kennedy Locust has a death wish. I should report him to a hotline or something so he can be put on suicide watch. Luckily my teammates are up here with me to keep me out of trouble.

But Jake is whispering to Haley. Red is too busy accidentally bumping into Leslie and then pretending to save her from falling off the float. I glance back at Leo, and he quickly looks away from me and out at the crowd.

"Look." Kennedy elbows me in the ribs, then points to Jake and Haley. "Someone's stealing your girlfriend…"

"She's not my—" I stop mid-sentence when I see Haley poke Hammond in the side. He flashes her a grin that clearly says, *I'm thinking about you naked.*

"And there's the game changer," Kennedy whispers. "You

don't want her, but you can't let someone else have her. That's so cliché, Tate."

"You know what?" I say to Kennedy through my teeth. I do my best to fake a smile and wave when we pass the Spark Plug, which has the biggest crowd out in front, probably due to the hot coffee and pastries. "I think you need to mind your own fucking business."

"Do I?"

"Aren't you supposed to be smart?" I step closer and stare down at him. I'm a whole head taller. "This is about the stupidest thing you could do right now."

An arm shoots out between us. I turn around and Leo is shaking his head.

"Dude, enough."

It takes me several long seconds to realize that he's talking to me. He's shaking his head at *me*. How is he not ready to toss Kennedy onto his ass on the street?

"Listen," Leo says while we're huddled near the goal. "Happy is pushing seventy. Don't need to worry about him scoring."

Lewis Happenstein, aka Happy, is one of the oldest alumni in town. I lean out of the huddle and catch Happy at the other end of the rink, his gray hair patchy and wild, his skating still smooth and sharp but slow. His knees are clearly shot. I swallow back a gulp of nerves. If Happy scores on me, I'll never hear the end of it.

"My dad's been training," Hammond says. "His slap shot is still game."

The seats in the ice rink are quickly filling. The

cheerleaders are standing across the first row of bleachers leading chants. Tons of people have signs with numbers they're cheering for, either supporting the alumni or the current Otters. In this famous yearly shoot-out, no one cheers for the goalie; no one thinks about the goalie unless he screws up. Except, with me in full gear and everyone except the alumni goalie in regular clothes, no pads, I feel more visible than I'd like.

"Tate, what about your dad?" Cole Clooney, our only freshman, asks.

My mouth goes dry. Dad is laughing with Rhett Hammond, all while tossing a puck from the end of his stick and catching it there. Everyone in our huddle waits for my response. I shake my head. "I'm not…I'm not sure."

"Then let's assume the worst, okay, T-Man?" Leo looks right at me, like he's trying to read my mood, to see if I'm on my game or not. Technically this is supposed to be for fun, not high pressure like regular season games and playoffs. But already, I'm sweating, my stomach in knots, my head working way too hard despite all Mike's advice. Maybe I'm freaking out over nothing. I mean, this is supposed to be fun, right? If I screw up during the shoot-out, that shouldn't be grounds for a town lynching, right? No college scouts. Aside from my dad, of course.

"Pratt's gonna score," Owen Jensen states flatly. Then he glances at me and adds, "He's playing juniors. No one will expect you to beat Pratt."

Leo gives the guys some pointers on Ricky Stone, the alumni goalie, who is under thirty and played college hockey for four years. He's probably decent.

Coach Bakowski, who's playing referee today, blows his whistle, signaling that we should get into positions soon. Leo loses the toss and the alumni choose to go last. The Otter radio announcer is miked up, his voice booming through the arena, introducing our first shooter, one of our senior forwards, Ryan Colter. His shot is rushed and Stone easily stops it. Boos and cheers erupt along with the scoreboard lighting up.

0–0

Happy uses the door to get out onto the ice, instead of climbing over the side like everyone else. The crowd claps and whistles for him. He takes his time circling the ice, waving while the announcer gives us his history and stats from back in the day. My stomach flips and flops so many times I lose count waiting for him to actually take a shot. When he does, the doubts fall away. I drop to my knees and let the puck bounce off my pads back out onto the ice. Happy surprises me by skating up and holding out a hand to me. I remove my helmet and glove and shake his hand.

"Leave it to Happy to keep things family-friendly at the annual Past and Present Otter Shoot-out," the announcer says. "Next up for the Otters is sophomore Owen Jensen, playing in his first shoot-out…"

Owen makes a decent attempt at his shot but comes up empty. After him, Larry Jones is announced. I block Larry's shot almost as easily as Happy's. Then Jake pulls off a shot I've never seen and sinks it into the net. All the young people in the crowd explode with cheers and wave their #37 signs.

"That's where it's at!" Leo shouts.

The scoreboard changes showing: 1–0.

"And next let's welcome our state senator Mr. Rhett Hammond, who is about to showcase what happens when hockey players take desk jobs."

Rhett Hammond gets into position at center ice, and I'm feeling pretty good about my chances of blocking him. But when I anticipate the slap shot Jake mentioned, he makes a quick turn and taps the puck right into the net. I spin around staring at it, shocked.

"And the Hammond family seems to have the scoring bug today! Too bad we're out of Hammonds."

Rhett skates past me, grinning big. "With age comes wisdom, son. Never underestimate the power of a good setup."

I glance over at the bench, holding my hands up as if to say, *What the hell?* Jake slaps a palm to his face and then mouths, *We got played*.

I shouldn't have let Jake's insight influence me, but all I could think was *slap shot* and…well, yeah, we got played. Before I can even fully process this, the scoreboard changes to say: 1–1. Then my dad is at center ice.

"Playing is his third Otter shoot-out as an alumni," the announcer says, "going head-to-head with his own flesh and blood, let's welcome the man stolen from Juniper Falls by the Wolverines and then the Hawks, someone who loves the game more than anyone I know…Keith Tanley!"

He gets the loudest cheers thus far, and he takes even more time than Happy did to soak it all up. Watching everyone yell for him, wave their signs, whistle, seeing that cocky grin on his face like he's got no doubt I'll fall short, I get pissed off all over again. It's like there's boiling water inside me, the same as when Ron and Stewart started talking shit at the carnival. The tension ripples down my body, and when my dad finally takes his shot, I dive to my right and snatch it up with my glove.

When I pull myself upright again, Dad is only a couple of feet away, so I can clearly see the smirk drop from his face.

"Oh! What a catch by young Tanley! This is the future of our town, folks. Looks like knowing your competition has its advantages."

I'm breathing hard, my pulse pounding. Dad snatches the puck from my glove and stares me down. I can't tell if he's pissed that I blocked his shot or surprised. All I know is that I want him to go back to center ice and do it again. And again.

"It's been well over a decade since the alumni have seen defeat in the annual shoot-out, but this could be the year for our young players."

The score remains 1–1, even after Leo takes his shot and another alumni from after Dad's time takes his turn. Cole Clooney had been shoved to the last spot just in case we closed the deal early and didn't need him. Positioned at center ice, his back to me, Cole looks really small.

"Is it me, or are these new Otters getting more scrappy every year?" the announcer jokes.

My helmet is off, so I get a clear view of Cole leaning forward then taking off with such speed and precision, it's obvious we're seeing another Jake Hammond type in development. When Cole sinks his shot, our entire bench erupts. I almost rush over to join the celebration, but Pratt hops onto the ice and I'm back in the game.

"You go, little man!" Jamie shouts from the first row of the stands where he and a lot of the other guys are watching.

"Okay, now that was a surprise! I think the young Otters put in a ringer." The announcer turns to Coach. "Got anything to say about that? Freshman in the annual shoot-out? What's next? Grade school kids? Girls?"

A lot of laughter follows that, along with some boos.

"Former Otter, State runner-up, and leading scorer for his junior team down south in some state we can't remember because who cares…?" Several people shout *Arizona* at the announcer, who seems to be enjoying the drama. "Wearing his former number twenty-one jersey is Mr. Luke Pratt!"

I snap my helmet into place and dig my skates into the ice.

"A score here will tie things up, and we all know what that means!"

"Round two!" the crowd yells.

"The last time we went into round two was 1986."

All I can think about when Pratt skates at me is Claire leading him up the steps, his hand in hers, his filthy gaze roaming up and down the back of her…and her red eyes later. I shake the thought from my head and focus on Pratt's shot. I skate forward, farther from the goal, anticipating his move.

He surprises me with a late shot. The puck heads for the goal, over my shoulder. I turn around and throw my body in front of the goal, feeling the puck smack against my chest. I come down hard on the ice, half my body inside the goal, the other half outside of it.

Bakowski blows the whistle, sharp and short, before skating toward us. He stops in front of me, ice flying through the holes in my face mask. He rolls my body halfway over, revealing the puck beneath me. The entire arena is quiet. I blink, trying to get rid of the stars flashing in front of my eyes. I hit the ice pretty hard.

Bakowski straightens up and gives a signal to the announcer.

"No goal!" the announcer says, getting a huge response from the crowd. "Tate Tanley has morphed into The Flash and actually succeeded at being in two places at once. I need to see a replay of that amazing save! The young Otters take the shoot-out victory for the first time in years!"

I get to my feet and take off my helmet, only to be rushed and knocked over by Leo, Jake, and the other guys.

"T-Man!" Leo thumps me on the back. "What the hell was that?"

As a tradition, the winners of the shoot-out get to throw pie in the face of the losers. Cole is paired with Happy and instead of pieing him, he hands it over and Happy scoops a chunk of cherry pie, offering it up to Cole. Rhett Hammond snatches the pie before Leo can shove it in his face and throws it at Pratt. "You were the money shot, kid; what happened?"

Pratt shrugs, like he doesn't care, but he looks as embarrassed as my dad. Leo steals my pie, and a food fight breaks out on the ice. Finally Bakowski uses his whistle to stop us, and the announcer calls the shoot-out over.

"And let's hear it for our goalies today! They had to stay on the ice the whole time." The voice of Otter radio looks over at me. "I don't know about the rest of you, but I'm putting my money on Tate Tanley getting us to State this season; who's with me?"

I think it's supposed to be a peace offering to the town who's been freaking out since Steller walked in the first home game, or maybe a snub at Mike. But I catch Mike's dad, glaring at the ice, and then he storms down the bleachers and heads out of the arena.

My dad puts up a front, like he's happy I didn't screw up, but every time he looks my way, the grin is gone. I don't care what he thinks or what he may have expected me to do, I'm done hanging out in his shadow. In fact, I hate his fucking shadow.

"Let's hear it for our father/son duos," the announcer says, shoving Dad and me beside each other, along with Jake and his dad.

"Pratt went easy on you," Dad whispers to me. "So did I. You're gonna have to step it up."

I stand there holding perfectly still, my muscles twitching to move, to break something or throw something. But I don't.

"Bakowski says you're a head case," Dad continues. "He can't push you like he needs to."

Finally, I turn to face him. "Thanks for the encouraging words."

"You need to know, Tate. You'll thank me later." He skates

away and waves at the crowd.

The excitement from earlier is long gone. I glance over my shoulder and catch Clooney ducking his head, suddenly very interested in his stick. Did he hear any of that?

Pratt hadn't gone easy on me and neither did my dad. But knowing this doesn't make things different. My dad being selfish and insecure offers me no security or comfort at all. Quite the opposite.

Chapter 24

−CLAIRE−

*S*evere encephalitis is rare but not unheard of.
It could be the result of a viral infection or his weakened immune system.
We're treating him with anti-viral drugs and steroids.

The conversation floats around me like a dream. My neck is stiff and angled funny in this hospital recliner, but I can't seem to wake up enough to convince myself to move.

Encephalitis…

His brain is swollen.

Finally, I gain enough consciousness to open my eyes and stretch. My mom and Uncle Ned are standing right outside the room, in the brightly lit hallway of the hospital. Dr. Weaver—the woman who removed Dad's inoperable tumor—is beside them, her long white coat dangling in my line of sight. Another doctor, probably a doctor-in-training, is next to her, and they're taking turns speaking.

It took three days, a helicopter flight, and four very scary seizures to be able to say the word: encephalitis.

I glance over at Dad, my insides tensing at the amount of tubes and cords surrounding him. And the ventilator. Uncle Ned is right; he hates that thing. He was on one right after brain surgery and in what little speech he was able to produce after they removed the device, he basically said, *Never again.* And here he is again. A tube jammed down his throat, a machine expanding and deflating his lungs.

I want my dad back.

After wiping the drool from my face and smoothing down my hair, I get up and pat Dad's hand before joining everyone in the hall. I heard them while I was sleeping. I wonder if Dad can hear them?

Uncle Ned smiles when he sees me and wraps an arm around my shoulders. "Hey, Princess. You ready to go back home with me yet?"

He's been asking me that for three days and I keep saying no. He and Aunt Kay have been taking turns watching the bar. I'm pretty sure Ned basically closed down his towing business to help out this week, and no one in my family can afford losing even one day's work. But I keep thinking if I leave, something bad will happen.

Maybe it doesn't matter what I do.

"Hi, Claire," Doctor Weaver says, giving me a genuine smile, unlike the doctor-in-training beside her. He's got that *I'm eager to slice open brains and I don't really want to care about the patients* look on his face. I should know. I've spent enough time in this place with nothing to do but people watch. "How's school going?"

Mom speaks up first. "She's headed back in January."

My conversation with Tate on the floor of the storeroom comes back to me, along with the "please pay tuition balance by…" date looming in the near future. How can I pay that bill? How can I leave now with everything like this?

Dr. Weaver returns to her medical speak, and after she concludes with the ambiguous *we'll have to wait and see* outcome, I refuse Uncle Ned's invitation for a ride back to Juniper Falls and instead head for coffee in the cafeteria.

It's six in the morning, so I'm surprised to get a text from Tate this early. My phone is nearly dead, since I left it in the back pocket of my jeans all night.

TATE: *everything ok? Still at hospital?*

We've been playing this game for a few days now. He checks in on me, I give him a short conversation-ending answer, and then anxiously wait for the next time I hear from him. Neither of us mentions our kiss last Saturday night. It's beginning to feel like a phantom memory, like I'm not sure if it was really as great as I think it was or if the excess whiskey (which I totally regretted the next morning) created this delusional version of the event. Part of me is screaming, *Then do it again and find out!* And the other part is wagging a disapproving finger at me and saying to pretend it never happened.

I dump a bunch of sugar in my coffee and then type a reply to Tate.

ME: *currently "waiting and seeing." And yes, still at Mayo.*

There. That should keep him away for a while. That should keep me nice and lonely for a while.

I sink into a cafeteria chair and let the weight of the big school question press down on me. It was only supposed to be for one quarter. And then I would be back at school, back with my friends and my classes and professors. But it feels like we're right where we were after Dad's surgery. Except more broken.

I grab my laptop and open the Northwestern website. My

heart sinks, just looking at the front page—tickets on sale now for the fall production of *Chicago*. Tears prickle in the corners of my eyes. If I could teleport myself there right now, I would. But how can I even think that? What kind of daughter am I to want to be somewhere else while my dad is here?

God, I hate this. This monster inside me with big, fat, selfish dreams. None of it matters. None of this is important in the grand scheme of things.

Furiously, I pound the keys, typing an email to my adviser. Then I pull up my winter quarter class schedule. One by one, I check the box beside each class.

And then I hit Cancel All.

Chapter 25

–TATE–

"Take your pads off, Tanley," Coach says.

Thanksgiving was yesterday, so I'm still in a turkey coma and slow to catch on. Is he kicking me out of practice?

"Leave your helmet and leg pads. Get the rest off."

Wait…what? "Excuse me?" I say, confused.

"You heard me," he barks. "We'll let Hammond send a few slap shots your way without protection and see if that gets you to use your glove."

I glance around at my teammates, and the concern on all their faces is enough to send me over the edge. My hands shake, but I drop my stick onto the ice, pull my helmet and jersey off, and hand over my chest pads. All that sits between the puck and my midsection is a thin long-sleeve undershirt.

With my helmet and glove back on, I skate in front of the goal. Coach blows his whistle, indicating my teammates should proceed with taking shots on goal like they'd been doing moments ago.

I stand there trying to breathe normally. At first, no one moves. Then Coach blows the whistle right in Leo's face.

"Coach, we've got a game in a couple of hours—"

"A game I'm about to bench you in," Bakowski snaps.

To Leo's credit, he shoots hard but low stick side.

Coach shakes his head. "High, boys! Glove side!"

Over the next several minutes, he keeps blowing that fucking whistle, rattling everyone. When Hammond is up, Bakowski rips him apart until he pelts one at top speed. Scared shitless, I dodge it. Bakowski has a field day with that. "Oh, sure, Tanley, just let the puck go right into the net. Great plan, son."

He makes Hammond shoot again, and I dodge it again, but the puck loses speed, misses the net, and ricochets off the crossbar, hitting my right side hard enough to knock the wind out of me.

I lose count of how many pucks I dodge, a couple more bouncing into me without anyone noticing. My dad's words after the shoot-out come back to me: *Bakowski thinks you're a head case. He can't push you like he needs to.*

The fear quickly turns to anger. Like *wanting to shove that whistle down Bakowski's throat and rip his fucking head off* anger.

But eventually my glove does what it's supposed to. And after fifteen or so saves in a row, not a single shot touching my midsection, Coach holds his hands up in the air, like a preacher on the altar. "Thank you, Lord. Tanley can use a glove."

He ends our pregame practice on that note. And I use the break time to ice my side, which is quickly turning dark shades of purple and blue.

...

"Dude, you survived," Leo says in the locker room after the game. It's nearly cleared in here and we're both showered, dressed, and gathering up our equipment. "A shutout is always something to brag about."

"Don't get too cocky," a familiar voice says from behind me. Bakowski. "You've got guys like Hammond and Red clearing the puck for you constantly."

I duck my head and continue stuffing pads into my hockey bag. My face flames.

"And you…" He points his clipboard at Leo. "We should have had at least two more goals tonight. When Hammond hands over the puck to you, you sure as hell better make the most of it."

Leo's mouth forms a thin line, but he keeps it shut. Both of us zip our bags and head for the exit.

"Well, that fucking sucks," Leo mutters.

I let out a nervous laugh, nodding my agreement. I mean, we won. They didn't score. He could have saved the negative feedback for practice tomorrow.

In the crowded lobby of the ice rink, Stewart approaches Leo and me, extending his hand. "Good game, T-Man."

I stare at his hand but I don't slap it. Not after the way he and Ron harassed Claire at the carnival. Leo looks back and forth between the two of us but must decide to leave it alone because he says nothing.

And then Jamie comes out of nowhere, launching himself onto my back. "The T-Man gets a shutout. Dude, I've got a six-pack with your name on it!"

I drop my equipment bag from my shoulder and wrestle Jamie to the ground. We're tangled up, with him sitting on my stomach, when I look up and see Roger, only a foot away, talking to Mr. Stevenson.

Shit. Did he hear what Jamie said about the six-pack?

Roger catches my eye and lifts an eyebrow. He heard. Then his forehead wrinkles and he's leaning over me, staring at my stomach. "What happened?"

Jamie jumps up and pulls down the bottom of my sweater. *Okay, this is getting a little awkward.* Jamie's goofy grin dissolves.

I glance at the blue and black bruise streaking across my side and then shove my sweater down and push off the floor, getting back on my feet. My teammates are shifting around, all looking uncomfortable. I'm not sure what makes me lie, maybe old habits resurfacing, but I shake my head and mumble, "Nothing."

Roger glances over his shoulder at my mom and Olivia, chatting with Haley's mom. He lowers his voice before asking, "Did you get in a fight?"

Leo elbows me in the side, but I'm not sure what he wants me to do. Roger never played hockey; he won't get it. I take a second to bend down and retrieve my bag before glancing from Jamie to Leo. "We've got plans, so, guess I'll see you later…"

Jamie gives me a small push from behind, and then he and Leo and I are heading outside into the cold.

"Why didn't you say anything?" Jamie asks. "Did you think Coach would bench you?"

"Yeah." I guess it hadn't seemed like a big deal to me. I guess I really wanted to play.

Leo's grip tightens on his stick. "Fucking Bakowski."

Jamie shakes his head. "I'm fucking sorry, T-Man. I didn't know you got hit. And you played like that?"

Leo and I both stare at Jamie. He's never this serious. His

face is contorted like he's in pain or constipated. Both Leo and I burst out laughing, and then we're all three piled up on the parking lot ground, beating the hell out of one another.

A few minutes later, we toss our bags into the back of Leo's truck and then drive around looking for food. We load up on snacks from the Quick Stop and end up at Juniper Falls Pond with Jamie's stolen beer, Red's stolen vodka, and a giant pan of Mrs. Hammond's enchiladas.

"Since when does your mom let you out of the house with her fine dishware?" Red says, his mouth full of cheese and red sauce. We're done with our pickup game of pond hockey, so we're all hanging in the back of Jake's truck, the beer and food piled in the center.

Jake shrugs. "I was supposed to drop it off at the O'Connors' but they weren't home."

My stomach drops, and I suddenly become aware of my phone poking out of my pocket. Should I text Claire again and check in? I did that yesterday and a bunch of days before that. I should wait a few more hours. Maybe until the morning.

Leo digs his fork into the pan. "That's pretty asshole of you, Ham."

For a second, Jake looks guilty, then he shakes his head. "What was I gonna do? Leave it on the doorstep? My mom would freak if she knew they weren't eating this fresh."

"Never mind, then," Leo snorts. "Nice work, Ham. You're such a do-gooder."

When Leo stands and says he has to get his phone from his truck across the street, I stand up, too, and say, "I'll go with you. I've got to use the bathroom…"

"Duh," Jamie says. "Go in the woods."

I shrug and follow Leo. We walk through the field and then across the street, into the high school parking lot. He keeps glancing around, and then I notice someone leaning against his truck.

Kennedy Locust.

Leo catches my eye and quickly says, "I told him he could hang with us."

Before I can even fathom why Leo would agree to this, we're too close to Kennedy to ask that question.

"Nice glove work tonight, Tanley," he says.

I stand there perfectly still, waiting for the punch line, but it never comes. And Leo never grabs anything from his truck. He keeps looking at me, like he's challenging me to say it out loud. But I'm not. It's complicated. Everything about this is complicated.

Leo and Kennedy quickly dive into conversation about the game and the opposing team. Right before we cross the street to head back to the pond, I glance over at O'Connor's Tavern and see someone walking up the steps leading to the upstairs apartment.

Claire.

She's home.

My heart skips and I'm right back in that storeroom with her, my mouth on hers, her fingers in my hair. And the last words she spoke to me before her mom called for her: *Don't leave.*

Leo smacks me in the chest with the back of his hand and I realize that I stopped walking. His gaze follows mine.

He nods in Claire's direction. "Go."

I study his face to see if he's being sarcastic, especially considering all of *his don't get involved* warnings, though he seems to be backing off a little on that lately. "I don't want to deal with Haley's crew talking shit—"

"I'll cover for you, T," Leo says.

I look over at Kennedy, who is pretending to be interested in his fingernails.

"Don't worry about him."

The look on Leo's face tells me everything I need to know without a single word spoken. He's keeping my secret and I'm keeping his.

I take off in a jog, reaching the bottom of the staircase just as Claire reaches the top.

Chapter 26

−CLAIRE−

"Claire!"

I drop my key from the lock and spin around. At the bottom of the staircase, wearing his varsity letter jacket and a very worried expression, is Tate. I don't turn my back to him right away, and I think he takes that as an invitation, because soon he's charging up the steps and is breathing his steamy air right in front of me.

My stomach does flip-flops and my fingers are all tingly, my thoughts drifting back to that night in the storeroom and Tate's steady voice and perfect words... *This is me being a grown-up.*

"Hey," he says, looking me over.

"Hey." My face warms and I turn quickly, jamming my key back in the door. I push the door open and walk inside, flipping the light switch on. I've got exactly fifteen minutes before I need to be downstairs at the bar. I've got to make this place look presentable for a potential renter coming first thing in the morning.

I don't know how to deal with these conflicted Tate Tanley feelings on top of everything else going on in my life, so I do what I do best now: deflect.

I toss my coat on the desk chair, my duffel full of dirty clothes onto the floor, and work on smoothing out the down comforter on the bed.

"How's your dad doing?" Tate has slowly shuffled inside without permission and closed the door behind him, but he's leaning against it. Unsure if he should move any closer.

I blow air out of my cheeks and throw two decorative pillows onto the floor. "He's off the ventilator. Finally. But still sedated. So I don't know."

"What about your mom, is she still in Minneapolis?"

"She has to be there for this test he's getting done on his spinal fluids or something and it's Friday night and a home game..." The panic I had during the long drive home returns. I haven't done inventory or anything with the books for well over a week. Who knows what's going on with our finances or what damage the part-time staff created in our absence? My chest tightens and I quickly return the pillows to the bed—this is as good as the apartment will get—then I open my overnight bag and dig for the apron I stuffed in here last week. "Tate, I've got to get downstairs. I have a million things to do here and then I need to go home and sort through all the mail..." Mail meaning bills. Lots of bills. Oh God, this should be a good day. Dad is off the ventilator. I need to focus on that. But I can't. I've ignored too much for too many days.

I try to breathe evenly and finally get my fingers around a green apron. I stand and toss it over my head. I stare at Tate, still leaning against the door. It's like he represents the reality that I need to face right now. And because he's right in front of me, all my anger gets directed at him.

"Let me guess?" I reach behind my back and fumble around, trying to find the ties for the apron. "You want to talk about what happened in the storeroom?"

"Well—"

I cut him off. "Everybody needs something from me. I can't deal with you and...*that* right now." I look away from him and add, "Besides, I never give much credit to anything that happens under the influence of large amounts of Jack Daniel's."

Hurt flickers across his face. I'm hit with a massive punch of guilt. Especially when I replay the way his fingers glided so gently over my skin, the things he told me about the fireworks on New Year's, my palm against his racing— *Stop!* I squeeze my eyes closed and shove it all away. "Tate, don't look at me like that. I've hardly slept in more than a week and I'm just..."

He smooths his expression and then takes a few steps toward me. One hand reaches out for mine. "Come here."

I'm rooted to the spot, staring at those green eyes. I shake my head, refusing any Tate Tanley touching. "I have to go," I whisper.

He ignores me and moves closer until suddenly I'm enveloped in his arms, the warmth inside his unzipped jacket seeping out, drawing me in even more.

I attempt to slide back, out of his grip, but he holds on tighter and I can't refuse anymore. My cheek rests against his shirt, just below his chin. His face touches the top of my head; his hands glide over my back and through my hair. I close my eyes and allow my nerves to light up, the tingling to return to my fingers and toes. I hold my breath and wait for it to stop.

"Breathe, Claire," Tate whispers into my hair.

I inhale, my lungs starving for oxygen, my senses memorizing his smell. Soap. Fabric softener. Firewood. Winter air.

Since Dad has been in the hospital again, I've gotten a lot of hugs—from Mom, Aunt Kay, Uncle Ned. Even Doctor Weaver hugged me this morning. But none of those were for me. Not *just* for me, anyway. They were for Mom or Dad.

This. Right here. This is for me. And as much as I hate to admit it, I need it.

I slide my hands through Tate's jacket and around his waist, squeezing tight. I hear him sigh, and I try not to think about kissing him again.

"You know, you're allowed to have this," Tate whispers, his breath on my ear.

A shiver runs up my back. "Have what?" *Physical contact with my friend's little brother?*

"Friends." He rubs his hand over my back and I'm not thinking friendly thoughts. "You know, people who help you with things?"

At the mention of things, my mind shoots right back to the huge to-do list, and the panic returns. My entire body tenses and I attempt, yet again, to step away. But Tate keeps his strong arms around me.

"Repeat after me," he says. "Tate, do you mind helping me out tonight?"

I lift my head and look up at him, my forehead crinkling. "Huh?"

He smiles. "I'm not busy. You're extremely busy. It makes perfect sense to me. What can I do?"

"Seriously?" I say, trying to hide my doubt. Finally he releases me, and the cold that rushes between us is more than unwelcome.

Tate reaches behind me, easily finding the strings to my apron and pulling them into a bow. "See? I'm handy. Just don't corner me in the storeroom and we'll be fine."

For the first time in I don't know how many days—it

feels like forever—I'm laughing. I shake my head, completely confused and amused. "Okay, goalie boy. You are totally going to regret this."

He places his hand on the doorknob and opens it. "Ten bucks says I don't."

I wipe sweat from my forehead and skid into the kitchen, snatching two orders Manny has finished filling. I've never seen a post-game rush this big before, not even after a winning night like tonight. It's after midnight and we're still serving food. We're packed, so there's no closing the kitchen on time tonight. From a business standpoint, it's great—especially with Late Night at O'Connor's having been on hold for two weekends in a row. But my huge to-do list is calling out to me. I wrote it on the ride from Minneapolis and pinned it onto the bulletin board in the office, but I've been waiting tables nearly the entire night, not even able to look at it again, let alone complete any tasks.

Table twelve is eagerly awaiting their food when I drop the orders in front of them. I fly past the bar, shouting to Petey. "Another Guinness and a Bud Light for twelve."

I look around for Tate, but he's nowhere in sight. I haven't seen him in the dining room for at least two hours. Maybe he got tired and went home out the kitchen door. I don't blame him. He had a game tonight. He's probably exhausted. And bored. Doing inventory isn't exactly the most exciting job. Plus it's freezing in the storeroom.

"I think we're ready to order drinks," one guy at the table says before they're all even seated.

I force a smile. "Of course you are. Go ahead."

Petey is done with twelve's beers when I hand over the new drink orders.

A couple of minutes later, Mike Steller walks in, glancing around until his gaze lands on me. My body tenses. Several tables have noticed Mike's presence, and whispered conversations break out. I take a breath and cross the room to stand in front of Mike. A few people even glare in our direction.

"Wow, the place is hopping tonight." Mike taps his fingers on the wooden hostess stand and ignores the buzz all around us. "I heard your dad is doing a little better?"

I nod, feeling the relief from this morning all over again, when I'd watched that tube come out of his throat. "Yeah, he's coming around. We'll know more in the next few days. What are you doing here so late?"

He shrugs. "Just got off work. Leo told me Tanley was here, so I figured I'd stop by, see how he's doing."

Mike's voice drops to nearly a whisper when he mentions Leo and Tate. Guess Bakowski still has his Mike Steller ban up and running.

And me, well, I'm frozen to the spot, not sure what to say. Maybe Tate left. But if he didn't, am I supposed to say he's not here? I know Tate thinks he and Haley are done, I just don't know if she and especially the rest of the town knows this. I've been too preoccupied to really think about what the kiss in the storeroom could turn me into—the other woman.

"Relax." Mike looks me over and laughs. "I'm glad you guys are hanging out. Or whatever you're doing."

"Hanging out. That's all." My face heats up. "Oh…yeah, so I'll go see if Tate's still around." I point to a booth near the back. "You might want to hide out over there."

I head past the bar, toward the kitchen doors, and call over my shoulder to Petey. "Can you close out three and four for me? Pretty please?"

Petey fake sighs, like super lazy, then flashes me a grin.

The second I'm out of the dining room and in the kitchen, I hear the sound of a drill coming from the office. I sprint down the hall. Tate is kneeling on the desk, a power drill in his right hand. My eyes widen. "What are you doing? I told you to count stuff in the storeroom!"

He glances over at me and smiles like this isn't totally ruining my night. "How's it going out there? Still busy?"

"It's fine." I shake my head. "Why are you putting holes in our wall?"

Tate hops down from the desk and grabs a piece of wood leaning against the wall. "This shelf was sitting here and there was a Post-it here…" He taps the wall above the desk. "It said, *new shelf here*. So I figured I'd put the new shelf here." He scratches the back of his head. "Bad idea?"

"That's been there for months," I say. "Since my dad…"

"I figured." He nods. "All the more reason to get it done."

"I guess." I blow out a breath and stand there watching him set the wood in place, creating a perfectly level shelf. Then he uses a mini-broom to brush the dust from the desk. "Did the inventory get boring?"

He snatches a few sheets of paper from on top of the file cabinet and holds them out for me. "I finished that a while ago." He pops open the laptop and spins it to face me. "I also entered the numbers into the spreadsheet labeled *inventory*, so you might not need those papers."

I lift an eyebrow and Tate manages to look a little guilty. "You really shouldn't use your birthday for a password."

He knows my birthday?

My gaze travels to the wall with the bulletin board where I pinned my long to-do list. I walk closer and look it over. Tate has crossed off seven items. "Did you really Google recipes for Irish potato soup?"

He spins again and hands me a stack of printed pages.

I give the papers a quick glance and then place them on the desk. Okay, so I'm in shock. I didn't even think he'd get through inventory. I knew he could take toasters apart but I didn't know he could enter stuff and print stuff and build stuff. What else don't I know about Tate Tanley?

I have no choice but to reach into my apron and hand over a ten-dollar bill.

Tate takes the money from me, smirking the whole time he's removing his wallet and placing the bill inside. "Impressed you, huh?"

Um, yes. "Do you have a bunch of elves shoved in a closet or something? They hopped out and went around fixing things?"

"Yeah, we call them the JV hockey team. They were in here a while ago, doing all your chores." He steps closer, his gaze flitting to the open door and back to me. My heart gives a quick *thud, thud.* "I sent them over to your house to fold your underwear."

"Funny." My neck gets hot, just looking at him this close up. I back away a step, but my heel makes contact with the wall and I can't go any farther. My throat turns dry.

Tate places a hand on the wall beside my head. My arms are pinned at my sides, my heart so loud the dining room noise is nonexistent.

"One question…" He lifts his free hand to my cheek. My skin warms under his fingers.

"What?" I manage to whisper, lifting my eyes to meet his.

"Have you overindulged in whiskey tonight?"

I squeeze my eyes shut, the punch of guilt hitting me again. "Tate, I'm sorry. I didn't mean to—"

His mouth meets mine, his lips so hot and yet so soft. My

insides turn to mush. I sink farther against the wall, my legs weakening.

It wasn't the whiskey.

I didn't imagine anything the first time. It really was amazing. It *is* amazing.

But it's over too quick. He pulls away, gliding his fingers across my cheek, then leans in to kiss the side of my face.

"I'll come by again tomorrow," he whispers, right next to my ear. "After practice."

I rest my head against the wall and let the air rushing into the now-empty space between us cool off my face. My eyes are closed when I feel a tug on my apron.

"Claire, you okay?" he teases.

"Hmm," I mumble. "Tomorrow. Yeah. We can do this again."

Tate laughs and leans in to kiss me again. "Yeah? All of this?"

"Grown-up Tate. Such a smooth talker." I open my eyes and rest both hands on his face. "You still look like you, ya know? Curious. Stubborn. Sweet. Adorable. Just with more…" I stroke his cheeks with my thumbs, feeling the stubble. "Facial hair."

He breaks out the killer grin. "So you did have a crush on me."

"Um…no. Sorry." I laugh at that thought. I mean, he was little Tate Tanley. Then the laughter dies quickly when Tate covers my mouth with his again. Something pulls at my thoughts, through the haze of this killer kiss. I shove him back a few inches. "Wait…what am I doing here?"

Tate's face turns dead serious. "Relax, okay. Don't think about it too much. Let's just focus on tomorrow. And then move from there."

I shake my head. "I mean here in this office. I came in to

tell you something and now I can't remember what." I jolt upright, remembering suddenly. "Mike. Steller."

Tate's playful expression drops, his forehead wrinkling. "What about him?"

"He's here. For you."

I push off the wall and grab the front of Tate's sweater, pulling him out of the office. I can't be alone with him anymore. I don't trust either of us to be good. Besides, I left Petey with all my tables plus the bar customers.

Jesus Christ. I forgot about my tables.

I hurry out of the kitchen and into the dining room. I can't help but watch the silent exchange between Tate and Mike. Tate glances at him and then walks straight out the front door. I check on my tables and deliver more drinks and then Mike finally gets up and goes out the door.

Trying to be discreet, I drift casually toward the window facing the parking lot. Mike and Tate are walking side by side. They pass up Mike's truck, but he snatches skates and a hockey stick from the back and then both of them head straight for the side entrance to the ice rink.

What are they doing at the ice rink at nearly two in the morning? I pull out my phone and send Tate a quick text.

ME: night skating?

TATE: something like that. Don't tell anyone, pls

ME: you hockey boys and ur secrets…

TATE: not with u. U know all my secrets

My heart squeezes; my insides are all warm and fuzzy. I stare at Tate's text for way too long before going back to my tables.

Chapter 27

−TATE−

"I know a lot of you are worried about checking." Dad skates in front of the line of kids here for the winter break clinic. "But some of you probably can't wait to reach Bantam so you can pin someone against the boards legally."

A few of the kids nod. One tiny girl on the end lifts a hand in the air like she's pledging her allegiance to knocking over boys on the ice.

"Body pinning is what we're going to learn today..." Dad continues.

He goes on with details of the partner drills he wants the kids to do. My eyes wander and land on Claire in the lobby of the rink. She's setting up tables. O'Connor's is catering lunch for the kids. Claire catches me watching and smiles, just enough for me to notice.

"...unfortunately my only partner option for a demonstration is a goalie and probably very out of practice."

I snap my head around to face Dad again. What demonstration? At the other end of the rink, Jamie, Leo, and Stewart are working with the youngest kids and have spent the morning doing basic skating and shooting drills and giving lots of high fives.

The kids on our end are laughing and looking at me now.

I've got basic gear on today, not my usual goalie gear, but for some reason the idea of me in any other position has become comical. It's not like I didn't play other positions before high school. Everyone does.

"Think you can handle a little pinning demo?" Dad challenges.

My entire body stiffens. "Maybe we should—"

"Come on, Tate. You're not afraid to take on an old man like me, are you?"

The kids laugh louder. My heart pumps hard against my chest. Red flags wave in front of my eyes. "Fine," I snap.

As soon as the word is out of my mouth, Dad passes me the puck. I stop it with my stick but stand there near the wall like an idiot, not sure what I'm supposed to do next. The laughter dies the second my dad pins me against the boards. His side digs into my back and my helmet presses against the glass. My heart pounds faster, my breaths coming quick and ragged.

"Make sure your leg is placed between your opponent's," Dad says.

I'm trapped in place, my skates slipping and sliding. Panic sets in, followed by the instinct to fight, to get out of his hold. I shove him back and take control of the puck again. He comes at me, attempting a check.

"Sloppy form, Tate," Dad practically growls into my ear. "Come on, don't hold back."

The fire inside builds and pushes me over the edge. I hit

Dad hard from behind, causing him to stumble back, to lose his balance. I freeze, my heart drumming so fast I can't hear the kids cheering us on. Dad stares at me for a beat, like we're complete strangers, and then he charges forward, snatching the puck away from me. I skate backward, switching over to defensive mode. The kids yell louder, cheering. But I can't focus on anything besides Dad.

"Get your head up," he tells me. "Can't be afraid of a little contact."

I look him right in the eye, and then I turn in a circle and steal the puck the second it gets a few inches out in front of his stick. I break away toward the empty goal and the kids part their line, making room. I'm about to take a shot when Dad plows into me from behind. The stick gets caught beneath me and I slide on the ice, flat on my stomach until my helmet bashes into the post, clanking loudly against the metal surface.

I lay there for several seconds, my ears ringing. When I get to my feet, I pull off my helmet and glance around. The kids all still look excited. But at the other end of the rink, Leo and Jamie have stopped their game and are watching us. I turn in a circle and my gaze stops on Claire in the lobby. Her eyes are wide, mouth hanging open.

I look back at Dad. He's got the puck now and he's sliding it back and forth, completely calm. I drop my helmet and head off the ice, mumbling that I'm gonna find more pucks in the equipment closet. When I get inside, I lean against the door, closing my eyes, allowing my heart and breathing to calm down. That was a cheap shot from Dad, but a little longer, and I may have done the same thing. Everything inside me feels so out of control right now.

Chapter 28

−CLAIRE−

My hands shake while I drop chicken fingers onto paper plates in the lobby of the ice rink. I can't believe Keith did that. I had no idea things were that bad between him and Tate. It's not right.

And today, my dad is coming home from the Mayo Clinic. He's doing so much better. On the phone this morning, he said my name. I could hardly tell him good-bye or hang up because I was choking back tears. It should be a happy day.

The kids all crowd around the open exit of the rink, heading toward the tables we have set up for their lunch. I speed up my food distribution as more hungry kids drop into chairs around me. The chatter of thirty to forty voices all at once creates a buzz in the arena that drowns out some of the panic I'm feeling at the moment. I glance at Tate, looking him over. He had disappeared into the equipment closet a little while ago, but he's since returned and put up his front again.

Tate, Jake, and Cole jump in and help me out with all the

requests for ketchup, barbecue sauce, drinks. I slip past Tate, and he catches my waist, resting his fingertips there. My entire body warms at the touch. I'm already imagining sinking back against him, letting those fingers slide—

"You look pretty," he whispers into my ear before stepping aside, putting a good two feet between us.

When I refocus on the lobby, I catch Cole Clooney watching us. He drops his head, squirting a pile of ketchup on a kid's plate. Tate sees this, too, and hesitates like he might want to pull Cole aside and question him, but then his gaze drifts away from the tables, over to where Jamie and Leo are leaning against the boards. Talking to Keith. Tate's forehead wrinkles, his body tensing.

And soon Keith is walking toward me. My mind drifts back to that night in the parking lot, Keith's very different tone and the way he looked at me, like my presence was ruining everything. He was wasted, probably doesn't remember a thing, but today, when he pulled that illegal check on Tate, he seemed completely sober. That's not right.

"So…" Keith flashes me his famous smile that has fooled an entire town of six thousand. "Are you feeding coaches, too? Or just kids?"

I clamp my jaw shut, the frustration building inside me. "Help yourself."

The reply comes out too loud, too sharp, too angry. Keith looks taken aback. "You sure?"

Jake Hammond is standing across from me. He stops pouring juice and looks up.

"The order was for forty kids and eight coaches," I snap. I turn quickly and head over to the buffet I have set up. I toss a pile of chicken fingers and fries onto a plate and march it over to Keith, practically thrusting it at his chest. His mouth falls open like he wants to ask me what's wrong, but Tate takes my arm and steers me away.

"We're out of cups," he says, pulling me in the direction of the concession stand. When we get to the counter, he leans in and whispers, "What are you doing?"

I take a breath and glance over my shoulder. If the guys are watching us, they hide it well, busying themselves when I look at them. I drop my face into my hands. "I didn't know it would be so hard to see him after…"

"Yeah, I know." Tension fills Tate's voice.

I glance sideways at him. He's stressed. I'm adding to that by not keeping my feelings in check. "I'm sorry. I just want you to go back on the ice and knock him on his ass. Is that horrible?"

He leans on his elbows, looks at me, and the tension seems to fall from his face. His pinkie finger hooks around mine, and then he leans closer, his nose grazing the side of my face. Heat crawls up my neck. I close my eyes, enjoying this feeling for a brief moment. "Tate…"

"It's okay," he whispers. "The guys won't say anything. Hockey secrets and all."

The moment ends too soon. We both slide several inches apart. "I haven't seen you play anything but goalie in years."

"I play defense sometimes, on the pond. Offense if I'm on Hammond's team. He makes me look like a pro at assists." Tate gives me that half smile, and then it fades. He looks at his hand. "My mom's making me visit SMU this weekend. Hammond and me."

Takes me a second to catch up. "Wait…like, as in visit your dad?"

"I've been putting it off forever."

I don't care. Put it off longer. My stomach twists with nerves. "Jake's going with you?" He nods. "What about Jody? She'll be back tomorrow. Can't she come?"

It seems better if Jody's there, but I can't really pinpoint why.

"She might come."

More protests try to work their way out, but I hold my tongue, and we stand there silent for a couple of minutes. I stare at the side of Tate's face, his dark hair and serious expression drawing me closer. "I think I'm starting to understand that whole *let's run away together* expression."

He turns, a slow smile spreading across his face. "I'm gonna help you tonight with that party-prep stuff..." He glances sideways, checking to see who's watching before leaning closer. "And then we're going somewhere. Alone." I lift an eyebrow. "For at least five minutes. Maybe six..."

"Don't push your luck. Plus, we've got about a thousand *taquitos* to roll." I give him a shove in the direction of the ice—the kids are preparing to head back out. "Now go teach sticking or tripping or whatever."

I try to keep the smile on my face, but I know it vanishes the second Tate is too far to see me. I have a bad feeling about this trip to Minneapolis.

Chapter 29

−TATE−

"Jake Hammond..." Coach Redeck says, glancing over the contents of a yellow folder resting on his desk. "A 3.0 GPA. Impressive."

Jake and I both look at each other, but neither of us has an answer to the looming question: What the hell is this?

"Um...yeah—I mean, yes sir, that's correct," Jake says.

Dad stands in the back of the office, arms folded over his chest, not an ounce of concern on his face.

Coach Redeck flips a page in the folder. "Please tell me the two of you managed good ACT scores? And be honest. I like to know upfront what I'm dealing with. I can only do so much if I don't have all the facts."

He stares at his paper for a moment and then at me, one eyebrow lifted. "A twenty-nine?"

I turn around, looking at my dad for help—he does nothing—before facing Coach Redeck. "I'm taking it again. I haven't even done the prep course yet—"

Dad's boss releases a low whistle. "A thirty-two on math and science. Keith, whatever you're doing with your boy, it's working. And a 3.4 GPA. Taking trig and honors physics and English courses. Since when is Juniper Falls grooming academic scholars?"

Since forever. My sister is one. Claire O'Connor is another. But neither of them is a hockey player, so I guess he wouldn't know about that.

"His mom makes him study," Dad chimes in. "She's always been serious about education."

Another shared look with Jake, and we're no more clear on this little meeting than we were several minutes ago.

Coach Redeck folds his hands on top of his desk and glances from Jake to me. "How would you boys like to see the ice rink, meet a few of my players?"

I wait for my dad to object or make up an excuse for why we can't stay any longer, but he doesn't. Jake and I have no choice but to follow Coach Redeck out of his office.

In the hall, we bump into two of the Hawks's top players. Coach introduces us, and Jake and I just stand there awestruck. Both dudes look way bigger in person than on TV.

"You guys wanna try out the ice?" the Hawks's leading scorer asks us.

"Sure," I say at the same time Jake says, "Really?"

I text Jody on the way to the rink. She hasn't even made it to the library yet.

ME: we r gonna grab our skates and try out the ice if u want to come

JODY: pass. The library is huge. And empty

"Tate," Coach Redeck calls after Jake and I have been on the ice for a few minutes, skating around in our jeans. "Since you're here, why not let Penbrook take a few shots."

And this.

This is why I don't want Jamie and Leo playing for this team. It isn't just Dad dancing around a gray area.

I look from him to Dad. "So…you want me to watch him shoot?"

Coach Redeck leans forward and lowers his voice. "I want you to block his shots." He looks at Dad. "If that's all right with you, Keith?"

Warning bells sound inside my head. Bakowski prepared us for recruitment from day one. I'm familiar with all the rules. "I don't have my gear."

"We've got plenty of gear."

Dad stares at me, sending a silent message—*do what he says; don't fuck this up*. My hands shake and my stomach feels sick, not from nerves but from all the wrong. We're treading into official territory, and that's not okay. I mean, technically I came here on my own dollar, so to speak—my mom gave us gas money. If I could trust my dad completely, I wouldn't worry about this, but I can't.

Some guy whose name I will never remember leads me over to a giant closet full of hockey gear. He starts handing me stuff to put on, and then Jake appears in the doorway. I shake my head, silencing him until we're alone.

"Are you… I mean, did they tell you to—"

"Yep." I tug furiously at my shirt, yanking it over my head. "Do me a favor?"

Jake nods, checking over his shoulder.

"Make up some emergency in a few minutes." I hand him my phone. "Text Jody and tell her we need to go home today." We were supposed to stay overnight at my dad's place.

He takes my phone without question and follows behind me. I'm sure Jake doesn't get everything going on with my dad, but he gets why it's not easy to just tell them no even though Coach Bakowski has made it clear—no visits until senior year, coaches go through him, we don't talk to a college or pro coach without our parents. He has his own system, one our town backs 100 percent. My dad might be here, but my mom isn't. Neither is Mr. Hammond.

"Looking good, Tate." Coach Redeck taps the SMU jersey I've been loaned as I take the ice. I give Dad one more long look and shake my head. I can't believe he's doing this. "Let's see what your boy can do, Keith. Besides math equations."

All I can think about, when I take my place in front of the goal, in the arena where so many hockey greats have played— it's Juniper Falls's Wall of Fame times ten thousand—is how long I've imagined a moment like this and how it's completely tainted now.

Chapter 30

−CLAIRE−

'm dumping the last of the late-night dishes when I spot a familiar pair of legs poking out from under the stove.

"Tate?" I walk closer and give his sneaker a little kick. "What are you doing here?"

He's supposed to be in Minneapolis right now. Both he and Jody sent me a text when they left town before nine in the morning. And if I recall, an overnight stay was supposed to be part of the trip. Even if it wasn't, it's two in the morning. Not a typical hour for stopping by unannounced.

Tate slides out from under the stove. Black grease speckles his face and hands. He glances down at his fingers and then wipes them on a cloth resting beside him. "Your mom let me in before she left. She mentioned the stove was messed up the other day. Figured I'd stop by and check on it. I think something is wrong with the gas line."

"Okaay…" Still doesn't explain his change in plans or the late-night visit. I lean against the counter and watch him work for a couple of minutes. Obviously his being here at this hour isn't just about the stove, but when Tate doesn't supply any more info, I decide to give him space. "I'm gonna go lock up, okay?"

He stays hidden from me. "Yeah, sure."

Once the doors are locked, I crank up the radio at the bar. I sing along to whatever song comes on while I get the tables wiped down and reset for tomorrow and the floors swept. After a while, even with music blaring, the loud clanking of metal hitting metal comes from the kitchen. I rush in there in time to hear Tate string eight different swearwords together.

He emerges from under the stove and kneels in front, craning his neck to look at a pipe or something. "Fuck." He shoves a hand through his hair and then tosses a screwdriver onto the kitchen floor. "Fucking hell."

"What?" I demand.

Tate gets to his feet and grabs the towel. He attacks a smudge of dirt on his forearm with such force, I decide to keep a few feet between us. He kicks the pipe-looking thing gently with one of his boots. "See that part? It's gonna need to be replaced. I thought I could patch it."

I'm not sure what to do. He wants to talk. That's why he's here. But how do I open that door between us? He'd been so good at this when it was me, half drunk on the storeroom floor.

Maybe I should give him a bottle of whiskey.

He releases a breath and continues the battle with the grease on his hands. "I never should have told your mom— Jesus, that's, like, a three-hundred-dollar part—"

In two quick strides, I reach him and rest my hands on his cheeks, forcing him to look at me. "Hey, forget the stove, okay? What happened, Tate? Something happened in Minneapolis, didn't it?"

His eyes close briefly, and when they open again, he's

studying me, maybe trying to decide if he can tell me. He takes my hands from his face and gives them a squeeze. "There's one more thing I can try…"

I sigh but move over to let him under the stove again. "Tate."

He's buried beneath the stove only seconds later, but he takes my hint and starts talking. "Coach Redeck, my dad's boss…he showed Jake and me around—the locker room, the ice rink, the training room and gym."

"That's good, right?" I have no idea what Tate wants to do after high school. Why have we not talked about this before?

"Sure." Sarcasm drips from his voice. I sit down on the kitchen floor beside his boots and wait. "Assuming no one will count that as an official visit. Because that would be illegal. At least until the first day of my senior year."

"But your dad works there," I argue. "Isn't that, like, a special circumstance or something?"

"Probably." He reaches for a tool beside my leg. His fingers brush up against me. "Except the innocent-visit claim went out the window when Coach Redeck asked me to suit up and play goalie for a couple of the top SMU Hawks."

I sink back on my heels. "It didn't go well?"

Tate laughs, the tone derisive and angry. "Nope, it went great, actually."

"What?" I grip his ankle, squeezing it tight. "So you could get a scholarship? Did they offer you anything?"

He drops the wrench and sits up again, facing me. "Everything went exactly how I've always imagined a big tryout to go. I could have turned into a total head case and I didn't. And Coach Redeck…he flipped out over my and Jake's grades, our ACT scores. He said we've both got the whole package."

I sit perfectly still, waiting for him to explain his obvious anger over what should be good news.

"It's tainted," Tate continues. "All of it. Anything I do in terms of pursuing college hockey—it's all ruined." He shakes his head. "I should have walked out of there; it's partly my fault. But my dad just sat there and let it happen. He knows better than anyone that this could come back and bite me in the ass. He could make it bite me in the ass if he wanted to. That's the big problem; he's not exactly on my side. He's on his own side."

My stomach flips over, Tate's worry falling quickly onto my shoulders. "What about Jake? Did he play, too? And Jody? Where was she when this was happening?"

"Jake didn't play, and he won't say anything," Tate replies so firmly I push aside those concerns. He knows his teammates better than I do. "Jody went to the library. I couldn't tell her what happened." He wrings his hands and stares at his lap. "I told Jake to make an excuse that we had to head home tonight instead of sleeping over. I couldn't stay there…"

The guilt from the other day, when I witnessed Keith and Tate's little showdown on the ice, doubles in size. It's like a sour apple sitting in the pit of my stomach.

"I hate him. I hate him so much it makes me hate myself." He whispers the words with his eyes still closed, like it's wrong for him to say them but yet he needs to. Of course he needs to.

"God, Tate, I'm so sorry."

He sighs and goes back under the stove. "Okay, so I patched this temporarily. I'd say you've got three, maybe six months before you need the part replaced. Or do you want to get it right away?"

I'm too busy stewing over the other stuff to respond to Tate. Eventually, he sits up again and looks at me. "Claire? The part?"

"Oh." I shake my head. "Wait. Definitely wait."

He nods slowly, probably forming more questions regarding my family's finances. Tate gathers up the tools, tossing them in a box, and then he rights the stove back to its before-repairs state.

Turning, Tate looks at me and shifts from one foot to the other, his gaze flitting to the door and back to me. "I'm keeping you here, aren't I?"

"No, no, it's not that. I'm just so…" God, how do I explain what I'm feeling? Conflicted? Guilty? Obligated?

"Busy?" Tate supplies, looking guilty himself.

His biceps flex in response to him pushing off the floor. I let my eyes drift from his arms to his chest and abs, where the formfitting long-sleeve shirt he's wearing displays perfect outlines of muscles. Tate catches me staring, and the sexy half grin slides over his features. "Checking me out, huh?"

My face flames. "No."

"It's okay." He laughs. "I had a great view of your ass from under the stove."

I shove him in the chest, but of course he grabs my hand and brings me closer. Not even a second later, his mouth is on mine, and I'm drowning in Tate Tanley and his soft lips and gentle hands.

"So this is why you stopped by," I say, breathless, my legs turning to jelly.

"No."

He wraps an arm around my waist and lifts me up onto the counter. I must look shocked or surprised because he freezes a few inches away from me. "Is this okay? I mean, I know we haven't really said what this is, and you're leaving in January…"

I think it's the mention of January and what I still have to face from canceling my registration that has me spilling out words I'd been trying to sort through for careful insertion into the conversation. "You have to tell Jody."

His forehead wrinkles. "About us? She knows. In fact, it made for a miserable drive—"

"About your dad."

Silence falls between us. Tate's entire body stiffens.

"Hear me out, okay?" I say, and his face changes. He gets it. He doesn't nod, but he doesn't stop me, either. "Maybe your dad popping up so much lately is a sign. You took all those feelings, that anger, and you've buried it. Didn't you think that someday, you'd tell your mom and Jody everything?"

He's already shaking his head.

"Tate, come on…your mom practically forced you to go to Minneapolis to see him. Do you think she'd do that if she knew what he was really like?"

"I don't know—"

"And Jody's oblivious to anything that you've been through. Wouldn't you want to know if it were the other way around?"

"He would never treat Jody like he does me." Fear is in his eyes now. I've put it there.

"Last year, you were willing to tell my dad. For me. Because it was the right thing to do. I should have let you. I have to do the right thing this time. Even if it ruins my relationship with Jody."

"This is insane." Tate presses his hands to his face. "He's never around. I can handle him now. Why would you—"

"You don't have to do anything. I'll talk to Jody. I'll explain everything." I touch his hand but he jerks it away. "It'll be okay."

"How do you fucking know that? He's supposed to be at the game on Friday and…" He lifts his hands up. "I came over here to get away from that, not…I can't do this right now."

I call after him, but he still walks away, heading right out the kitchen door. I lock it behind him and then make my way to the office before sinking down into the desk chair. I bang my head against the wooden surface a few times and then remove my phone from my apron pouch. I send him a quick text.

ME: She's ur sister. She should know the truth

TATE: and ur dad? U want him to know, too?

My heart practically stops. I didn't think about that. I guess maybe with Dad's situation now, it doesn't seem the same as it did before. But why? Because he might not physically be able to kill Mr. Tanley? I wouldn't put it past my dad to get ahold of a handgun and take his best shot. He does have one fully functioning side of his body.

ME: this is what we need to talk about. But u can't just shut down on me.

TATE: We can talk. But I'm not gonna change my mind. It's none of anyone's business

ME: u don't want to talk. That's what u really just said

TATE: yeah. I guess so. But if you need to clear ur conscience...

ME: thanks for giving me permission. Thanks for listening and not getting pissed off

TATE: what do u expect? It's my life ur screwing with. Of course I'm gonna be worried. Maybe pissed.

ME: Maybe pissed?

TATE: Yeah I'm pissed. Happy?

No. I'm not happy. But thanks for asking, Tate.

Chapter 31

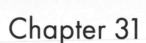

-TATE-

"**S**o your dad is coming in tonight?" Roger says from the other side of the table. We're sitting around drinking root beer Roger brewed himself, killing time before the ball, while Mom and Jody are out picking up a tux for me, despite my protests against attending the dance.

"Uh-huh." Since my fight with Claire the day before Christmas Eve, I've been avoiding any and all thoughts of the New Year's Eve ball. But that's about to end soon. Despite my claim to Haley a while back, I'd be a dead man if I skipped out on the big event.

The front door opens and Mom and Jody stand there in winter gear, fresh from the car, both assessing us, both wrinkling their noses at the mess.

Mom has two suit bags on hangers draped over one arm. "All right, I've got one black tuxedo for Roger. And one black suit and green skinny tie for Tate."

"Why green?" I ask, going back to my manual.

"Leslie is wearing green shoes," Jody explains. "She doesn't have a date, either. You guys are going to match."

I look up at both of them again. "How did that happen?"

Jody shrugs. "Mom arranged it."

"It's tradition," Mom argues, probably anticipating my protests. "The girls wear white dresses and colored shoes and the guys wear a tie to match their shoes."

Right. How could I forget?

"How do you know the green tie you rented is the same shade of green as Leslie's shoes?" I lift up the book and turn to the index in the back. I'm just messing with them, but both Mom and Jody start to panic.

"Did she say Kelly green or forest green?" Jody asks Mom.

Mom's eyes widen. "I don't know. I'd better call Linda…" She rushes off into the house.

"So…" Jody swings her arms from her spot in the doorway, then she steps through and closes the door behind her. "Claire and I have been texting back and forth this morning."

My heart speeds up, but I pretend not to care. "Cool."

"About plans for tonight. After the ball," Jody prompts, waiting a beat for me to jump in. I don't. "I suggested that we invite you to go out with us, since you and she are…well, whatever you are." Her nose wrinkles, but she shakes her head and continues. She's taking the news better than I expected. "But then she said you probably wouldn't want to come. So what's up?"

"Nothing." I set my drink down and examine a spot on the table.

Jody gapes at me. "Seriously?"

When I don't respond, she sighs and then sits down between Roger and me.

Looking at the two of us, Roger gives me a serious look. "Everything okay with you and Claire?"

"It's fine," I say automatically.

Roger waits until he's taken a drink of his soda, swallowed, and let the air still. "I can tell you from experience, terminal illness cuts into families in a way that no one can anticipate."

I shift in my spot. Roger would know. I've seen the picture in Olivia's room, the woman with the same blond curls and blue eyes as his daughter.

"I imagine Claire really needs someone like you right now," Roger adds, letting me off the hook from bringing up his own family tragedies.

That last part sinks in hard. He's right. Claire needs someone. I sigh and then stand up, brushing dirt off my pants. "Guess I should go get ready for the ball."

Roger pulls out his cell and glances at the screen. "Shit, me, too."

The second I see Claire on the stage in town hall, wearing a skin-tight long green dress, I can't even remember what we argued about. I can't remember seven minutes ago, let alone seven days ago.

Roger and his band are all sporting traditional black tuxes. Above the stage, a black and gold sign hangs for everyone to see. It reads: Music Sponsored by O'Connor's Tavern.

The Women's League president turns her back on the sash- and antler-wearing gang, and I quickly move over between Red and Leo. All around the completely transformed town hall, former Juniper Falls Princes and Princesses wear smaller versions of Leo's antler crown. Including both my parents, who have made an effort to remain on opposite sides of the room.

A row of tables traveling the entire length of town hall is spread out in front of us. Black and gold paper was used to decorate the tables, but it's hard to notice because the entire mile of table surface is covered with cookies. Every cookie you could possibly imagine and then some.

"This is my childhood," I say to Red and Leo. I barely remember any crowning ceremonies from any other New Year's Eve or the music or dancing. Just the cookies.

"Damn straight." Red shakes his head, his eyes full of sugar lust. Then he looks around, grabs a paper plate, and takes off, even though we were instructed not to move from our spots.

I glance sideways at Haley, wearing Jody's white dress and pink shoes. Before I can look away, she catches my eye, holds my gaze for a beat too long. There's a sadness in her eyes despite the excitement of the night. It's possible news has traveled around about Claire and me. But I have a feeling that I know what she's thinking about. And it isn't Claire.

Last year, before the ball, my mom and Jody were busy helping with setup and preparation duty. I had the house to myself for nearly six hours. And I knew I would be alone. Haley knew, too. And she'd planned on coming over. We'd planned on having sex for the first time.

It was a big deal for both of us and after, when we finally made it here, we were completely absorbed in each other. It was kind of perfect. I didn't think I could love her more than I did then, and I didn't think I'd ever love her less, either. How did we get from there to here? And is that something that's always going to happen? Does that mean it wasn't important? Would I take it back? Honestly, I have no fucking clue. But I do know that Haley and I both *wanted* to feel like that; we wanted to play house together, to have her alone in my bed. We wanted to feel grown-up. To imagine ourselves twenty years in the future and still here in Juniper Falls living out our glory days.

With Claire, it's the complete opposite, like some outside force is hurdling us toward each other, and both of us are taking turns putting on the brakes, trying to skid to a stop. Or at least slow this down, whatever it is. But I'm not sure we can.

I turn away from Haley, putting Claire and her long green dress in my line of sight again, and tonight, I'm not sure that I want to slow anything down. Even if I could.

But her neutral expression, when she catches me staring, is a reminder that she's still pissed at me for being pissed at her. She isn't having the same stomach-fluttering, pulse-pumping revelation that I'm having right now.

I don't want her to go out with Jody and their friends tonight. I want her all to myself. I want to be able to kiss her as many times as possible. And I want to get my fingers on the zipper holding her dress together—

I shake that vision from my head. I should have texted her an apology earlier, before she got onstage and left her phone behind.

The lights in the great room dim, and Roger clears his throat before leaning in to the mic. "We're going to start things off with a classic…"

A couple of the kids from marching band join Roger's crew, and they begin playing a Frank Sinatra song. Claire stands behind the keyboard, her gaze focused downward. She looks nervous. For someone who's been in much bigger productions, it's a little surprising.

"Yeah, that's exactly what I open with when I'm hitting on a woman."

I glance around, having heard Dad's voice loud and clear nearby. Sure enough, he's breezing past me, two of his buddies trailing him.

"My wife left me for the town exterminator and his garage band," Dad finishes.

My jaw clenches, and I swear under my breath. *Stay put. Don't move.* He's out of earshot moments later. I close my eyes and breathe deeply.

Since when do I feel obligated to defend Roger?

Dad and his gang settle at a table not too far away. They're all eating up whatever bullshit Dad's feeding them. And I can't help thinking about those photos hanging here in town hall, the speech my dad gave in the locker room the night of the carnival.

I love playing hockey. But it's never completely belonged to me. It's what we do here. It's a machine, and I'm just another preassembled product running down the conveyor belt. Even dating Haley, to everyone here, it was what made sense. And now that college hockey is tainted for me, it makes me want something all my own, that nobody can take away from me.

And Claire. The girl who has never really fit in here, whose talent is beyond the realm of what people around here know. I want her to be mine, and that won't make a whole lot of sense to anyone else.

Olivia races past me in her puffy red dress and little black shoes. A few girls are with her, probably friends from school. I assume they're about to swipe cookies from the table, but then Olivia lifts up her dress and proceeds to show off the new *Frozen* panties she got for Christmas. My neck heats up. I glance around for my mom or Jody, and when I don't see either of them, I have no choice but to head that way.

Haley beats me to it. She slides right behind Olivia, tugs her dress down, and whispers something in her ear. Olivia straightens up, eyes wide. She and her little friends slow their walk to the cookie table, their backs upright.

Haley catches me watching, and when she gets close enough to me, she whispers, "Princess policy. Keep your panties a secret."

I stifle a laugh. We should probably get a memo out about that because I'm not sure everyone's aware of the policy.

"I can't believe how good they are," Haley mutters, like she's still in shock about her dad joining Roger's band. "I didn't even think of playing Sinatra. That's brilliant. The Women's League ladies will love it."

"I bet Claire can't wait to get back to Northwestern," Leo says, chancing a glance at me.

My stomach twists, but I shove it aside. I need to make things right with Claire. The rest, I'll worry about later.

"I know, I was just thinking that," Haley says to Leo.

Okay, she definitely doesn't know about Claire and me.

Roger introduces the three marching band kids on the stage with them, then the actual band one at a time. Claire keeps her eyes on the keyboard, even when he says her name.

Silence fills the great room. Roger and his band seem to be waiting for something. Beside me, Haley tenses. "She nailed this song in rehearsal."

Finally, after what feels like an eternity of silence, Claire takes a deep breath, her eyelids fluttering shut. And then she sings the first line of the song. No music. Nothing but her voice—pure and perfect, ringing from the walls and ceiling and everywhere.

The words, the sound, all of it wraps around me. I lock my gaze on Claire and her lips brushing the microphone.

In my head, I silently say *I'm sorry*, hoping she hears me. It reminds me of when I was eleven, and we were making New Year's wishes in my backyard. She was the New Year's wish I couldn't write down. Midway through the song, Claire opens her eyes and she glances at me. And doesn't look away.

I can't believe I wasted a week being mad at her. We only have a couple of weeks left.

Leo elbows me in the side. "Dude, might want to downplay a bit."

Claire's mom is now beside Haley, an arm around her shoulders. She gives her a squeeze and whispers, "Thank you for letting her do this."

"Are you kidding?" Haley says. "I'm making music-committee history. I should be thanking Claire."

"Nervous about the results?" Claire's mom asks Haley.

"Um…yes. I'm about to barf."

Nervous? Oh, right. The results.

I move forward, closer to the stage. To my surprise, Claire's mom follows me. She makes a plate of cookies and hands me one with sprinkles on top. "Haven't seen you hanging around lately."

My face warms, and I duck my head, stuffing the cookie in my mouth. "Yeah, I know."

I brave looking at Claire again, and I feel Mrs. O'Connor's eyes on me. "She's better around you, you know?"

The cookie crumbs sit like sawdust on my tongue because I'm pretty sure I've caused some not-so-pleasant moments for Claire recently.

Mrs. O'Connor glances over her shoulder at Haley and then back to me. "You're allowed to be happy. Both of you."

Happy. Definitely a word I haven't used much lately. I imagine Claire hasn't, either. When's the last time I've seen her completely carefree and happy? She was happy in my memory, when we set off those fireworks in my backyard after the ball years ago. Jody's words come back to me… *She really believes in this stuff.*

I glance back at Leo and then head over to talk to him. "Think you can do me a favor?"

I explain my plan for later tonight and after he agrees, I walk around the great room until this year's Prince and Princess are announced—Haley and Jake. Claire exits at stage right after the announcement. Mr. Stevenson takes over the keyboard, and I force myself to stay where I am. Until they start playing a song that says exactly what I'd like to say to Claire right now: "Break Your Plans" by The Fray. I glance around and then head for the space behind the stage where Claire just disappeared to.

Chapter 32

−CLAIRE−

My feet are killing me and my throat is dry. I slip out the back part of the stage, hopefully unnoticed, and head for the drink and snack table set up for the band. I grab the first water bottle I can reach and start chugging. Roger is still talking, doing his between-song filler—something he's gotten much better at as the night went on.

When the next song begins, the lights dim even more, allowing the spotlight on Jake and Haley to shine brighter. She's being Haley and crying and he's being Jake Hammond and not crying.

I bend over to fix the strap on my shoe and immediately recognize the quiet steps and even breathing behind me. I straighten up, my stomach doing flip-flops. Warm fingers land gently on my shoulders and slide their way down my arms. Goose bumps form all over my skin, and I know I'm not going to fight this. I close my eyes and lean into the heated body. His lips press gently against my shoulder, then my collarbone, then my neck.

"Dance with me." Tate's strong voice echoes over the music and the thud of my heart.

"Here?" I whisper, my eyes still closed.

He answers by slowly turning me around until we're face-to-face. All I can do is focus on those bright-green eyes and enjoy the feel of his arm snaking around my waist, pulling me closer until our bodies are touching. He takes my free hand and holds it against his chest. I lay my head on his shoulder, my lips dangerously close to his neck. And then we're swaying to the song, cords from all the equipment running between our feet. Neither of us says a word, just the rise and fall of breaths and the movement of Tate's fingertips over my skin speaking everything loud and clear.

I feel like we're completely alone. Alone and naked.

Tate buries his face in my hair, and then his mouth drifts to my cheek and chin, to my neck, to the scar below my ear, hot lips gliding over hot skin until I'm ready to explode.

The song comes to a close and Roger starts the countdown to midnight. Each second he shouts into the mic is punctuated with another kiss from Tate, another spot of bare skin brushed over by his mouth. Until the shouts of "Happy New Year" fill the room and I lift my head, my gaze meeting Tate's again.

"I'm sorry I pushed you," I whisper. "We don't have to… I mean, just promise you'll keep talking to me. We'll start there, okay?"

"Okay, I promise." His eyes are intense, heated when he says, "Don't go out with Jody later." And I hear his words between those words: *I want you.*

My insides melt and our mouths melt together and the kiss is long and slow and so deep it hurts to breathe. Whatever this is, it makes staying in this spot seem easy. It makes being here in Juniper Falls seem easy.

"I want you," I mumble against Tate's mouth. My cheeks flame; my eyes widen. "I mean I want to…you know, break my plans. With Jody."

One corner of his mouth lifts up in that sexy half smile. "Yeah, me, too."

"You know that apartment above O'Connor's Tavern?" I say, and Tate lifts an eyebrow. "Well, we haven't been able to get a tenant yet."

"So it's available." Tate nods. "For tenants."

"And for people looking for a place to…" I swallow back nerves. "Hang out."

"I like hanging out," Tate adds.

"Me, too." I exhale and return my head to his shoulder, not able to brave looking at him.

'm turning the key in the lock when Tate appears at the bottom of the steps. My heart picks up, my hands shaking. But I don't get a second to overthink. He's right behind me in no time, an arm tight around my waist, the other hand pushing the door open, closing it behind us while his mouth finds its way back to my neck.

It's dim and cold in the apartment, but the bed is made even though I've halfway moved in over the past couple of weeks—so many parties and events to cater had me up late and early prepping food and supplies. I've got clothes in the dresser and bathroom supplies scattered everywhere.

Tate slips my coat off my shoulders and lets it fall on the floor, stepping over it gracefully. Now that it's past one in the morning, I should be exhausted, but I'm so keyed up I can hardly form a complete thought.

"I haven't texted Jody yet," I say, but then I turn around and I'm distracted, slipping my hands inside Tate's warm suit jacket. "We were supposed to meet up—"

"Shhh." He presses his mouth against mine, and I'm falling all over again, losing my balance and waiting for Tate's arms to hold me firmly in place.

"What about your mom? What did you tell—"

"Shhh," he says again. "Everything is fine. I promise. I took care of it."

He looks so genuine and sincere, I know he's telling the truth, but still, I reach into my purse, digging for my phone. Tate snatches it from my hand and tosses it several feet away, letting it land softly on top of my coat.

I lay a hand on his chest and try to push him back, but he doesn't budge. "Bossy much?"

He grins, looking so sexy and also so much like Tate, like he's keeping a dozen secrets from the entire world. "You want me. I'm making it happen."

My cheeks flush. "That is not what I said."

He lifts an eyebrow. "You did, too. I heard you loud and clear."

"Okay, that's not what I meant. I corrected myself."

"Freudian slip." He studies the updo on my head, touching the French twist gently, like it's another piece of clothing to remove. "Don't be embarrassed. You can blurt out all your random subconscious thoughts…the fantasies, too. Especially the fantasies."

I'm trying to be angry, but instead I laugh. "Who are you?"

He leans in to me, kissing my mouth gently. "The guy who wants you. Probably not the only one." He pulls away and looks me over. "Not in that dress. But I'm the only one you have plans with, so that makes me special."

"Does it?" I take a step back and fold my arms over my

chest. I'm stalling. I know I'm stalling. And it's partly because it's fun and partly because I do want him and that's scary. "Why does it feel like you've already got my clothes off in your head?"

Tate nods. "Oh, I do."

My face and neck warm again. "You're one of those people who is completely comfortable walking around in your underwear, aren't you?"

Actually, I've seen nine-year-old Tate in his underwear. But it occurs to me that I don't even know what grown-up Tate looks like shirtless.

He tugs my arms apart and pulls me close again. "Underwear is optional."

I press my nose against his shirt and laugh. I can't help it.

"Claire, I'm only teasing." He kisses more bare skin. "Well, more like projecting my feelings onto you. I want you. Okay?"

For so long, relationships were limited to my imagination. And inside my head, perfect words were always spoken at the perfect time. But I don't think the words matter as much as I'd thought. It's the actions. It's where you've been and how you got to this moment. I think he could say just about anything to me and I would know—I would feel—the sentiment behind the words.

I lift my head to look at him. "Okay."

The grin fades, and he stares at me for a beat and then both of us are in motion—kissing, touching…anything we can get our hands on. I slide off his jacket, his tie…he yanks his shirttails from his pants with one hand while gripping my face with the other, slipping his tongue into my mouth. He tastes like sugar cookies.

I work my fingers through the buttons of his shirt, allowing it to fall open, giving me a clear view of his chest. I have to stop kissing him just so I can stare. Not only because this isn't the chest of skinny Tate, cannonballing into the public pool, splashing Jody and me while we attempted to get Florida-resident tans in Minnesota. But because this part of his body is full of new marks and scars, stories that I don't know about. Pieces of Tate Tanley that I have yet to become friends with.

I place my index finger over his heart, feel the steady but fast drum and then slide it down, over a faded scar and the rippled abs. I slide the shirt off him and toss it into the pile we've made of his clothes thus far.

His gaze shifts to the jacket, shirt, and tie lying several feet away and then back to me. "A bit uneven, don't you think?"

The smallest trace of insecurity leaks through his voice. But his fingers skillfully locate the zipper on the back of my dress and tug it down. I'm breathing so fast the room has started to spin all around me, and my pulse is pounding in places I hadn't realized it could reach.

The dress falls at my feet in a heap and then my bare skin is against Tate's and I'm going crazy. Crazy and falling backward, my feet having just been lifted a couple of inches off the ground by Tate. My back hits the cold surface of the blue and white bedspread. Tate slides beside me, one hand traveling from my neck to the space behind my knee until he's got my leg around him and his mouth is back on mine.

He leans over me and kisses my neck and slides lower and lower until his lips rest on the bow plastered to the front of my black bra. He reaches around behind me, fingers on the clasp of my bra, and I'm already visualizing the next step, needing it. *Jesus Christ, I can't think*.

"Tate… Wait…" Words fall out of my mouth in a rush. "Maybe we should slow down a little…"

He lifts his head and looks at me. "I'm not… I mean, I've done this—"

I cover his lips with two fingers, not needing any further details. "But I haven't."

For the briefest second, his eyes widen, and we're frozen in place, both our heartbeats screaming in the silence.

The idea that Tate, like Haley's gossiping friends, thought Luke and I had—

I shake the thought away. It doesn't matter. He knows now.

He gives the tiniest nod, acknowledging that he heard me. And then we're kissing again, my heart ready to burst out of my chest. I've never felt so perfectly content yet so unsettled at the same time. The heat barely works in this apartment and usually, whenever I stay here, I can't even lie under my thick blankets without three layers of clothing.

And here I am on top of the covers, and beads of sweat are forming on my neck and back. We could lay in the center of the ice rink next door like this and I'd be perfectly warm. Tate covers my body with his, and warm turns to hot.

I reach for the buckle of his belt, unfastening and tugging it until the end emerges through the last loop. My gaze follows the trail of hair from his belly button down to the waistband of his pants. When I touch the same trail with my finger, his breath catches, and he watches my thumb hook into his waistband. He takes my hand, brings it to his lips, and then turns me on my back again.

We kiss forever, pressing against each other until I can't take it any longer. Until my nerves are ready to explode. He's whispering my name, saying it in a way that's become familiar. The tone radiates through me, filled with emotion, with determination, and my heart squeezes.

He might as well tell me he loves me. That's what his voice feels like.

•••

"Are we meeting up with Jody?" I ask when Tate pulls up to his house. He wouldn't tell me where we were going, just that it involved some mutual friends who were waiting on us and it involved going out in the cold again.

"Not exactly." He parks the minivan in the driveway, but instead of leading me inside, we head around to the back.

Down by the lake, I spot Jamie, Leo, and Jody sliding around on the ice in their tennis shoes. "A party?"

But before he can answer, I catch sight of the patio table, recently cleared of snow. At least a dozen of the good—illegal—fireworks lie on the table, plus duct tape, paper, and pens. "Not a party." I smile at Tate. "Fireworks and wish-making. Are you trying to change the events of the past? Wish fulfillment for your eleven-year-old self?"

"Absolutely," Tate says with a straight face.

The guys and Jody head over when they see us.

I settle in to write my wishes, stuck as to what I should write. I glance over my shoulder to make sure Tate is occupied, and then I break my own rules and sneak a peek at his paper.

1. RAISE MY ACT SCORE FROM 29 TO 30

2. MAKE IT TO STATE

3. ASK CLAIRE TO MARRY ME

Tate looks up at me from the fire pit, a sly grin on his face. He points a finger at me. "I knew you read other people's wishes. Cheater."

"Jesus, Tate." I cross off his number three.

I stare at my blank paper again. It's one thing to play along while everyone else makes wishes but completely different to attempt it myself, even just for show. I should be doing this with my dad. A lump forms in my throat and I discreetly wipe away a couple of tears. A minute later, Tate is beside me, his face filled with concern. "This was supposed to make you happy."

"It does," I lie. "I'm just not sure what to write."

He studies me for a long moment. "Maybe go for something a little less…tangible. Something broad. Like this…" He takes the pen and writes a new third wish.

3. CLAIRE

That gets me to smile. "So I should write 'Tate'?"

"Only if it's true." He tapes his paper to the firework and tosses it to Jamie. "Fire it off."

I put my wishes on hold and turn to watch Tate's firework. He comes behind me, his arms snaking around my waist, pulling me against him.

"Can I tell you a secret?" he whispers.

"Hmm." I lean my head back against his shoulder.

"Last time we did this," he says, "I wanted to write a third wish, but I knew you or Jody would see it."

"What's that?"

He kisses my cheek. "Same as right now. Claire."

I smile to myself and enjoy the feeling of my insides warming. "So…if you were holding back before, you're probably holding back now. Surely you want something bigger than another point on your ACT."

"And Claire," he reminds me.

The firework explodes above us, blue and pink streaking across the sky. "And Claire. But what else?"

"Honestly?" He snuggles closer, his lips right beside my ear. I nod. "I want to play a game where I'm excited instead of freaked out about screwing up. How do I put that into words?"

I lift a hand, resting it on his cheek. "I think you just did."

"Here's the thing," Tate says. "Hockey...it's not really mine. It's everyone's. My loss is the entire town's loss; it's like I don't get a choice."

I tilt my head up. "So choose it. Or don't. Screw everyone else."

"Even my dad?" he whispers.

My entire body tenses. "Especially your dad."

When we break apart so I can finish my rocket, Tate is looking at me like...well, like he's telling the truth about wanting to write *Claire* down for his third wish when he was eleven. And suddenly I want to go back in time and see that night for what it was. But I can't make my younger self feel those things for Tate or see him like that. All I can do is let myself feel them now.

Eventually, after I can't think of anything else, I wish to be able to make wishes again. Whatever that means. I grab the pen and jot it down, then snap a quick picture with my phone.

Tate takes the firework from me and I'm rooted to my spot, watching him light it, watching it soar up high. He runs back to me, holding me close again, and the second the green and blue explode in the sky, it occurs to me that I might have ruined the chances of my wish coming true. Especially for my parents. I know they've never wished or dreamed about their only child canceling her registration, giving up a big scholarship, to stick around town, serving beer and balancing checkbooks.

I have to tell them. I have to tell someone.

My head turns on its own, my lips right beside Tate's ear. I'm about to come clean with someone. But then the back door opens and Roger steps out. "Any of you interested in some early morning ice fishing? Might be a better place to set off fireworks. No sleeping neighbors."

Chapter 33

–TATE–

Olivia's skates come out from under her, and I lunge forward and grab her under the arms, preventing a fall. Roger releases a breath and nods to me. "Ten more minutes, Livi. Then you have to warm up."

Teaching a six-year-old to skate is easier said than done.

I stay closer to the kid while Mike and Roger set up a table and "skin" the fish. We work on widening our rink and spend a couple of minutes out of earshot of Mike and Roger. When we're closer again, they're deep into a serious discussion.

"You did the right thing," Roger says. "No matter what he promises, it's not likely he'll stop bullying you, trying to control your life. He isn't going to accept you and Jessie and probably not your kid, either."

"You sound like you're speaking from experience?" Mike prompts.

Roger looks out at Olivia and me. I quickly turn my back to them.

"I am," Roger says. "My dad…well, let's just say he wasn't very nice. But try and convince anyone else of that…"

The hair on the back of my neck stands up, goose bumps pop up all over my arms. I scrub them away with my gloves. It's not the same for me. My dad isn't like that, not exactly. Right?

I'm stuck in this argument with myself until it's time for Olivia to go sit by the fire. I step inside the ice-fishing cabin Roger inherited from his dad when he died. After putting my boots back on, I'm suffocating from the space and the people inside. Jamie and Leo had the grand idea of riding here on my snowmobile, probably because they were too buzzed to drive a car. I talk Claire into going for a ride with me. Of course this earns many snide remarks and *oooh*s.

But really? What are we gonna do? Get naked in the middle of the forest somewhere when it's a whole five degrees outside?

"You sure this is safe to drive on the ice?" Claire asks after she's seated in front of me.

"An entire cabin is sitting on this ice," I say, laughing. "You've been inside it for hours."

"Okay, fine."

I point across the lake. "If we cross here and head that way, we can see the frozen waterfalls."

Luckily we're both dressed warm, because the wind is killer riding across the open lake, no trees to block anything. I slow to a stop a little ways from the falls. Claire hops off before me and shakes the snow from her jacket. I take her hand and tug her through the trees. I pull her in front of me and spin her around.

"Holy…" Claire's voice trails off.

Only a few feet away sits what looks like a canyon now because the waterfalls are frozen. Hanging from the canyon edges are the biggest icicles I've ever seen. They reach all the way to the bottom of the canyon where mounds and mounds of snow have gathered.

Claire moves closer, leaning down to get a better look. "I feel like we could jump and land in a pile of fluffy clouds."

I hook an arm around her waist, holding her in place. "Lots of sharp rocks hiding in those fluffy clouds."

She turns around to face me. "You okay? You look, I don't know, spooked or something."

"I'm gonna miss you." My eyes close and I touch my forehead to hers. "When do you leave?"

With Claire in my arms, it's easy for me to feel her body stiffen. I open my eyes, expecting her to look stressed or maybe frustrated because that's how I feel. But I don't expect her to completely break down.

Which is what happens.

Tears stream down her cheeks. She ducks her head, pressing her face against my jacket.

"Claire… Hey…?" I take her face and lift it up again, forcing her to look at me. "What? What's wrong?"

She shakes her head and then squeezes her eyes shut. More tears tumble out. "I did something…bad. Really bad."

"What?" I demand. When she doesn't answer, I prompt her again. "Just tell me."

I back up until I'm close enough to a tree I can lean against, and then I bring Claire with me.

She takes a breath, trying and failing to compose herself, then a string of apologies follows. "My dad was on a ventilator… I didn't know if he would…" She chokes up again. "…And then the bills, I couldn't just leave them."

Okay, what? Did she make a deal with the devil? Borrow money from a mobster?

"I canceled my registration for winter term," she says all

in one breath. "I haven't told my parents. I did it without their knowing. I haven't told anyone."

Relief rushes over me. I rest my hands on her face. "It's okay. This can't be the end of the world. So you reregister."

"I tried to make some extra money to cover it but even with all the catering and parties, there's no way we can pay the tuition. And I don't know about my scholarship. They probably gave it to someone else. Why wouldn't they? I didn't even talk to financial aid, I just hit cancel. I wanted to fix everything for them…"

She starts crying again, and this time I let her press her face against my jacket. I don't say anything for a while, just stand there running a hand over her hair.

"Tate, you don't know what it was like for me. When I got that phone call from my mom and I was hours away. I can't do that again. Ever."

I squeeze her tighter, press my face against her hair to block out the cold. Roger was right, this is even harder for Claire than I realized.

"It'll be okay," I whisper. "You'll tell them soon, and it'll be okay."

As I say those words, I keep my fingers crossed that I'm right. Claire's parents love her; they want her to be happy. She doesn't have to be in college for that to happen.

Now I know why she didn't want to write down her wishes. Probably she's wished for lead roles and solos in the past, things that don't happen to people who stay around here. And she feels guilty for wanting anything that doesn't keep her here helping them.

"I know you," I tell her. "You did what you had to. What you're doing for your family, it's pretty amazing. You gave up so much to be here."

She takes a deep breath, lifts her head. "That's the

problem. My parents don't want me to make sacrifices for them. They want me to just take off and not worry about them, but how can I do that when they've given me everything?"

There's nothing else I can say to reassure her. Instead I dry her cheeks with my jacket sleeve and then kiss her, long and slow and with as much distraction as I can offer. It isn't until our tongues and hands are tangled together that I really allow myself to process the idea that Claire isn't leaving.

Chapter 34

-CLAIRE-

I walk with Tate over to the ice rink, hoping my face is finally rid of the red puffiness from my lengthy sob fest in the forest. Tate holds my hand tight in his until we're right outside the locker room. He gently nudges me until my back touches the wall and our mouths are only an inch or two apart.

"I have a feeling, in a little while, I'm gonna bang my head against the wall for going all crying drama queen on you," I admit.

"Stop," Tate orders, leaning down to kiss me. A couple of his teammates walk by us and whistle, but Tate doesn't look away from my face. He touches his forehead to mine and gives me one more quick kiss before pushing away from the wall. "See you later, Claire."

I had planned on heading home, but I get stopped several times by the skate rental girls who want to talk about the ball. Then, Renee who runs the concessions tells me all about her daughter's wedding that's coming up on Valentine's Day. She wants to know if O'Connor's caters weddings.

I'm still talking to Renee when Coach Bakowski and the varsity team take the ice. I let her continue on about buffet and cake options, while I witness Bakowski run those boys into the ground. The skating, turning, stopping, shooting, and hitting people goes on and on. I figured since Tate was always guarding the goal, he didn't have to do any of the regular player stuff, but he's right beside Jake Hammond, sprinting from blue line to blue line. There is an obvious difference in the skating abilities of each player. But still, they move as one machine, hitting a mark, twisting in place, hitting the next mark.

When one of the boys looks ready to collapse, Bakowski stalks over to him, tennis shoes moving with ease on the ice, blows his whistle sharp in the kid's ear, and yells until he finds the energy to move again. The only varsity freshman, Cole Clooney, bends over beside Tate, resting his hands on his knees. Despite Bakowski's directions for them to skate again, the kid pulls off his helmet. His face is a dangerous shade of red.

In the front of the bleachers, a woman jumps to her feet and shouts at him. "Get your damn helmet back on, Cole!"

The kid sways, losing his balance. Tate grips the back of Cole's practice jersey, holding him up. When Bakowski turns his head to talk to the assistant coach, Tate leans down and whispers something to Cole. He bends over farther, shakes his head, then stands upright. Jake Hammond reaches over and shoves the helmet back on the kid. Bakowski blows the whistle again and both Jake and Tate push Cole Clooney forward.

A few minutes later, Bakowski gives them thirty seconds to get water. I spot Cole Clooney leaning over a garbage can, heaving up nothing. Leo grabs a water bottle, takes it over to him without any eye contact or exchange of words. The whole practice is eerie in its silence. Its intensity.

Watching Cole Clooney skate until he nearly passes out is nothing compared to seeing Tate behind the goal. Bakowski lets all the boys take hundreds of shots, pucks flying at Tate constantly. I jump and wince every time the puck smacks into the glass or against the crossbar.

Finally, Bakowski blows a whistle, stopping all the shots. Everyone is silent, watching him stalk over to Tate. He sticks a foot inside the goal and sweeps out a puck.

"That's the game-winning shot at Sections," he says, his voice lower than usual but somehow more intimidating. He sweeps out another puck that had gotten past Tate. "And that's the shot that knocks us out of State in the first round. At this rate, we'll be the laughingstock of high school hockey." He turns to face all the boys. "Thanks to Tanley, we're gonna lose State."

My heart is about to beat out of my chest. I can't imagine how Tate feels.

"What do you think, boys?" Bakowski says. "Think Tanley needs another round of shots minus the chest pads to get his head out of his ass?"

The boys now have their helmets tucked under their arms. None of them responds to Bakowski's threat.

"How late can we stick around here?" Bakowski shouts at the assistant coach across the rink.

The guy is young and looks almost as stricken as the players. I remember his name now. *Ty.* He's ordered takeout from us before. Mushroom burger on rye, I believe. No coleslaw.

"Ten," Ty responds back.

"Ten," Bakowski repeats with a nod. "It's six now. I'll tell you what, boys. If Tanley manages to stop your lame-ass shots in the next five minutes, we'll finish up at eight. If not, we'll end practice with an extra two hours of suicides. Got it?"

"I think I just figured out why his mom never watches practice," I say.

"You're telling me," Renee replies, whistling under her breath. "It's always worse after the holidays, when they're gettin' ready for the playoffs."

Bakowski blows his whistle, getting ten or twelve of the boys to quickly form two lines, preparing to shoot at Tate. At the far end of the rink, Ty has taken the sophomore backup goalie and a few of the varsity defenders and is running them through shooting drills. Even from my spot far away, I can tell the temperature at that end of the rink is at least twenty degrees warmer. That's probably where Tate would be right now if Mike Steller hadn't walked out during that first home game.

One by one, the boys all take shots on goal. Tate is everywhere, covering high corners and low corners, his stick and glove working overtime. Bakowski decreases the time between whistle blows, sending the players to shoot at shorter and shorter intervals, until Tate is a blur in motion. I stand there mesmerized. I don't know how he can keep track of where the pucks are when they're coming so fast. If he's afraid right now, I'd never be able to tell.

All the boys rotate through the line, then take a shot at the other end, with the backup goalie. Pucks are sliding past the backup kid every five or six shots, but Bakowski shows no interest in his mistakes.

When Tate snatches one of Leo's shots out of thin air, Bakowski grabs Leo's jersey and gives him a shove so hard he falls over his stick and slides several feet across the ice. "Get your damn head out of your ass! You shoot like that at State and you'll be headed nowhere fast next year."

Leo is back on his feet in two seconds flat. I glance at Tate and see that his gaze has followed Leo despite his rock-solid focus thus far. Jake Hammond skates toward the goal and Tate snaps his attention forward again. He manages to cover the goal, the puck bouncing off his leg pad.

"Maybe I didn't make myself clear," Bakowski says. "Tanley misses and we all stick around for a late night. But you keep shooting like pansy-ass freshmen, and we'll have a late practice all week."

He gets right up in Cole Clooney's face, yelling at him to use a more difficult shot. "You ready to go back to JV yet, son? Wish you hadn't come into my office pledging your allegiance to my team...*I'm ready, Coach. I can handle this.* You'd better start proving it, or I'll find someone to replace you for the playoffs."

Bakowski takes the shooting drills up a notch by having the second line of players act as defenders, trying to shove the other around, hoping to mess up his shot. It means they're all in motion constantly. Skating, checking, shooting.

Tate is making some spectacular saves, in my opinion. But Bakowski keeps yelling at him, saying he's hesitating or that it was a lazy shot. Then he yells at the player with the lazy shot.

After dozens and dozens of rounds of this, Jake Hammond knocks Jamie Isaacs right on his ass and pulls off the most amazing shot I've ever seen at a high school game. It bounces off the crossbar, then slides right between Tate's legs into the net.

Bakowski blows the whistle again, but this time long and sharp. They all seem to know this means stop. The entire rink is frozen again, while Bakowski digs out the rebellious puck that made it through.

He holds the puck in his hand, tosses it up in the air, and then catches it again. "I don't know if I should be thrilled that we've got one player who can score a goal or worried that our goalie can't block a single trick shot. And that's with clear sight, no one screening him. How about I just declare myself pissed off about both these things? How about we have a nice long night together, boys."

Tate draws in a deep breath, his chest filling but not deflating.

Bakowski tosses the puck at Jake Hammond. "You made the shot. You can go home now if you want. Your choice."

Jake doesn't move.

"The rest of you can thank Tanley for the ass beating you're about to get."

My heart drops to my stomach.

"Well," Renee says, shaking her head. "Come back here and help me get these water bottles ready."

She opens the little door off to the side, allowing me to go behind the concession counter.

Renee is busy pulling items out of a storage closet. "When they get going long hours, I usually make up my special mix. A bit of Gatorade, some water, and then that god-awful Pedialyte stuff they give to babies. I read on the internet the NHL players use it to keep hydrated."

I hurry up and help her with the water bottles, following her mixing instructions carefully. She tells me that last year, around this time, two players ended up in the hospital needing IV fluids. The way rumors spread around here, I'm surprised I hadn't heard about this before. And then there's Renee, the way she's prepared for this, even anticipating it. For the first time ever, I'm seeing a side of varsity hockey that's much different than the king-of-the-world, screw-any-girl-I-want side.

Maybe this is the only way to have a winning hockey team.

Chapter 35

–TATE–

Getting closer to Sections and State means cheerleaders on the bus with us. More specifically, Haley on the bus. Haley, who hasn't spoken to Claire or me since New Year's Eve. Maybe today is the day to break the ice. For Claire's sake.

I take my time stowing my hockey bag underneath the charter bus, and I'm one of the last people to board. I drift down the aisle, my gaze wandering, looking for the blond ponytail.

I spot her backpack on a seat. She's sitting alone, scrolling through her phone. I reach for the backpack, preparing to lift it so I can sit beside her.

She raises her head, hand shooting out to grip her bag. Kayla ducks under my arm from behind and scoots right into the seat beside Haley. I sigh and walk down the aisle. Leo waves at me, and I head for the very back to sit beside him.

Leo tugs his headphones down around his neck.

"You're glad it's over, right? I know she was the one who wanted to take a break…"

"I'm glad it's over," I agree. "But we had our moments, you know? It wasn't all bad."

Leo snorts out a laugh. "Yeah, I know. I've seen more of those *moments* than I'd like to admit. If I could erase certain things from my memory, believe me, I would."

I glance around, making sure the rows in front of us are still empty. "Why? You weren't, like, jealous, were you?"

Oh, shit. That just came out, didn't it?

Leo stares at me, shock written all over his face. "You went there. I can't believe you fucking went *there*."

I scrub a hand over my face. "Yeah. I did. Sorry."

Leo faces forward again, pulling his headphones back into place. "Relax, T-Man, you're not my type."

"But I am sort of your type." I glance at him, lowering my voice. "Wait, so you mean, like, me specifically? I'm not your type?"

He turns to me. "This is really bothering you? You need me to tell you you're hot stuff or what?"

"No," I snap. "Jesus. I don't fucking need you to tell me anything. I was just making conversation."

Leo laughs, and we both sit in silence while the bus pulls out of the school lot and heads down the road.

"Thanks," he says quietly. "For, you know, being cool."

"Yeah, sure," I say. And then I add, "But Kennedy—please tell me you have other options."

Leo shakes his head, still laughing. "How about you spend less time thinking about my love life and more time thinking about the game?"

"Right. The game." My stomach is in knots all over again.

The game is all I can think about for the entire bus ride. So, when Bakowski holds me back in the locker room, I'm already on edge, already near cracking.

"We win tonight, Tanley, and we've got a shot at the best seat going into Sections," he says.

I nod. I get it. We need to win. I need to not let the other team score. Easy, right?

"Believe me, you want that better seat. Takes the pressure off the first couple of games in the playoffs."

That's probably the most logical, nonthreatening thing Bakowski has ever told me. And somehow it changes my perspective. I'm not as afraid of the ridicule that comes with losing; instead I'm thinking about the benefits of winning. We're ranked number one in our section right now, but a loss would put us back to second or third. Then we'd have to play the top team much earlier in the tournament.

My glove is working overtime the whole warm-up, my teammates probably worried that I'll mess up again and forget how to use the damn thing. But luckily, it's working for me today. Inside my head, I'm still a fucking mess, doubting every move, but my body seems to know the drill. It should after all the extra hours of practice we've had this week.

And while our sophomore backup goalie takes a turn warming up, I study the other team's shots, trying to absorb as much data as possible. This proves to be a useful tool during the first period. They've got a small handful of good shooters but I'm ready for all their shots, keeping that 0–0 score.

Near the end of the third period, one of their younger players gets ahold of the puck, breaks away, and my heart is pounding so hard I can't even hear the crowd. He's flying toward me with so much speed I can't think. This kid is faster than Hammond. I shift back and forth, preparing for his shot.

He slaps it hard and fast. My body reacts on instinct, diving in front of the goal. The puck lands in the pocket of my glove, but the kid who took the shot is coming at me, too fast to dive out of the way. His skate pushes forward. He's bracing himself for the fall. The blade of his skate jams into my chest and both of us are sliding backward, the goal moving with us until it hits the boards with a jolt.

The lights flicker in front of my eyes and eventually go completely black.

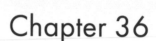

Chapter 36

−CLAIRE−

"Oh my God," I say at the same time Jody says, "Shit!" Number four from Homebrook took a shot and then kept going. He and Tate are now tangled up in the goal. My heart thuds, my stomach dropping.

"He caught it, right?" Jody says. "I can't see the puck."

Number four manages to disentangle himself from Tate and stand, but Tate hasn't moved. My hands lift up, covering my mouth. "Oh God, I think he's knocked out. Is he knocked out?"

"No way." Jody shakes her head, but she doesn't sound completely sure. "He didn't even hit his head."

"Maybe he hit it on the ice." I glance around. Is there a way down there? Wait, we can't go running out on the ice to check on him.

Jamie Isaacs skates over to Tate, along with Leo and Jake Hammond. Tate is still curled on his side, his glove resting on the ice. Oh my God. He *is* knocked out.

Move, Tate.

Beside me, Jody mutters the same words, "Fucking move, Tate."

The ref pulls off his helmet just as Bakowski makes his way out on the ice. I hold the air in my lungs, waiting for someone to move out of the way so I can see. We're pretty high up in Homebrook's stands.

When Bakowski holds a phone to his ear, I nearly scream out loud. *Please tell me they're not calling an ambulance, please.* I've seen it happen at games. But it's never made me feel this panicked before.

The ref shifts sideways, and finally we can see Tate's head. His eyes are open.

"Thank God," I say, my legs weak with relief. I'm hit with a wave of dizziness so bad, I have to sit down.

Jody plops down beside me, her own sigh of relief mixing with mine. "Jesus freakin' Christ. Why did he take so long to move? He's probably into the drama of it all."

I laugh, tears prickling at my eyes. That's so not Tate, and we both know it.

The people in front of us sit back down, and by the time we get a clear view of the ice, Tate is sitting up and slowly getting back on his feet, or skates, actually. But he's hunched over, his hand clutching his stomach.

"He's not gonna keep playing, is he?" I ask.

"Don't they have some rule about not playing if you were unconscious?" Jody chimes in.

"He definitely got knocked out," I agree, wanting nothing more than to see Tate on that bench. "It might have only been a few seconds." It felt like an hour.

Sure enough, Tate ends up on the bench moments later, the sophomore second-string goalie now in his place. I don't even watch the game. I keep my eyes on the team doctor hovering over Tate, shining a light in his eyes.

"Dammit," Jody says, staring at her phone. "I'm gonna have to call my mom, right? What should I say? 'He was knocked out and stabbed in the stomach with a skate blade, but he's awake now'?"

"I could text Roger," I offer. "Let him break the news to your mom."

Jody flashes me a grin. "Do it. Let's take bets on how long before my mom calls me after you text Roger. I'm gonna say four minutes."

"I'll give her ten." I quickly punch in a text. "Let the countdown begin." I pass my phone to Jody in case she wants to reply.

While my eyes are glued to Tate on the bench, Jamie Isaacs manages to score a goal and the game ends at 1–0. Us.

It takes seven minutes for Jody and Tate's mom to call her. She's on the phone with her the whole time we're making our way out of the stands, and then she forces Jody to wait for the guys to come out of the locker room so she can check on Tate herself. Of course I'm not complaining about seeing him up close, making sure he's okay. But I'm not looking forward to his teammates seeing me checking up on him.

"What kind of catastrophic injuries are possible if he's walking and talking?" Jody says to her mom. Their exchange goes on for a while until the team finally begins to file out of the locker room and head toward their bus outside.

I push off the wall, anxious to get this over with. Leo comes out before Tate and makes his way over to Jody and me.

"Some of the guys are carrying him; they'll be right out," Leo says, all casual.

"What?" Jody and I both shout.

Before he can answer, Tate walks out of the locker room. Completely unassisted. His heavy bag on his shoulder.

"You asshole." Jody punches Leo on one shoulder while I shove his other shoulder. "No, Mom, no one is carrying him."

Tate approaches us and mouths, *I'm not talking to her.*

He stops in front of me and sets his bag on the ground. I turn to face him and look him over, but I don't move to hug him or anything. "I'm afraid to touch you."

"He's making a lasting impression on you already," Leo says, breaking free of Jody's grip.

"Mom wants to know if you blacked out or not?" She pauses, listening to her mom on the other end. "I'm not shining a damn light in his eyes."

Tate moves closer to me, his fingertips grazing my arm. "Hey," he says, his mouth right next to my ear. "I'm glad you came."

This is not a catastrophically injured Tate. I smile at him and whisper, "You're really okay?"

"That kid is fast." Tate shakes his head. "He's gonna be a nightmare to deal with next season."

I grasp the sides of his jacket, tugging him down to my eye level. "Are you okay?"

He nods. "My stomach is killing me."

It takes me a second to realize he's talking about the blade that jabbed into his abdomen, not any signs or symptoms of nausea that could be a result of a concussion. I reach for the hem of his sweater and dress shirt below, slowly lifting them up.

"Do not grope my brother right in front of me," Jody says from behind me.

She's about to dive between us but instead decides to chase after Coach Bakowski, who has just entered the lobby. "Coach, my mom would like to talk to you."

He barely gives Jody a two-second glance, and then he yells over his shoulder, "Ty, phone call for you!"

I turn my attention back to Tate, pulling his sweater all the way up. The entire center of his stomach is bright red, bruises already forming. "Talk about battle wounds..."

I continue to stare a few seconds longer, and then Tate pushes his clothes back down. "I'm fine, I swear." He dips his head again, planting a kiss on the side of my neck. I sigh and get two more kisses from Tate before he says again, "I'm glad you came."

Aside from watching him get knocked out, I don't hate this hockey-girlfriend gig as much as I thought I would. I kind of loved watching him play tonight. Maybe I even kinda loved watching all the Otters play.

When Tate steps away from me, bending over to lift his bag, my eyes meet Haley Stevenson's all the way from across the lobby. She's not glaring like I'd expected. She's staring at us, though. She holds my gaze for a beat longer before turning away and pushing open the door. Nerves flutter in my stomach. I don't know what she's thinking, but I know she's thinking something about me. I have to make this right, but how? What do I say that makes it okay? *Tate and I have this thing that goes way back to when he was eleven*? 'Cause that's not weird.

I turn to Jody, who is waiting impatiently for Ty to talk to her mom. But then when Kyle Stewart and Red stand near her, laughing about something directed at her brother and me, after my face flushes hot, she shoves both of them and tells them to go fuck themselves. An insult I'm sure her mom probably hears, too, from the other end of the phone.

Before he walks out the door, Tate glances over his shoulder one more time, giving me another smile.

Jody catches this, too, and with her phone back in her hands, she steers me out a different door. In the parking lot, Haley is standing around her group of cheerleaders, hands on her hips, speaking emphatically.

"Look, I don't care if it's a competition or not, you don't wave at random guys while we're in the middle of a cheer. All you're doing is adding fuel to the cheerleader stereotypes. We're better than that."

Jody elbows me in the side as Haley breaks away from the other girls. "You should talk to her."

"Right." I nod, taking a deep breath. I have to jog a bit to catch up with her. She spins around to face me, and her eyes widen. "Look, Haley…I just—"

She lifts a hand to stop me, and her eyes close for a moment. "Don't. Seriously. I can't think about this—I don't know what I'm supposed to think."

I take a small step back. "I'm sorry."

A few tears trickle down her face. She wipes them quickly. For a split second, I can't help wondering if Tate is nuts for not getting back with Haley. She's beautiful and smart and strong. Maybe stronger than me.

But then it occurs to me that she doesn't know the Tate I know. She can't, because he's never let her see all of him. In my mind, I conjure the memory of Haley and Tate kissing at my going-away party. It was cute and full of curiosity and new—new everything. But he'd walked away from her that night, went back to O'Connor's, and he became the Tate I know.

Haley swallows back more tears. Her voice comes out barely above a whisper when she says, "Okay."

And then she turns around and heads for the bus. I stand there for a few too many seconds, I think, because Jody eventually hooks her arm through mine and she's tugging me toward the car. "I know what you need," she says.

"What's that?"

"Hot fudge and double-chocolate ice cream…" She

continues to give detailed descriptions of our favorite dish from a great ice cream joint in Homebrook that we've hit up before during an away game.

"I kinda feel like I don't deserve any treats." I glance at Jody and hesitate before adding, "Not just because of Haley... Something else."

"Let's have a confessional dessert, then. You'll spill all your dirty little secrets and I'll do the same." She wiggles her eyebrows. "There's this TA for my U.S. history course; nothing's happened yet, but we've totally been dancing on the line. And now I'm not his student anymore..."

I squeal a little too loudly and then glance around to make sure no one is listening. On the way to get ice cream, Tate sends me a text from the bus.

TATE: want to hear a secret?

ME: ok

TATE: it was different today. The game. Hockey

ME: yeah?

TATE: more mine or maybe its always been? idk

Yeah, I know. But I don't tell him his love of hockey is obvious. Watching him play, it was like seeing someone fall in love. It almost made me want to play hockey. Or hop up on a stage and deliver a heartfelt solo. But Tate needs to come to these conclusions on his own. That's really what's it about. Finding his own thing. Despite his dad.

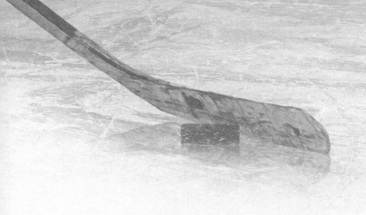

Chapter 37

–TATE–

"Andi?" I repeat, glancing at Leo and then back at the baby through the glass window.

Leo nods. "Like a girl Andi."

"I figured, considering the pink blanket and hat." The babies trapped in little glass boxes are moving around a lot. Some are red-faced, their mouths open, but any sounds of crying are confined to the other side of the window, which is kind of weird, to see it and not hear it.

"God, it's just weird," Jamie says on my other side. "That thing was, like, a big bulge under Jessie's shirt just the other day."

I snort out a laugh. "Yeah, it's a real scientific miracle."

"I just can't believe Steller has a kid," Leo says. He holds up his phone, zooms in on Andi, and snaps a picture. "Big-ass hands; think she'll be a goalie?"

Andi's hands are like the size of a quarter. "I can't believe he's not getting out of here, you know?" I look around, suddenly regretting my words. "I don't mean it like that; it's just people around here aren't exactly Mike Steller fans. That sucks. They couldn't even show their faces on New Year's Eve."

Jamie has walked away to find a vending machine, so I wait for Leo's opinion on this. They were seniors together. A year ago, this couldn't have been Mike's plan for senior year. Or after.

"Think about it this way," Leo says. "People will get over Steller walking out. Being a hockey player who doesn't go anywhere, having a kid really young with your high school girlfriend…kinda makes him fit in just fine around here. People like me, on the other hand…"

He doesn't add any more. I turn my attention to the babies again. I don't know what else to say. I mean, I know of people in town who are presumed to be gay, but not many are open about it—definitely no hockey players. But that's not just here. I don't know of any openly gay NHL players. Not that Leo has been open about anything yet. Not that Leo has plans to be in the NHL. But college…

The thought of college sends my stomach twisting into knots—for Claire and what she's going to have to spill to her parents at dinner tonight, for me and what Dad did over break, and for—

"You're gonna sign with Michigan in April, right?" I ask Leo. It's been at least two weeks since the last time I asked this. Both Jamie and Leo held off on signing any letters of intent during the early signing period. They'll have a week in April to decide.

"I'm waiting on one more decision," Leo says. "But Michigan still feels right."

Jamie has returned, so I ask him the same question. He shrugs and doesn't elaborate more than that. Leo and I both press him until he admits the truth.

"I kind of…sort of…" He plasters on one of his famous goofy grins. "Might not graduate."

"What?" Leo and I say together. We're so loud, a pregnant lady and her husband walking the hall glare at us, like we're wild teens loitering in the maternity wing.

Jamie shrugs again and looks at the babies. "It's fine. I probably just need to do summer school and then I can play."

We badger him for several minutes about this, but when we've gotten all we can out of Jamie, I ask, "So neither of you are considering becoming an SMU Hawk…?"

"Not a bad team, but I wasn't feeling it there, you know?" Leo explains.

Yeah, I know.

Jamie opens a pack of Skittles, which earns him a glare from a different pregnant lady in a hospital gown, wheeling an IV. "I'd play more for St. Cloud."

I sigh with relief.

Leo looks at me. "Why? What's going on?"

Ever since my "unofficial" tryout, I've wanted to tell Jamie and Leo about it. I almost did, like, five different times, especially on New Year's when I got tired and we were all hanging out together.

"No reason." I shrug. "Just kinda got a bad vibe over there…"

Leo turns to face me, arms folded across his chest. "What kind of bad vibe?"

I glance from Leo to Jamie, deliberating. Jamie's jaw has gone slack, mid-chew. I keep my head down and my voice low. My hands are shaking all over again. "The coach…he basically shoved me out on the ice and I— Well, I played. And he told me what to do." I look up at them, hoping they see the regret on my face. "I mean, he coached me—that's illegal, right? I'm not a senior."

Leo's forehead wrinkles. "Did he make an offer?"

I shake my head.

"Dude, where the hell was your dad?" Jamie hisses, keeping his voice low.

I dig my fingers into the railing below the glass window. "He was there. He didn't do anything—I think he wanted it to happen."

My legs are shaking now, too. I've never said anything like this to either of them. But Hammond had been there.

Silence falls between the three of us. I think Leo is about to say something, but Mike comes down the hall, sees us, and lets out a yell, complete with a fist pump.

"You guys made it!" He's wearing a huge grin, though he looks scruffy and tired. "Look at my kid; she's, like, the best one in there, isn't she?"

I have a feeling hockey players will soon be banned from the maternity wing.

While Mike gets Jamie and Leo all riled up, I glance at my phone—it's almost time to head to Claire's for dinner. But when I turn around, Roger is standing less than three feet away, a big package of diapers in his arms.

Shit. Oh shit. Did he hear any of that? Why didn't Leo notice him standing there?

I force a grin and clap Mike on the back. "Congrats, man. I gotta go meet Claire."

He opens his mouth to respond but then spots Roger. "Hey, you heard! And you brought diapers. Thanks, man."

I'm not sure how taking off quickly will change the situation if Roger did overhear the conversation, but I do it anyway because what the hell else can I do? I guess the theory is, if we don't talk about it then maybe he'll assume he misunderstood. Maybe none of it will be anything to Roger.

I make it down one flight of steps before I hear my name called. At first I pretend not to hear, but then Roger takes the volume up several notches and I'm forced to stop. He thunders down two flights of stairs, the sound echoing in the empty stairwell. He's in better shape than I expected.

"Tate…hold up."

I stretch my arms out as if to say, *I'm here, what do you think I'm doing?*

He reaches me finally—slightly out of breath—but keeps an empty stair between us. "Does your mom know?"

"Know what?" Nope, not admitting anything.

"About the coach working with you?" He looks me over, like he's suddenly concerned for my well-being. Which is probably bullshit, but why would Roger care about NCAA eligibility? "Did you see anyone recording it? Did the university pay for anything like meals or…"

My dad bought lunch. Surely that won't count against me. Will it count against Jake? Was that the real purpose of the visit? Maybe we're forced into being uptight about all of these eligibility rules and no one really cares.

Maybe it's fucked up that I even have to worry about it with my dad there. He should be protecting me; he should be worrying about all of this for me.

"Tate?" Roger prompts.

I shake my head. "I don't—I don't think so."

"Your dad shouldn't be using his position to pressure you into attending his school." Roger pauses, waiting for me to jump in. I don't. "Is that happening?"

I clamp my jaw shut tight and stare out the tiny window over Roger's shoulder. I keep my face calm and cool, but my heart races.

Roger holds up his hands in surrender. "I'm not a coach. I couldn't care less about hockey. I'm not gonna turn you in to the NCAA eligibility center. Whatever is going on, you can tell me."

"It's fine—" I start, but he interrupts me.

"Look, I've seen you go out of your way to avoid your dad on several occasions. I'm not an idiot, Tate." He keeps his voice low. "I'm just saying, if something is going on, you can tell me. Consider me a neutral party, all right?"

If all the issues with my dad weren't bubbling to the surface right now, trying to burst out, I could drop the defensive attitude, put on a happy face, and tell him thanks for the offer. But my heart is still pounding, too many memories I'd rather forget swirling inside my head.

I point a finger at the final flight of steps below. "I gotta go; Claire's waiting for me."

He attempts to respond, but I don't wait. I take off down the stairs, and this time Roger doesn't follow me. I have to be more careful around him. He's seen too much already.

Chapter 38

—CLAIRE—

Tate is uncharacteristically jittery sitting at my dining room table, eating pot roast with my parents and me. Maybe it's the fact that the last time he saw my dad was probably when Dad decided to take a late- afternoon stroll in his underwear. But Tate knows he was sick that day—his brain swelling, fever rising—we just hadn't discovered it yet. And he's not insane tonight.

I rest a hand on Tate's bouncing knee. It's causing a clicking sound from his boot hitting the leg of the table. *Relax.* I attempt to send him the one-word message telepathically. In five minutes, I've scarfed down half my dinner. I was starving. I look over at Tate's plate. His mashed potatoes and meat have a small dent in them, but the carrots and salad are still untouched. Same goes for his bread. And freshly baked bread is the one thing my mom makes better than Dad. The whole house smells like it right now. It's amazing.

My mom reaches over to slice the meat on Dad's plate

even though it's so tender it's practically falling apart. My dad is in a surprisingly good mood today. Instead of glaring at her, cutting his food like a child, he leans back on his elbow and watches with amusement.

When she's finished, it takes some work for Dad to get the fork from his plate to his mouth, but he manages eventually, and then after chewing and swallowing, he also manages to say, "It's good."

Mom beams. She's come to expect critique in the form of narrowed eyes or glares at the dinner table. Not because Dad wanted to insult her cooking, but because he always had a suggestion or tip for her or me and he didn't really have a way to communicate this.

"It's very good," Tate says, and then his neck turns pink. What is up with him today?

My mom rescues him by saying, "Thank you."

Dad manages another bite of mashed potatoes, but when he goes for his glass of Diet Coke, I have to reach across the table to steady it. He waves a hand at Tate, who goes all wide-eyed and alert. Then Dad holds the marker beside him in his fist and begins writing a word on his notepad. He forms what looks like an *H*, and my mom leans in to get a closer look.

"How are you?" Mom guesses.

Dad shakes his head and scribbles out the word he'd been trying to write and starts a new word.

"Puck," Mom reads, her forehead wrinkling.

"He wants to know how hockey is going this season," I say to Tate and then look at Dad for confirmation. He nods and goes back to leaning on one elbow, his fork taking a break. It isn't only his motor skills affected but also processing information. According to the therapist, right now it's impossible for him to think about eating and the movements required to complete the task *and* listen to someone talk at the same time.

Tate clears his throat then takes a long drink from his glass of milk. "Oh, yeah. Hockey. It's going well right now. Mike Steller isn't playing; did you know that?"

Dad shakes his head and then throws an accusatory look at both Mom and me. Mom holds up her hands. "I can't possibly keep up with all the neighborhood gossip and the high school hockey team. You know how my memory gets."

This is true, except that with Mom and me covering most of the O'Connor's shifts, she's keeping up with hockey just fine. Especially with all the added Late Nights at O'Connor's.

"Anyway…" Tate keeps glancing my way, taking deep breaths. "We have Sections coming up soon and I'm playing goalie. The tournament starts next month. The weekend of the fifteenth." He looks at me one more time and then drops his eyes to the plate in front of him.

Oh shit. Is he trying to start this conversation?

"The fifteenth of next month," Mom repeats. "Isn't that the weekend of auditions for the spring musical? That's too bad. Otherwise maybe you could have made a trip home for the weekend."

The shell-shocked look I must be wearing sends Mom out of her seat and into the kitchen. She returns with a flier from Northwestern's theater department. "Opening night for *Les Mis* is May tenth; auditions are February fifteenth."

Tate's eyes are burning a hole in the side of my face. I can practically hear his silent chant: *Do it, Claire. Now. Tell them.*

But God. They're doing *Les Mis* this year. Back when I thought I'd be at school this year, I promised my roommate, Keisha, that I'd at least audition for the big university production this year. And it's *Les Mis*.

I've been staring so long at the back of the green paper in Mom's hand that I half expect Tate to kick me in the shin or something, but instead he takes my hand under the table and gives it a squeeze. I look over at him, channeling my thoughts: *But it's Les Mis*. My dream show with my dream role.

It doesn't matter. Because I'm not a student there anymore and I don't know when or if I will be again.

And God, what is wrong with me? This is all so petty and trivial—the audition, even winter quarter classes. Buried anger rises in me. Instead of lashing out at the town about ridiculous things like winter carnivals, this time I'm pissed off at me. What the hell am I doing even thinking about the audition?

I glance at Tate one last time, then back at my parents. Both are staring at me.

"About winter quarter…"

Chapter 39

−TATE−

"What about winter quarter?" Mrs. O'Connor drops into her seat. It's like she knows something big is coming.

Say it, Claire.

"I'm not going back." She squeezes her eyes shut, waiting for the impact.

Silence falls. Dead silence. My body aches from being stiff and not moving.

Finally Claire's mom lifts a hand to her mouth. "Oh God… you're pregnant."

Davin glares daggers at me, his mouth contorting with all the words he can't spit my way.

I lift up a hand. "I didn't— I swear—"

"What?" Claire drops her fork onto her plate, causing a loud *clank*. "No, God, no!"

I release her hand under the table and wipe away the beads of sweat from my forehead. Right above Claire's parents' heads is Jesus. Hanging on the cross. For a brief second, Mrs. O'Connor glances at him and then sighs with relief.

Davin finds energy he didn't have moments ago. His hand is around the marker, the black tip pressing hard against the notepad. Claire and I both tilt our heads to read.

GOING. YES.

Claire lifts her gaze to meet his, and silent communication happens between them. I hold my breath. Slowly Claire shakes her head. "I canceled my registration already. I'm not going."

Davin's face twists with anger. He shakes his head much more firmly than Claire had. Claire's mom speaks up. "I'm sure you can un-cancel. We'll make some calls."

"No. It's over." Her voice rises, and I reach out my hand to her again, but she tugs it away. "We don't have the money. We haven't had the money for a long time. I decided this a while ago." She looks at her dad. "When you were in the hospital."

Davin squeezes the marker in his hand, then he pounds the tip against the paper over and over.

"Dad, stop," Claire pleads. "Please."

The marker stills, and he tries to get a few words out and when he can't, he swings his bad arm hard into a glass of water, the saltshaker, and plate with butter on it. All the items fly into various parts of the room.

I jump out of my chair so fast it tips over. Claire's mom tries to calm Davin, but he fumes a few more seconds and then he storms into the kitchen. Claire must sense my panic during all this because she wraps her fingers around my wrist while looking right at her mom. "I'm sorry."

"You can't make decisions like this without us," Claire's mom says. "What were you thinking? You could ruin your scholarship eligibility. What about your education?"

"My education?" Claire shouts, surprising both me and her mom with the rise in temper. "My education consisted of analyzing patterns of music notes, contemplating whether or not Tennessee Williams was an alcoholic in a five-to-seven-page paper, and singing show tunes. Jesus Christ, it's not like I was learning to cure cancer!"

Claire's mom flinches and gives the Jesus behind her another quick glance. "You've worked your whole life for this—we all have. You can't just throw it away."

"You make it sound like I've decided to develop a drug addiction." Claire's face is bright red now, from anger or frustration. "I'm staying here. I'm helping you out, working. There is nothing wrong with that. You and Dad didn't go to college. You didn't live in a big city. No one told you you were throwing your life away!"

A look of defeat takes over Mrs. O'Connor's features. She lowers her voice to practically a whisper. "You're not us, Claire. You're special."

"I'm not you," she agrees. Most of the anger drops from her voice. "But I'm not special. None of that matters. It's… inconsequential."

I look at Claire, waiting for her to add on to that or correct herself. Is that really what she believes? The spark she had while she sang at the ball has dimmed in a short time.

Mrs. O'Connor looks like she has a million things to say, but she just exhales and holds up both hands. "We'll talk about this again later." She nods toward the kitchen. "Give him some time to settle down, okay?"

Claire stands and starts to pile up the dinner plates, but her mom lays a hand on top of hers. "Leave me with him for a while."

A few tears fall from Claire's eyes, but she nods, and then she's tugging me toward the front door. The glass plate and saltshaker hitting the wall play over and over inside my head, but I still put one foot in front of the other.

"Claire…" I prompt once we're inside the minivan. I don't know what to do.

She closes her eyes and shakes her head. "Just go. Anywhere."

I start driving even though I have no clue where to take her. Everything is hazy inside my head. Each breath Claire takes beside me is magnified, my ears ringing.

Warm fingers land on my knee, squeezing it gently. "It's not the same, okay?"

"What?" I glance at her and then back at the road. "What's not the same?"

"My dad. His…behavior," she says gently. "He's not mad at me. He's not mad at anyone. He can't speak. It's like he's trapped inside himself. You have to understand—"

"He looked mad," I say, even though I don't want to admit the reason for my panic. I know Davin O'Connor. At least I thought I did. But people think they know my dad, too.

"He's mad at himself," Claire agrees. "I think I broke his heart. I just don't get how any of that can be so important to them. After everything…"

"But it is kind of a big deal," I say quietly, not wanting to fully open this can of worms right now. "You aren't just a regular college student." I catch her eye for a second. "You're so much more than that."

"I don't know," she mutters. "I don't know anymore."

She turns her head to face the window, but I still catch her wiping away more tears. I lay my hand on top of hers and keep driving—another time we'll dig deeper into this.

"Where should we go?" I ask after a few minutes of driving. She's gone somewhere else, looking out that window. "Milkshakes at Benny's?"

I make five more suggestions and get no response from Claire. While I keep glancing her way, waiting for her to say something, I have to clamp my jaw shut to keep from saying the three words I'm dying to whisper in her ear.

I love you.

Something shifted in me—in us—tonight. Or maybe it grew. If she turns the question around, asks *me* where I want to go, I'll probably answer with: *I love you.* And it seems too soon. How long has it been? Two months? Maybe a little longer.

Or maybe it's been years.

When I'm near explosion from the silence and the guessing, Claire turns her head toward me, her gaze heated. "Let's go somewhere alone."

I have to work to keep my focus on the road. I don't know if it's tonight's tension and seeing Claire hurt or the promise inside her words, but next thing I know, I'm pulling up in my driveway, telling Claire to wait in the car.

The kitchen is dark, but the glow of the TV is bright in the living room. Mom and Roger are curled up on the couch. I tiptoe down the hall, but Jody, who is coming out of the bathroom, stops me. I hold a finger to my lips. I don't want to get caught up in another chat with Roger or a *where are you going, who are you going with* inquisition from my mom.

Jody nods. She'll cover for me.

I unlock my bedroom door and wait for her to head down the basement steps before I sneak into my mom's bedroom. I stare at the silver key for a beat and then snatch it off the nightstand. In my own room, a strip of condoms gleams at me from its place in my top dresser drawer. I go through a dozen different arguments in my head, but eventually, I tear off three condoms and zip them into my coat pocket. Better safe than sorry.

I make it all the way to the kitchen door before my mom calls my name. I freeze, my heart slamming against my chest. I clear my throat. "Uh...yeah."

"Not too late, okay? Or call if you're staying somewhere else."

Jesus Christ. "Okay, yeah. I will."

I head out the door and drop into the driver's seat.

"Why do you look like you just robbed a bank?" Claire asks.

"Huh?" I sit up straighter, attempting to wipe the guilt from my face. "Oh...just my mom and her inquisitions."

Maybe this is wrong. Maybe the timing is off. I look over at Claire before putting the van into drive. "Jody's home. Would you rather—"

Claire shakes her head. "She's going out. I don't feel like being social. Is that okay? I just—"

"It's fine." I smile at her. "It's perfect, actually."

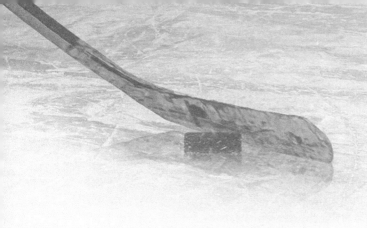

Chapter 40

−CLAIRE−

figure he's taking me to the apartment above the bar, but then we head just outside of the Juniper Falls city limits. Tate pulls off on a side road in the middle of nowhere.

I glance around, bewildered. "Guess I should have specified the words 'indoor place.'"

"Yeah, I figured," he says, his tone way too serious for this particular moment.

Through the dark, I can barely make out the outline of a trailer sitting on the very east end of Lake Estella. Roger's cabin.

"Does he know we're coming here?" I ask.

Tate shrugs. "You heard him before; he said to let him know if I wanted to come back and fish. He'd give me the keys."

I decide not to push for details because honestly, this is exactly what I had in mind when I asked him to take us somewhere. No locals to remind me of my life and the turns it's taken, no bar below us to suddenly have a crisis that needs my attention—like running out of paper towels. That happened last weekend.

Tate pulls the van off to the side of the road before reaching the trailer. He shifts into park but doesn't cut the engine. I lean back against my seat, my gaze following the headlights pointing into the forest. "Is this why you looked all freaked a few minutes ago?"

"No," Tate protests immediately. Then he exhales and adds, "Okay, maybe." He looks at me, so hard and intense, I swallow back more nerves. "Just because I have the key doesn't mean we need to use it. If you don't want to be alone here, I completely understand."

"No, I do." I turn to face him and let out a breath. "Can we just… I mean, can we not be serious?"

"Not serious?" Tate stares at me, his forehead wrinkling. "Like casual dating?"

He spits the words out with disgust. I shake my head so hard I give myself whiplash. "No, no, no. I'm serious about that. Very serious. I mean right now. This. I don't think I can handle it with all those deep, intense looks you're so gifted at and that weight in the air. Especially after dinner tonight. I just want this one thing with us to be easy."

He arches one eyebrow and then nods. "Yeah. Okay."

"Let's not make a big deal of it." I exhale and open the door.

True to his word, Tate is completely cool after opening the door to the cabin. Of course it's freezing in here, and he has to get a generator started. He's outside fiddling with stuff when the lights come on, revealing the nice-size place—it's much bigger with only two of us in here this time. At one end is a small wood-burning stove with a stack of dry logs beside it. Tate gets a fire going right after he comes back inside. We can still see our breaths, it's so cold in here.

The fire is blazing quickly, thanks to those useful starter logs. Tate opens a few of the wooden cabinets and pulls out various items—two decks of cards, a Monopoly game, a pad of paper, and a couple of pens and pencils.

"Entertainment," Tate says simply.

It's not quite warm enough to remove anything yet, but I take off my coat and shoes regardless and make the climb up to the full-size bed hanging from the ceiling. "It's stable, right?"

No one tested it out the other day. But the blankets and pillows look warm and clean.

"Oh yeah, the thing can hold, like, a thousand pounds." He ditches his coat and shoes, too, and then flops onto the bed beside me, stretching out like we're about to discuss trig homework or something. The comforter is ice-cold beneath me, but the heat from the fire and the generator begins to drift up this way. I can tell he's working to hide the concern from his face. He probably wants to ask how I'm feeling after the drama.

How am I feeling? Relieved. Because I told them. They know. Heartbroken. Because I told them. Now it's real.

And then there's Tate. I'm here with him. I get to stay with him. That's not exactly the worst thing in the world.

He rests his arms behind his head, relaxed and completely at ease. I smile at him and pat his knee. "You're doing really well with this non-serious thing."

"So I shouldn't light a few candles and draw you a bath?" He rolls on his side and props up on one elbow. His fingers touch the hem of my shirt lightly. "Then I thought maybe after your bath, I could sketch your portrait, and then we could make love, smearing pencil shavings all over our—"

I slap a hand over his mouth even though I'm laughing

too hard to hear him finish the sentence. "Stop. Now."

He fakes disappointment. "Too much?"

"The candles and the bath? Definitely too much. Especially considering the lack of bathtub." The cabin has an airplane-size bathroom with a teeny-tiny shower that is most likely filled with frozen water. "But the sketching I could handle."

I only said that as a joke, but Tate leans over the bed, eyes the pad of paper and pencils that were meant for keeping score in card games, I'm sure. Then he looks back at me. I laugh. "I was kidding."

"No, I can do this. If this is what gets you off, then who am I to—"

I reach out to shove his shoulder—I said I could handle it, not that it turned me on—but he's too quick. He flashes me a devious Tate Tanley grin and then hops down from the bed, not even bothering with the ladder. He's back seconds later with paper and a pencil. He moves down to the end of the bed, near my feet, and leans against the wall. The top of his hair brushes the ceiling.

For some reason, I play along and lay still. "Should I lift my arm up like Kate Winslet in *Titanic*?"

"No idea what you're talking about, but whatever you want." He assesses me like he might actually make an attempt at this request. God, this is weird.

"Do you even draw?"

"All the time," he says. "In kindergarten. Maybe a little in first grade." He angles the notepad so that I can't see it and then instead of drawing, he stares at me for a long minute.

"What?"

"Something's not quite right." He scratches his head, then reaches for my foot and tugs off my sock. "There. That's much better."

I shake my head when the pencil starts moving.

"Are you seriously sketching me?" I'm waiting for him to stop this charade any second now and start kissing me.

This non-serious Tate is pretty adorable. I kind of needed this, too. An escape from reality. I quickly itch my nose with the sleeve of my sweater and then return to my pose. "You really seem like you know what you're doing. Am I gonna be shocked by your talent?"

He flashes me a dimpled smile. "Well, I do have a beautiful subject."

Heat creeps up my neck, but I return the smile.

A bit more glancing and scribbling and shading ensues, along with lines and more lines. Then Tate looks up at me. "I think I'm finished."

"I have to see this." I push up to my knees, keeping my head ducked to avoid collision with the ceiling, and move across the bed until I'm close enough to reach for the notepad.

"Wait." Tate holds it tight against his chest. "Just a fair warning. This might change things."

I roll my eyes. "You spent less than ten minutes on it; how much change could this drawing possibly provoke? I want to see it."

He holds my gaze, looking way too serious. Especially when I demanded the opposite. "You're sure?"

"I'm positive." I fold my arms over my chest. "You gave me three boobs, didn't you?"

Tate hesitates before slowly turning the notebook around.

My arms fall to my sides as I take it in. There's no stick figure. No figure at all. He didn't draw me.

A large shaded heart touches the edges of the paper. And in the center, he's written the words:

I LOVE YOU

I draw in a quick sharp breath and sink back onto my heels.

"Kind of a game changer, huh?" Tate says tentatively. Less confident than he'd been while creating this artwork.

I'm still staring at the words. I can't look away. But I nod. "Yeah, kind of."

My gaze shifts to his face. He looks so serious and worried. It's exactly what I didn't want to see, except I do now. I really do. I reach out a hand and touch the words in the center of the page.

"You should sign it," I suggest, my voice barely above a whisper.

Tate keeps his eyes on me while reaching for the pencil, and then he initials the bottom right corner of the page. Slowly, he tears it from the notebook and it floats in the air between us. I don't want to get up now, but I can't risk it crumbling underneath us. I slide off the bed and make my way down the ladder, paper in hand. I tuck it carefully under the Monopoly board.

He's in the same spot, perfectly still, when I return and kneel in front of him. "You made me pose for nothing."

"I did," he says.

I push my hands under his sweater, tugging it up over his head. I don't know why I thought this would be hard. It's not. But it's not easy, either.

It's…*inevitable*.

How long have we been walking toward this very moment without knowing? Years, I bet.

Something inside me calms, and I'm no longer wanting to rush, thinking that I'll chicken out. *It's inevitable.* All the threads of my life, my future, have changed or been pulled away from me, but this… This bridge between Tate and me somehow emerged in the midst of everything falling apart.

Despite how much I tried to stop it. Despite how afraid I was to make that leap with someone for real. Not just a fantasy built to unrealistic measures. Tate is real, and his life is messed up, and my life is more real and messed up than ever. But his heart is beating beneath my hand, and I didn't ask for it, but he's given it to me. And there are some gifts you just don't turn down. There are some threads that you hold on to as tightly as possible.

I work through the buttons on Tate's shirt, and then I unbutton and unzip his jeans. He kicks out of his jeans and reaches for my sweater. After my sweater is off, my shiny purple bra still on, Tate pushes me back until I'm lying down again.

He unsnaps my jeans but struggles to pull them down.

"Did you paint these on?" Tate's still tugging and pulling at my skinny jeans.

I laugh, watching him study my pants like a mechanical object he needs to take apart. "I think you just have to let them turn inside out."

He shakes his head. "Maybe if you lift your hips ten degrees…"

I'm laughing harder now. "Is this how it's gonna be, goalie boy? Should we get the notebook again and map out a few plays first?"

"You want to have a strategy?" He lifts an eyebrow. "I can do that."

My pants are quickly abandoned while Tate grabs the notebook and both pencils, before flopping onto his stomach beside me.

Okay, then.

I remove my own damn pants and then roll over on my stomach, our hips touching. It's definitely getting warm in here.

Tate smirks at me and then quickly draws a line with a circle on top, then arms, then legs. He puts an X in the spot right between the legs. "The X represents the places I'm going to make contact."

"Now you draw people?" I tear the paper out and toss it off the side of the bed. "No plays."

I look over at him. My cheeks burn and my gaze roams to Tate's bare shoulders, then down his back, the muscles moving along with the pencil. But I don't stop at his back; I drift farther south, taking in his ass, hugged by the navy striped boxer briefs. A shiver runs down my spine.

Tate holds my face with one hand, gently directing my attention back to the notebook. "Focus, Claire. I know how much I can distract you…"

Tate picks up a pencil again and writes: I REALLY WANT TO KISS YOU NOW

My pencil presses to the paper, forming a reply.

OK

Tate leans closer, his warm breath on my neck, his lips grazing the bare skin. Goose bumps burst from every bit of flesh near his mouth. A fire builds in my stomach. He lifts an arm across my back, leaning over me and sliding the notebook in front of us. I tilt my head, allowing him more skin to kiss. He kisses my neck and collarbone. I close my eyes and enjoy the feel of Tate's moving fingers and lips and whatever else he can use over my neck and back. He unfastens the clasp on my bra. My breathing hitches when his hand drifts under me, brushing lightly over my boobs. I grab his hand beneath me and hold it to my heart, forcing him to drape his body over me, all the bare skin touching bare skin. Tate nibbles on my ear while he writes something else.

You smell so good

He slides down my body, his thumbs latching onto the

waistband of my panties. But he doesn't take them off. He's carefully moving his lips over my skin, making a straight line from between my shoulder blades to the lowest, lowest part of my back.

My stomach flutters as Tate slides the straps of my bra down my arms. I try to roll over, but he's pressing too much of his weight against me now and planting too many amazing kisses on my shoulders and back for me to give my body any kind of directions. He slides another hand underneath me, dragging it down my stomach. He makes gentle strokes over the front of my underwear.

"Feel good?" he whispers.

I pull back a little from Tate's hand, my body stiffening.

His hand stills, his heart pounding against my back. "It's okay if you…*you know*."

I rest my forehead on my arm and let my hips press back against his hand. I can't help it. It feels so good. "It's better if I wait."

"For what?" Tate says, and I hear the smile in his voice. "You're that close, huh?"

I grab his wrist and yank his hand out from under me. "Don't get cocky." I shake my head, not surprised by Tate's laughter that follows. "Bad word choice."

"Can I be completely honest?" he says, the teasing dropping from his voice.

"Only if it's literal honesty." I turn my back to him and pull both his arms around me so we're spooning now. Except Tate is very careful to keep his pelvis a couple of inches from touching me.

"I'm putting every single bit of brainpower I have into not losing it," Tate says, his voice low and sexy in my ear, but in his tone, I hear the nerves, the vulnerability. I relax further into him, sliding his hands over my breasts. "I'm not exaggerating when I say this… I'll be surprised if I even… I'm just too— You're too—" He draws in a sharp, ragged breath, and I take a few seconds to relish in the fact that I've obviously driven him to this point. This is extremely good for my ego. "I'm sorry, I know you probably have big ideas and—"

I place a hand over his mouth, covering it gently. He's not allowed to apologize for things that boost my ego. Then I close my eyes and listen. Tate relaxes a bit, his fingers wandering over the front of me again. "Let's make one more rule, okay?"

"What's that?"

I turn my head, getting a view of his profile over my shoulder. "We lose it when we lose it, and we don't worry about which thing is happening right then."

"Thank God," he mutters under his breath.

And then I'm suddenly pulled tighter against him, Tate's hand drifting inside my panties. The hazy, *I don't care about anything but this good feeling* air is engulfing me, and I know everything is about to explode. I stick a hand behind me and reach for the band of his underwear. He instinctively pulls away, but I get my hand around him anyway. There's moisture at the tip and for a second I hesitate, too many health and religion class lessons explaining exactly what that bead of moisture contains popping up in my head. I shake off the thoughts because no baby-making zones are currently being invaded without armor. We're okay.

I hold him tight in my hand, my head falling more to the side with each movement of his hands on me. Heat is bursting from the places his fingers touch. I bite down on my lower lip. He plants more kisses against my neck, and I'm gone. Lost in this place where self-consciousness rarely exists. I grip him tighter and move my hand up and down a few times until he comes.

My muscles relax, my eyes closing, nothing but my

pounding heart to listen to. I feel Tate's kisses, light and sweet, all over the back of my neck and shoulder.

"Don't move," he whispers.

I hold perfectly still while he plucks a tissue from the little built-in shelf by our heads and wipes off my hand. I turn over on my back, looking up at Tate. "Would that technically be called sex?"

He balls up the tissue, resting it on the shelf, and then reaches for a bottle of hand sanitizer. Once the bottle is in his hand, he buries his face against my neck. "I'm sorry."

I laugh. "What are you sorry about? You know how many friends I've had to listen to whine about how long it took for them to give a guy a hand job? I know a girl who passed out one time from low blood sugar."

"Stop right there," he warns. "I know one of your friends a little too well."

"I wouldn't go there."

A huge glob of blueberry-scented hand sanitizer lands in my palm. Tate rubs my hand with both of his, then he grabs me around the waist and drags me underneath him. My now-calm body is already stirring again, looking right into those green eyes and the tousled hair. His forehead touches mine and he breathes out the words, "I can think clearly now."

"Good for you." I comb my fingers through his dark hair. "I feel kind of drunk."

"Good." He smiles. "Because I have something I need you to tell me." When I nod, he continues, leaning into my hand while it drifts through his hair. "When you pictured how this would go—you and me—what exactly did you picture?"

I tilt my head, pretending to think hard about this. "Well, we were on a stage and you were wearing a Romeo costume—"

"You pictured me in tights?"

"Leggings," I correct.

Tate stares at me until I finally concede to the lie. "I guess I didn't exactly picture it. Not all the details."

He nods and then kisses my forehead. "Okay, close your eyes." I squeeze them tight and Tate continues to kiss my face in several different places. "We're having sex—"

"Really? I can't feel a thing."

"Be serious," he says, but I hear the smile in his voice. "Imagine we're having sex."

"Are you wearing a condom? What color is it? Neon?"

"Claire," Tate groans, and then he dips his head and tugs at my earlobe with his teeth. "Humor me."

I roll out my shoulders and smooth my expression. "Okay. We're having sex."

"So what do you see?"

I work hard to imagine it for real this time. But I don't really see anything tangible. Real-life Tate begins kissing me, and in my imagination, my legs wrap tight around his waist and my fingers press into his back. We're so close, so connected. My breath gets caught in my throat.

"You're blushing," he says against my lips. His mouth moves to the front of my neck. "Your pulse is racing. Tell me."

So I do. I spill out all the words I just thought, and when I finish, Tate is staring at me, wide-eyed. "That's it?"

I nod, my cheeks still hot.

"No Romeo?" he asks.

I slide my hands from his hair to his face. "You'll do."

Without releasing me from his tight hold, Tate reaches toward the end of the bed, fishing around in the pocket of his jeans. He drops three condoms on the bed beside us. "We're gonna use these."

I lift my eyebrows. "All of them?"

"We might."

The lines of *will we* or *won't we* blur in a tangled web

of kissing and touching and Tate using his teeth to drag my panties all the way to my ankles when I bet him that he couldn't do it. Eventually, after his underwear is on the floor, he sits up. He holds up one of the condoms and tears it open. I watch him roll it on, into place, and my stomach does flip-flops, expecting him to jump right to it. But instead, he takes his time, working his mouth over my body again and again.

And then Tate is positioning himself between my legs, but still I tense up, even before he's gone anywhere inside me.

He must sense my nerves because he waits, kissing me longer, rubbing my neck and shoulders with both his hands.

"Relax," Tate whispers, his voice filled with a calmness that washes over me. "I can stop if it hurts. It's no big deal. We'll do it again tomorrow. Or in an hour. Or five minutes…"

A laugh builds in my throat until it emerges, my whole body shaking and loosening. My eyes flutter until I close them completely. And in the haze of laughter, I feel Tate pushing inside me and then the laughing cuts off. I open my eyes. I'm sure they're huge with surprise. Did that really just happen?

Tate stops moving, holding himself in place. "Are you okay? Does it hurt?"

Okay. So it hurts. A little.

It takes me several seconds to absorb everything—the feeling of Tate inside me, on top of me. The sting of pain is already fading. I must have been quiet for too long because concern fills his face. "Claire?"

"I'm okay." I slide my arms underneath his, wrapping them around his back. "Just…go slow."

He frees one hand from behind my head and slides it down my leg, pulling it around his back. He does the same thing with my other leg. "Like this?"

Yes, like this. It's just how I'd pictured it in my head. I knead my hands into Tate's back and eventually slide them south, pulling our hips together even more. He makes long, slow movements that build one on top of the other. And still it's not enough. Something isn't enough.

Tate stills again, dipping his head, lips on my ear. "I love you." His eyes meet mine again and he's breaking all the rules. So am I. There's so much intensity on his face when he repeats those three words again. "I love you."

And there it is. That perfect bubble of heat and emotion and holding each other tight that I saw—and felt—inside my imagination.

I love you.

I love you.

I press harder into his back, bringing us closer together, more connected. We kiss and kiss until my body is on fire again, and then Tate deepens his movements, not much but enough for me to feel him come inside me.

He shudders for several seconds and then his mouth crashes into mine. *I love you. I love you.* I don't know if he's saying it or I'm saying it. It doesn't matter. We don't even need to say it. It just is.

flash of my dad, pissed off and shoving me toward the truck, hits me hard.

I swear to God, kid, if you ever touch my goddamn keys again...

I'm still bracing myself for yelling, at the very least, when Roger says, "I wish things were easier for you, Tate. I really do. The last thing I want to do is scare you off. I won't push you anymore, but if you need to vent about anything, or if you need advice, you know where to find me."

At first I can only nod slightly and turn around to leave, but I stop myself before I'm out the door. I spin around again and Roger waits for me. "I shouldn't have taken the keys without asking. I'm sorry. Won't happen again."

"The place is still standing, right?" He waits for me to nod and then adds, "Catch any interesting fish?"

Uh...

My face heats up again. I scratch the back of my head. Roger laughs. "Yeah. That's what I thought."

"Sorry," I repeat.

"How about you help me get the oil changed on the minivan and we'll call it even?"

"Yeah, sure." I nod. "The tires haven't been rotated in a while, either."

Roger looks at me and lifts an eyebrow. "Looks like we've got an afternoon of work ahead of us, then."

We work in peace for a good hour before my dad's truck rolls into the driveway. I know Roger sees the truck, but he takes my cue and neither of us stops what we're doing.

It takes several minutes for Dad to appear in the garage, Jody beside him. "Get clean," Jody demands. "We're going out to dinner."

I'm already spinning excuses in my head. Dad opens his mouth to chime in. "It's your sister's last night in town..."

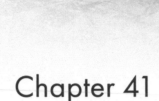

Chapter 41

−TATE−

When I spot Roger in the garage, cleaning the back shelves, I don't even think about the stolen keys in my pocket or the fact that I should probably use this as an opportunity to put them back. I head right in and ask him what he's up to.

Hearing my footsteps, he turns. "My cabin keys…have you seen them?"

My face and neck heat up. I look anywhere but at Roger. He already knows. I can tell. "Uh…"

"Let me guess." He continues wiping his hands, speaking calmly. My heart is pounding, anticipating an angry reaction from Roger. "You didn't ask me for them because you didn't want to talk about what I brought up yesterday at the hospital?"

Yeah, pretty much. I keep my mouth shut. But I do take the keys from my pocket and hand them over.

Roger pulls himself up to his feet and accepts the keys. A

"You guys go ahead, then. I'm— I've got homework to do."

Dad waves a hand. "You don't need to worry about any of that—you heard Coach Redeck. You're already a top academic recruit; no need to lay it on so thick."

"That is not good advice." Jody shakes her head. "Maybe you *should* stay home and study."

Dad rolls his eyes. He seems like he might be drunk or maybe just buzzed. He's probably been somewhere watching Sunday football with Larry Jones and those guys.

"Tate," Roger says, meeting my gaze. "I thought you were taking Olivia to that birthday party? At the movie theater?" He looks at Dad and Jody, dead serious. "I've got a rabid squirrel I have to deal with over at the Gleason farmhouse. Those jobs can take hours."

"Right, the party," I say, following Roger's lead. "Can't wait to spend the evening supervising six-year-olds."

Dad looks like he wants to protest, his gaze flitting to Roger, but then he must decide it's not worth it because he waves a hand and leaves with Jody. I release a breath the second I hear the truck back out of the driveway.

Roger keeps his eyes on the car parts in front of him but says, "Everything is fine there, huh?"

Fear sinks into me. It's not fine. It's so far from fine, but I'm barely treading water and I'd rather not have someone else pressing my head under.

He seems to realize this and returns to being less invasive. "There really is a birthday party. No rabid squirrel, but if you did take Olivia, I could bring your mom some dinner at work…"

I look at him, like, *Are you serious?* He is. If it weren't for him being so cool about the keys and getting me out of dinner with Dad, I'd probably tell him no way. Instead I sigh and prepare myself for lots of singing. And whining.

Chapter 42

−CLAIRE−

make it to the game by the beginning of the second period. I would have been here sooner, but with this being the last game before Sections, the one that can seal our spot as number-one seed, lots of prep is needed over at the bar. It'll be a busy night.

Of course, to add to the tension, the score is 2–2. From what Tate's told me, this team is supposed to be an easy win for us. If he let two goals in during the first period, he's not playing his best. I scan the bleachers, looking for signs of Mr. Tanley, but my attention is brought back to the ice where Tate has just lost his stick. I suck in a breath as the opposition prepares to take a shot. Cole Clooney sweeps in and steals the puck out of thin air and takes off for the other end of the ice. Jamie grabs Tate's stick and tosses it at him, and I can finally release the air I've held in for way too many seconds.

"Come on, Tanley, wake up," I hear someone mumble from behind me.

I spin around and squint into the shadowed corner of the rink near my special side entrance. Mike Steller is standing there—dressed in all black, a baseball cap pulled way down low, concealing part of his face—like a celebrity hiding from the paparazzi. "What are you doing in my secret spot?" I say to Mike.

He smiles and puts a finger to his lips. Then he reaches for my arm and pulls me into the shadow with him. "How are you? How's the baby?" I ask because I haven't seen Mike since New Year's Day. Though I have sent plenty of soup and casseroles his way.

"Good," he says, then he grips my shoulders and slides me halfway in front of him. Probably as another hiding method. "Bakowski will have a fit if he sees me in here."

I want to ask him why he's here if it's such a risk—we do have Otter radio—but Mike seems to read my mind.

"Leo and Jamie were worried about Tate. I guess he had a shitty pregame practice. I had to come see for myself. In case I can help."

Definitely not the attitude of a selfish, stubborn former hockey player that nearly everyone in town has made him out to be. Not that I ever agreed.

"He's not doing well, is he?" I can't hide the worry from my voice. I turn my head to see Mike's reaction.

He shrugs. "He's rattled right now. Playoffs are stressful as hell for everyone, but especially for goalies. Honestly, he's better than I was this time last year."

That can't be true. Mike Steller had NHL scouts watching him play in the state tournament last year. And he was only a junior. I turn back to the game, and we both watch in silence— well, not silence with this crowd and noise level. Tate pulls off a couple of good saves, and Jake Hammond makes a killer pass to Leo, who scores another goal. While the home crowd is on their feet cheering, the pep band playing, Mike steps to the side of me and nods.

"They got this," he says, completely confident. "Claire?"

I look away from Tate and glance at Mike again. "Yeah?"

He moves to the door, and I automatically shift to block anyone's view of Mike. "It's cool you guys are together," he adds.

Before I can tell him thanks, he slips out the door, quiet as a burglar. I wonder how many games he's watched like that. I wonder when people around here will get over the fact that Mike chose responsibility and family over pursuing his hockey dreams. I didn't realize until this moment how much he and I had in common. And the thing is, unlike Mike, I *did* get to leave. I experienced an entire year of college in a new city, three different student-run stage productions, band ensemble concerts, final exams. I've earned college credits. I should be grateful to have gotten even this much. I *am* grateful.

"Isaacs and Rose are as good as signed."

I jump when I hear Keith Tanley's familiar voice. From the corner of my eye, concealed by the back side of the rink, I spot Tate's dad pacing, his cell pressed to his ear. I tuck myself into the hidden space Mike just abandoned.

"Clearly you underestimate my ability." Keith laughs. "Just send them a few small gifts from the pros, ask them about it innocently, then offer to keep the violation quiet as long as they agree to sign with us in April."

My heart bangs against my chest. I sink farther into the shadows, pressing my back against a wall.

"These are not typical hockey parents. They're pretty clueless. It's almost too easy."

Oh my God.

The conversation shifts to other names I've never heard of, probably from different towns. I hold perfectly still, keeping myself hidden, my heart racing, my chest constricted from the attempt to breathe quietly. Finally Keith Tanley leaves to go back to sit with his buddies. My hands are shaking now, but I do the only thing I can think to do. I pull out my phone and send Tate a text he won't get until after the game.

ME: come find me when u get done. It's really important.

Chapter 43

−TATE−

After the game, I head over to Claire's house. I figured she'd be at the bar, so I was surprised and worried when she messaged me, saying she had to run home. Her dad sent her a text.

Through the kitchen window, I can see Claire and Davin talking at the table. I decide to let myself in the kitchen door so neither of them has to get up.

The second I enter the house, Claire's mom rushes in from the other room, holding a stack of photo albums.

Claire jumps out of her seat, her voice immediately escalating. "I told you, I don't want to look at photo albums!"

Davin taps his marker hard against the notebook in front of him and looks at his wife, who speaks for him. "We've already got Uncle Barry drawing up the paperwork for a second mortgage. We'll be able to get a check to Northwestern in time for the spring quarter deadline."

Shit. What did I walk into? I glance over my shoulder at

the door and debate backing away before anyone sees me. I should have knocked. I always knock.

Davin spots me and lifts his chin like he's glad I'm here. Uh-oh. The last thing I want to do is get involved in the *Claire's going back to college* chat.

Claire drops her face into her hands and groans. "Why would you do that? We'll never recover from that hit. I bet the interest rates were—"

Davin lifts a hand, and Claire stops talking. Her mom and Davin exchange looks, and then Mrs. O'Connor nods before turning to Claire. "You dad—both of us—we're worried about you."

"You're worried about me? What does that mean? Like my health? I'm fine." Claire stands and begins gathering her stuff, lifting her coat off the back of the chair. She tosses a glance in my direction, pleading for me to whisk her away again, I think.

My thoughts drift back to last weekend, in the cabin. The hair on the back of my neck stands up. I'm ready to get Claire alone again. Tension rolls over her in big waves, and all I want to do is make her feel good. Whatever that takes.

"…you aren't happy," Claire's mom says, forcing me back to the room. "You aren't enjoying yourself."

I'll volunteer to help with this task.

Claire laughs. "Seriously? You guys are insane. Stop worrying about me. I'm a big girl now."

Mrs. O'Connor shakes her head. "This is my fault. I should have never let you come home in the first place."

"Are you kidding me?" Claire snaps. I move toward the door, but she grips my coat sleeve, holding me in place, before turning back to her mom. "What did you expect me to do? Keep going to class and play rehearsals while Dad was having his inoperable brain tumor removed?"

"Of course not," Claire's mom says. "But that was months ago. It's time for things to go back to normal."

"This is normal!" Claire throws her hands up, obviously exasperated. Something inside me is coming undone or snapping into place, I'm not sure. Claire stuffs an arm into her coat. "I can't do this now. The bar is jam-packed—"

Davin scribbles furiously on his notepad. All three of us freeze in place, watching the words form.

Not LIVE.

Not live?

Claire says the words out loud, her forehead wrinkled.

"Not living," Mrs. O'Connor corrects, earning a nod from Davin. "This isn't normal. This is you not really living." Her mom's face changes, the words obviously becoming hers, too, not just Davin's. "You're eighteen. You can't keep living the life of someone who's more than twice your age. We won't let you."

Davin flips furiously through pages in a photo album, revealing dozens of images of Claire playing a giant guitar, Claire in brightly colored dance costumes. She reaches over and slams the album shut. "Enough."

She gets her other arm in her coat and flings open the door. Before exiting, she calls over her shoulder. "Do not sign whatever Uncle Barry is drafting up for you."

Like last time, I follow Claire outside, but it's like my legs are made of lead. And the house is a giant magnet pulling me back inside. She's all the way down the walkway before she realizes I'm no longer right behind her. She spins around and looks at me. "Tate?"

I come to a complete stop, my boots now buried in snow that hasn't been cleared from the sidewalk. My tongue is tied up and twisted.

"Sorry I made you come here," she says. "But I really do

need to hurry, and we have to talk about something—"

I glance back at the house, and this seems to stop her. "Maybe you should go back in there."

Suspicion fills her face. "Don't tell me you agree with any of the crap they just said?"

I open my mouth to protest, but I can't say the words that would reassure her.

"Fine." She turns and walks quickly away. Instead of getting into her mom's car, she strides down the block like she's preparing to walk to the bar.

This gets my lead legs working, and I jog to catch up with her.

"I can't believe you, Tate. You're supposed to be on my side. Is that so much to ask?" The anger is a cover-up. When she glances sideways at me, there's a look of desperation on her face. She's begging me to let her have this. But why?

"Just stop for a second, Claire." I reach out to grip her arm gently, halting her forward movement. We've made it four houses away from hers. "I'm on your side. Always."

She meets my gaze and exhales. "Thank you."

"But…" I hesitate only a moment, but it's long enough for her to groan. "What if your parents are right? What if you're not letting yourself really live?"

"Why are you doing this to me?" she pleads, and I'm hit hard with a punch of guilt.

"Why are you so dead set against listening to what they have to say? Maybe they've got it worked out better than you think…" I have no idea what I'm saying, but I have to say something.

"And what if they do?" Claire shakes her head. "So what if they find the money, everything is great on the financial front…my dad can barely speak, he can't get himself places, his tumor could come back."

I lay both hands on her arms and start to slide them around her. "He's getting better. Every time I see him, he looks stronger. Why don't you at least think about it, maybe even for next fall—"

She jerks out of my grip. "Why don't I? Because it's not fair!"

Tears trickle down her cheeks. She backing away. I've made her cry, and now she's about to run off. *Well done, Tate.* "What's not fair? Your dad's tumor? The money stuff?"

Claire squeezes her eyes shut. "It's not fair for me to be doing something that…that…"

"That you love," I finish when she doesn't. Her parents were right. She's sentencing herself to some kind of purgatory. Out of guilt. And what does that make me?

Silence falls between us, the cold night wind swooping right through the space between us. Instinctively, I reach for her, and for a second, she lets me. "What if you regret not going back to school?"

My arms were around her, but the moment pops like soap bubbles, and Claire's entire body stiffens. She moves away from me.

"I'm never going to regret that," she says firmly. "But you know what I regret?"

I shake my head.

"Being hours away when my dad thought he may only have weeks to live, or when he had an eighty percent chance of dying on the operating table," she says. "And then he almost died again, and you know where I was?"

My stomach knots, not just from seeing more tears fall from her eyes but because I know where this is going.

"I was drunk and making out with you in the storeroom!" And the look she gives me is one of pure regret. It hits harder than I expect.

I try to keep my voice steady when I speak. "Claire, don't do this. Don't push me away again."

We are so past this. I know we are.

"I just think we should talk about this," I add as gently as possible. She's too far away. Too ready to flee.

"Like when I wanted to talk about your dad?" Claire points out, one eyebrow shooting up.

"This isn't the same."

"You asked me to back off, and I did," she says. "So I'm asking you to do the same."

I'm about to concede and just go along with it for the present, but my hesitation speaks loud enough for Claire to hear. And a minute later, when her uncle drives past us in the tow truck and stops to check on Claire, she asks for a ride to the bar and then hops in the truck, not even giving me another glance.

I stare at the taillights of the tow trunk until they're out of sight. I think I'm beginning to understand that guilt thing Claire's feeling. And I'm always going to wonder if she'd be better off not here. What happens next year when I'm deciding about colleges? Will I feel guilty every time I think about the possibility of leaving just because Claire is still here? My mom's van is now a whole block away, and while I'm walking back to it, I get a text from Claire.

CLAIRE: *I'm not pushing u away. Not if u let this go, ok? Just let it go and we'll be fine*

My thumbs hovers over the keypad on my phone, preparing to give her the reply she wants, but again, I hesitate.

And standing right there in the middle of the icy road, I can see her. Climbing behind the wheel, the tiny trunk and backseat loaded with boxes. Claire driving away. Out of Juniper Falls. My gut twists just at the idea of her leaving, of us not being…us. But still, it doesn't feel wrong. Quite the opposite. Maybe if she's strong enough to leave again, if I'm strong enough to let her go, we'll be okay. It's not the craziest plan ever. People do it.

I stare at my phone again. I'm gonna have to be the strong one first. I swallow the lump in my throat and tuck the phone back into my pocket without replying.

Chapter 44

−TATE−

C laire has stubbornly kept her word and not talked to me for days. I'm trying to do the same, be as firm as she is, but I'm close to caving. I would do anything she wanted me to if we could just talk about all of this. Maybe her parents have succeeded in getting through to her and she hasn't had a chance to tell me yet. But I doubt this is true.

Maybe avoiding me is yet another method of Claire punishing herself. But I still don't understand it. Why is she punishing herself? Because she's healthy and her dad isn't? Or maybe it's like a temptation…she's afraid if she gets a tiny dose of happiness, she'll want more and more and eventually decide her responsibility to her family isn't as important. Jody spit out a bunch of psychobabble to me on the phone last night that was way over my head. The only phrase I caught was "survivor's guilt." But I thought that only happened when someone died. I don't know.

All I *do* know is a week apart and I'm trying not to go

crazy from missing her. And trying to study everything I can relating to Sections coming up. Mike has been helping me this last week. He told me to watch the game tapes from last year's Sections.

I pause the tape and then get my notebook and pencil ready to keep count.

After only a couple of minutes of watching on my laptop in the school library, something catches my attention. I back up forty-five seconds and watch the play again.

"What are you doing, Steller?" I mutter to myself. He's left a hole wide open. This can't be what Mike wanted me to see.

The opposition takes a shot, and it isn't Steller who makes the save, it's Hammond. His stick pushes forward, protecting our goal at the very last possible second.

I hit play again. Engrossed, I watch the entire first period of the game, rewinding several times. I've got a tally sheet, counting any goalie errors. Knowing very well what Bakowski considers a goalie error, I've calculated thirteen in the first period alone.

The most I've had in any single game period this season is nine.

I lean back in my chair, mulling this over. I'm better than he was last season. But I'm not better than he would have been this season. I know there's still next year, but I'm not looking forward to the possibility of screwing up Sections for the sake of a learning experience. I need to be Mike Steller right now. This year. Today.

The bell rings, signaling the end of the school day, and I'm forced to abandon the tapes and head to the gym for a make-up health test—I've been out with a stomach virus for two days.

"Take your exam over to the bleachers," Mrs. Seville says after I've seated myself comfortably in the gym, leaning against a mat-covered wall. "We've got cheer practice starting in a minute."

Ten minutes into my exam, the cheerleaders have rolled out mats that cover more than half the gym floor, and Cole Clooney is now beside me with a test of his own.

"Stomach flu?" I ask him, and he nods. "Are you doing health, too?"

"No," he says. "Badminton."

I go back to my sex-ed questions until the loud music distracts me. Cole looks up, too, his forehead wrinkling, then his gaze zooms in on Haley, who has just done a complicated series of flips and is now front-and-center, shaking her ass in a pair of those super-tiny shorts. Cole's jaw goes slack, and I snort back a laugh.

The laughing catches me off guard, and then I'm hit with that wave of regret all over again. Claire would get a kick out of this Cole story. Maybe being without her to prove a point isn't worth it.

"Uh-oh," I hear from below us. Jamie has just walked into the gym and probably taken in Cole and his one-sided staring contest with Haley. "You should shift your attention up higher, little man."

Mrs. Seville cuts off the music just as Jamie is saying this, and all the girls stop and look this way, a few of them laughing.

Cole turns bright red and ducks his head, the pencil in his hand moving at lightning speed. Jamie climbs up toward us but sits two rows down. "You guys ready to head over to the rink?"

We've got an hour before practice, but usually I would be over there, grabbing a snack and hanging out. "Gotta finish this test first."

"Bummer," he says, but he stays seated.

"Girls, you are not listening to the counts!" Mrs. Seville

yells. "Everyone except Haley and Leslie is off."

She makes Haley demonstrate the little dance sequence in front, and I catch Cole looking up at her again. Jamie tosses me a glance, his eyebrows lifted. "Little dude's got a crush."

Cole shakes his head and looks down again. Then he glances at me and says, "I don't. I swear."

I lift my hands. "Doesn't matter to me either way."

The music blares again, and I whip through the rest of my test just to escape it as soon as possible. On my way out of the gym, I walk past the far side of the cheerleaders' mats in time to see Haley land with her ankle turned. I'm right beside her, so I don't miss the pain on her face. But she finishes the routine and zips in front of me, heading for the drinking fountain in the hallway. The second she's away from everyone, her walk turns to a limp.

I follow her over to the drinking fountain. "You okay?"

"Go away, Tate." She leans over and takes a long drink.

"I saw you twist your ankle." I lean against the wall beside her, waiting for her to straighten up and look at me. "You can't hate me forever, you know."

Haley stands up, turning to face me. "I never said I hated you."

"You don't?" I ask. "You look pissed. Like, even right now you look pissed while saying that you don't hate me."

"I am pissed." Haley drops her arms to her side, the movement contradicting her words. "You're so different now, Tate. You're so different with Claire. But I think maybe you're not different, you just didn't trust me enough to let me really know you."

"That's not true—" I protest.

But she lifts a hand to shut me up. "It is true. And it sucks because I didn't hide any parts of me from you. I put everything out there."

She chokes up and then stops abruptly, probably not wanting to fall apart. I lean my head against the wall. She's right. I know she's right. I've known it all along. I never had to pretend with Claire. "You're right. But I didn't know I was doing that; I just knew I couldn't do it anymore." I close my eyes and take a breath. "Give me some time and…we'll talk, okay?"

"Okay." Her voice breaks again, and I open my eyes just in time to catch Haley swiping away a few tears. Both of us glance around, making sure we're still alone in the hall. "I don't know how to be me. Like me without you. I get that it's over, I just don't know how to…"

I reach for her and let her rest her head against me. Haley is so tiny, her forehead is level with my heart. "You'll figure it out. Think about it. Do you really want to be one of those forty-year-old women who wakes up suddenly and realizes she doesn't have an identity of her own?" I press my face against her hair and whisper something I should have told her so many times. "You are so much more than that, Haley."

And so is Claire. This is why I'm suffering without her.

Haley pulls away and gives the hallway another check. I take the hint and turn to walk in the other direction.

I head over to the ice rink, my laptop in tow so I can watch more game tapes before practice starts. When I pass by Coach's office, Leo walks out. The door is still cracked open, and I can clearly see my dad seated in one of the chairs across from Bakowski's desk. Leo grabs me by the arm and steers me toward an empty corner of the lobby.

"Look, I didn't tell Bakowski anything," he says right away.

"About what?" My gaze flits to the now-closed office door, then back to Leo's face. "You mean my visit in December?"

Already my heart is racing.

Leo's forehead wrinkles. "No, of course I didn't say

anything about that. I mean about what Claire—"

He stops abruptly, probably realizing I have no idea what he's talking about. Then after another glance back at the still-closed office door, he lowers his voice and tells me about a conversation Claire overheard two weeks ago.

My entire body tenses, the anger building inside me to a point so high that when Dad emerges from Bakowski's office—despite Leo's protesting—I take off after him. He glances over his shoulder, sees me, and then stops. I nod for him to follow and head all the way to the far side of the rink. The place where he most likely made that phone call Claire overheard during the game.

Once we're alone, I spin to face him. "I know you tried to blackmail Leo and Jamie."

"Whoa." He holds up his hands, the charming Keith Tanley smile on his face. "What are you talking about, buddy?"

I can't remember the last time my dad called me "buddy." That one word hits me hard. It's so phony. He doesn't care about me. And that means he definitely doesn't care about my teammates. "I'm talking about you trying to ruin their eligibility."

I'm on fire now. Too much is pent up inside me to keep things in control. If I could go one-on-one with him on the ice right now, his ass would be dead.

The careful front drops from Dad's face. And he's the drunk man in the parking lot again, dragging me toward his truck. Instinctively, I take a step back.

"Don't meddle in the grown-up stuff, Tate," Dad says in his most condescending voice. "You have no idea what you're dealing with."

"I know you're cheating." I fold my arms across my chest and glare at him. "What more do I need to know than that? I could tell—"

"Go ahead." Dad steps closer to me, lowers his voice. "But don't forget you've been doing a little cheating yourself. Coach Redeck has been training you, hasn't he? He's got you playing with the boys on his team. And I think someone spotted you having dinner with that coach from Southeastern Minneapolis University. Did he pay for the meal?"

My jaw drops, the anger falls from me in one second flat, and it's replaced by panic and…well, hurt. "Why would you…?"

He looks me over, a hint of regret in his eyes. "I'm not gonna do anything like that. Just keep your mouth shut and plan on signing with Southeastern Minneapolis College next November."

I'm so fucking tired of not saying anything, not doing anything. I shake my head. "No… No way."

"SMC is a great school," Dad argues. "You're getting a full ride with my being on staff and your playing hockey. Coach Redeck is practically foaming at the mouth to get you and Hammond signed. Especially with Jamie and Leo turning us down."

"Hammond?" Shit. It's not going to end. I exhale, feeling like I'm backed into the smallest corner possible. I look up at my dad. Maybe he's right, SMC is probably a good school, and I won't have to worry about paying for it. Jody had to jump through dozens of hoops to get enough scholarships to cover her tuition. The essays alone were weeks of work. And she's already taken out student loans, too. Based on what my dad is telling me, I won't have to do any of this. But I don't want it like this. I want it to be my own. Hockey. College, if I decide to go. I can't keep playing if it's not my own.

I can't keep playing.

What if I don't play? If he knows I'm not bluffing about him backing off… I'm stuck with his reputation in town; I've been stuck with it my whole life. The son of the Great Keith Tanley. All those words. All those false words. And I just sat there and let them happen. My win is always his win, too. That needs to end.

"You know what?" I tell him. "No one can sign me if I'm not playing."

He opens his mouth to protest, but I step around him and head straight for the locker. And yes, I realize I'm taking a note from Steller, but this will be different. Game one of Sections isn't until tomorrow night. We're the number-one seed, which means we play the worst team.

It'll be fine.

But I have to wait. Hold off until the last minute to tell Coach I'm not playing. Otherwise Jamie and Leo will talk me out of it.

I'm positive that this is the only way to stop my dad and his manipulation. It's the only way to make hockey mine again. Maybe the only way to protect my teammates.

Chapter 45

—CLAIRE—

I wipe down yet another empty table. It's like the first home game all over again. I'm dreading the aftermath, dreading the celebration. Dreading the Late Night at O'Connor's I've already agreed to host. Not that the money won't be great for us—it will. I hate the wall between Tate and me. It seems to have created this barrier between the hockey team and me. Guess I can't have one without the other.

I sigh to myself and drop the wet rag into a bucket of soapy water. Soon my family and Tate will both realize that I'm here to stay. And maybe we can go back to being us. Forgiving Tate, loving him, is not the problem. The problem is getting him to let go of this responsibility he seems to have put on himself.

But then again, maybe it won't be the same. If we were together again. Maybe there's too much between us now.

I can't begin to worry about this, because the door to the bar opens and my dad walks through it.

For the first time in months. For a moment, every worry, every doubt, and bit of tension between us falls away. And I just stand there, stunned to see him in this place again. In his place.

The wet rag dangling in my hand drips water onto the floor, but I don't move. Dad heads in my direction, his weak side lagging behind the other. He grabs a dry towel from the bar and drops it onto the floor where water now forms a puddle. He uses his shoe to push the towel along the floor, drying it. I get a flash of Dad doing this the night before I left for college when a glass of water tipped over while he was busing a table. He takes the wet rag from me and motions for us to sit down at a table.

I can't believe he's here. He's refused to come in for so long, part of me believed it would be forever.

A tiny notepad emerges from his back pocket along with a pen. He flips to a page, revealing words he's already written: Not ANGRY.

I glance up at him, my throat already tight from the sight of him seated at a table. This is where he used to do the financials, during the down times. He preferred it to the office because it made him available in case anyone needed anything.

"You're not?" I ask.

He shakes his head, flips a page over, and reveals a new word: PROUD.

My eyes fill with tears. He turns another page, revealing an entire sentence, lots of scratching out and fixing words. It must have taken him a long time to write.

WE CAN PAY FOR SCHOOL. Got It WORKED OUT. DONE.

I shake my head, wiping away a few tears. "It's okay, Dad. I don't need it. I'm okay, I promise."

He doesn't get angry this time when I refuse. I watch as he turns another page.

I LEARNED FROM tHIS.

He tilts his head and runs a finger over the scar from his brain surgery. Then he turns another page.

MUSt. LIVE. NOW. ALWAYS.

I force a grin. Force myself to brush off the deeper meaning. "Are you a poet now?"

He nods and underlines NOW. Okay, that's not what I meant.

Not JUSt FOR YOU, his next message says. FOR ME.

I lift my head, my gaze meeting his. For him.

For him.

A new kind of guilt sweeps over me. *For him.* I take a deep breath. "But why do I have to go back so soon? What's another year?"

He flips back a few pages and underlines the word NOW again.

JUSt tHINK ABOUt It. PLEASE.

Because he's my dad. Because he's given me everything, I nod. With hand gestures and Aunt Kay's help interpreting, he ushers me out of the bar, telling me to take a break before the crowds come. I don't know how I decided what to do or where to go, but minutes later, I'm upstairs, opening the storage part of the apartment, crawling inside and hiding among boxes of my childhood.

My dad is proud of me. He's proud of me and I'm holed away in an attic, sorting through the remains of my dreams. I used to think all of this wasn't real and Juniper Falls was just my life before it got real. Now everything I wanted before, it's all just unicorns. Shiny, gratuitous unicorns.

I stumble on my old keyboard and a box of songbooks from every musical a preteen and teenager could possibly be interested in. I stare at the music and the keys long and hard before I give myself this one bit of enjoyment. Just a few minutes alone with the unicorns and then I'll go back to my real life. I plug in the keyboard and grab the *Wicked* songbook. This is one of my most worn books, and two pages are stuck together from a jelly doughnut incident while I was learning how to play "Defying Gravity." Years ago, I'd wanted to sing that one almost as much as Éponine's famous solo, "On My Own," from *Les Mis*.

"Your dad told me you were up here."

My hands freeze over the keys, my heart jumping up to my throat. Haley's blond hair swings into view from the tiny half door of the storage area. She's dressed in her cheer uniform, which means it must be close to game time. How long have I been up here?

I look at her, my eyes probably wide with surprise. "Hey…"

And oh my God, Haley is here. And she doesn't look pissed off. A little uncomfortable but not angry, at least. She ducks through the half door, coming inside to sit in the only empty place available.

"I love *Wicked*. It's my favorite musical," she says.

Okay. So far this is friendly. What's going on? Oh Jesus, surely she isn't here to confess that she and Tate—

"So…I have a proposal for you," she says. "I'm in charge of party prep and The Pizza House canceled last minute for the post-game celebration party—"

"The game is over already?" I move to get out of this little cave, but Haley holds up a hand to stop me.

"Still two hours from starting. We're playing the worst team in our Section. We'll be celebrating later." She releases a breath. "I know you've mostly handled pregame dinners and this is a little different, since we've got families plus the team, but I think O'Connor's can handle it. The boosters donated way too much money for this..." Haley rolls her eyes. "It's only game one of Sections. But if we have to hand it over to anyone, I want it to be O'Connor's."

"Haley, I'm sorry. I didn't mean—"

She stops me again and shakes her head. "This year has been really hard for me so far and honestly, when we were working on the music committee together..." She takes a breath and closes her eyes for a second. "I really needed that. I liked it. Can we just go back to that?"

I release a short laugh, relieved. "Yeah. We can."

"I know you didn't plan on stuff happening with Tate," she admits, forcing his name out with great effort. "I know you wouldn't have done it if you thought things might not be over. That's kind of how I figured it out. That things were over. That's why it was so hard for me."

"I'm sorry." I don't know what else to say.

"It's okay." She shakes her head. "Well, it will be. Eventually. I'm working on it. I think I have a lot of things to work on."

Silence falls between us, and then I remember what she came up here for. "Oh, the party. Yes, that would be awesome to host it. Just tell me what to prepare. Lots of chicken wings, I'm assuming?"

"I've got a list right here." Haley pulls a folded piece of paper from her purse and holds it out for me. "I guess there is a tiny possibility of us losing this game with Tate not playing."

I turn around so fast I knock over the keyboard. "Wait... what? Why isn't Tate playing?"

"You didn't hear?" I shake my head. Haley mimics the motion like she's trying to believe it herself. "He quit the team. Just, like, an hour ago. For personal reasons, apparently."

She stares at me, staying silent, probably looking confused as hell because that's how I feel, and says, "Do you know why he quit?"

Um…no freakin' idea.

Chapter 46

–TATE–

"We were told by Bakowski that Tanley's out with the flu, but rumor is, he's turned in his jersey."

I pace back and forth in the tiny walking space available in Roger's cabin. Yes, I'm torturing myself by listening to the game on the radio. Yes, I'm hiding out. If I don't hide, I'll end up at the ice rink, back in my uniform. And I knew Dad wouldn't find me here.

"This isn't good for the Otters, but surely, as the number-one seed in the section, they can hold their own against the last-place team."

God, I hope so. Losing this game would be a historical level of humiliation for our team and town. My phone is shut off for now. It's been blowing up all afternoon. I don't know what my mom is thinking. I don't know if she's looking for me. Most likely, she's heard that I'm not at the game. Even if she's still at work, someone's told her by now.

The radio continues to dictate the game play-by-play,

telling me everything I'm missing. The team—my team—is more a part of me than I realized. I just haven't ever had to give it up.

"Oh no! The Otters let a goal through…they should be pushing for a shutout against a team seeded last."

And to think, I didn't even want to go in during that first home game. No, that's not true. I was afraid to go in. But I wanted to. I've always wanted to play.

During a break between periods, I go outside and sweep snow from the ice until my hands and feet are completely numb. I have to move; I have to do something with this pent-up energy.

Finally, near the end of the third period, I turn my phone back on. I skim through the many texts, but I only read one person's message: Claire.

Just seeing her name on my screen does something to me.

CLAIRE: *don't let him take this from u.*

Is that what I'm doing? Am I handing over something I love because my dad owns part of it? I guess that's true, but he needs to know I'm making my own decisions. Now that I've shown him, I need to find him and make sure the message is received.

Chapter 47

—CLAIRE—

I made the mistake of telling Haley about my dad pushing for me to register for spring quarter. She keeps looking at me from across the dining room, and I can tell she's forming her persuasive arguments in her head.

But right now, all I can think about is Tate. Where is he? How is he doing? This stuff with his dad has gone too far. He needs to talk to someone. Besides me. More than me. Maybe I need to take a note from my dad. Maybe I can lead by example, face my own obstacles with the hope that it will drive Tate to do the same. That's what Dad had done earlier by coming in here. He was trying to show me that things are getting better. That he's getting better. That maybe I don't have to handle as much.

I shove that thought aside and focus on bringing out more orders of chicken wings and cheese sticks to the long tables of varsity hockey players and their families, plus most of the alumni guys—including Luke Pratt. And unfortunately, Luke has brought some of his scummy friends with him. Even when I still had a crush on him, I'd hated his friends.

After I drop off the food, when I'm leaning against the bar, Jamie and Leo corner me.

"Where is he?" Leo demands.

Jamie nods toward a table where Roger and Tate's mom have just sat down. "They're freaking out over there. His mom thought we would know; we thought she would know. What the fuck is going on?"

My heart races. Where is he? Why don't his best friends know anything?

My dad sees us huddled near the bar and glances my way. He looks concerned, but he doesn't move to get up from the table near the back where he's rolling silverware one-handed. I still can't believe he stuck around for the big crowd. He must really want me to think he's okay. My mom and Aunt Kay keep making excuses to check on him. We're all on pins and needles having him here again. But he does look stronger today. Every week he's away from chemo he'll get stronger. That's what his doctor told us.

"Claire!" Leo repeats, jolting me back to our little huddle. "Where is he?"

"I don't know," I admit reluctantly. "We haven't…we haven't been talking."

"We can't play the next game without him." Jamie leans over and bangs his head against the bar counter. He stands upright and looks at Leo. "If we were T-Man, where would we go?"

Leo looks at me. "This is about his dad, isn't it? What's the deal with that?"

I shake my head, still loyal to Tate despite every ounce of me protesting.

"Come on, I know something happened. He flipped out

right after I told him about the eligibility stuff," Leo says.

The guys at Luke Pratt's table are glancing around like they're looking for someone to bring them something. I push past Jamie and Leo. "I gotta work."

When I pass by one of Luke's friends I don't recognize from our school, he sets a hand on my waist and flashes me a big grin. "Look at you, right at my service…"

I move away from him and walk around to the other side before taking their drink orders. My phone vibrates inside my apron. I pull it out just enough to read the name on the screen: *Tate*.

I ditch Luke's table mid-order, walk far enough away from them before answering the call, my voice barely above a whisper.

"Where the hell are you?"

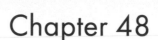

Chapter 48

−TATE−

He was just outside of town when I caught up to him. Both of us had pulled into a gas station and got out of our cars. He almost looked like he'd expected this encounter from me when I first saw him.

"Is this what you wanted?" My dad lifts his hands. He's standing in front of me now. "To humiliate me? Job well done, Tate."

"It's not about you." Rage built up from months—no, years—of holding it in, putting on the brave, happy face, is bubbling to the surface. I'm losing control. I need to find my way out of this so I can say what I need to. "In fact, I don't need anything from you. I'll find another way into college if that's what I want. I love hockey, but I'll give it up in a heartbeat if it means keeping you from manipulating my teammates and me."

"You have no idea what it's like in the real world," he snaps. "Juniper Falls is an alternate reality where boys like you are made to believe you're special. Well, I can tell you right now, you're not special. If you don't want it badly enough, if you aren't willing to do what needs to be done, then you'll never make it anywhere with hockey."

"Fine." I shrug. "Then I won't. You mess with Jamie and Leo again or try to drag me into some illegal coaching session, I'm gonna turn you in to someone."

He folds his arms over his chest and smirks at me. "You make it sound so easy. Just wait until you're right there, ready to show any disloyalty to your team or your town—you won't go through with it. Why do you think we keep secrets so well around here? You're damaging more than just my reputation."

That message hits harder than I want it to. Still, I wave a hand, already ready to leave. "Whatever. You heard me. We're done here."

I delivered the message. He's unsure enough about what I might do that he'll back off. I get in the van and head down the two-lane highway. After a minute or two of driving, I'm reaching for my phone and calling Claire.

"Where the hell are you?" she says in a hushed voice the second she answers.

I give her a brief recap of the conversation with my dad. I don't know if she and I are okay, but I do know now that we can do this—disagree and still be there for each other. "Tell my mom and the guys I'm on my way there."

"Yeah, sure." She exhales and then her voice turns to its normal volume. She must have gone in the office or somewhere away from everyone. "This is messed up. Your dad, what he's doing."

"I'm handling it—I handled it," I say. "I called him out on his bullshit. This is what you wanted, right?"

Even saying the words to Claire, I'm aware of this ball of ugly building in the pit of my stomach.

Why do you think we keep secrets so well around here?

"You handled it alone. Again." Claire's tone is gentle, but it might as well be a slap in the face. "These feelings you're having, they don't just vanish because you stood up to your dad. If Stewart or Ron messed with you right now, you wouldn't pick a fight with them?"

I did something big today. It's a step in the right direction. Why can't she see that?

I want to play in game two of Sections; I want a shutout and another shutout in game three. I want to play at State for the first time. I hope to God Bakowski lets me back after I pissed him off by turning in my uniform today. But he told people I was out with the flu, so he must have held out hope I'd be back. That's a good sign.

Claire sighs on the other end of the phone. "Tate, you can't keep doing this. Making excuses not to tell anyone."

"I promise you, I'm okay." The words come out snappier than I'd meant them to. This leads to an abrupt end to our conversation.

But while I'm driving down the dark two-lane highway, I can't help thinking, if I'm okay, why do I still feel on the verge of snapping?

Chapter 49

−CLAIRE−

Tate's mom and Roger seem like they want to ask me a dozen more questions and so do Jamie and Leo, but I tell them Tate's on his way. I hate this feeling. Knowing he's not okay and knowing he thinks he is. Despite Tate's big show of action today, there's no way Keith is done doing his damage to Tate and the team.

The crowds in the dining room, coupled with all the stress from today, has me volunteering to take the garbage out a little while later, just to get some air. I make it all the way to the Dumpsters in the back alley alone, but as soon as I finish tossing the bags in, I hear footsteps behind me. I sigh and rest my face in my hands.

"Who is it? Jamie or Leo?"

"Neither," a deep, scratchy voice says. One I heard minutes ago at the table with Luke Pratt's friends.

The hair stands up on the back of my neck. I spin around fast and gasp when I'm practically nose-to-nose with a guy who I thought left right after my phone call with Tate. I saw him head out the door. He never opened a tab, so I don't even know his name.

His breath smells like beer; his clothes reek of dead fish. Luke apparently has made some fisherman friends who like to corner girls in a dark alley.

This is like a scene straight out of a horror movie.

Don't panic.

Statistically, there's a 95 percent chance that he's here to tease, maybe flirt inappropriately, but not the ax murdering, body dismembering I'm imagining. I've never even heard of anyone being intentionally dismembered in Juniper Falls. Ever.

I force a grin, my legs already shaking. "Oops, sorry, I thought you were someone—"

A hand claps over my mouth and my back slams into the Dumpster before I can even think about stepping around the guy or running.

Oh God. Not good. My heart pounds, my brain unable to form a plan, to remember any fucking thing from that ridiculous self-defense class my mom made me take before I left for college. Only now I'm thinking it wasn't so ridiculous.

Grab the hand that grabs you.

I tug on his pinkie finger and manage to lift his hand an inch off my mouth, exhale a short-lived scream, before he presses it down again, harder this time.

Step on his foot. Do it now!

I lift my black boot and smash it onto the guy's foot as hard as I can. His face twists and he lets out a yelp. I push him away with my free hand and take off. I make it two steps before the hand is over my mouth again. His arms hug me tight from behind, binding my own arms to my sides.

Oh God. This can't be happening. Think, Claire. Think.

"I'm not going to hurt you," he breathes into my ear. "But

I am sick of you ignoring me and shaking your ass in front of me all the time. I at least deserve a minute alone with you."

"What the fuck!" I hear someone say.

I don't bother squinting into the dark to see who it is. The voice has created a distraction. The guy turns his head, his grip loosening. I free my elbow and jab him hard in the groin. He grunts before releasing me. I take off running.

I smack into Leo, my entire body in panic mode. And then I see Tate flying past me, his eyes blazing.

Leo grips my arm and leans down. "Are you hurt?"

My mouth falls open, the words lodged in my throat, when a beer bottle smashes against the pavement. Even from twenty feet away, I see Tate's body stiffen and then, before the dude can run away, he's launching himself at him.

I can't fight this off. Can't fight the flashback to last fall in this very same spot. If I can't shake it, what's happening to Tate? Especially after—

"Claire!" Leo yells at me. "Are you hurt?"

I shake my head. I'm not hurt. Except something warm and sticky is trickling down my lip. Leo releases me and sprints after Tate.

"Get help!" he calls over his shoulder.

My brain is all screwed up, and for a moment, I can't move. Tate smashes his fist into the guy's face and then gets him down on the ground.

Fumbling in my apron, I get my phone and start to call 911, then stupidly realize that the sheriff is inside right now, enjoying the free appetizers at the hockey party. I drop my phone on the pavement and sprint toward the doors. I don't even have to go inside; Roger is already outside, looking around for Tate, I assume.

His eyes go wide when he sees me, and all he has to do is make one motion through the window and Sheriff Hammond is out here, sprinting ahead of us in the cold.

Chapter 50

—TATE—

I can't see anything but red. I ram my fist into the asshole's face again. Maybe the red is his blood. I don't fucking care.

"You are so fucking dead." I lay a punch into his stomach and he curls up and groans. Red is smeared all over my fist. Maybe his nose is bleeding? I don't fucking care.

"Okay, kid. Give it a rest," Sheriff Hammond says, but I don't listen.

It takes both Leo and Roger to pull me off the guy, and even with both of them holding my arms, with Roger's arm wrapped across my chest, preventing forward movement, I still manage to kick the sick bastard hard in the balls.

Sheriff Hammond takes my place, tackling the guy, but less aggressively than I had. Maybe because he's no longer moving. Good. Fucking good.

Sheriff Hammond cuffs him and then presses two fingers to his neck.

Why does this feel like my fault? I can't think right now,

can't process the information properly to get an answer, but somewhere inside my head, I know it's my fault.

The guy attempts to roll over, his eyes focusing on me. The beer bottle smashes against the pavement over and over again inside my head.

"Hey... Hey!" Sheriff Hammond says when I succeed in breaking away from both Roger and Leo.

I get another kick in and then sink down, ready to tackle the guy again. He shouldn't be awake. He shouldn't be able to see straight.

"Tate!" My mom's voice rings from somewhere nearby.

Then Jamie jumps in front of me, blocking my way. He's bigger than Leo and harder to get around. Before I can figure it out, Roger is holding me back again, along with Leo.

"Tate, stop!" My mom has moved closer; she's tugging on my arm.

Sheriff Hammond looks up at Claire, his foot still pressed on the asshole's back. "What happened?"

I relax for a second and stop fighting Roger and Leo. Claire is standing between both her parents. She's shaking, her teeth chattering. My heart lurches.

"He...he..." She swallows and then forces out the words clearly. "He grabbed me by the Dumpster. He covered my mouth, and when I got away, he grabbed me again from behind. Tate and Leo came out and they distracted him and I...I elbowed him and ran."

He touched her. He fucking touched her.

Fury spills over again. I tear away from the guys holding me back, but they stop me again. From the corner of my eye, I see Davin O'Connor attempt to break away from his daughter and wife and head toward the bastard on the ground.

Claire grabs his arm. "Dad, no!"

I'm breathing so hard that spots are forming in front of

my eyes. The anger won't fade. I have to do something.

A squad car pulls up in the parking lot, blocking the scene from others who have spilled out of the bar. Two male cops tell everyone to stay back. Another squad car comes barreling through and a female cop gets out and stands beside the sheriff.

The dude on the ground turns his head again, and I swear to God he sneers at me. I kick and twist, trying to break free.

Leo and Jamie both shove me hard and keep pushing until I'm seated on the bottom step of the staircase leading up to the apartment above the bar.

Sheriff Hammond pulls the dude to his feet and looks over at me. "Relax, kid, justice will be served. I promise."

I try to stand, but Roger shoves me down again. "Forget justice. Toss him back onto the ground and get out of here. I'll take care of him."

"Tate, enough!"

I glance at my mom for a split second and do a double take. Her eyes are wide, hands covering her mouth. She looks absolutely petrified. Of me.

My stomach sinks, a sick feeling washing over me. I let my eyes glaze over and watch everything move in front of me in a blur. Leo squats down and stares at me. "T-Man, shake out of this. It's okay."

"Talk to me, man," Jamie says, moving beside Leo. "You okay? Did you get hit?"

I don't know. I don't remember. My hands are shaking. It's freezing out here. Snow is underneath my butt. Jamie reaches a hand toward me, like he's about to lay it on my shoulder. Some buried instinct causes me to scoot back, away from him. Away from anyone's touch. What the hell did I just do?

I can't look at Claire. What if she's scared of me like my mom is? I'll never be able to erase that image. I push up to my feet, and before Jamie and Leo can shove me back down again, I turn the other way. "Just…" I can hardly talk without getting winded, without feeling this crushing weight on my chest. "Just give me a minute, okay?"

I act like I'm gonna walk around the building, but I take off in a jog toward home. I'll go the back way, off the street. I don't trust myself to stay here and not do anything else wrong. I need to reset or something.

Chapter 51

-CLAIRE-

I break away from Mom the second the squad car disappears with that asshole locked up in the back. I'm looking around everywhere. The parking lot is crowded with nearly everyone who was inside the bar. For a second, I catch Luke Pratt's eye from a distance. He's standing still, his mouth hanging open in shock. *Yeah, that's right. Make new friends, buddy.* I can't think about him or anything related to him at the moment. But I do hear him tell someone nearby, "I don't even know that guy. I don't even know his last name. We just started working together."

I shake my head and force his voice to fade into the loud chatter happening in the parking lot right now. My dad is shaking, his face twisted with rage. I grab his arms. "Dad, you have to go back inside. You need to sit down." I glance over at my mom. She's got that look like she needs to hold on to me again, just in case. "Mom, I'm okay. Bring him inside, please?"

She takes a sharp breath and nods. Then Dad puts an arm

around her shoulders and they both lean in to each other while walking toward the doors. I move quickly, looking some more. I spot Jamie and Leo talking in low voices.

"Where's Tate?" I ask.

Jamie runs around the building and Leo, after seeing me shivering, sheds his coat and puts it around my shoulders.

"He's okay," Leo reassures me.

He might be physically okay, but I need to see his face. I need him in my personal space right now. Something broke in him. I saw it with my own eyes. And God, this was a long time coming. But it shouldn't have gone down like this.

"He's gone," Jamie calls, coming back around from the other side of the building. "Maybe he went inside?"

That's unlikely, considering the crowd that's now formed near the front doors of O'Connor's. I feel around for my phone, preparing to call him, but it's not in my apron or my hand. Leo is already on it, his phone pressed to his ear. He waits for a minute and then shakes his head.

Tate's mom moves beside Roger, whispering something. And then she walks toward me. "I'm so sorry, Claire. I don't know…I don't know what that was…"

I shake my head and zip up Leo's letter jacket. "I saw that guy earlier. He did the usual teasing, but nothing—"

"I mean Tate," she says, tears bubbling in her voice. "I've never seen him like that. I don't know where it came from."

My eyes meet hers. I try to make my voice firm and assertive even though she's the adult. "He was protecting me."

"I know." Her head bobs up and down, but her tone contradicts the movement. She's not sure. "Of course he was."

"We need to find him," I tell her. I'm starting to panic. "He's scared and…well, I don't know what else he is, but he shouldn't be alone."

"She's right," Leo says from beside me.

"He wouldn't let us near him," Jamie adds. "He just kept backing away."

"Maybe it's best if we let him cool off for a little while," Tate's mom says. "I can take Olivia to your mom's house," she tells Roger.

"If you want." Roger turns to Jamie and Leo. "Let's go find him."

I jump right behind them. "I'm going with you."

Roger shakes his head. "Your dad will pummel me. You need to warm up. Get inside and I'll call you as soon as we find him, okay?"

I open my mouth to protest, but Haley appears in front of me, holding out my phone. "Found this in the parking lot."

I'm dialing Tate before I even have a chance to thank her. It goes straight to voicemail. Dammit.

"Tate's gone," I tell Haley.

She gets her arms around me, and suddenly I'm craving the human contact. I rest my head on her shoulder.

"My lip is throbbing. Does it look really big and fat?"

Haley laughs, but her voice is nearly as shaky as mine. "Can we go upstairs? We can get you cleaned off."

"Yeah, sure."

Sheriff Hammond must have heard Haley mention going upstairs because he nods his agreement and says, "I'll come up in fifteen minutes and get your statement, all right?"

"All right." I'm not looking forward to repeating the whole event. It was hard enough the first time.

I lead Haley upstairs, and she goes into the bathroom to get something to wash off my hands. My stomach drops, remembering what Jamie and Leo said about Tate not wanting them to get close. "Where do you think he is?"

"I don't know." Haley appears with a wet washcloth. "He was pretty upset?"

"I'm not sure what he was." I sink down onto the bed, my worry growing by the second. "Whatever he is, he needs someone."

"I know it must have been awful to see Tate in a fight like that…but his mom was so…" Haley shakes her head. "Weird. Not together. I don't get it. It's like she was upset with him."

I avoid her eyes, but she catches on quick. "What, Claire? Why did she react like that?"

"This is just a guess, but I think maybe she was making an association between Tate and her ex-husband."

If Haley is shocked, she does a good job of hiding it. "Tate's dad got in fights?"

"Honestly, I don't know." He got in fights with Tate. That much I do know. And once with Tate and me. I glance at my phone, willing it to ring. Willing Roger to tell me he found Tate. "But I've seen Tate's dad angry before. Seen him violent."

"Because you were friends with Jody?"

I shake my head. "No, she doesn't really know that stuff. It's kind of been a secret between Tate and me for a while now."

"A while?" Haley lifts an eyebrow. "You mean while he's been in town recently? To watch the games?"

I look down at my hands. "I mean since right before I left for Northwestern."

It feels so weird to finally say it out loud. Not that I really gave specifics, but God, it was something at least. It's time.

Haley hands me the washcloth and sinks into the spot beside me. "That's what he was going to tell me. He said—"

"Wait." I spin to face her. "He said he was going to tell you that?"

"Well, no." Her forehead wrinkles. "He said he knew that he hadn't trusted me with really getting to know him and that he wanted to trust me now. As friends," she adds quickly, concern filling her face. "But he needed some time."

My heart breaks all over again. He's really trying. He's trying to be ready to do this. He got what I said. That he can't wait any longer. He has to do this now—

Oh man… I cover my face and groan.

"What?" Haley jumps. "What's wrong?"

I lift my head and look at her. "Just what my dad said today…you know, the *do it now* speech."

"Yes," Haley says, nodding. She's obviously wanted to push me on this since I spilled about this afternoon.

I get up from the bed and start pacing. I'm so completely scared. Scared of where Tate is. Mentally more so than physically. I can't focus on this too much.

There's a knock on the door, and then my mom enters with Sheriff Hammond.

"Where's Dad?" I ask.

Mom's face fills with concern. "He insisted on walking home. Wouldn't let me talk him out of it."

My panic rises several notches. "He walked home?"

"Ned is going to follow him. He'll be fine," Mom reassures, moving closer to touch my hair. "He's very upset. He wants to be able to protect you, and he can't now. Not like he could have before. But he needs to accept reality. That isn't something we can help him through."

My heart sinks again. Just when Dad was able to find peace with everything, he's shaken up again with what he can't do. Those feelings can be more crippling than the actual physical limitations he's been forced into.

Haley stands up and looks between Sheriff Hammond and me. "Do you want me to go?"

"No," I say right away. And I mean it. I want her here.

"Okay." She flashes me a smile and returns to sitting on the bed.

In my hand, my phone vibrates. My heart jumps up to my throat.

ROGER: *found him. He's ok. Give us a few minutes, ok?*

I sigh with relief. Then I look at Sheriff Hammond. "Let's get this over with."

Chapter 52

—TATE—

When Roger walks into the garage, my whole body is shaking, my stomach flipping over and over. I'm not sure if I'm about to puke or pass out. Sweat trickles down my neck and back. I sit on the floor and lean against the back shelf.

Roger rests a hand on my shoulder, and I have that instinct to pull away again, but I'm too sick and dizzy to move. "I'm sorry," I say.

He squats down in front of me, looking me over. "What for?"

I shake my head. "I don't know—everything. I don't know if…" My face drops into my hands. "Claire told me I wasn't okay. I should have listened to her—I don't know if I would have stopped. If you and Leo hadn't been there."

The sickness increases, but it feels like I just coughed out a piece of that toxic part of me buried inside. It's ugly in there. It's a hole I want to seal off for good. But I'm not sure

I can. Especially knowing that it's been festering inside me for so long.

I pull in a sharp breath, needing to release more. "I think…I think I would have killed him. I wanted to so badly. I was completely blind. I couldn't see two seconds in front of me. I didn't care. It was just now. Now."

Finally, I brave looking up at Roger. His face is full of concern.

"That's why my mom looked so freaked out, isn't it? She's afraid of me."

"Your mom has some of her own demons to work through," Roger says quietly.

Her own demons?

"I'm turning into him." Another exhale of toxic thoughts.

"Your dad," Roger says, no question in his voice.

He knows. He sits down on the floor across from me. My gaze meets his and I'm desperate for the truth, no matter how awful it is. "You said you knew my dad in high school. Was he like me? Or am I like him?"

I lift my hand to my cheek. My face is wet, but I don't know if it's tears or sweat.

Roger leans against the shelf of tools behind him and pulls up his knees. "You know who you remind me of, Tate?"

I shake my head.

"Me in high school," Roger says. "Every time I woke up hungover after a party or lost my temper, I worried that I was turning into my dad. I had all these emotions—I'd go from scared and depressed to feeling nothing but rage, and there was nowhere to put any of these feelings."

His dad. He told Steller about him. *He wasn't nice.*

My throat constricts and I can't say anything. I wipe my eyes and look away from Roger.

"Tate." His voice is so firm, I force myself to look at him

again. "You're not a murderer. And you're not like your dad."

"I don't know." I shake my head. "I don't know anymore. I could be."

"You can tell me," Roger says. "Whatever happened between you and him, you can tell me. I promise you, it'll stay between us."

I squeeze my eyes shut and press the heels of my hands over them. Claire's right. She's been right all along. I need to do this. I can't keep living on the verge of explosion. I'm going to hurt someone. I'm going to do something even worse than tonight. Something I can't undo. "What has my mom… I mean, has she told you anything? About him?"

"She's told me bits and pieces. Most of which I've had to work very hard to extract over many months. From what I've perceived, he was verbally abusive to her. And on at least one occasion, he put your life in danger."

I lift my head, surprised. "She said that?"

"She told me he drove drunk with you in the car," Roger says.

All these years, I just thought she was mad about him drinking too much. I didn't know she had realized that my life was in danger.

"It didn't stop after they split up," I admit. "Well, not all of it."

"No?"

I'm not sure if I can do this. Once I tell him, I can never un-tell him. "How bad was it with your dad?"

Roger stares at me, maybe deciding if he's going to allow the change in subject. "Sometimes it was fine. My dad was a very smart man. I was an only child, so he put a lot of pressure on me with my grades and school. One minute I would be glowing with pride from something he said and the next I would feel worthless. That was the worst part for me. That power he held wasn't something I could take back. And he knew how to use it against me. The physical abuse was infrequent enough that no one would have suspected."

"You didn't tell anyone?" My voice is hoarse, barely audible.

"No." Roger exhales, like he's being forced back in time. I know that feeling. "He died of a heart attack when I was sixteen. And that brought on all kinds of other doubts, like maybe I was a difficult kid and he would have been easier to get along with if he'd lived long enough to watch me grow up. That maybe I missed out on the good parts."

I drag my finger across the dusty garage floor. "I might never want to talk about it again. Or tell anyone else."

Roger seems to understand what I'm asking because he nods and says, "Okay."

"Claire knows. Most of it, anyway."

He lifts an eyebrow, surprised by this, but he doesn't interrupt me.

I'm focused on my hand again, watching it shake. "Before Claire left for Northwestern, we had this party for her over by the pond. I had to leave to watch football with my dad at O'Connor's…but later, we were in the parking lot. I took his keys and he was drunk and pissed off, trying to shove me in the car. And then Claire came outside—"

His eyebrows shoot up. "Claire was there?"

"Yeah," I say, worry twisting in my stomach all over again. I force it back. I have to finish this. If I don't, I might never have the courage to.

Roger doesn't say anything for a long time. He just listens; any emotions or thoughts he might be having are carefully concealed from his face. It takes me a while to give him the details of that night and then the events that followed, including my confronting Dad tonight.

"So when I saw Claire in that parking lot, sprinting away from that dude…" My throat tightens again. I swallow the lump. "And then he picked up the beer bottle and smashed it. It was all so familiar. The dark, the cold, the same pavement, the same glass shattered everywhere." I use my sleeve to wipe my face. "And all I could think about was how I needed to keep her safe and watch out for her like she watched out for me that night. I needed to get it right."

Roger moves closer. His hands land on my arms, gripping them tight. "Look at me, Tate."

I make myself look at him.

"It's not your responsibility to keep Claire safe. It's not your fault that she got hurt."

"But why couldn't I stop?" I ask. "You told me to. Sheriff Hammond told me to. He had the guy cuffed already, and I couldn't stop."

Roger releases his hold on my arms but doesn't scoot away. "I'm not a murderous person, Tate, but if that were your mom or Olivia who got attacked tonight, I sure as hell wouldn't have stood around waiting for justice to be served. I would have beat the shit out of him. You saw Davin O'Connor, didn't you?"

Vaguely I recall the twisted rage on his face. He would have killed that guy if his muscles had worked properly. Maybe even now, if Claire hadn't held him back.

"Claire told me that she kept things from Jody because her dad would have killed mine."

"Jody doesn't know?" Roger asks.

"No." I inhale my first non-ragged breath in, like, an hour. "But Claire thinks she needs to know. That's what we fought about before New Year's. I just wanted to forget about it. I'm not afraid of him now. I hate him being around here so much now, but I don't even think he'd attempt to hurt me. It's the kind of thing you do when you want power over your kid. But now he's messing with my head about college and messing with my teammates." I study Roger's face, trying to decide if he's keeping anything from me. "Did you know already? About my dad? It just seemed like you knew—"

"It nearly killed me to stand by and watch you going through something that I knew had to do with him," Roger says, his jaw tensing. "But I didn't know any of what you just told me. It was pretty obvious to me that you and Jody had very different relationships with your father. The stuff with Bakowski threw me off a little. I thought maybe he was the one causing the problems."

"I don't understand why my mom doesn't hate him the way I do." I sniff again. "Why doesn't she have the urge to kill him? She looked more afraid of me tonight than she ever was of him."

"I'm not gonna lie to you," Roger says. "Your mom has a lot of things to work out still, but take it from someone whose mother stood by and did nothing—she probably would still be doing nothing if my dad hadn't died years ago—telling him to leave, being alone, raising two kids alone, that was very brave of her."

I finally gain the courage to ask the question I've been avoiding for too long. "What about Claire? Did you see her after I took off? Did she look like my mom?"

Roger shakes his head. "She's worried about you. She tried to come with me to look for you, but I wouldn't let her." He smiles a little. "Actually, she kind of bit your mom's head off when she apologized for you acting on your feelings."

I rest my head against the fender and close my eyes. My mom felt the need to apologize for me. That's great.

Right on cue, my mom enters the garage through the side door, Jamie and Leo trailing in behind her. And the first words to exit my mouth are, "I'm sorry."

Sitting on the floor feels too vulnerable and exposed. I'm less dizzy and sick now, so I stand up again. My mom isn't wearing the same scared-of-me look, which is something positive, at least. She assesses me and places a hand on my face.

"You look terrible...clammy and pale." She shakes her head. "What happened?"

"I'm sorry," I repeat. My throat is tightening again, my eyes burning. "I just thought...I thought he was going to hurt Claire. Like, really hurt her. And I got so..."

"Fucking pissed?" Jamie says, then he glances guiltily at my mom and mumbles an apology. "Seriously, T-Man, you should be pissed."

Mom catches sight of my bloody knuckles, and her eyes go wide. "I'm gonna get some peroxide. For your hands."

The second she leaves the garage, Jamie turns to me. "You know whose ass we need to kick right now? Fucking Luke Pratt."

"What's he doing making friends with some psycho?" Leo adds, picking up on Jamie's thoughts like they've been conspiring over the last half hour or so.

Before I can open my mouth to comment on the guy being Pratt's friend, Roger jumps in. "I think you've done enough ass-kicking for one night."

"And," my mom says in her warning voice as she returns with the peroxide, "getting a beating does not absolve someone of sexual assault. There are steps that need to be made..."

My heart flies. I look around among all of them. "Is that what happened? I mean, she said—"

"No," Leo says firmly. "She doesn't even know if he would have really hurt her. He tried to overpower her and she got away. That's it."

"I need to see Claire." I don't know who I'm talking to exactly, but someone needs to loan me a car.

"We'll take you," Jamie says.

I'm shifting back and forth the whole thirty seconds my mom is cleaning my knuckles. She looks like she wants to protest my leaving, but she must see that I'm not going to listen.

We head outside again, and before we can hop in Leo's truck, Jamie comes at me, his arms spread wide. I take a step back, eyeing him. "Dude, what are you doing?"

"I'm fucking hugging you." He doesn't stop. He keeps moving closer. Jamie gets his arms around me and gives my back a huge thump with his hand. I pat his awkwardly. Over his shoulder, I glance at Leo. He shrugs like he's as confused by this as I am.

Finally Jamie releases me. "We heard what you told Roger."

I stop, my limbs frozen. A rock sits in the pit of my stomach.

"Dude." Leo glares at Jamie.

Jamie throws up his hands. "What?" Jamie turns to me. "We were standing outside for a while before your mom got home and let us in. We didn't mean to hear. We can't just fucking pretend like we didn't. And you should know that we know."

I still can't move or speak. This isn't something I'd have told them. Probably ever.

Leo puts a hand on my chest. "Look, Jamie's right, we were waiting outside, didn't even know that you were in the garage until we heard you talking. But you know what? If you don't fucking trust us to keep your shit quiet, then we've all been wasting our time hanging out."

"Yeah." Jamie nods. "What he said."

After taking several deep breaths of ice-cold air, my limbs regain their ability to move and I've processed and accepted this piece of information. What the hell else am I supposed to do? "Okay."

"Okay," Leo repeats, dropping his hand from my chest. He leans against the truck, making it clear they have more to say. "We thought you had someone better than us to talk to. We knew you were dealing with shit, but we assumed maybe Haley…and then you weren't with her anymore."

"Then Haley told us she had the same thoughts about us," Jamie adds. "That you were keeping things from her and telling us. She went on and on about how you trusted us more than her."

"Then we figured out that you weren't talking to anyone." Leo shakes his head. "That sucks, man. We should have known. God, we fucking worshipped your dad."

"Fuck that," Jamie says, disgusted.

I'm speechless. I don't know if I should be angry, embarrassed, or thankful. I think maybe I'm a little bit of each.

"I got issues, too," Jamie says. "I make Leo sit down and listen to me bitch until I'm done."

"By bitch, he means admit his infatuation with a certain student teacher," Leo says. "And then he describes in great detail what he'd like to do with her if he could get her alone in the library or the janitor's closet."

"The library would be my preference. And this guy…" Jamie nods in Leo's direction. "He tells me all about his man-love—"

"Do not call it that." Leo shuts his eyes, clearly disturbed by Jamie's vocab.

"Think I want to listen to that shit?" Jamie says. "But I do it because he's my fucking friend. Well, not like my *fucking* friend as in the verb—but that's what we do."

I still don't know what to say, so I don't say anything.

Jamie releases a breath. "We're done with this feelings shit, right? I can't take anymore tonight."

Leo and I both laugh. Leo spreads his arms open to Jamie. "Wait, let's hug first."

Jamie shoves him, snatches the keys, and jumps into Leo's driver's seat. "Get the fuck in the back. Both of you. I fucking hug you and you fucking make fun of me."

"I think he's serious," I say.

Leo groans. "Yeah, I know."

We both climb in the back, preparing for Jamie to floor it just so we can get a little more ten-degree wind blistering our faces. While we're driving, I turn my phone back on and type a quick text to Roger.

ME: *if you want to tell my mom, you can.*

I hit send before I can chicken out.

Chapter 53

−CLAIRE−

"What's this?" Haley asks.

I look up from staring at my phone, willing it to ring. She's holding up the green flier. For the musical auditions. "Where did you get that?"

"It was laying on the floor." She glances around and then lifts my duffel bag. "I think it fell out of your bag when you got clothes out."

Earlier I gave her some sweats so she could change out of her cheer uniform, which is now hanging on the back of the door along with Leo's varsity letter jacket.

"*Les Mis*," Haley reads from the paper. "Isn't that, like, your dream musical? I remember you did that song for the talent show—"

"Did my parents put you up to this?" I ask, only half joking.

She shakes her head. And I stop her before she dives into a Catholic-girl lecture about signs. I tuck the flier back into my bag and return to my position alternating between staring at the phone and the door.

"I tried to read *Les Mis* last year," Haley says. The two minutes of silence must have gotten to her. Or she's trying to distract me from worrying. "But I only made it through a couple of chapters. The musical is way better. Tate read the book, you know? For honors English this year."

"Summer reading list, I remember." I sink onto the mattress. "Where are they? I thought Jamie and Leo were bringing him over here."

"They will," Haley says firmly. She keeps looking me over, like she's checking for signs of shock or something. "Wow, Northwestern musical auditions. That must be a big deal, huh? Like major freak-out worthy."

"Yeah, I'm sure." But honestly, it would be a breeze compared to facing tonight's drama. I cross the room and peek through the blinds for, like, the fiftieth time, hoping to see headlights.

Nothing. Not yet anyway.

I sigh and return to my spot just in time for my phone to ping. I literally dive for it, my fingers fumbling over the screen, sliding right.

MOM: your dad made it home fine. He's calmed down. Getting some hot tea and soup in him now.

ME: good. Then make him go right to bed! He's got to be beat after that walk. Also, tell him to never ever do that again!

MOM: done ☺ How's Tate?

ME: idk.

After promising to call my mom later and update her, I put the phone down and let Haley distract me with her chatter about pretty much everything going on around town.

My phone blinks, and the background pic I have of Jody and me flickers into view. We're both holding up a giant fish that Mike Steller caught in Roger's cabin. My stomach sinks all over again thinking about Jody.

She needs to know about what happened tonight, at the very least, but it will have to wait until later. I need a second to breathe. And I need to see Tate. Desperately.

"...I've thought about trying out for college cheerleading, but it's gonna have to be out of state. Minnesota is seriously lacking in this NCAA sport. But out of state means way higher tuition," Haley says, continuing whatever she's been going on about when my mind drifted back to worrying. "But you know what? People get scholarships all the time. Like you. All I need to do is make lists and keep a positive attitude. I'm doing these visualization exercises. Have you heard of Doctor Shrener's book, *Mental Toughness Training for Athletes*?"

"I bet you drove Tate nuts with all your assertiveness and positive thinking." I lift my head. "He hates being told what to do, doesn't he?"

The grin falls from her face and she sighs. "I drove him nuts. And I knew I was doing it and I still did it. I just don't understand why."

"I didn't mean it that way. It's not a bad thing." I feel horrible now. She's been so nice. "Look, Haley, someone is going to want that."

"I know." She nods, obviously employing some of her positive-thinking techniques. "It took me a while to get it, but I get it now. Tate and I... We were in love with being in love."

My mouth falls open, but I don't let myself say anything. Until Haley stares. "What?"

"Nothing." I sigh. "Well, it's just that he said the same thing. About being in love with love. He said it was easy for you guys."

"I guess it was," she admits. "Until it wasn't."

"So...you and Jake Hammond?"

She shakes her head. "It was a bad idea. Drinking too much will do that, though. I mean, we used to take baths together when we were babies. It's weird. And I think our parents would enjoy it too much, and that would suck if we broke up. I'm a lot more aware now of how likely breakups are in high school. Plus, Jake is so..." She shifts her gaze, thinking. "Perfect, maybe? Too perfect, I think."

"Hmm..." I lean against my pillows again. "Everyone has flaws. Maybe he just hides them better."

She shrugs, but the discussion ends because someone knocks on the door. Haley jumps to her feet. She presses her ear against the door. I guess I'm not the only one shaken up from what happened practically right below this apartment.

Sheriff Hammond already let us know who the guy was—Dale something—and that he's from two towns over and he has a bit of a drunk-and-disorderly record—again, *get some new friends, Luke*—but no assault charges. Most likely he would have backed off his attack on me, but still, he's gonna get in a shit-ton of trouble because of the past record. Actually, Sheriff Hammond thinks his sentence will be so bad that he'll gladly take the ninety-day-rehab option, and I should expect an apology letter sometime soon as part of his twelve steps.

"Who is it?" Haley says.

"Leo," a voice calls from the other side.

"And Jamie."

"And Tate."

Relief washes over me. I push over the lock and fling open the door. Tate is last to come in, and when he does, I throw my arms around him before he can even make eye contact. He stiffens and then hugs me back. I think fighting with Tate is the worst activity I've ever engaged in.

"Okay, so we're gonna take off now," Leo says when it's obvious that we need to be alone.

Tate buries his face in my hair, inhaling.

"Need a ride, Stevenson?" Jamie asks Haley.

"Sure." She grabs her uniform, and Leo takes his jacket from the hanger I placed it on.

I pull away from Tate long enough to say thanks to Haley, and then they're gone and the door is closed. Tate's mouth finds mine instantly, our breaths mingling. My heart is up to my throat, beating so fast. With great effort, I pull back again, looking him over. "Are you okay?"

"Kind of. Kind of not," he says. "Are you okay?"

"Yeah, I'm just—I'm sorry." I kiss him again. "It couldn't have been easy for you to side with my parents."

He holds on to my face and looks me over. "I'm on *your* side, Claire. No matter what. Always. Okay?"

My forehead scrunches up. "Did you get to talk to your mom?"

"Not her." He slides freezing-cold hands under the back of my shirt and brings me closer until we're pressed together. "I don't know if I can talk about that stuff anymore tonight, but later…"

A wave of emotion hits me and my eyes burn with tears. He did it. He told someone. Either Roger or maybe Jamie and Leo. God, I'm so relieved. I can wait to hear the details.

I walk backward toward the bed, bringing him with me. "We can talk later."

He kisses me again but stops abruptly. "Tell me the truth. Did that guy…did he do anything more than what you said outside?"

"No, I swear. That was it." I quickly fill him in on the details the sheriff was able to provide thus far. "And as much as I want to keep hating Luke, you should have seen him. He was completely freaked. I don't think he knows the guy that well."

He touches his forehead to mine and sighs. "I'm so sorry, Claire. I keep thinking, what if Leo and I hadn't come outside…"

"You can't do this to yourself. It's like last fall all over again. That wasn't your fault and neither was this." I watch his face carefully. I want to see him get this. But he looks like he's trying to fight off several different emotions. Like he's trying not to break down. And honestly, I want Tate to fall apart if that's what he needs to do to get past everything. And this is not just about tonight. It's way beyond tonight. Tonight was the big wakeup call.

He draws in a deep breath, and then those intense green eyes are full of heat and longing when he asks, "Are we alone?"

I glance at the door, making sure the dead bolt is locked. "Yeah."

His mouth crashes against mine, fingers tugging at the hem of my T-shirt. My breath comes in short bursts, and it only worsens when Tate tosses me onto the bed and his lips travel the length of my body. Everything is rushed and urgent compared to last time. And yet, not a single bit of my skin is left untouched by Tate when we've stripped off all our clothes and he's lying on top of me.

At the points I should be experiencing the most euphoria, it occurs to me that if I agree to go back to school, then I've agreed to leave Tate. To be without him. Without this.

Chapter 54

−CLAIRE−

It's not even seven in the morning when I get home, but still, I'm sure it's obvious to both my parents that I stayed out all night with Tate. Or stayed in, I guess. Sure enough, after I step out of the shower and head for my room, Mom is right on my heels.

"Just getting in?" She's in the doorway of my room, not even attempting to keep quiet. I must look freaked out because she adds, "He's not home. Ned took him to get his blood work done this morning. So…?"

"Um…" I knot the tie on my robe and then busy myself untangling my wet hair. "Well, we went—" I start and then stop again. "I mean Tate—"

"I know where you were." Mom stretches out on my bed, calm and cool—the polar opposite of me right now. "You're being safe?"

I nearly drop the brush. My cheeks are flaming hot. But I manage to nod and say, "Yes."

"Good." She looks me over like I'm different now. "You really love him?"

"Yes." This time I don't blush. I leave my hair alone and stretch out beside Mom on the bed, tucking my cold feet under the quilt. "Is that crazy?"

"Why would it be crazy?" She shifts the pillow so I can rest my head beside hers. "I like Tate. So does your father. He used to talk about him all the time...smart kid, respectful, wish his dad treated him better..."

I look at Mom, surprised by this. "Wait, you guys knew about Keith Tanley? For how long?"

"I don't know, honey." She sighs. "Your dad has seen a lot of people's worst sides. Occupational hazard. He mostly tries to forget those things. Keep it separated. But I know he liked to keep a close eye on Tate."

Tate told me about all the times Dad had pulled him aside to show him the beer taps or some other mechanical device. Suddenly my silence over the last year and a half seems even worse. I should have told Dad that night. We should have gone straight to him. He would have known what to do, cared enough about Tate to not go on an ass-kicking rampage involving Keith.

Lines of worry crease Mom's forehead. I take a deep breath. "I have to tell you something..."

And then I spill the whole story about last fall. Every bit of it. From taking Luke Pratt upstairs, to Keith Tanley breaking that beer bottle, to Tate's broken arm, to the hour Tate and I sat in the car eating Benny's and sealing our future together.

I use the sleeve of my robe to wipe tears from my face. "It was stupid, keeping it secret. You and Dad would have known what to do."

My mom is on the verge of spilling her own tears. "You

should have told us. But what's done is done. It's not a mistake you'll make again. Let me think about whether or not to tell your dad, okay?"

"Yeah, okay." I rest my head on her shoulder, exhausted from everything but also free. "What do you think I should do about school? Spring quarter starts in March—I mean, that's just around corner."

"We really do have it worked out for you to go back." She gives my shoulder a squeeze and we lay there for a minute in comfortable silence.

"This will make Dad happy?"

"Without a doubt," Mom says.

"Okay, then. I guess it's settled." I'm going back to Northwestern. Next month.

She rests her head against mine. "You know what would really make your father happy? What I would love for us to do?"

"What?" At this point, I think I'd do just about anything for them.

"Take a few days off," she says. "And make a trip to Chicago for that audition—"

I open my mouth to protest—the audition is next week, which is way before spring quarter starts—but Mom lifts a hand to stop me.

"I called. I checked into it. You can audition." She looks at my skeptical face. "He wants to see you on that stage, trying, doing something big."

I bite down on my bottom lip. It doesn't seem like that big of a deal but… "I don't really feel prepared, you know? I've been out of that competitive mode for so long."

"So don't compete," Mom says simply. "Just let him have this. Since the day you left for school, your dad's talked about going to see you in a show at school. He was disappointed when you didn't audition for anything but the small student-run shows last ycar. Hc won't admit it to you, but it's true. So let's go. Together. Let him have this one thing. What if you don't get a part or you don't want to audition again? Or what if…" She swallows back the words neither of us wants to hear. What if he isn't around?

Even though she hadn't said it out loud, the impact is just as hard. I'm thinking about that phone call from my mom months ago and how it could have gone so differently. And then I start crying and it takes me a while before I can stop. I swipe my sleeve over my face again before answering my mom. "Okay, let's go to the audition."

She tears up again and kisses my forehead. "You have no idea how much your father needs this."

Maybe I need it, too. Maybe I need to know that there's always someone who wants to see me do something I love.

My thoughts immediately drift to Tate. I reach for my phone and send him a quick text.

ME: *meet me somewhere?*

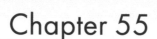

Chapter 55

−TATE−

"Consider yourself on probation," Bakowski says.

He's pissed. Yelled at me for twenty minutes about missing the game, so I force myself to not smile with relief. But I am. Relieved. I mean, I figured he'd let me back on the team, but he's not exactly the forgiving type.

"I assume you're done throwing your little teenage tantrum?" he says.

I refrain from correcting him. Bakowski isn't the type of coach you confide in. Truth is, he really doesn't want to know what's happening in my life. He wants to coach a winning team. That's it.

"Yes, sir," I tell him.

He narrows his eyes at me from across the desk, then points to the pile of uniforms I'd turned in the other day. "You've got no strikes left, Tanley. Not a minute late for practice, first one on the bus before and after games… understand?"

"Yes, sir," I repeat.

Finally, I'm allowed out of his office. I check my phone and read a quick text from Claire about meeting up.

ME: by the pond? 10min?

I head outside, across the street. In the daylight, the parking lot of O'Connor's seems less of a bad memory than it had last night. I still have this knot in my stomach, but a weight has lifted off me just opening up to Roger. He asked me how I was doing when I came home this morning, and it wasn't awkward like I thought it would be. We even worked on my snowmobile for an hour, put in the new carburetor.

Claire arrives at the bench near Juniper Falls Pond in only seven minutes. Right away, it's clear she's worried, has something big to tell me. I wait several seconds while she stands in front of me, twisting her hands.

For some reason, I'm not worried at all. She loves me. I love her. We'll figure it out. Nothing can be as difficult as what we've gone through the past year—her with her dad and us with our buried secrets.

"I'm going back to Northwestern," she says finally.

A grin spreads across my face. I grab her hand and tug her down beside me. "Good."

"Good?" she repeats but then seems to need to spit out the rest. "And I'm going to that audition. This weekend. So I can't see you play at Sections."

I put my arm around Claire, lean in to kiss her temple. "I'm really proud of you."

We sit there for a few minutes, the tension starting to leave her body. "I wish you could come with me."

"You know what?" I say, remembering something. "Maybe I can. Someday. Maybe I'll apply to Northwestern next year. They have a hockey team, right?"

She looks up at me, hopeful. "I believe they do."

I rest a hand on her face and kiss her for a couple of minutes.

Despite my happiness at the moment, sadness sweeps over me. She really is going to leave, and I'm still here. And there's so much to figure out still. I'm scared about this, about Sections, State—assuming we make it there—and dealing with my mom, who is probably dealing with my dad. And Claire must be petrified to leave her dad knowing what could happen and guilty as hell about it, too.

But there's not much we can do except plunge ahead. Keep putting one foot in front of the other.

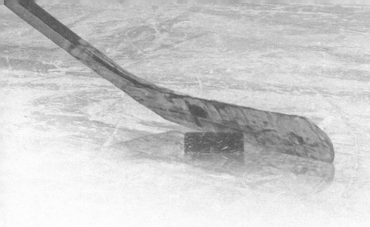

Chapter 56

−CLAIRE−

pace back and forth backstage, shaking my arms out. It's been a long day. I hadn't anticipated making callbacks, and now all I can think about is the fact that it's taking forever. And my dad has been sitting in a hard auditorium chair for way too long. He must be in a lot of pain. The physical therapist told me that sitting in one position for extended periods is extremely difficult for him because the weak side forces the stronger side to hold it up. And to make matters worse, he slept in a cheap hotel bed last night. Between me, my parents, and Aunt Kay and Ned, we all pooled our credit card points to cover a hotel stay and restaurant gift cards. But it's been really nice. My mom was right. We needed this.

"The girl who killed it earlier with 'Don't Rain on My Parade' got a callback, too," my mom says, appearing beside me backstage with a half-eaten deli sandwich.

"Oh, good. You guys found somewhere to grab lunch."

Mom nods and then continues her assessment of my

competition even though she told me not to compete. "The blonde will be tough to beat. The Asian girl was amazing. But way too trained; the way she moved, it was so calculated."

I smile down at my feet. I'm not really worried about the blonde or the overly trained girl. But I let her give me all the details. Let her think I need to hear all this and that it's the most important moment of my life. A year ago, it probably would have been.

"How's Dad doing? Is he getting all cramped up? Have you given him any pain meds?"

"This is what gets you riled up." Mom sets her sandwich down on a table and grips both my arms. "Where is the drama queen who follows a careful list of backstage rituals?"

She's exaggerating. Well, I did have rituals, but I was far from a drama queen compared to other theater-type kids. The thing is, I just never really had anything big to worry about outside of me and my goals.

Until I did.

"Dad is okay?" I ask again.

Mom smiles at me and gives both arms a squeeze. "He's having the time of his life. This is probably the second nicest thing you've ever done for your father—you know that, right?"

I suck in a breath, forcing down all the emotions. My mom's eyes get all bright and shiny. "No crying," I warn. "Someone made me wear stage makeup. If you cry…"

"Okay, okay." Mom pulls herself together and releases me, then grabs her sandwich again. "He really needed this. Doctor Weaver said depression is common with tumor patients but—" She shakes her head. "Worrying about you, trying to help get you back here, I think it's made him better."

I stare at her, confused. "How? It's more stress."

"But he has purpose again." Mom shrugs. "Maybe in all our efforts to protect and shelter him, we underestimated the importance of having purpose."

I let that sink in for a moment and turn to watch the girl before me onstage. Purpose. I think that's what I lost when I couldn't figure out what to wish for. Or maybe I didn't lose it, but I felt guilty holding on to it. Never occurred to me that my dad may have lost his purpose, too, not being at work. Not doing the things that Mom and I took over for him. "Maybe we did underestimate it."

"You know what the best thing you ever did for him was, don't you?" Mom asks.

"Coming home," I say without a doubt.

"That's right. He says he hated that you took time off school, but I bet it was hard on him because it was a very adult thing to do. Maybe he wasn't ready for you to be so grown up. He might not ever be."

"Two minutes," the assistant director tells us when she breezes past Mom and me, talking softly into her headset.

"They're asking everyone questions before they start," Mom adds. "Just stuff about the part and the character."

"A quiz. Great." It is a university. Guess that's to be expected.

"Maybe you should get your hair wet." Mom scrunches up her face like she's trying to imagine me with wet hair. "It's raining when Éponine sings this song."

Despite the worry about Dad out there in the audience, I smile. "That's the movie. No rain on this stage."

"Oops. You know what else would make your father happy?" Mom says. I turn to look at her. "Seeing you enjoying yourself. Not just going through the motions. It's okay to love it. It doesn't make you selfish or ungrateful."

Despite my earlier efforts to keep my eyes dry, they well up about thirty seconds before I have to go onstage. What she's telling me to do, I don't think my mom realizes how hard that is for me right now. "You know at the ball, how I had trouble getting started with that first song?"

"You were nervous," Mom says gently. "Totally understandable. Big crowd. You were out of practice."

I glance at the stage, checking to make sure I've still got a few seconds, and then I turn around again to face Mom. "I wasn't nervous. I just"—I take a breath, working hard to keep my emotions in check—"wasn't sure I could do it. You know, let go. Be in the moment. It felt wrong. Eventually I talked myself into it by thinking about the money and how we needed it."

"Claire…" Mom rushes over, giving me a big hug. "Enough of that, all right? We are done with all of that, understood?"

"Yeah, okay." I use my thumbs to wipe under my eyes. "Okay."

My name is called from the table in the auditorium where the director and faculty advisers are seated. I don't step out onto the stage right away. I take a second and make sure I'm in the right mind-set, here. Right now. Not worried about anything else.

Except Tate. And the game.

Enough, Claire, I tell myself, trying to imitate my mom's voice inside my head.

I take my place at the *X* marking center stage where a microphone stand waits. I try not to squint into the audience. Two men and a woman sit behind a table a ways out in the audience. The director leans in to the shared mic on their table. "Claire O'Connor. Thank you for coming today."

Finally, I spot Dad a few rows behind the director and off to the right. I lift a hand and wave. Unprofessional, I know, but I can't help it. Dad is grinning big. He really does look okay. A weight lifts off me, but when I shift my focus back to the table in front, all of them are turned in their chairs, probably trying to figuring out who I'm waving at.

I lean in to the mic. "I brought my dad with me. I hope that's okay."

It better be because I doubt he's leaving.

All three of them nod, and the woman waves at Dad. He looks a little embarrassed but returns the wave.

One of the men slides the mic toward him. "Can you tell us why you think you deserve the part of Éponine?"

At first I assume it's a trick question. Of course I don't deserve this part. I've been out of school since last summer. A year ago, I would have said that I've wanted this role since I was a little girl. That I played young Éponine in a local community theater and now that I'm all grown up, I want to play the grown-up version. It would have been a cute answer, probably received a couple smiles, maybe a laugh.

I adjust the mic before answering, surprised at the clarity in my voice. "I guess maybe I understand Éponine—" I almost say, *better now*. But realize quickly that it won't mean anything to these strangers because they don't know my view of the world from a year ago. Before my dad, before so many things. "Well. I understand her. But as far as deserving the part, I'm just here for…" I catch my dad's eye again. "I'm here for this. Right now. I'll let all of you figure out the rest."

"Thank you, Claire," the director says. "Let's hear you sing Éponine's solo and then we'll move on to reading for the part. Please, feel free to make it your own. Put some of you into it, okay?"

The intro to the music plays, and for a moment, glancing out at my dad again, I nearly panic. What if this is happening because he won't be here to see me perform another day? What if—

I clear those thoughts from my head and instead think

about what my mom said only minutes ago: My dad is having the time of his life right now. I'm giving him purpose. Whether it's for a day or a decade. And I'm giving *me* purpose, whether it's for a day or a decade. Because I don't really know what's coming. I don't know anything except this song, this moment. Right now.

And how much I love to do this.

Chapter 57

−TATE−

It's still dark out when Mom pulls up to the ice rink. The bus isn't here yet, but I reach for the door handle anyway. "I can wait outside."

My mom reaches out a hand to stop me. "No, stay in the car. It's cold."

We sit in silence for a few seconds, then she turns the radio down and faces me. "I told him not to come to the game."

"Who?" I say, even though I'm sure I know who. My heart picks up, the fear of another uncomfortable chat looming in the air.

"Your dad," Mom manages to spit out.

I stare at my hands. "Did he say… I mean, did he ask why?"

She shakes her head slowly. "I think he knew why. He knew something had changed."

There's nothing for me to say to that. I'm pretty stunned, actually. She could be that vague and he didn't protest.

"He will be confronted about his misconduct. He will have nothing to do with your hockey stuff, especially where college is concerned," Mom says firmly. "But my first concern…" She closes her eyes and takes a breath. "Is you. Having him around is not helping you, and putting a stop to him reliving his hockey glory days through your games is only one step of many to come. Okay?"

I'm still so uncomfortable with this topic. I don't know if that will ever change. But I brave looking up at her. "Okay."

"Are you sure you want to play today?" she asks, just as our red and blue charter bus is pulling into the parking lot. "Maybe you shouldn't."

I look at her, surprised. "Why?"

And then, before I'm able to hop out of the car and pick a good seat on the bus, my mom completely loses her shit. "I'm so sorry, Tate. I always thought if things had been really bad between you and your dad, you would have told me."

I force the bubbling emotions back down—I can't fall apart again right now. Not before this game. Not after I promised Bakowski I'd be the first one on the bus.

"I probably should have," I tell her truthfully.

We're both quiet for a long minute, then Mom wipes her face and pulls herself together. She pops the trunk where my hockey bag is stored and pats my hand. "It's going to be okay. We're going to make it okay."

She might be an embarrassing emotional wreck, but I recognize her tone. It's the one that comes from the version of Mom who knows how to take care of things. The experienced nurse who's always on top of her work. The organized Mom who never lets her kids get away with anything. She's that person 90 percent of the time. So I believe her this morning. Some more of that weight I've carried for way too long lifts off my shoulders as I'm exiting the car and heading toward the bus.

. . .

"What's on your mind, T-Man?" Leo asks me.

We're standing on the ice, all twenty Juniper Falls Varsity Otters lined up, preparing for the national anthem.

I'm about to say hockey. The game. But that isn't completely true, and Leo and Jamie have made it very clear that I need to be real with them, that I *can* be real. So what's on my mind? Claire. Her audition is happening now. Then there's Jody. My mom will talk to her soon, if she hasn't already. I don't know what she'll think, how she'll react. Will she be angry at me for not telling her? Plus Leo and Jamie—I want April to come so they can sign their letters and I'll know for sure that they're moving on to something better.

And of course there's my mom breaking down in the parking lot of the ice rink this morning.

"You know what I'm thinking about?" I say to answer Leo's question. "Everything. Fucking everything."

"Yeah, I bet." He glances sideways at me, looking me over before nodding. "But when the whistle blows, just shut it all down. It's us and that puck. Nothing else. Got it? I want this win, too. Really fucking badly."

I nod my agreement. I'm afraid to say it out loud, but I want another shutout. I want to have a day where nothing goes wrong, and for me, that means no goals.

I clap Leo on the back. "You guys better score a fucking goal today, because that's the only way to win."

Leo laughs. "That's right. I'll win the game for us; you just keep from losing it for us."

The national anthem plays, and then we're all in position, the referee blowing the whistle. And there's nothing I want more than to be right here, right now. In this game. I've been so afraid of screwing up that I haven't even let myself enjoy the success so far. We're one game from qualifying to State. We have the best fucking record in the state.

And something about knowing that Claire is out there, having her own moment like this...it makes me happier than if she were here watching the game. I think we can do this long-distance thing. I think I'll love her even more knowing she's strong enough on her own, knowing she's using every part of herself every day, not hiding it or stuffing it away because she feels guilty being happy. And I don't want to hold back, to not get everything I can from this game just because my dad loved it. I just want Claire and I to be us. A 110 percent us.

The puck slides over the ice, the opposition already pushing it in my direction. Then everything inside my head disappears and I'm in position. I'm ready for whatever this game throws at me.

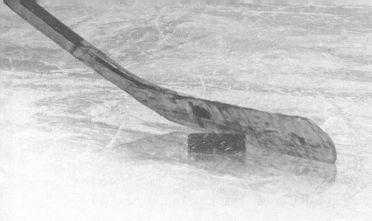

Chapter 58

−CLAIRE−

ONE MONTH LATER

Roger walks outside, a phone charger in each hand. "Need an extra?"

"Sure." Tate snatches one of the chargers and tosses it into the passenger seat.

I busy myself arranging items in the backseat while eavesdropping on Tate and Roger's conversation. They're discussing which interstates to take to Chicago. Which is weird because, duh. GPS.

"...You know Randy Lippman?" Roger asks.

"I think I played hockey with his kid," Tate says. "Why?"

"He wants to get rid of his seventy-three Datsun—"

"No way?"

I glance over at Tate. He looks like he's about to go into cardiac arrest. Then disappointment is all over him when he asks, "How much?"

It started with snowmobile tweaks and oil changes in the garage, now they're moving on to full-on fixing up old cars.

Roger shrugs. "Haven't negotiated yet, but he owes me a favor, so…" He bends over to check something on the tire. "We could work on that one. Together. If you're up for it?"

Tate stares at Roger for a beat, something more than car-fixing plans passes between them, and he says, "Yeah, I'd like that."

"Good." Roger rubs a hand over his bald head, then he nods. "We'll work it all out when you get back next week."

After Roger heads inside, I hold the keys out for Tate to take again, but he shakes his head. "You drive first."

Tate shoves the last box into the car. It's packed so high I'm not sure if I'll be able to see out the back.

After Tate runs inside to say a quick good-bye to his family—I already had my very long and tear-filled good-bye with my parents earlier this morning—Tate and I climb into the car and I start the engine.

Once we're on the road, I decide to bring up the car conversation with Roger. "Sounds like you've got a new hobby. Junk car makeovers or whatever."

Tate lugs his overstuffed school bag from the backseat onto his lap, to avoid eye contact, I think. "It should be fun."

"Admit it." I give his shoulder a shove. "You like your new stepdad. You hang out with him all the time."

It's true. They're always ice fishing or going to some junkyard to dig through stuff and coming back smelling like oil and gasoline—scents that have become weirdly attractive to me.

"I never said I didn't like him," Tate protests. "He's cool."

We've had more serious chats over the last six weeks than I've had in practically my entire life, so I don't push him to talk more. It's spring break. We're on vacation. Which is why I lift an eyebrow when Tate pulls out his physics book. "You're studying? On spring break?"

"Why? Do you wanna pull over and make out?"

I laugh and shake my head. "Not yet. Maybe after we get on the interstate."

"I found a couple more scholarships through Northwestern." Tate's flipping through the textbook now, looking for the right page. "But I need a 3.75 GPA, and I've got a 3.5 right now, so this semester I need all A's."

"It'll be worth the extra work. I hear the girls are incredibly hot at Northwestern." I wiggle my eyebrows at him.

He leans over and plants a kiss on the side of my neck, and I'm about ready to pull over right now. And we've gone a mile. "Just one hot coed. With a single room."

"Single room for a week," I remind him. Keisha is rooming with me again. But she's gone for spring break. I wouldn't be headed back to school until next week except that rehearsals start tomorrow.

I got a part in the ensemble for *Les Mis*. And to my own disbelief, they cast me as understudy for Éponine. Which means I'll perform that role in two of the afternoon shows.

The shock of actually winning a part took a while to wear off. I really hadn't given the musical much thought after I left the stage. My parents were so happy they got to watch, we all kind of forgot about the results aspect. I got the call while we were driving home, and Mom immediately went online and purchased tickets for her and Dad to see the musical opening night and the following afternoon when I'll play one of the lead roles.

Tate catches me biting my nails, and he takes my hand from my face and holds it. "You okay?"

I exhale and focus on today. It's hard dumping on other people all the jobs I've been doing for months. My mom said to just take it one day at a time. They'll call when they need me to explain something or whatever. But it's still hard to leave them. Much more difficult than it was the first time I left, and that was no picnic, either.

At least I get to hold my very hot boyfriend captive in my single room for his entire spring break. Tate needs some R&R after having just completed the state tournament and the hockey season.

"Do you think you'll want to talk to the coach while you're on campus?" I ask after a little while of my driving and Tate studying.

I've recently learned the ins and outs of NCAA recruiting rules, and Tate is free to visit schools on his own dollar, unofficially, and he can talk to the coaches, too. Coach Bakowski of course has his own rules—he wants the guys to wait for senior year and for coaches to go through him first.

He closes the book and looks over at me. "I don't know. What do you think? Think second place at State will hurt my chances? Maybe it's too fresh and I should wait a while."

I laugh. I can't help it. "First off, second place at State is amazing. And next, that's the team's result. It's only part of the picture."

And Jesus. Minnesota is probably the most competitive state for high school hockey. And it's not Tate's fault they lost. He played amazingly the whole tournament. But unfortunately, he got plowed over by Cole Clooney, who was attempting to help Tate by stealing the puck from the other team, and as a result Tate got knocked out during the game. For the second time this season. Bakowski had no choice but to put in the cold sophomore goalie. And of course, the other team took advantage of our disadvantage. We lost by one.

Tate still looks worried, so I add, "You've already had tons of junior team coaches contact you, right?"

Tate reaches in the front of his bag and pulls out what looks like a stack of business cards. He fans them out for me to see. "Eight junior teams. Hammond got fourteen."

He tucks the cards away and places a hand on my thigh, rubbing it gently. "Part of it is our town. We get more scouts watching us at State. They'll compare me to every other supposedly good goalie soon enough, and my name will fall off a bunch of lists."

"Maybe, but maybe you are really good."

He shrugs. "I want to go to college. The classes sound cool and so does living in another city, at least for a while."

I'm excited about the classes I'm taking this quarter, too. I'm excited about being a student again.

"And you never know...if the leading girl for your character breaks a leg and you're in the show..." Tate flashes me a grin. "And then some Broadway scout sees you and wants to drag you all the way to New York City..."

"You are clearly insane." I roll my eyes. "And Broadway scout? Is that a thing?"

"What I'm saying is..." Tate continues massaging my leg and I'm now looking for an exit to take soon. "Both of those things are a problem for future us to worry about. Present us is doing exactly what we need to be doing."

Oh. The right-now thing again.

"No we're not." I spot a sign for a rest stop and steer the car in that direction. Tate's eyebrows shoot up, but he makes no protest when I park the car in the very back behind a tree.

There are still traces of snow on the ground, but March has brought some sunshine and warmth, which means twenty degrees, sometimes thirty. I cut the engine, and Tate is already leaning over in his seat, unbuckling my seat belt and pulling me close.

I sigh against his lips. "Now we're doing exactly what

we're supposed to be."

"I like how you think." Tate slides a warm hand inside my jacket.

"We have to build up a bank of awesome make-out sessions over the next week so I can survive without you."

"Agreed," Tate says. "But I love you, so that's like a bottomless bank."

Warmth fills my insides. I touch my mouth to his again. "I love you, too."

"Yeah, I'm still waiting for my picture," he teases. "If you mean it, put it in writing like I did."

I use my finger to trace *I love you* all over his cheek and chest and back. It's there for good; it's not going anywhere.

No matter how many miles we have between us.

ACKNOWLEDGMENTS

Super special thanks to Roni Loren and Erica Haglund for all your help. I would never have gotten this book to its final state without your help and encouragement. Thanks to my agent, Nicole Resciniti, to whom I dedicated this book mostly because she's the only person to have all nine or ten versions of the story. I'm sure she is just as shocked as I am to see it finally released. Thanks to Liz Pelletier and the amazing team at Entangled Teen—all of you are constantly surprising me with your fresh ideas, encouragement, and energy. Thanks to the dude who makes those hilarious Hockey Hair videos each year during the Minnesota State high school hockey tournament. You have provided so much inspiration for this series through your YouTube videos. Lastly, thanks to my readers, new and old; I hope you love Claire and Tate's story and come back for the next Juniper Falls romance.

GRAB THE ENTANGLED TEEN RELEASES READERS ARE TALKING ABOUT!

SECRETS OF A RELUCTANT PRINCESS
BY CASEY GRIFFIN

At Beverly Hills High, you have to be ruthless to survive…

Adrianna Bottom always wanted to be liked. But this wasn't *exactly* what she had in mind. Now, she's in the spotlight…and out of her geeky comfort zone. She'll do whatever it takes to turn the rumor mill in her favor—even if it means keeping secrets. So far, it's working.

Wear the right clothes. Say the right things. Be seen with the right people.

Kevin, the adorable sketch artist who shares her love of all things nerd, isn't *exactly* the right people. But that doesn't stop Adrianna from crushing on him. The only way she can spend time with him is in disguise, as Princess Andy, the masked girl he's been LARPing with. If he found out who she really was, though, he'd hate her.

The rules have been set. The teams have their players. Game on.

ISLAND OF EXILES
BY ERICA CAMERON

On the isolated desert island of Shiara, every breath is a battle.

The clan comes before self, and protecting her home means Khya is a warrior above all else. But when obeying the clan leaders could cost her brother his life, Khya's home becomes a deadly trap. The council she hoped to join has betrayed her, and their secrets, hundreds of years deep, reach around a world she's never seen.

To save her brother's life and her island home, her only choice is to turn against her clan and go on the run—a betrayal and a death sentence.

OTHER BREAKABLE THINGS
BY KELLEY YORK AND ROWAN ALTWOOD

Luc Argent has always been intimately acquainted with death. After a car crash got him a second chance at life—via someone else's transplanted heart—he tried to embrace it. He truly did. But he always knew death could be right around the corner again. And now it is. Luc is ready to let his failing heart give out, ready to give up. A road trip to Oregon—where death with dignity is legal—is his answer. But along for the ride is his best friend, Evelyn. And she's not giving up so easily.

Life After Juliet
by Shannon Lee Alexander

Becca Hanson was never able to make sense of the real world. When her best friend Charlotte died, she gave up on it altogether. Fortunately, Becca can count on her books to escape—to other times, other places, other people...

Until she meets Max Herrera. He's experienced loss, too, and his gorgeous, dark eyes see Becca the way no one else in school can.

As it turns out, kissing is a lot better in real life than on a page. But love and life are a lot more complicated in the real world... and happy endings aren't always guaranteed.

The companion novel to *Love and Other Unknown Variables* is an exploration of loss and regret, of kissing and love, and most importantly, a celebration of hope and discovering a life worth living again.